Jean-Baptiste Lully
and the music
of the French baroque

This volume of essays on Jean-Baptiste Lully and his musical
legacy honors the distinguished French baroque scholar James R.
Anthony.

Jean-Baptiste Lully, court composer to Louis XIV, served as the
principal architect of what would become known as the French
style of music in the baroque era. The style he created strongly
influenced the great musical figures in England (Purcell and
Handel) and Germany (Bach and Telemann), but Lully's music
itself has received little attention. Recently, through the efforts of
scholars and musicians concerned with the performance practices of Lully's time, Lully's own music has begun to come alive
in performance and recording.

These essays, all by important baroque specialists, cover significant aspects of Lully's life and works and the French tradition
he influenced. They constitute the first post-war collection of
studies centerd on Lully and form a fitting tribute to Professor
Anthony whose own *French Baroque Music* provided a stimulus
for the work of an emerging generation of scholars.

JEAN-BAPTISTE LULLY
AND THE MUSIC OF
THE FRENCH BAROQUE:

ESSAYS IN HONOR OF
JAMES R. ANTHONY

EDITED BY
JOHN HAJDU HEYER

In collaboration with
CATHERINE MASSIP
CARL B. SCHMIDT
HERBERT SCHNEIDER

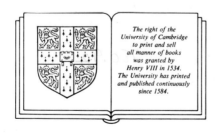

The right of the
University of Cambridge
to print and sell
all manner of books
was granted by
Henry VIII in 1534.
The University has printed
and published continuously
since 1584.

CAMBRIDGE UNIVERSITY PRESS
Cambridge
New York   New Rochelle   Melbourne   Sydney

Published by the Press Syndicate of the University of Cambridge
The Pitt Building, Trumpington Street, Cambridge CB2 1RP
32 East 57th Street, New York, NY 10022, USA
10 Stamford Road, Oakleigh, Melbourne 3166, Australia

First published 1989

Printed in Great Britain at the University Press, Cambridge

British Library cataloguing in publication data
Jean-Baptiste Lully and the music of the
French baroque: essays in honor of James
R. Anthony.
1. French music. Lully, Jean-Baptiste, 1632–
1687. Critical studies
I. Heyer, John Hajdu II. Anthony, James, R.
780'.92'4

Library of Congress cataloguing in publication data
Jean-Baptiste Lully and the music of the French Baroque: essays in
honor of James R. Anthony/edited by John Hajdu Heyer: in
collaboration with Catherine Massip, Carl B. Schmidt, Herbert Schneider.
p.   cm.
Bibliography.
Includes index.
ISBN 0 521 35263 0
1. Lully, Jean Baptiste, 1632–87 – Criticism and interpretation.
2. Music – France – 17th century – History and criticism.
I. Anthony, James R. II. Heyer, John Hajdu.
ML410.L95J4 1988
780'.92'4 – dc 19   88–2625

ISBN 0 521 35263 0

ME

Contents

List of illustrations   *page* vii

Preface   xi

Glossary   xiii

Introduction   1
PAUL HENRY LANG

The first opera in Paris: a study in the politics of art   7
NEAL ZASLAW

Michel Lambert and Jean-Baptiste Lully: the stakes of a collaboration   25
CATHERINE MASSIP

Chronology and evolution of the *grand motet* at the court of Louis XIV: 41
evidence from the *Livres du Roi* and the works of Perrin, the *sous-maîtres*
and Lully
LIONEL SAWKINS

The sources of Lully's *grands motets*   81
JOHN HAJDU HEYER

Some notes on Lully's orchestra   99
JÉRÔME DE LA GORCE

The Amsterdam editions of Lully's orchestral suites   113
HERBERT SCHNEIDER

Parnassus revisited: the musical vantage point of Titon du Tillet   131
JULIE ANNE SADIE

The residences of Monsieur de Lully: a west side story   159
MARCELLE BENOIT

The geographical spread of Lully's operas during the late seventeenth and early eighteenth centuries: new evidence from the livrets   183
CARL B. SCHMIDT

How eighteenth-century Parisians heard Lully's operas: the case of *Armide*'s fourth act   213
LOIS ROSOW

La Mariée: the history of a French court dance   239
REBECCA HARRIS-WARRICK

A re-examination of Rameau's self-borrowings   259
GRAHAM SADLER

A musician's view of the French baroque after the advent of Gluck: Grétry's *Les trois âges de l'opéra* and its context   291
M. ELIZABETH C. BARTLET

A bibliography of writings by James R. Anthony   319
DORMAN SMITH

Index   323

Illustrations

The first opera in Paris

Plate 1. The printed scenario from *Il giuditio della Ragione tra la*   *page* 18
Beltà e l'Affetto, Dramma in musica, 1643 (Vatican Library)

**Chronology and evolution of the *grand motet* at the court of
Louis XIV**

Plate 1. Title-page for one of the *Livres du Roi* – a quarto volume   53
designed for the royal family (Bibliothèque Municipale, Valenciennes)

Plates 2a, b. Title-pages of the *Livres du Roi* in the smaller formats –   54
probably intended for the congregation (Mme Hélène Charnassé
and Bibliothèque du Conservatoire royal, Liège)

Plate 3. Lalande, *Deitatis majestatem*, 1682 (Bibliothèque Municipale,   72
Versailles)

Plate 4. Lalande, *Dixit Dominus*, 1680, his first setting (Bibliothèque   73
Municipale, Versailles)

Appendix 2. Texts of works by Colasse in the *Livres du Roi*, 1686   76

The sources of Lully's *grand motets*

Plate 1. J.-B. de Lully: *Motets à deux choeurs* (Paris: Ballard, 1684),   84
Premier dessus du petit choeur, p. 1. GB-Ge: R. b. 11–13 (by permission
of the Euing Music Library, Glasgow)

Plate 2. J.-B. de Lully: *Motets à deux choeurs* (Paris: Ballard, 1684),   85
Premier dessus du petit choeur, p. 1. B-Bc: Réf. 15145Z (by permission
of the Conservatoire Royal de Musique, Bruxelles)

Plate 3. J.-B. de Lully: *Motets à deux choeurs* (Paris: Ballard, 1684).   86
Cover of partbook with Lully coat of arms for *Premier dessus du petit
choeur*: F-Pn: Vm^1 1039 (by permission of the Bibliothèque Nationale,
Paris)

Plate 4. J.-B. de Lully: *Motets à deux choeurs* (Paris: Ballard, 1684).   87
Manuscript corrections in F-Pn: Vm^1 1039 (by permission of the
Bibliothèque Nationale, Paris)

Plate 5. J.-B. de Lully: Motets. Manuscript copy in the hand of   92
Scribe E, F-Pn: Rés. F. 669, p. 4 (by permission of the Bibliothèque
Nationale, Paris)

Plate 6. J.-B. de Lully: Motets. Manuscript copy in the hand of   96

Scribe A, B-Br: Ms II 3847 (by permission of the Bibliothèque Royale
Albert 1er, Belgium)

Some notes on Lully's orchestra
Plate 1. Costume designed by Jean Berain for Act I, *Thésée*   101
(by permission of the Musée du Louvre, Collection Rothschild, Paris)
Plate 2. From the studio of Jean Berain for Act III, *Isis* (by permission   102
of the Musée du Louvre, Collection Rothschild, Paris)

The Amsterdam editions of Lully's orchestral suites
Plate 1. Title-page from the Pointel edition of the *Amadis* suite   116
(the British Library)
Plate 2. Title-page from the Heus edition of the *Amadis* suite   117
(the British Library)

Parnassus revisited: the musical vantage point of Titon du Tillet
Plate 1. Nicolas de Largillière, portrait of Évrard Titon du Tillet,   132
1736 (by permission of the Bibliothèque Nationale)
Plate 2. Jean Audran, engraving of the Parnasse François after   135
Nicolas de Poilly, 1723 (by permission of the Bibliothèque Nationale)
Plate 3. Nicolas Henri Tardieu, engraving of the Parnasse François,   136
after Jean Audran, 1730 (from *Le Parnasse François*, 1732)
(by permission of the University of London Library)
Plate 4. Alexandre Maisonneuve, engraving of the Lully medallion   137
(from the *Description du Parnasse François*, 1760) (by permission of
the Bibliothèque Nationale)
Plate 5. Alexandre Maisonneuve, engraving of the Parnasse François   139
in a garden setting, after Jacques de Lajoüe (by permission of the
Bibliothèque Nationale)

The residences of Monsieur de Lully
Plate 1. Lully's signature at the bottom of the lease for the Rue-   161
Neuve-Saint-Thomas, 6 June 1664 (Archives nationales, France,
Minutier central, XLVI–91)
Plate 2. L'hôtel Lully, Rue Sainte-Anne. Reconstruction and   163
drawing by Edmond Radet in *Lully, homme d'affaires, propriétaire et
musicien* (Paris: Librairie de l'Art, 1891)
Plate 3. L'hôtel Lully, Rue Sainte-Anne; detail of the facade.   164
Present-day condition (Photo: Nobuko Uchino)
Plate 4. The house built by Lully on Rue Royale in 1676; present-   165
day condition; now 10 Rue des Moulins (Photo: Nobuko Uchino)
Plate 5. Vestiges of Lully's house on the Rue de la Madeleine in la   170
Ville-l'Evêque, incorporated into an eighteenth-century building.
Present-day condition; now 28–30 Rue Boissy-d'Anglas
(Photo: Nobuko Uchino)

Plate 6. *Grand Plan de Paris et ses environs*, by Jouvin de Rochefort,   172
c. 1675. Planche IX, 'Les environs de Paris'. From east to west:
la Ville-l'Evêque and Vaugirard; Puteaux and Sèvres; Saint-Germain-
en-Laye, and Versailles

Plate 7. The village of Puteaux in the seventeenth century.   173
On the right, the sixteenth-century church; facing on the right,
the presumed house of Lambert and Lully (Archives nationales,
N III Seine, 345, detail)

Plate 8. Le Pavillon Lully at Sèvres, before restoration   176
(Photo: Christian Decamos, 1985. General inventory, Société de
Propriété Artistique des Dessins et Modèles)

Plate 9. Le Pavillon Lully at Sèvres. Panoramic view. Present-day   177
condition (Photo: Nobuko Uchino)

Plate 10. Vestiges of Lully's mausoleum at Petits-Pères (now Notre-   181
Dame-des-Victoires); present-day condition (Photo: Nobuko Uchino)

La Mariée: the history of a French court dance

Plate 1. The first figure of Pécour's choreography *la Mariée* as   242
notated by Feuillet (Paris, 1700)

A re-examination of Rameau's self-borrowings

Plate 1. F-Pn Estampes, Hennin 8343. Anonymous engraving (1739)   263
(by permission of the Cabinet des Estampes, Bibliothèque Nationale,
Paris)

Plate 2. Passage quoted by Cahusac (*Les fêtes de Polymnie*, 1753 revival)   271
from Voltaire's *La princesse de Navarre*, 1745 (by permission of the
Bibliothèque Nationale)

Preface

A decade and a half have now passed since the publication of the first edition of James R. Anthony's *French Baroque Music*. That book, having already undergone extensive revision and translation into French, has become a milestone in its field. More importantly, as the citations in this volume testify, *French Baroque Music* now serves as a springboard for all studies on French music from Beaujoyeulx to Rameau. When it appeared, Anthony's book presented the first comprehensive study devoted to the vast musical product of France's great age. Earlier baroque surveys had struggled with the problems of French music in France's classical age. Paul Henry Lang, Anthony's teacher, had written perceptively and at length in *Music in Western Civilization* as had others, most notably Bukofzer in his essay on 'French music under the absolutism' in *Music in the Baroque Era*, but little enthusiasm for the music can be found in the pages of student textbooks. Now, with the fruits of the labors of Anthony and his colleagues, and with the recent achievements of musicians, including the performance and recording of splendid productions of works by Lully the greatness of French music in the *grand siècle* may, at last, be comprehensible to more than a few cognoscenti.

Anthony's *French Baroque Music* and other writings, particularly those for the *New Grove*, provided timely stimuli for the work of an emerging generation of scholars, many of whom present the products of their research here. Thus, in 1984, during a post-session discussion among some of those scholars at a conference on the French motet in Paris, the conversation turned to Lully and to the three hundredth memorial year in 1987. It was mentioned that the memorial year coincided with James Anthony's sixty-fifth birthday and it was suggested that a festschrift should be prepared. This resultant volume holds studies that survey French music from the important advent of opera in Paris in the mid-1640s through the culminating study of Grétry's 1778 retrospective on the 'three ages' of French opera. Within that survey of a century and a half appear more detailed studies on the other great French figure of the thoroughbass era, Rameau, on one of Anthony's favorite figures, Titon du Tillet, and, happily, on that most distinctive dimension of French musicality, the dance.

Certainly the greater effects of James R. Anthony's past work are yet to be felt, and we can hope for much more from one whose productivity appears to increase with the passing of time. So with this volume, Jim, we offer a cordial and affectionate birthday salute and our best wishes for many more productive years.

The following libraries have kindly granted permission for the reproduction of the plates: Bibliothèque Nationale, Paris; Musée du Louvre, Collection Rothschild, Paris; Bibliothèque municipale, Valenciennes; Bibliothèque municipale, Versailles; Bibliothèque du Conservatoire royal, Liège; the National Archives of France, the Euing Music Collection in Glasgow University Library, the Library of the Royal Conservatory in Brussels, and the Bibliothèque Royale Albert 1er in Brussels. Library references throughout the book follow the RISM sigla.

I want to express my gratitude to the University of California, Santa Cruz Faculty Research Committee for its support in preparation of the typescript, and to the following individuals who have contributed to the completion of this volume: to my collaborators Catherine Massip, Carl B. Schmidt, and Herbert Schneider who served as readers and offered important advice and valuable counsel; to Carl B. Schmidt, particularly, for calling to my attention many details that otherwise might have been overlooked; to Miriam Ellis, for translation work under severe time constraints; to Caroline Wood for additional translating; to my colleague Sherwood Dudley for assistance clarifying certain points regarding the translation; to Neal Zaslaw for his good advice; to Sandra Heyer for her assistance in the proof-reading stages and in the translation of Herbert Schneider's article; to Thomas Bauman for assistance and many good suggestions on the translation of Schneider's article; to Andrietta Hunter and Peg McCray for help with the typescript; and, most certainly not least, to James R. Anthony, who gave the editor and several contributors his wise counsel not even knowing the articles in question were destined for this volume.

John Hajdu Heyer

Glossary

The following definitions of terms found in this volume may be of use to the general reader.

Académie-Opéra: the Académie d'Opéra, established by Perrin, Cambert, and the Marquis de Sourdéac in 1669 under the protection of the king came under Lully's control in 1672. Lully renamed the organization to Académie royale de musique, and produced his *tragédies en musique* through it during his career. The organization continued through the eighteenth century, then underwent a series of name changes at the time of the Revolution. With the construction in 1721 of the Paris Opéra, the terms Académie and Opéra both continued to be associated with that building.

Ballet de cour: French court ballet that flourished from the time of Henry III through that of Louis XIV. The genre included *récits* and *vers*, *entrées*, and a concluding *grand ballet*. These lavish ballets were generally prepared by court musicians, poets, and a machinist, around a theme (e.g. the seasons, the triumph of love, etc.) often determined by the king, who would then take part in the performance.

Comèdie-ballet: a unification of stage play and ballet developed by Lully and Molière in works including *Le mariage forcé* and *L'Amour médecin*.

Double: a variation following a vocal air or an instrumental dance. The *double* was generally characterized by the use of smaller note values.

Entrée: in a *ballet de cour* the term referred to a group of dances unified by a subject. The *entrées*, therefore, functioned like scenes in the acts of the ballet. A *ballet de cour* usually had twenty to thirty *entrées*.

Grand motet: a large-scale choral piece on a religious text (most often a Psalm) officially inaugurated by Lully, Robert, and Dumont on the express order of Louis XIV.

Livret: libretto. Livrets were commonly published in the seventeenth and eighteenth centuries. In addition to the text of the operas, they often included names of performers and other information on the production for which they were printed. The term generally refers to these small printed books rather than to the poetic text of the opera, for which the term *libretto* is retained.

Parties: individual orchestral or vocal parts.

Partition: orchestral or orchestral and vocal score.

Partition réduite: a conducting score reduced by the elimination of the *remplissage*.

Récit: in seventeenth- and eighteenth-century France the term designated passages for solo voice or instrument. In the primary sources the term usually appears as a rubric over any solo passage, from brief introductions for ensemble movements, to fuller, aria-like movements. The term, therefore, is not synonymous with *recitative*.

Remplissage: the inner parts of an orchestral score in seventeenth- and eighteenth-century French practice, specifically, the *haute-contre de violon, taille de violon*, and *quinte de violon*, or those parts between the *dessus* and the *basse continue*. The attention given to melodic writing in the *dessus*, and to the flexible basso continuo style, placed a lesser degree of importance on these internal parts. Lully is known to have had others 'fill out' the *remplissage* after he completed the *dessus*, *basse*, and leading imitative entries.

Simphonie: Brossard (1703) maintained that in France the term applied generally to all compositions written for instruments *and* voices. The term usually appears in manuscripts and printed scores as a rubric over any strictly instrumental passage, including introductions, and interludes.

Sommeil: the musical characteristics of a slumber scene introduced by Lully in his ballet *Les amants magnifiques* became common to many such scenes in later ballets, *tragédies lyriques*, oratorios, and, even, motets. The effective *sommeil* scenes achieved a high degree of popularity in French opera.

Sous-maître: musicians responsible for the composition and preparation of music for the Royal Chapel.

Tragédie lyrique: see *Tragédie en musique*.

Tragédie en musique: the term Lully applied to his serious operas. In the eighteenth century, the term *tragédie lyrique* became common. Inaugurated by Lully and Quinault with *Cadmus* in 1673, the form of a prologue and five acts on mythological or chivalrous subject matters became characteristic of French opera, and was adopted by subsequent composers, including Campra, Rameau, and, eventually, Gluck.

Introduction

PAUL HENRY LANG

The *grand siècle* of French culture, when contemplated from our historical perspective, divides itself into halves. In the first half it seems as though writers, scholars, artists, and statesmen, not to speak of the *grandes dames*, deliberately came together to prepare the second as the golden age of the French spirit. In the history of French civilization and culture, consciousness has always carried considerable weight, the French have always admired order and rules that can be learned and propagated, and intelligence has often vied with imagination and fantasy for the principal role, for supremacy. The achievements of the century in literature, philosophy, rhetoric, and the theatre were extraordinary, but this great age had no real poetry; the alexandrine tied the poets' tongues – except Racine's.

In this animated era, French music, also largely bereft of real poetry, moved slowly. In the aristocratic homes the lute was the favorite instrument, yet it took the French composers a long time before they ventured beyond transcriptions to original compositions. We note the same hesitation in keyboard music; the clavecin literature took its inception long after there was a rich repertoire for harpsichord in Italy and England. And there was no Frescobaldi among the French, though of course the Couperins, Marchand, Chambonnières, and all the others later made French keyboard music a world success. The music all these composers cultivated was in the sign of the dance, so congenial to the French, with its neat little forms, pregnant rhythms, great surface attraction, and in tone and structure so much in harmony with the spirit of the age. This music, though slight and short-breathed, was elegant and so different from any other that the whole of Europe became enamored of it. The forms of dance music, with their well-regulated steps and rhythms, permitting equally elegant gestures and movements, particularly appealed to the French upper classes and was diligently cultivated at court and by the king himself.

The fourteen-year-old Florentine youth who immigrated into this scintillating realm of *Le spectacle*, as the *ballet de cour* and the other genres based on the dance were called, discovered a world such as he had never seen. Young Jean-Baptiste Lully contemplated all this with sharp attention, as well as with inordinate ambition; he watched, measured, and planned, taking his time and rarely making a false move, for he wanted nothing less than to become Cardinal

1

Mazarin's counterpart in music, the uncrowned head of the French musical world. In this ascent to a commanding position he deftly used everyone from the king down. The *lettres patentes* and the *privilèges* he secured from the king were so outrageous that they could not have stood the slightest legal scrutiny, but they could not be scrutinized because they came directly from the king. This adroit manipulator did succeed in becoming the virtual dictator of French musical life, but he became more than that: a mighty force to contend with not only in France but wherever there was a serious musical culture. For this masterful intrigant was also a great artist, and in that capacity he remained uncompromising and absolutely true to his vocation. Once more, the entire first half of the century seems to have conspired to clear the decks for a superlative captain and artist who embodied the *grand siècle* in music.

Much has been made of Lully's Italian origins, but whether or not one agrees with Taine on the influence of environment, it stands to reason that a fourteen-year-old boy, not well educated in music until he learned theory and practice from French teachers, could hardly have brought with him even the simplest Italian operatic ideals and aesthetics. After initial uncertainty, Lully methodically acquired the themes, ideas, forms, and motives of French arts and letters, from which he developed his own aesthetic and dramaturgical views that more and more diverged from his Italian heritage. Earlier historians overlooked Lully's exceptional powers of observation and his singular devotion to a dramatic/theatrical concept. He watched the unsuccessful efforts to acclimatize Italian opera in France and recognized that the French musical theatre could not be based on Italian elements; it had to be grounded in native sources, notably in the highly developed French literary language and theater. Indeed, the original name of French opera was *tragédie en musique*, a term that plainly declared it to be a literary genre despite the music added to it. It took a long time before the French followed all other countries calling their music dramas 'operas'. It used to be said that Lully returned to the style of the opening of the seventeenth century, that is, to the Florentine melodrama. He did return to genres fashionable early in his century but they were French sources and all of them connected with the dance. He collaborated with Molière in creating balletic spectacles, but soon realized that Molière was really closer to middle-class taste while he himself, by temperament and ambition, preferred the pseudo-classic heroism of the serious French theatre. It was this that made some historians believe that Lully returned to early Italian operas which also took their subjects from classical antiquity. On the contrary, Lully steadily distanced himself from Italian opera despite this similarity; titles prove little, the whole libretto must be carefully studied. Wherever we look we see Lully codifying French tastes, conventions, and aspirations. He examined the welter of materials, the various forms of the ballet, the chansons, the pastoral plays with music, and concluded that while some of these elements were usable, they almost completely lacked the dramatic quality which he envisioned for his future stage works. He saw the dramatic in the serious spoken theater despite its cothurnus and the glacial peaks of wit and rhetoric. And he saw even more there as he felt that some of the heroes, though imitation

Greeks, were true men and women ravaged by love or honor. Lully also took a close look at Cambert's operatic experiments and found them not viable without considerable modifications. When Lully secured the royal patent for the establishment of the Académie royale de musique for himself, the potential rival Cambert, then stripped of his livelihood, fled to England. Lully suffered no competition.

There is always something in a national art that a foreigner does not understand or fails to appreciate, but Lully (like Handel in England) was no longer a foreigner, and his eyes penetrated to the core of the French *esprit*. He clearly saw that the key to the future French music drama that he was nurturing in his mind was the language and the declamatory pathos of the French theatre, which had to be transferred and adapted to the musical stage if the kind of French opera he hoped for was to take root in a nation with a highly developed spoken theatre. The problem was one that France shared with England and Spain, both with a rich literature for the stage, but while Lully solved the problem for France, England imported Italian opera, and the Spaniards settled on the operetta-like zarzuela. Interestingly enough, while the majority of French literary critics and philosophers staunchly refused to accept opera ('parceque la musique ne sait narrer'), Lully was not one to see anything as impossible, yet he immediately ran into serious obstacles: musical declamation could not be solely based on the alexandrine, which was almost the only poetic verse form of the heroic theatre. The alexandrine had an intellectual rhythm, classically simple and with crystalline transparency, yet from the musical point of view it was a drum roll, a metronome. With his fine ear Lully found a way to break through the monotony of the alexandrine with the sophisticated rhythms and inflections of the single words; the resulting melodic line has a remarkably varied and complicated quality. Indeed, these melodies of the erstwhile Florentine observe the most intimate laws of the French language; his lines of declamation are unsurpassable to this day, the wonderfully flexible musical settings of the words remain models for all time. It is thus that the French recitative was born, a musical speech fully the equal of the declaimed pathos in the Comédie Française, and thus the new musical theater remained a form of tragedy, though a tragedy with and in music.

What remained to be done was to fill this marvelous musical diction with dramatic life. At this juncture Lully met Philippe Quinault, a playwright who filled the void between Corneille's silence and the appearance of Racine. He wrote poor tragedies, somewhat better comedies, was a good literary craftsman, and ended by being elected, like many other mediocre poets, to the Academy. Lully's searching eye discovered a talent in Quinault that the poet himself was not aware of: his ability to write lyrics for singing. Naturally, he was immediately annexed by Lully for his own purposes, and just as inevitably on Lully's terms. The partnership was successful and lasted until a year before Lully's death. The delighted librettist, praised even by Boileau, gave up all his commitments in order to keep Lully provided with books on whose form and tone, down to individual words, the composer kept close control. Posterity has dealt harshly with this dramatic poet – as it has with Metastasio – and in both instances has been wrong. The modern literary critics were looking for a Racine or a Tasso instead of recognizing the new and highly original theatrical genre in which the words are 'servants of the composer' as Mozart would say in the next century. Quinault could place an air, or dance, or recitative exactly where it suited the composer's plans and wishes. And, an unusual distinction: Quinault's librettos could be read even without the music; Voltaire still thought highly of them.

Lully knew the value of stylistic consistency better than most composers active in his time. Almost everything is serious in this style, which is hard yet transparent. He gave up the long soaring sentences of the Italian Baroque, its convoluted constructions, and created a light, pellucid, beautifully organized musical texture admired by everyone who could understand the perfect marriage of words and music. Italian opera of the baroque with its glorification of the singing voice and its acceptance of the castratos' excesses, minimized the verisimilitude of the drama. Lully expelled the cadenzas, roulades, and most other ornamental fretwork – there were no castratos in French opera – yet the *tragédie lyrique* did not escape the fate of Italian opera. It is difficult for us to believe that Greek gods, Roman emperors, or Egyptian queens are real dramatic figures as they were seen to be in Lully's time. But this is largely the fault of our misguided concept of the style in our performances.

The *tragédie lyrique*, like the spoken theater, did not permit the passions of the admired Attic drama to appear naked in their carefully groomed and highly moral theatre, yet the Euripidean lode was rich and inviting. Since the text avoided showing passions openly and to their full extent, Lully found an entirely novel way to indicate the presence of passions and the undeniable eroticism that flowed like a mysterious ether through the conventional scenes in which queens confessed their secret loves to their confidantes and the warriors did their courting with the most exquisite politeness. Lully's inspired solution was to compose little dream symphonies for orchestra without the words that would make them too explicit; Quinault always found the right spots into which to insert them. Some were martial, some balletic or pastoral, but it was the *sommeil* and other mood pieces that really carried the 'ether'. These delightful descriptive musical poems enthralled musicians and public alike. We must admit that Charpentier was a more adventurous harmonist, and Delalande a greater contrapuntist, but no one else had Lully's driving force and faith to pursue and realize an idea, the power to direct and codify a national style that reigned for a whole century.

James Anthony realized that Lully's overwhelming presence on the scene should not make us forget the many able French composers who worked in other fields of music. He saw that keyboard, chamber, orchestral, and sacred music flourished largely independent of the norms laid down by the *tragédie lyrique*, and in his many excellent publications cleared the imbalance by revealing the important roles discharged by these composers. Among the happy results of his work, and valuable supplements to it, are the enlightening contributions to this elegant volume of *hommage au maître*.

As can be seen, much has been done and much still remains to be done to give this colorful era its comprehensive historical picture, and to eradicate the last vestiges of the malediction that emanated in the eighteenth century from the 'Queen's corner' and still lurks in the background. Fortunately, Professor Anthony's zeal and dedication are unimpaired and the partisans of the *grand siècle* are growing in numbers, so we can look to future scholarship in this field with confidence and large expectations.

                                                        Lakeville, Connecticut

The first opera in Paris:
a study in the politics of art

NEAL ZASLAW

Jules Mazarin, né Giulio Raimondo Mazzarini, played a principal role in the drama of the early years of the reign of Louis XIV. After the deaths of Louis XIII's minister Richelieu (December 1642) and of Louis himself (May 1643), Mazarin emerged as the confidant and favorite of Louis's widow, Anne of Austria, wielding great power right up to his death in 1661, even after Louis XIV (b. 1638) had attained his majority. As the ambitious Mazarin accumulated political and economic power, he pursued two interrelated objectives: to bring France politically and culturally closer to the papacy, and to be a great Maecenas, like the Barberinis who had been the patrons and mentors of his youth. The intersection of these two ambitions resulted in extravagant efforts on Mazarin's part to bring Italian art, architecture, music, and drama to Paris. This attempt at politico-cultural colonization constituted nothing less than the introduction of the baroque style to France, where it was, at least initially, considered to be an exotic intrusion.

Mazarin scholar Madeleine Laurain-Portemer has succinctly summarized the cardinal's attitudes in these matters:

Two principles guided Mazarin in the realm of the arts: first, the necessity for patronage as an ornament of politics; then, the excellence of baroque art as a stimulus to renewal. As soon as he could do it, Mazarin put into effect these postulates drawn from his daily observations of the Barberinis, and became a convinced propagandist in the Roman style of his generation. . . .

From the moment when the Palais Mazarin was transformed into a bastion of Italianism, concerts or operas came to be heard in Paris, while Bernini was invited there several times. Painting, music and architecture–sculpture represented the three parts of a co-ordinated, intensive, continued operation – in a word, of a program in favor of baroque art.

When he lived in Rome, Mazarin had verified the prestige that the pontificate of Urban VIII drew from artistic patronage. Already there was for him no glory without statues, without paintings, without melodies. Indeed, in showing the child Louis XIV the political importance of patronage, he prepared the way for the *grand siècle*.[1]

[1] Madeleine Laurain-Portemer, *Etudes Mazarines* (Paris, 1981), pp. 177, 261.

Deux principes ont guidé l'action de Mazarin dans le domain des arts: d'abord la nécessité d'un mécénat comme fleuron de la politique, puis l'excellence de l'art baroque comme ferment de renouveau. Dès qu'il l'a pu, Mazarin a mis en oeuvre ces postulats tirés de ses observations quotidiennes auprès des Barberini et n'est fait un propagandiste convaincu du style romain de sa génération, tel qu'il l'a vu s'épanouir sous ses yeux. . . .

That Mazarin had arrived at these precepts for the politics of art as early as 1636 emerges from a letter to his patron Cardinal Antonio Barberini, advising him about a proposed campaign to convert the British monarch, Charles I, to Catholicism, 'In such a case I should like to be the purveyor of the Berninis, the Cortonas and the best musicians, because they would erect statues, paint pictures and create melodies to exalt the glory of such a king.'[2]

Then there was another, darker side to the importation of musicians: travelling virtuosi had long served as spies, for, when they were good courtiers as well as good musicians, they frequently had easy access to the private chambers of those in power. Thus, James Anthony correctly suggests that Mazarin 'saw Italian opera in France as a potential source of secret agents and as a smokescreen for political maneuvres'.[3] One singer, Atto Melani, imported by Mazarin for his first opera, was at the beginning of a long career as a spy, and another, Leonora Baron, was heavily involved in papal politics.

Art historians have thoroughly chronicled Mazarin's importation of Italian art and architecture to France,[4] and, indeed, even today, three centuries later, the long-term results of this transalpine influence are still visible in parts of Paris, at Versailles, and in French museums. The musical results of his campaigns proved more ephemeral, however, in part because the remains of any performing art are, by their nature, evanescent compared to buildings, statues or canvases; in part because, subsequently, the works of Jean-Baptiste Lully (né Giovanni Battista Lulli) so thoroughly subsumed earlier attempts in the field of opera in France that most of those pioneering efforts vanished, leaving scarcely a trace.

Many years ago Henry Prunières presented, in a classic study,[5] much of what is known of Mazarin's musical activities in France. More recently, James Anthony ably reexamined those activities in his indispensable survey of French baroque music.[6] The most visible results of Mazarin's undertakings were performances of several operas accompanied by ballets as entr'actes or afterpieces. Table 1 lists these performances.

Au moment où le Palais Mazarin se transforme en bastion de l'italienisme, concerts ou opéras se font entendre à Paris, tandis à maintes reprises le Bernin y est invité. Peinture, musique, architecture-sculpture représentent les trois parts d'une action coordonée, intensive, continue en un mot d'un programme en faveur de l'art baroque.

Lorsqu'il habitait Rome, Mazarin avait constaté le prestige que le pontificat d'un Urbain VIII tirait de la protection des arts. Déjà, il n'etait point pour lui de gloire sans statues, sans peintures, sans mélodies. En révélant à Louis XIV, enfant, l'importance politique du mécénat, il a, en réalité, préparé le Grand Siècle.

[2] Letter of 26 March 1636 (Vatican Library, Barb. lat. 8040, fol. 65), as cited in Laurain-Portemer, *Etudes Mazarines*, p. 261 note. 'Io vorrei in tal caso esser il conduttore degli Bernini e Cortonesi e migliori musici perchè si ergessero statue, si facessero pitture e si formassero melodie per celebrar la gloria d'un tanto Re.'

[3] James R. Anthony, 'Mazarin, Cardinal Jules', in Stanley Sadie (ed.), *The New Grove Dictionary of Music and Musicians,* vol. XI (London, 1980), p. 863.

[4] For the standard English-language account, see Anthony Blunt, *Art and Architecture in France 1500 to 1700*, 2nd ed. (Baltimore, 1970), chapter 6: 'Richelieu and Mazarin 1630–61'.

[5] Henry Prunières, *L'opéra italien en France avant Lulli* (Paris, 1913, repr. 1975).

[6] James R. Anthony, *French Baroque Music from Beaujoyeulx to Rameau* (London, 1974; 2nd ed., New York, 1978, pp. 45–51; 3rd ed., Paris, 1981 as *La musique en France à l'époque baroque*, Beatrice Vierne (trans.), pp. 67–75).

Table 1 'Opera' in France during Mazarin's ascendancy

Title (première)	Acts (genre)	Composer	Librettist	Performances (non-Paris in CAPS)	Ballet	Occasion
*La finta pazza (Venice 1641)	prol+3 (commedia)	F. Sacrati	G. Strozzi	14-xii-1645 Petit Bourbon (several perfs.)	G. B. Balbi	Advent
*L'Egisto, rè di Cipro (Venice 1643)	prol+3 (favola)	F. Cavalli	G. Faustini	13-ii-1646 Palais royal (?4 perfs.)	[?none]	Carnival
Achebar, roi du Mogol	? (musique récitatif)	Abbé Mailly	?	1647 Alessandro Bichi's CARPENTRAS	?	Carnival
*L'Orfeo	prol+3 (tragedia)	L. Rossi	F. Buti	2-iii-1647 Palais royal (8 perfs.)	G. B. Balbi	Carnival
†Les amours d'Apollon et de Daphné	prol+3 (comédie en musique)	C. Dassoucy	C. Dassoucy	pubd. 1650 but prob. never perf.	?	?
*Le nozze di Peleo e di Teti	3 (commedia)	C. Caproli	F. Buti	14-iv-1654 Petit Bourbon (9 perfs.)	Lully/Benserade Les nopces de Pélée et di Thétis (3 entrées)	?
Le triomphe de l'Amour sur des bergers et bergères	4 scenes (pastorale, idylle)	M. de La Guerre	C. de Beys	†21-i-1655 Louvre (?1 perf.)	?	Carnival
La muette ingrate	? (comédie en musique)	R. Cambert	?	†1658 concerts	?	?
$La Rosaura, imperatrice di Constantinopoli	?5 (commedia)	?	D. Locatelli	Carnival 1658 Petit Bourbon (several perfs.)	(4 entrées)	Carnival
Pastorale	5 (comédie en musique)	R. Cambert	P. Perrin	iv/v-1659 ISSY/VINCENNES (9-11 perfs.)	?	?Carnival

Table 1 (cont.)

Title (première)	Acts (genre)	Composer	Librettist	Performances (non-Paris in CAPS)	Ballet	Occasion
Ariane, ou Le mariage de Bacchus	3 (opéra)	R. Cambert	P. Perrin	1659, not perf. [several public rehearsals, Hôtel de Nevers, 1669–70.]	?	?
*Xerse (Venice 1655)	prol+3 (tragedia)	F. Cavalli	N. Minato	22–xi–1660 Louvre (several perfs.)	Lully Xerxes (6 entrées)	Louis XIV's wedding
L'inconstant vaincu	5 (pastorale en chansons)	?	?	pubd. 1661 but prob. never perf.		
La Mort d'Adonis	? (opéra)	J.-B. Boesset	P. Perrin	†c. 1661 petit coucher du Roi	?	?
*Ercole amante	prol+5 (tragedia)	F. Cavalli	F. Buti	(1 perf.) 7–ii–1662 Tuileries (more than 5 perfs.)	Lully/Benserade Hercule amoureux (18 entrées)	Carnival

*Sponsored by Mazarin
†This perf. not staged
§ Not all-sung

Mazarin's campaign, which, through his direct or indirect patronage, caused six Italian operas to be brought to France between 1645 and 1662 (along with Italian singers, dancers, instrumentalists, and stage designers to realize them) may be viewed as a success or a failure, depending on the criteria employed for making such a judgment. Mazarin succeeded insofar as all-sung opera eventually did take root and flourish in France, in the form of a native hybrid that cross-pollinated the *ballet de cour* and *air de cour* with those elements of Italian opera amenable to bending to the exigencies of the French language and tastes. Table 1 chronicles not only the Italian imports sponsored by Mazarin, but also the French responses to the Italian productions. The latter includes seven more or less capable attempts to counter Italian opera by adapting domestic genres, especially the pastorale with chansons and the *ballet de cour*, to make them more like operas.

But Mazarin may be judged to have failed insofar as he was not able to generate enough sustained French patronage to maintain a permanent Italian troupe in Paris, so that, after each set of performances had ended, the laboriously assembled artists returned to their native land. Mazarin's final Italian opera, *Ercole amante*, planned in the last years of his life but performed only after his death, marked the end of this experiment; without Mazarin to organize it, Italian opera as such vanished almost totally from the French scene, even as it was conquering the rest of Europe. Aside from one last attempt (Paolo Lorenzani's *Nicandro e Fileno*, on a libretto by Mazarin's nephew F. Mancini-Mazzarini, duc de Nevers, produced at Fontainebleau in September 1681) Italian comic opera was not staged again in Paris until 1729 (Orlandini's *Il marito giocatore e la moglio bacchettona = Bajocco e Serpilla*), and Italian serious opera, not until 1811 (Paisiello's *Pirro*).[7] Nonetheless, the limited long-term success of the Italian operas that Mazarin sponsored should not obscure the fact that his vigorous advocacy permanently altered the course of musical and theatrical history in France.

The scope of Mazarin's musical patronage, impressive by almost any standards, is the more noteworthy when one considers his origins as a commoner, who rose to a position of power and wealth in the Catholic Church and French government by sheer force of personality and wits. And as striking as the contents of table 1 may be, they do not convey the full measure of Mazarin's efforts on behalf of Italian opera, for besides the six operas starred, there was another, unidentified work brought from Italy before *La finta pazza*. Prunières first collected systematically the evidence for this earlier production; the account that follows expands upon his excellent research, to which this study is indebted.[8]

[7] Alfred Loewenberg, *Annals of Opera 1597–1940*, 2nd ed. (London, 1955), cols. 40–1, 71, 137, 439. This refers to public performances of all-sung opera, and leaves aside the *commedia dell'arte* troupe active in Paris between 1682 and 1697, private performances of Italian cantatas and operatic scenes, etc.

[8] *L'opéra italien en France avant Lulli*, pp. 45–66. Prunières had discovered a copy of the bilingual libretto of *Nicandro e Fileno*, which bore no indications of date, place, composer, or poet, and he suggested that this was the work in question (pp. 62–4). Later, having correctly identified it as Lorenzani's work, he withdrew his initial suggestion without coming up with an alternative. See Henry Prunières, 'Un opéra inconnu de Paolo Lorenzani', *Congrès d'histoire de l'art organisé par la Société de l'Histoire de l'Art français, Paris, 26 Septembre – 5 Octobre 1921, Compte-rendu analytique* (Paris, 1922), pp. 180–2; Prunières, 'Paolo Lorenzani à la cour de France (1678–94)', *La revue musicale*, III/10 (August 1922), pp. 97–120.

Mazarin arrived in Paris for the first time in December 1634, as nuncio extraordinary from the Vatican. He was thirty-two. Two years later he was called to Avignon, then to Rome where he served as an unofficial French agent. By the end of 1636 France had nominated him for a cardinalate, and at the end of 1639 he returned to Paris officially to enter France's service as a naturalized citizen. Almost at once he became the protégé of and chief aide to Richelieu and later, on his mentor's recommendation, heir to his position as prime minister of France. By 1641 Mazarin was importing Italian songs, arias and cantatas to entertain his French patrons. Prunières conjectured that this may explain the origin of a manuscript in the Bibliothèque nationale (Vm^7 59102), which contains works by Rossi, Marazzoli, Carissimi, Savioni, Caproli, Boccalini, and others. This repertory must have met with some success, for a letter of January 1643 from an agent of Mazarin's in Rome reveals grander plans afoot: to bring the musician Marco Marazzoli to Paris.[9]

Marazzoli (*c.* 1605–62), popularly known in his lifetime as Marco dell'Arpa, today receives little more than a footnote in the history of music, but this does him an injustice. In the mid-seventeenth century he distinguished himself as a prolific composer of high-quality 'cantatas', oratorios, operas, and also church music (for he was a priest and member of the Papal choir). Marazzoli's graceful, post-Monteverdian idiom can be examined in several modern editions of his music even if not to any meaningful extent in live performances or recordings.[10] If Mazarin sought an outstanding Roman composer to further his political and artistic ends, Marazzoli was the logical choice.

The struggle to arrange for Marazzoli's visit to France, along with the experienced singers necessary to perform his music, stretched out over two years. Its ups and downs can be traced in Mazarin's correspondence.[11] Planning was halted by Louis XIII's death on 14 May and by the period of mourning that followed. This temporary setback proved a blessing in disguise, however, because unlike her late husband, Anne of Austria, who became regent during the minority of her son Louis XIV, enthusiastically admired Italian music. Mazarin continued to work behind the scenes, corresponding with his agent in Rome,

[9] Letter of 4 January 1643 from Elpidio Benedetti to Mazarin. Paris, Archives du Ministère des affaires etrangères, Correspondance diplomatique, Rome 81, fo. 16v; Prunières, p. 47. 'Il S^r. Marco dell'Arpa, richiestone da me, va' spesso a trattenerlo e, se gli fosse permesso dal S. Card. Antonio, lo volentieri lo servirebbe anco nel viaggio nel suo ritorno alla Corte. Io cerco di servire il detto Sig^r. in quanto vaglio et essendo stato appunto questa mattina a vederlo, ho trovato ch'era con due architetti francesi, che pigliavano le misure di tutto il Palazo [*sic*] et me ha detto faceva fare per curiosità'.

[10] A complete list of Marazzoli's works, with modern editions indicated, is found in Eleanor Caluori, 'Marazzoli, Marco', *The New Grove Dictionary*, vol. XI, pp. 642–6. To this should be added a facsimile of twenty-one cantatas ed. Wolfgang Witzenmann, in Carolyn Gianturco (ed.), *The Italian Cantata in the Seventeenth Century*, vol. IV (New York, 1986); and another of *L'Egisto, ovvero Chi soffre speri*, Howard Brown (ed.) (New York, 1982) (=*Italian Opera 1640–1770*, vol. LXI). The sole commercial recording known to me is two scenes from *L'Amore trionfante dello Sdecno*, Piero Cavalli/Complesso Barocco di Roma, RCA Victor ML 40001–3 (=*Storia della musica italiana*, vol. II, record 3, side 2 (Rome, 1961)).

[11] Letter of 7 May 1643 from Elpidio Benedetti to Mazarin. Paris Archives du Ministère . . . Rome 82, fo. 174; Prunières, pp. 47–8. 'Si farà ogni diligenza per trovare li musici che V. Em^{za}. desidererebbe e di già ne ho parlato al s. Marc Marazzoli, che ha quasi affatto perduta la speranza di poter fare questo viaggio.'

Elpidio Benedetti. In addition to Marazzoli's post in the Sistine Chapel, he served in the entourage of Mazarin's old employer Cardinal Antonio Barberini, nephew of the pope, Urban VIII. Permission for Marazzoli to go to France proved difficult to obtain because, despite Urban VIII's generally pro-French policies, this was a period of difficult relations between the French court and the Holy See. In August Benedetti wrote Mazarin again:

I had finally resolved to petition Cardinal Barberini for permission for Signor Marco Marazzoli's leave of absence, and, having spoken frankly about it to Cardinal Poli, had found in him [Poli] the strong wish to please Your Eminence, when Signor Marco came to my house to let me know that he was free to make the journey and that he hoped to set out at the first possible moment.[12]

A week later, however, the hopes raised by this letter were dashed:

What will Your Eminence say when you learn that Signor Marco Marazzoli's projected journey cannot be realized? After having obtained Cardinal Poli's authorization and having gone to get permission for the leave of absence from His Holiness [the Pope] and from Cardinal Barberini, Marazzoli was given to understand that His Holiness would not wish to have him leave the [Sistine] Chapel. He [Marazzoli] cited numerous precedents including his own example (since he had spent eight or ten months in Venice), but to no avail.[13]

Benedetti added that Marazzoli favored the French cause, was upset at the Pope's revocation of his permission to travel, and still hoped to have the opportunity to carry out the proposed voyage. In a letter of November of the same year, Mazarin complained bitterly to Cardinal Alessandro Bichi (an opera patron whose name may be noted in table 1) that his former employer Barberini had prevented Marco dell'Arpa from going to France 'simply because I wished it', and this despite Mazarin's having facilitated the entrance into the Pope's service of the French engineer Petit.[14] At about the same time Mazarin's agent asked Barberini why he had refused to allow Marazzoli to travel to France. Barberini

[12] Letter of 19 August 1643. Paris Archives, du Ministère . . . Rome 82, fo. 312; Prunières, p. 49. 'Mi risolvei finalmente di supplicare il S. Card. Barb. per la licenza per il sigr Marco Marazzoli et havendomi rimesso al S. Card. Poli, S. Em. si mostrò m^to inclinato a compiacerre V. Em. et in q^to punto arriva da me il S. Marco a parteciparmi come è in libertà di fare il viaggio, epensa di mettersi in esso quanto prima.' For Marazzoli's continuing connection with Cardinal Barberini, see Henry Prunières, 'Les musiciens du Cardinal Antonio Barberini' in *Mélanges de musicologie offerts à M. Lionel de La Laurencie* (Paris, 1933), pp. 117–22.

[13] Letter of 25 August 1643. Paris Archives du Ministère . . . Rome 82, fo. 313; Prunières, pp. 49–50. 'Che dirà V. Em^za in sentire svanito il viaggio del Sr Marco Marazzoli? Dopo haverne questi ottenuta la licenza dal Sig. Card. Poli, et esser stato a licentiarsi di S. S^tà e dal S. Card. Barberino, gli fu fatto intendere che S. S^tà non voleva che abbandonasse

la cappella. Nè giovó l'allegare esempii in persona d'altri e sua, mentre era stato a Venetia 8, o 10 mesi, togliendo, se lieve, affatto ogni speranza. Mi dice il s^r Marco, che S^a S^tà si dolse seco de' Francesi, che voglino sempre continuare ad assistere il duca di Parma, che ben pensano a stare allegramente e far feste con lassare in mille afflittioni la sede apostolica e cose simili, che riflette poi nell' impressione del Papa e viene che gl'habbino fatto revocare la licenza di partire. Il pover' huono si è acquietato con la speranza che pur un giorno sia per succedergli d'havere questa buona fortuna, convenendo ancor' egli che frattanto non se ne faccia altro tentativo essendo troppo manifesta la contraria volontà di S. S^tà. Alcuni ne sono rimasti grand^te maravigliati, stimando che si potesse in gratia di V. Em. fargli questa gratia, che si è concess a tanti altri.'

[14] Letter of 20 November 1643. Paris Archives du Ministère . . . Rome 81, fo. 483; Prunières, p. 50.

responded that he was offended that Mazarin had not written to him directly.[15] Behind Barberini's obstructionism and transparent excuse doubtless lay an exercise in *Realpolitik*: with the deaths of Louis XIII and Richelieu, Mazarin could have fallen from power; instead, he rose to greater power and, as soon as his ascendency had become clear, his request for Marazzoli's visit to France was quickly granted. The composer arrived in Paris about the middle of December, and on the eighteenth of that month Mazarin wrote to his brother Michele, the Father Provincial for Rome, 'I again send most humble thanks to Cardinal Antonio for the permission that he granted Marco dell'Arpa to come for a while to this Court'.[16]

Next Mazarin had to obtain experienced singers. It would have been against his clearly enunciated principles to settle for anyone less than first rate in the artists whom he patronized.[17] One of the best singers in Rome, the extraordinary Leonora Baroni, known to all as Signora Leonora, had been a friend of Mazarin's in his Roman days. Since that time she had risen to a position of astonishing eminence. A combination of musical talent, striking appearance, and political savvy had made her a reigning figure in Roman social and political life. Among her other accomplishments, this remarkable woman – daughter of the equally extraordinary *bell'Adriana*, who had charmed an earlier generation in Mantua[18] – had a hand in the choosing of two popes. Although officially married to one Giulio Castellani, secretary to Cardinal Francesco Barberini, her true role was as mistress of Prince Camillo Pamphili. So strong was her position in Rome that she could hardly hope to better it by a trip to Paris. There was always the danger that returning to Rome after an absence she might find conditions changed and her former position filled by someone else. Thus it is not surprising that after initial enthusiasm for the idea, when it was first broached in the spring of 1643, she hesitated to leave. In November she was still hesitating, and a voluminous correspondence resulted. In the end, however, promises of large amounts of money and a personal invitation from the queen overcame these obstacles, and Leonora arrived in Paris around the beginning of April 1644. Her success at the French court was as great as Mazarin had anticipated, and she was soon on such intimate terms with the queen that the anti-Italian factions at court were much alarmed. The improbable panoply of Leonora's triumphs,

[15] Letter of 15 November 1643 from Elpidio Benedetti. Paris Archives du Ministère . . . Rome 82, fo. 394; Prunières, p. 50. '. . . havendo penetrato la causa, che glielo ha sin' hora ritardato. Era parso al S. Card. Antonio che, desiderando V. Em. il sud.to, havesse potuto scrivergliene un motto e per questo, non dichiarandosi bene S. Em. con Poli, se gli era poi fatto intendere che non partisse. Hora che il S.r Card. Antonio, con l'occasione della sua venuta in Roma, n'è stato pregato da me in voce per parte di V. Em. e fatto scusa s'ella non gliene haveva scritto, ha condisceso a permettergli che parta e mi sono veramente chiarito che il sig. card. Barberino non vi haveva colpa alcuna. Di che ne riceverà avviso

più certo col seguente ord.rio.'
[16] Paris, Bibliothèque Mazarine, MS 2217, fo. 200v; Prunières, p. 50; A. Cheruel and B. d'Avenel (eds.), *Lettres du cardinal Mazarin pendant son ministère*, vol. I (Paris, 1872), pp. 498–507. 'Rendo ancora humiliss.me gratie al Sig. Card.le Antonio della permissione, che ha data a Marco dell'Arpa di venire per qualche tempo a questa corte.'
[17] See Mazarin's letter of 8 August 1659 to Buti (Prunières, pp. 231, 395–6).
[18] For Signora Leonora's mother Adriana Basile, see Stuart Reiner, 'La vag'Angioletta (and Others)', *Anelecta musicologica*, XIV (1974), pp. 26–88.

musical and political, has been portrayed in colourful detail by Prunières. She remained at the French court until 10 April 1645, on which date she set out for Rome laden with jewels, money, and a lifetime pension. Thus, although she left Paris well before the performance of *La finta pazza* in December of that year, she was there for the crucial portion of Marazzoli's visit during which an 'opera' of his was done.

With Leonora and Marco dell'Arpa as cornerstones, Mazarin had still to build the rest of his company. His agent in Rome had made several abortive attempts to hire castratos, and similarly futile efforts were conducted through Cardinal Bichi. News of Mazarin's desire to 'guide to France castratos from Rome, and in particular some from the Pope's chapel, for a *commedia* or *dramma musicale*,'[19] and perhaps also news of the way in which Signora Leonora was being received, gradually spread in Italy, and musicians from various cities wrote to offer their services. Mazarin did not want self-nominations, however, but the recommendations of discerning princes. He wrote to Florence and, perhaps because the Medicis were then on good political terms with France, finally found there what he needed: Prince Mathias recommended a young castrato with an excellent voice, who had been sent to Rome for further training under Luigi Rossi's supervision. Thus on 5 October 1644 the eighteen-year-old Atto Melani, having received permission, left for Paris escorted by Mazarin's secretary, Alessandro Fabri. In Florence they were joined by Atto's brother Jacopo[20] and by Anna Francesca Costa, known as Signora Checca, an experienced singer in the service of Prince Gian Carlo Medici. This party reached Paris early in November.

The newly arrived trio was warmly welcomed by Anne of Austria, who delighted in hearing them almost every evening and rewarded them by lavish compliments and rich gifts. With the approach of Carnival, and with four virtuoso singers and a composer in residence, Mazarin found himself in a position to fulfill his long-standing wish to present the French court with an Italian opera. But the way in which this was done remains a source of great puzzlement. Despite years of struggle and great expense to assemble the first Italian troupe in Paris, no public event was given and (quite unlike the cases of Mazarin's six other Italian operas chronicled in table 1) the newspapers, diplomatic correspondence, diarists and writers of feuilletons kept strangely silent. If it were not for two passages, one from the *Gazette de France* and the other from a letter of Atto Melani's, there would be no way of being certain that anything at all had happened.

The semi-official report of the *Gazette* alotted more space to matters of court protocol than to the new artistic enterprise:

On [Shrove Tuesday] the 28th [of February 1645] the king [Louis XIV] gave a dinner for the Queen of England, the queen [Anne of Austria], the duc d'Anjou, the duc d'Orleans (who is the king's uncle), and Mademoiselle [the king's first cousin]. Her Highness

[19] Alessandro Ademollo, *I primi fasti della musica italiana a Parigi* (Milan, [1884]), p. 10; Prunières, p. 56. '. . . condurre in Francia musici di Roma per una comedia o dramma musicale et in particolare alcuni della cappella del Papa'.

[20] Concerning the musical activities of Jacopo, Alessandro, and Atto Melani and the vast correspondence generated by Atto's spying activities, see Robert Lamar Weaver, 'Materiali per le biografie dei fratelli Melani', *Rivista italiana di musicologia*, XII (1977), pp. 252–95.

presented the napkin to the king, as did also the duc d'Anjou to the Queen of England and Mademoiselle to the queen. In the evening there was an Italian comedy in the Great Hall [of the Palais royal] and a ballet danced by several noblemen of the court. After this the queen gave a supper in her great study for the Queen of England and for His Royal Highness.[21]

Everything that the young castrato Atto Melani thought necessary to relate about this event to his patron, the Grand Duke of Tuscany, was contained in four sentences:

We finally performed the opera, which is very beautiful, and Her Majesty wished to hear it again next Sunday. Each of us acquitted himself well in his role. In order to bring honor to Your Highness, I exerted myself so as not to do less than the others, and, by the grace of God, I succeeded beyond my dreams. Signora Checca managed as well as it was in her power to do.[22]

No further reports of any kind, not even any indication of whether the second performance mentioned by Melani actually took place on Sunday, 12 March – or did he mean '*the* next Sunday', i.e. 5 March (which, in either case, was during Lent, as Ash Wednesday fell on 1 March that year)? After the opera had been performed, Mazarin's Italian musicians gave a few more concerts in the queen's private apartments and then, on 10 April, Marco dell'Arpa, Signora Leonora, and her husband left Paris to return to their homeland, while the brothers Melani apparently departed not long thereafter.

After decades of uncertainty about which work of Marazzoli's might have been performed at the Palais Royal on the evening of 28 February 1645, Pier Maria Capponi's nomination of one in particular has been accepted by several specialists.[23] To investigate the nature of this work and to evaluate the probability that it is the work that was performed in Paris on 28 February 1645, we must turn back the clock two years to Carnival 1643 and change venue from Paris to Rome.

Among the entertainments offered during that Carnival for the delectation of

[21] *Gazette de France*, 4 March 1645; Prunières, p. 61 (with the second sentence omitted). 'Le 28, le Roi donna à dîner à la reine d'Angleterre, à la Reine, à M. le duc d'Anjou, à Mgr le duc d'Orleans, oncle de Sa Majeste, et à Mademoiselle. Son Altesse Royale ayant donne la serviette au Roi, comme fit aussi M. le duc d'Anjou à la reine d'Angleterre, et Mademoiselle à la Reine. Sur le soir, il y eut comédie italienne dans la grande salle, et un ballet danse par plusieurs seigneurs de la cour, apres lequel la Reine donna à souper, dans son grand cabinet, a la reine d'Angleterre et à Son Altesse Royale.' The idiom *donner la serviette à quelqu'un*, here rendered 'to give the napkin to someone', refers to a ceremonial presentation of a moist towel or napkin at the beginning of a meal for wiping the hands.
[22] Florence, Mediceo 5425, fo. 221; Ademollo, p. 19; Prunières, p. 61. As late as 1677, La Fontaine, in an anti-opera tract, still referred

to 'Les passages d'Atto et de Leonora', or, in one manuscript, 'Les longs passages d'Atto et de Leonora' ('Épître à M. de Nyert sur l'opéra' in Henri Begnier (ed.), *Oeuvres de J. de La Fontaine*, vol. IX (Paris, 1892), pp. 154–63, here p. 155).
[23] P. M. Capponi, 'Marco Marazzoli e l'oratorio "Cristo e i Farisei"', in Accademia musicale chigiana, *La scuola romana* (Siena, 1953), pp. 101–6; entries for Marazzoli and Buti in *MGG*, *The New Grove*, *Enciclopedia dello specttacolo*, *Der Grosse Lexikon der Musik*, *La musica . . . Dizionario*, etc.; or Michael Grace, 'Marco Marazzoli and the Development of the Latin Oratorio' (unpubl. PhD diss., Yale University, 1974), pp. 35–44; Giorgio Pestelli, 'Trionfo Barocco e Illusminismo alle Corti Europee' in Guglielmo Barblan and Alberto Basso (eds.), *Storia dell'Opera* (Turin, 1977), vol. II, p. 6.

il bel mondo of Rome was one entitled *Il giuditio della Ragione tra la Beltà e l'Affetto, Dramma in musica*, performed at the Palazzo Roberti. The distinguished librettist Giulio Rospigliosi, who was in the service of the Barberinis and later became Pope Clement IX, attended a performance and wrote to his brother Camillo of 'a beautiful *commedia in musica* . . . done in Count di Marciano's house this Carnival'.[24] A brief notice in the Roman *Avvisi* reported that 'A beautiful little moral opera entitled *Il giuditio della Ragione* [etc.] was sung many times . . . and it was highly praised by the listeners for being short, curious, and well performed.'[25] A printed scenario (plate 1), a manuscript libretto, and a manuscript score survive.[26] None of these bear attributions of the poetry or music, but the score originally came from Marazzoli's personal library.[27] Some four decades later a bibliography of Roman authors attributed the libretto to Francesco Buti,[28] and circumstantial evidence supports this attribution. There are three reasons to single out this work as the most likely one of Marazzoli's to have been performed in Paris: (1) it was the last such work he wrote before his French adventure; (2) the score, otherwise written on Italian paper similar to that used in his other scores, contains one sheet of French paper;[29] and (3) the circumstances of the work's Roman première suggest French sponsorship.

Il giudizio comprises a prologue and three acts, with two danced entr'actes and a *canzonetta del ballo* at the end. The characters and story of this 'beautiful little moral opera' (*Avvisi*) or 'beautiful comedy set to music' (Rospigliosi) or '*dramma ideale*' (Mandosio) appear in the scenario as follows:

The Judgement of Reason between Beauty and Affection
Dramma in Musica

Interlocutors

La Bellezza	Beauty
Vero Amore	True Love

[24] Letter of 7 February 1643, Vatican Library, Vat. 1. 13364. This information and that reported in notes 25, 26, and 28 was gathered by Margaret Murata and communicated to me by Thomas Walker. Walker, Margaret Murata, Lorenzo Bianconi, and Lowell Lindgren are compiling a catalogue and bibliography of opera in Rome in the seventeenth century. '. . . una bella commedia in musica . . . si fa questa Carnevale in casa del Signor Conte di Marciano'.

[25] 'Di Roma', 14 February 1643 (Vatican Library, Barb. lat. 6363). '. . . è stato più volte fatta recitare in musica una bella operetta morale intitolata il Giuditio della Ragione [etc.] . . . et per essere breve, curiosa, et ben rappresentata, è stata molto commendata dalli ascoltatori.'

[26] The libretto (Barb. lat. 3795) and score (Chigi Q.VIII.182) are at the Vatican; copies of the scenario are there (Barb. lat. 3795), at the Biblioteca Casanatense in Rome (Vol. misc. 2540.15), and at the University of Toronto (Italian Play Collection – Pamphlets). I have

compared photocopies of the Vatican scenario with that in Toronto and found them to be identical.

[27] Wolfgang Witzenmann, 'Autographe Marco Marazzolis in der Biblioteca Vaticana' *Analecta musicologica*, no. 7 (1968), pp. 36–86; (1970), no. 9, pp. 203–94; here pp. 75–7. Marazzoli's score is a professional fair copy with numerous autograph corrections and emendations (Witzenmann, p. 51). It was listed in the inventory of Marazzoli's library at his death as 'Un altra commedia intitolato il Capriccio, che commincia Prologo, e finisce [a]ma chi t'ama' (Rome, Archivio di Stata, Notari, segretari e cancellieri della R. C. A., vol. 2082, fo. 56v; Witzenmann, p. 40).

[28] Prospero Mandosio, *Biblioteca romana seu romanorum* . . ., vol. II (Rome, 1692), p. 45. Mandosio gives Buti's libretto the title 'Il Capriccio, ovvero il Giudizio della Ragione con la Beltà e l'affetto, drama ideale'.

[29] Witzenmann, 'Autographe Marco Marazzolis', pp. 59–61.

Plate 1. The printed scenario from *Il giuditio della Ragione tra la Beltà e l'Affetto, Dramma in musica*, 1643

Ragione	Reason
Gelosia	Jealousy
Capriccio	Caprice
Tempo	Time
L'Inganno ⎫ parti mute	Deceit ⎫ silent roles
Martello ⎭	Hammer ⎭
Damigelle della Bellezza	Beauty's maids-in-waiting
Choro della Ragione	Reason's chorus
Choro dell'Inganno	Deceit's chorus
Choro del Martello	Hammer's chorus

Argument

TRUE LOVE, despairing at the cruel treatment accorded him by his lady BEAUTY, leaves her, persuaded by REASON to withdraw to a solitary and peaceful life. In the meantime, BEAUTY, becoming enamored of a false lover called CAPRICE [and] perceiving that he does not return her love, has JEALOUSY bring TRUE LOVE back to her, in order to induce affection in CAPRICE through competition with the other rival. TRUE LOVE returns together with REASON to work on BEAUTY, with the result that TIME overtakes any conflict between them, which causes BEAUTY to recognize TRUE LOVE and to detest the inclination that she had for CAPRICE. She surrenders to the rightful superiority of REASON, who judges finally the difference between beauty and affection, resulting in perpetual peace.[30]

This peculiar description of the consummation of an amorous union – 'perpetual peace' – suggests that beneath the allegorical presentation of the pitfalls and triumphs of love lies a subtext dealing with the resolution of political strife. This suggestion finds indirect support in several recent historical studies of seventeenth-century opera, studies which have made it increasingly clear that the contents of staged works were usually taken to stand for current leaders and current events no matter how distant in time, place or overt subject the plots may have been.[31] This commonly understood double meaning goes a long way

[30] 'Argomento. / Il vero Amore disperato per le crudeltà usategli dalla Bellezza sua Dama, si parte da lei, così persuaso dalla Ragione, per ritirarsi a vita solitaria, e quieta. La Bellezza intanto invaghitasi d'un falso Amante detto il Capriccio, accorgendosi di non esser da esso amata, per indurlo con l'emulatione d'altro rivale à verace affetto, fa ricondurre à se dalla Gelosia il vero Amore, il quale per opra di costei insieme con la Ragione tornato, nel succeder tra loro qualche contrasto, sopragiunge il [T]empo, che fatto dalla Bellezza riconoscere il vero Amore, e detestare il Genio havuto de lei al Capriccio, constituisce nella sua dovuta superiorità la Ragione, la quale guidica finalmente le differenze tra la Beltà, e l'[a]ffetto, undendoli in perpetua pace.' The only modern reaction to *Il giudizio* calls it 'a droll [work] rich in an extraordinary humour realized with the most interesting musical invention' (Piero Capponi, 'Marco Marazzoli e l'oratorio "Cristo e i Farisei"', in *La scuola romana: G. Carissimi – A. Cesti – M. Marazzoli* [Siena, 1953], pp. 101–6, here p. 104: '. . . una comica ricca de uno straordinario umore realizzato con interessantissime invenzioni musicali . . .').

[31] For Britain see John Buttrey, 'The Evolution of English Opera between 1656 and 1695: A Re-investigation' (unpubl. PhD diss., Cambridge University, 1967) and Curtis Price, 'Political Allegory in late-seventeenth century English Opera' in Nigel Fortune, ed., *Music and Theatre: Essays in Honour of Winton Dean* (Cambridge, 1987), pp. 1–29; for France, Robert M. Isherwood, *Music in the Service of the King: France in the Seventeenth Century* (Ithaca, 1973); for Hamburg, Hans Joachim Marx, 'Geschichte der Hamburger Barockoper. Ein Forschungsbericht', *Hamburger Jahrbuch für Musikwissenschaft* III (1978), pp. 7–34.

toward explaining the great anxiety over the censorship of plays and operas. In some instances the political allegory was explicit, in others it remained hidden. A single instance of the former, near in time to *Il giudizio*, may serve to exemplify this form of entertainment *cum* propaganda. In 1643 H. Le Gras published in Paris a five-act play entitled *Europe, comédie heroïque*, an unabashed allegory of European politics written in a way destined to please pro-French sympathies. As a frontispiece, a key assigns each of the characters in the play to a country whom he represents in the action. *Il giudizio* presented no such key. The audience made its own interpretations, and today we are left with our educated guesses.

Precisely what political strife *Il giudizio* may have referred to becomes clearer from an examination of the political maneuvering to appoint a new pope after the death of Urban VIII (Maffeo Barberini) on 29 July 1644. Urban's reign had coincided with that of Richelieu in France and with the Thirty Years War in Germany. Far from wholeheartedly supporting the Catholic cause in Germany, however, Urban had generally pursued pro-French policies, in an attempt to weaken the Habsburgs, whose growing power in northern Italy he feared. This must have been a controversial policy, for the two leading candidates to replace Urban represented respectively pro-Austrian and pro-French factions in the Vatican. The candidate of the pro-Austrian faction and winner of the election was Gian Battista Pamphili, uncle of Signora Leonora's lover, who took the name Innocent X.

Mazarin, the Barberinis, and their entourages had supported Urban's pro-French policies and hoped to encourage them. The French embassy in Rome may have been housed in the Palazzo Roberti, where *Il giudizio* received its first performance.[32] Prior to the letter of 4 January 1643 cited above, that is, before the first performance of *Il giudizio*, Mazarin had already courted Marazzoli for a visit to France. Hence, even without a complete deciphering of the allegory, *Il giudizio* must be considered a pro-French tract, or, more accurately, a piece of propaganda urging strong ties between France and the Holy See. By this interpretation TRUE LOVE represents France, BEAUTY portrays the Vatican, and CAPRICE stands for Austria.

The career of the librettist of *Il giudizio* provides circumstantial support for this interpretation.[33] Like Marazzoli, Francesco Buti (1604–82) was in the service of Antonio Barberini, as Mazarin had been before being sent abroad by the Vati-

[32] Witzenmann, 'Autographe Marco Marazzolis', pp. 61, 77. I have been unable to confirm Witzenmann's assertion that the French embassy was housed in the Palazzo Roberti. This is not a well-known building, although a slightly later map of Rome shows a 'Palazzo Ruberti' (*Pianta di G. B. Falda* [Rome, 1676]: '439. P[alazzo] Ruberti Rione Sant' Eustachio'; facsimile in Cesare D'Onofrio, *Roma nel seicento* [Florence, 1969]). Pier Maria Capponi, who lists, in addition to the performance of *Il giudizio* in 1643, the works that were given at the French embassy during the carnivals of 1638 and 1639, states that the embassy was housed in the Palazzo Acquavivi ('Roma', *Enciclopedia dello specttacolo*, vol. VIII (Rome, 1961), col. 1114). To add to the confusion, Giulio Rospigliosi reported that *Il giudizio* was performed 'in Count di Marciano's house' (note 24 above). The French ambassador from 1641 to 1646 was François Du Val, marquis de Fontenay, dit Fontenay-Mareil (*c.* 1594–1665).

[33] See the entries for Buti in *MGG*, the *Enciclopedia dello specttacolo*, and especially the excellent article by A. Lanfranchi in *Dizionario biografico degli italiani*, vol. XV (Rome, 1972), pp. 603–6.

can. After the election to the papacy of the rival faction's candidate, Buti accompanied the Barberinis on their exile in France (1645), and, when the Barberinis returned to Italy (1653), Buti stayed in France to become one of Mazarin's servants and then to remain in France for some time after Mazarin's death. At various points Buti wrote librettos, in Rome for oratorios, cantatas and operas, and in France for operas and ballets (table 2). His life was thus spent serving

Table 2 *Librettos attributed to Francesco Buti*

Title	Genre	Composer	Première	Comments
Per la Purificazione della B^{ma} Vergine Maria	oratorio	?	Rome	
Il Giuseppe venduto, figlio de Giacobbe	oratorio	?L. Rossi	?Rome	
Il giusto inganno	commedia	?	?Rome	
Il Capriccio, ovvero Il giudizio della Ragione tra la Beltà e l'Affetto	dramma ideale	M. Marazzoli	Rome 1644/ ?Paris 1645	
Non v'è più chi non discerna	cantata	M. Marazzoli	?Paris ?1644–5	
Balletto di Psyche	comédie-ballet	J.-B. Lully	Paris 1656	Fr. texts by Benserade as *Psyché et la puissance de l'amour*
L'Orfeo	tragedia	L. Rossi	Paris 1647	see table 1
Le nozze di Peleo e di Teti	commedia	C. Caproli	Paris 1654	see table 1
L'Amor malato [?=Baletto degli spropositi]	comédie-ballet	J.-B. Lully [M. Marazzoli]	?Paris 1657	Fr. texts by Benserade as *L'Amour malade*
Ballet de l'Impatience	comédie-ballet	J.-B. Lully	Paris 1661	with Benserade
Ercole amante	tragedia	F. Cavalli	Paris 1662	see table 1

those who supported stronger relations between France and the Vatican, and it would be no great surprise if his masters had commissioned an allegorical text supporting their cause, hiding the controversial political message behind a carnival entertainment.

If correct, the identification of *Il giudizio* as the work performed at the Palais Royal on 28 February 1645, offers grounds for speculating about the nature of the occasion and about its influence. A text of this sort, with allegorical characters set in no particular time or place, did not require the same kind of staging as an opera based on mythology or history did: machines and changes of scene would not have been necessary. Rome had a tradition of presenting oratorios as tableaux, that is, placing the singers and instrumentalists on a stage, on a platform, or in a chapel, with fanciful, fixed decorations, but with no costumes or action. In this manner producers of oratorios could provide listeners with attractive sights, both inexpensively and without defying the (frequently ignored) papal ban on public opera performances. Even during periods when the ban on opera was lifted or was not being rigorously enforced, women were not allowed on the public stage; males usually sang all parts, with boys, falsettists, or castratos taking the high ones. Given her position in Roman society, Signora Leonora would most likely have been heard only in gatherings that, however large, were construed as private.

All the vocal parts of *Il giudizio*, for both the soloists and the choral voices (which were probably sung one to a part), are for treble voices notated in soprano clef. (Instrumental participation is limited to two violins and basso continuo.) With the exception of TIME, who makes only a brief appearance at the end and is limited to an octave, the soloists share almost identical ranges of roughly d′ to g″. As REASON, TRUE LOVE and JEALOUSY sing together in Act II, scene iv; REASON, TRUE LOVE and BEAUTY appear together in III, iii; but JEALOUSY and BEAUTY share II, i; four soloists are required. The Italian musicians in Mazarin's circle in late February of 1645 present a logical configuration for the Parisian performance of this work: BEAUTY, who appears in more scenes that any other character, would conceivably have been sung by the comely Signora Leonora; the other two important roles, REASON and TRUE LOVE, would then have been taken by Atto Melani and Signora Ceccha (although not necessarily in that order); and a carefully coached local soloist, or a fourth unidentified Italian, could have taken the three minor characters, CAPRICE, JEALOUSY, and TIME, who never appear simultaneously.[34]

This must have been a private semi-staged performance, attended by neither the public nor the whole court, but only by an inner circle – with 'several noblemen of the Court' for the ballet that followed, according to the *Gazette*. Signora Leonora would have been just as reluctant to perform in public in Paris as in Rome. Because Mazarin did not import an artist to paint scenery or an engineer to build machines, he had perhaps foreseen a small-scale performance from the start.

An account of just such a private performance, described in a rambling entry in the diary of Madame de Motteville (who was no fan of Italian opera), suggests something of the nature of this occasion:

> On Mardi gras of this year [13 February 1646] the queen caused one of these *comédies en musique* to be performed in the small hall of the Palais royal, where there were only the king, the queen, the cardinal [Mazarin], and the inner circle of the court, because the big crowd of courtiers were at the palace of Monsieur [the king's uncle], who was giving a supper for the duc d'Enghien. We were only twenty or thirty people in this place, and we thought that we would die of boredom and cold there. Entertainments of this sort require company, and solitude is not in keeping with the theater.[35]

The undertaking of a work of Marazzoli's in February 1645 must, therefore, have been a test of the viability of Italian stage music in Paris, an attempt by Mazarin to create enough interest to sustain the extraordinary expenses that bringing a fully-staged opera from Italy would entail. And it was a successful trial, for Mazarin then raised the necessary support to put on *La finta pazza* ten

---

[34] One must not rule out the possibility that one or more of the roles were performed an octave lower by a tenor. Cf. Monteverdi's madrigal, 'Bel pastor' (Book IX), in which the two voice parts are notated in soprano and tenor clefs respectively, but the work is labelled for two sopranos or two tenors. Marazzoli himself was a tenor but may have played the harp among the continuo instruments; I have been unable to ascertain the range of Jacopo Melani's voice.

[35] M. F. Rieux (ed.), *Mémoires de Madame de Motteville sur Anne d'Autriche et sa cour*, vol. I (Paris, 1855), p. 263; Prunières, p. 81. Mme de Motteville's remarks refer to the second item in table 1: *L'Egisto*.

months later. Furthermore, Buti continued to be asked to write for the French stage, and in a vein similar to *Il giudizio*'s, for his two collaborations with Lully, allegorical characters abound.[36] Finally, the French government granted Marco Marazzoli an annual pension of 1000 *livres*, which was still being paid in 1660[37] – fifteen years after the Paris performance of a work of his that probably was *Il giudizio*.

[36] Herbert Schneider, *Chronologisch-Thematisches Verzeichnis sämtlicher Werke von Jean-Baptiste Lully* (Tutzing, 1981), pp. 31–8, 62–72. I believe that Schneider may have misrepresented the nature of works such as *L'amour malade*, *Psyché et la puissance de l'amour* and the *Ballet de l'impatience*. Like *Ercole amante + Hercule amoureux*, these works were created double – that is, there were Italian librettist, composer and singers on one 'team' and French librettist, composer, singers and dancers on the other.

[37] Prunières, p. 88. I should like to thank Margaret Murata for reading this essay and making several helpful suggestions. See her forthcoming article, 'Alcuni antefatti della *Finta pazza* parigina', in L. Bianconi (ed.), *L'opera tra Venezia e Parigi* (Venice, Cini Foundation, in preparation). Professor Murata informs me that another manuscript copy of the libretto of *Il giudizio* is in the archives of the Doria-Pamphilj family, Rome, under the title *La Bellezza amata*.

Michel Lambert and Jean-Baptiste Lully:
the stakes of a collaboration*

___

CATHERINE MASSIP

Since the publication of the outstanding essays by Lionel de La Laurencie and Henry Prunières, Jean-Baptiste Lully's early years have received little scholarly attention. While seemingly just a series of anecdotal exploits revealing something of the man's origins and progress up the social ladder, a study of these years promises to shed light on the very foundation and wellspring of Lully's art.

In his article 'Recherches sur les années de jeunesse de J.-B. Lully',[1] Prunières presented Florentine documents regarding the composer's ancestry and disclosed the exact circumstances of his arrival in France with the retinue of the Chevalier de Guise, during February or March of 1645. The chevalier was fulfilling a precise mission: to present to his cousin, Mademoiselle de Montpensier, a young Italian capable of conversing with her in her native tongue. De La Laurencie and Prunières had previously sketched a picture of the composer's first thirty years in a study that remains a principal source for Lully bibliography;[2] drawing from contemporary documents such as the *Gazette*, Loret's letters, the livrets of the *ballet de cour*, letters of naturalization, and the musician's marriage contract, these two authors leave few unilluminated areas in an already rich biography. If one searches this primary material for the name of a music master or, at least, of an instructor, one finds only a 'cordelier' cited by Lecerf de La Viéville, who would have taught Lully to play the guitar, and three organists, Nicolas Metru, Nicolas Gigault, and François Roberday, mentioned in a late pamphlet in 1695. Michel Lambert, however, received little attention: the two great musicologists, fascinated by their young 'hero', were scarcely concerned with his 'mentor' and with the latter's true role.

However, the vindicatory comments that are found, for example, in Bourdelot's *l'Histoire de la musique et de ses effets* would have sharpened their curiosity; the historian does, in fact, group together Cambert, Lambert, 'and le Sr Lully, these famous composers [who] have further perfected Music through a new method,

* The content of the present article is based on research effected within the framework of the *Doctorat d'Etat en lettres et sciences humaines*, 'Michel Lambert (1610–1696): contribution à l'histoire de la monodie en France' (Paris, Université de Paris IV, 1985, 2 vol., typescript).

[1] H. Prunières, 'Recherches sur les années de jeunesse de J.-B. Lully', *Rivista musicale italiana*, XVII 3 (1910), pp. 646–54.

[2] L. de La Laurencie, H. Prunières, 'La jeunesse de Lully (1632–1662). Essai de biographie critique', *Bulletin français de la S.I.M. (Société internationale de musique)* (March-April 1909), pp. 234–42 and 329–53.

by taking what was most excellent in Italian Music and joining it to French Music, the mixture forming the good taste that we see reigning in music today'.[3]

Before Lully's ascent Michel Lambert had enjoyed exceptional fame among his contemporaries. This fame may be measured not only by much evidence gathered from collections of poetry, the press, and memoirs of the time, but also by considering the illustrious rank of his protectors, Gaston d'Orléans, Louis XIII's only brother, Cardinal Richelieu, and the surintendant Fouquet. Lambert is also situated at the heart of the literary and poetic movement developing in the salons and *précieux* society: his rich musical production of nearly three hundred airs is inseparable from that 'esprit galant' which permeated French literary life before 1660. In the network of subtle intellectual relations and influences that surrounded Lambert, we find several elements of interest related to the career and development of the young Lully.

The encounter between Michel Lambert and Jean-Baptiste Lully must have taken place early in the Florentine's life. We know of an 'official' date, January 1651. Loret[4] mentions the pension that the Grande Mademoiselle, Anne-Marie-Louise d'Orléans, duchess of Montpensier, gave to Lambert and his sister-in-law, the singer Hilaire Dupuis, future performer *privilégiée* of Lully's ballets with Anne de La Barre and Anna Bergeroti:

> Cette grande et haute pucelle . . .
> Donne une pension honneste
> Au seigneur Lambert et sa soeur,
> Afin que l'extrême douceur
> De leurs voix, belles à merveilles,
> Delectent souvent ses oreilles.[5]

At this time, Lully was still part of the Grande Mademoiselle's household but he may well have met Lambert some years earlier because the latter, recruited by Etienne Moulinié for the chapel of Gaston d'Orléans between 1625 and 1630, owed all his musical training to the house of Orléans. Well after the start of his independent career as a singing teacher in Paris, Lambert kept close ties with various members of the house of Orléans, whether with musicians like Pierre Bony and Jean Blaisot, or with poets like Jean Bouillon.[6]

A second important meeting took place between Benserade and Lully. It is not necessary to review the details of their well-known collaboration, important for the *ballets de cour*. But who could have put a very young musician in contact with a celebrated court poet? Here again the name of Lambert appears. In fact, the latter had been a close friend of Benserade since the 1640s: in 1642, when his

[3] P. Bourdelot, *Histoire de la musique et de ses effets*, vol. I (Amsterdam, Le Cène, 1725), p. 18.

[4] Y. de Brossard, 'La vie musicale en France d'après Loret et ses continuateurs (1650–1688)', *Recherches sur la musique française classique*, X (1970), p. 149, 1 January 1651.

[5] 'This great and noble damsel . . ./Gives a rea-

sonable allowance/To milord Lambert and his sister,/So that the extreme sweetness/Of their voices, wondrously fair,/May often delight her ears.'

[6] C. Massip, 'Le mécénat musical de Gaston d'Orléans', in R. Mousnier (ed.) *L'age d'or du mécénat 1598–1661. Actes du colloque international* (Paris, C.N.R.S., 1985), pp. 383–91.

wife Gabrielle Dupuis died, Lambert owed Benserade 150 *livres*.[7] A *Historiette* by Tallemant des Réaux[8] tells us that the poet belonged to that small group of literati and musicians who frequented the Bel-Air tavern on the rue de Vaugirard, owned by a certain Michel Dupuis, the future father-in-law of the singer. Benserade was to take lodgings for a while at this inn near the Palais du Luxembourg, during which time he wrote a poem about Lambert's matrimonial problems, as we learn from a marginal note to the poem, 'Que je meine une triste vie' ('How sad is the life I lead'): 'Lambert says that Benserade wrote these words for him and that Monsieur le Cardinal de Richelieu had forbidden him to marry "la fille de Bel-Air", forcing him to marry her six months later, however, when he no longer wanted to do so.'[9]

The third of these encounters involved Quinault and Lully. The beginning of their collaboration is dated by Etienne Gros[10] from 1664, when the poet circulated some 'musical words on airs by Lully' and other composers. In 1668 they signed their first collaborative work, *La grotte de Versailles*. However, as between Benserade and Lully, the signs of an earlier relationship with Michel Lambert exist, back to the time when the latter was already working closely with Lully on *ballets de cour*. In 1655, *La comédie sans comédie*, was presented at the Théâtre du Marais; this play 'brought together all types of theatrical genre: pastorale, comedy, tragedy, and tragi-comedy "à machines" could be seen in it'. For this, the young poet Philippe Quinault (b. 1635) chose a famous composer, Michel Lambert, to set to music the song 'Il faut aimer c'est un destin inévitable', which he gave to Amour to sing in Act v.[11] A revealing anecdote regarding the relations between Lully and Quinault deserves close analysis in the light of the triangular relationship Quinault–Lully–Lambert. This story is known through Charles Perrault, who related it in the *Parallèle des Anciens et des Modernes*.[12] Briefly, during the course of a dinner, Lully is reproached for his infatuation with Quinault's verses; the host is charged by those present to visit Perrault, faithful friend of Quinault, and set forth the terms of the argument. This mysterious host, called D . . . in the text, puts forth the point of view of those who criticized Quinault's operatic verse: 'They find that the thoughts are not sufficiently noble,

---

[7] L. Maurice-Amour, 'Benserade, Michel Lambert et Lulli', *Cahiers de l'Association internationale des études françaises*, no. 9 (June 1957), pp. 53–76. Ch. I. Silin, *Benserade and his ballets de cour*, Johns Hopkins Studies, vol. xv (Baltimore, Johns Hopkins Press, 1940; repr. New York, AMS Press, 1978). C. Massip, 'Michel Lambert (1610–1696): Contribution à l'histoire de la monodie en France' (unpubl. diss., doctorat d'etat, Paris-IV Sorbonne, 1985), vol. i, p. 35 (Archives nationales, Minutier central, xlvi, 29, 1643, June 6): 'inventaire après décès' of Gabrielle Dupuis, Lambert's wife.

[8] Tallemant des Réaux, *Historiettes*, La Pléiade (Paris, Gallimard, 1970), vol. ii, p. 495.

[9] C. Massip, 'Michel Lambert', vol. i, pp. 23–4:

F-Pn: Manuscrits, Français 19145, fo. 185v.

[10] E. Gros, *Philippe Quinault, sa vie et son oeuvre* (Paris, E. Champion, 1926), pp. 84–5.

[11] P. Quinault, *La Comédie sans comédie* (Paris, G. de Luyne, 1657), p. 81.

[12] C. Perrault, *Parallèle des Anciens et des Modernes en ce qui regarde la Poesie* (Paris, Ve J.-B. Coignard, 1692), vol. iii, pp. 239–42, cited in 'Dokumente zur französischer Oper von 1659 bis 1699', H. Schneider (ed.) *Quellentexte zur Konzeption der europaischen Oper im 17. Jahrhundert* (Kassel, Bärenreiter, 1981). Commentary by P. Lacroix in *Mémoires de Charles Perrault* (Paris, Librairie des bibliophiles, 1878), pp. xvii–xviii and by E. Gros, *P. Quinault*, pp. 114–15.

subtle or elegant; that his ideas are too commonplace, and finally, that his style consists only of a limited number of words that are constantly repeated.' Perrault's reply, which is addressed to the mysterious D. . ., reveals that the latter is a musician:

I am not at all surprised that people who do not know what music is express themselves in such a manner; but you, Monsieur, who know the subject perfectly and to whom France owes that delicacy and correctness in singing which no other nation yet possesses, do you not see that if one were to conform to their notions, one would devise words that singers could not sing and the audience could not understand?

Quinault scholars have tried to identify this anonymous figure: Paul Lacroix proposes, quite simply, Lambert; Etienne Gros suggests Pierre de Nyert. Both hypotheses are plausible; both musicians belonged, in the opinion of their contemporaries, to the same aesthetic movement – that of the *air galant* as opposed to the opera, a theme that their mutual friend Jean de La Fontaine developed in his *Epitre à Monsieur de Nyert*. Lambert owed much of his singing technique to Pierre de Nyert, as he acknowledged in 1660, calling him the 'god of song, to whom France owes all she has that is fine and touching in beautiful singing', a declaration quite close to Perrault's. Thus, around 1674–5, Lully and Lambert – or at least someone who was the latter's equal – seem to have been the heroes in a debate between 'Ancients' and 'Moderns', between partisans of French vocal art of the years 1640–60 and partisans of the young operatic art. How does this image correspond to reality? If one considers only biographical facts, we find a long list of activities in common, primarily in the setting of the court, to be followed by close ties of a private nature, confirmed by the marriage of Madeleine Lambert and Jean-Baptiste Lully. Lambert was introduced at court a short time before Lully: did he also present the younger musician there?

Although no official document, statement, or account is known to confirm it, in 1645 Michel Lambert declared himself to be 'chantre' or 'ordinaire' of the Chambre du roi. In February 1651, his name figures in the cast of the *Ballet de Cassandre*, then in May, in the *Ballet des fêtes de Bacchus*. For the first time, in February 1653, he appeared with Lully in the second watch of the *Ballet de la nuit*: he played the role of Pélée in a comical pantomime on the *Mariage de Thétis*. Until 1664, Lambert's talents as actor and dancer were to be utilized in comic or parodic scenes, as well as in travesty roles of the type that Lully liked. Lambert's physical appearance may have predisposed him to play characters who were completely opposite to his personality as a singer and composer of *airs galants* and at odds with his personal tastes, because he seems to have steadfastly refused to write even a single drinking song. Tallemant des Réaux tells us in fact: 'It's not only that Lambert grimaces horribly and is awful to look at in that state; he's extremely ugly even when he doesn't pull faces.'[13]

These are the roles that Lambert played in the *ballets de cour*: in the *Ballet de Cassandre* (26 February 1651), he appeared with a certain Robichon as the Count and Countess of Savoie (ninth *entrée*), 'des contes à dormir debout' ('a

---

[13] Tallemant des Réaux, *Historiettes*, vol. II, p. 524.

cock-and-bull story'), as the *Gazette* specifically described it. Certain ballet roles seem somewhat autobiographical: Lambert is one of the 'People searching for the Rhythm that wine has made them lose' who danced the ninth *entrée* of the *Ballet des fêtes de Bacchus*; he also performed a 'grotesque piece' in the fifteenth *entrée*, before appearing with the king as an 'ice man' in the twenty-second *entrée*. In the *Ballet de la nuit* (February 1653), he donned a merchant's costume in the first watch, then that of a beggar in the Court of Miracles; in the second watch, he played the role of Pélée; in the third, a witch in a sabbath – the corresponding costume designs have been preserved in the Bibliothèque de l'Institut.

On 16 March 1653, Lully received the charge of *compositeur de la musique instrumentale de la chambre*, made vacant by the death of Lazzarini. From then on, the names of Baptiste and Lambert were never missing from the cast lists announced in the livrets of the *ballets de cour*. In the *Ballet du temps* (3 December 1654), they played the Hours, then the Years and the Centuries together, while Lully subsequently appeared as a sailor and as one of the seven planets. In the *Ballet des plaisirs* (4 February 1655), Lambert played Hymen who, together with La Félicité, flanked the married couple, then an 'oublieux' and one of the court-iers of the last *entrée*, while Lully was in turn a satyr, an Egyptian, one of the *débauchés* who came out of the tavern (with the king), finally, the ridiculous old man who invited the 'oublieux' to drink. In the *Ballet des bienvenus*, produced in honor of Laure Martinozzi, Mazarin's niece, on the occasion of her marriage to the Duke of Modène on 30 May 1655, Lambert assumed the roles of a Venetian, of Justice, of a fictional hero; with Lully, he was one of the protagonists of the 'grotesque Italian tale, as much vocal as instrumental', which opened the second part, then he danced the grand final ballet. During the year 1656, particularly rich in *divertissements de cour*, ballets, *fêtes*, and masquerades, he played the role of Fear in the *Ballet de Psyché ou la puissance de l'amour* (third *entrée* of the first part), then, in the second part, one of the Bacchantes who tear Orpheus to pieces. He appeared once again with Lully in the *Ballet de la galanterie du temps*, among other dancers playing the Amours, dressed as buffoons. Involved in all the *fêtes*, he was called to Essones by Louis Hesselin to participate in a production in honor of Christina of Sweden. Did the clan rivalries characteristic of court life also influence the casting of ballets? The *Ballet des plaisirs troublés* would tend to suggest this: produced through the initiative of Henri II of Lorraine, duc de Guise, it numbered neither Lully nor Lambert among its musicians and dancers. On the contrary, the grand *Ballet d'Alcidiane* honored the return of the two comrades, Lambert as a subject of Alcidiane, then as a soldier, with Lully as his captain – a significant hierarchical relationship – finally, as harpsichord accom-panist for 'Moorish ladies who sing', if the publisher of the livret correctly printed the name Lambert (and not Cambert.)

In the *Ballet de la raillerie* (Carnival, 1659), Lambert created the characters of an old man and a soldier, roles which were more fitting to his age, now somewhat advanced for a comic dancer; the same holds true for the *Ballet de l'impatience* (Carnival, 1661) in which he played an awkward Muscovite and an old father who turns out his two good-for-nothing sons, impatient for their inheritance.

His last appearance was to take place in 1663, in the masquerade of *Les noces de village*, danced at Vincennes: 'The school master, who is something of a poet and "compositeur ordinaire" of village music (Lully) is invited to come with his pupils to entertain the gathering, and gives a second *récit*.' An amusing paradox: one of the pupils is none other than Lambert, a fact which opportunely reminds us of the comic function of antithesis.

These numerous assignments as dancer-mime are known to us only through the *Gazette* and the ballet livrets;[14] it is astonishing that Lambert was never employed in these *fêtes* as a singer, in contrast to his sister-in-law and star pupil, the famed Hilaire Dupuis, whose career exactly parallels his own. The same holds true for Lambert's participation as a composer, which, as will be discussed in detail below, was very restricted. This restriction may be explained by the character of the two men, Lully and Lambert, and by the ties that bound them. From May 1661, each held title to the two highest offices of the *musique de la chambre du roi*, a partnership that was to be sealed by the marriage contract of 14 July 1662. This famous document,[15] already closely studied by Fétis in his *Biographie universelle des musiciens*, was honored by three royal signatures: that of the queen mother Anne of Austria, of Louis XIV, and of the queen, Marie-Thérèse. Following them are the signatures of the Duke of Rochechouart-Mortemart, and of Jean-Baptiste Colbert and his wife, a group who, in some respects, formed the Mazarin 'clan': one can readily imagine that the minister's signature would have been next to these, had he still been alive. Musicians' names are conspicuously absent from this contract: only Pierre de Nyert, teacher of Lambert and Hilaire, Louis XIII's favorite singer, was present. The Dupuis tribe, the many maternal relations of Madeleine Lambert, was well represented. The illustrious royal patronage has always been explained solely on the basis of Lully's fame, but in 1662, he was only at the beginning of his career and had no reason to be the protégé of Anne of Austria. It is true that his talents had earned him letters of naturalization, a necessary preliminary to every marriage, because they permitted him to avoid the 'droit d'aubaine', which was levied against foreigners, and decreed that in the event of their death, their property devolved to the king. But it is surely also possible to interpret these signatures as honoring Lambert. Since the time when Cardinal Richelieu had, or so the chroniclers reported, 'arranged' his marriage, Lambert had enjoyed protection from the highest quarters. It should not be forgotten that two years previously, the post of *maître de la musique* for queen Marie-Thérèse had been offered to Lambert by Colbert,[16] despite the advice of Mazarin, who was supporting Jean de Cambefort; didn't Colbert's active protection of Michel Lambert, obvious in 1660,

[14] C. Massip, 'Michel Lambert', vol. I, pp. 80–4; M.-F. Christout, *Le ballet de cour de Louis XIV 1643–1672* (Paris, A. et J. Picard, 1967); Ch. I. Silin, *Benserade*.

[15] C. Massip, 'Michel Lambert', vol. I, pp. 100–3 (Archives nationales, Minutier central, XLVI, 85, 1662, 14 July and 23 July). This contract is discussed in L. de La Laurencie, H. Prunières, 'La jeunesse de Lully', pp. 351–2.

[16] H. Prunières, 'Jean de Cambefort (. . . – 1661), surintendant de la musique du roi d'après des documents inédits', *L'Année musicale*, II (1912; repr. Geneva, Minkoff, 1972), pp. 215–16. According to a letter from Jean de Cambefort to Mazarin, dated 19 April 1660, published in its entirety by H. Prunières, without indication of its location.

contribute to the double nomination of 19 May 1661, in which only royal intervention is customarily recognized? The post of *maître de la musique de la chambre* is not included in the 20,000 *livres* of dowry which in turn was divided into 12,000 *livres* cash down payment, 4000 *livres* in 'rings, jewels, clothes . . . and furniture', and 4000 *livres* to be paid against future appointments from the post of Michel Lambert, which itself remains, however, the exclusive property of Madeleine Lambert or her next of kin. As for the position of *surintendant* or *compositeur de la chambre*, it appears that Lully, as Lambert had to do for his post, was obliged to pay the sum of 20,000 *livres* to the widow of Jean de Cambefort and his children.

More surprising still was what followed this marriage. An extended family community was established, comprising at least seven people, to whom were to be added the six children born to the Lullys: the household included Michel Lambert, his sister-in-law, the singer Hilaire Dupuis, after 1669, his other sister-in-law, Agnes Dupuis, his two nieces, Catherine and Anne Morineau, who was soon to marry the singer Dominique Normandin, known as La Grille, Jean-Baptiste Lully, and Madeleine Lambert. This entire little group lived and changed residences together; they settled into the increasingly impressive dwellings that Lully rented until he undertook his great projects of real estate investment and construction. In 1662, they all lived on the Rue Notre-Dame des Victoires; in 1664 they moved closer to the Louvre Palace and went to live in Rue Neuve Saint-Thomas; in 1667, they moved once more to Rue Travercine; in 1675 came the purchase made in common by the three partners, Michel Lambert, Hilaire Dupuis, and Jean-Baptiste Lully, of a seignorial domain at Puteaux, on the banks of the Seine.[17]

The years of professional collaboration and physical cohabitation are tangible facts, but a definition of the Lambert–Lully relationship musically and aesthetically is more elusive. Two sources of information may help us in this approach: the ballets written jointly during the period 1663–5 and the testimony of Lecerf de La Viéville.

A first obstacle presents itself when we try to make a fair evaluation of Lambert's collaboration on the ballets conceived by his son-in-law, because the manuscript sources of the latter never carry Lambert's name, and the other sources that might allow us to attribute certain pieces to him are of unequal value. Only the three great dialogues which he himself inserted in his book of airs in 1689[18] can be attributed to him with certainty:

– *Ballet des arts* (January 1663): Dialogue de la Paix et de la Félicité: 'Douce Félicité ne quittons point ces lieux', sung by Mademoiselle Hilaire and Mademoiselle de Saint-Christophe (*Airs*, 1689, pp. 193–5, LWV 18/2b);

[17] See M. Benoit, 'The Residences of Monsieur de Lully' in this volume, and C. Massip, 'Michel Lambert', vol. I, pp. 357–8 and 104–9.

[18] *Airs a une, II, III, et IV parties avec la basse-continue composez par Monsieur Lambert, maistre de la Musique de la Chambre du Roy* (Paris, C. Ballard, 1689).

– *Ballet des amours déguisés* (1664): Dialogue de Marc-Antoine et de Cléopâtre: 'Doutez-vous de mon feu, vous pour qui je soupire?' (*Airs*, 1689, pp. 206–10, LWV 21/7);

– *Ballet de la naissance de Vénus* (1665): Dialogue des Trois Grâces: 'Admirons notre jeune et charmante Déesse' (*Airs*, 1689, pp. 201–5, LWV 27/22).

These dialogues are fundamental to our understanding of French opera. One may wonder about Lully's reasons for excluding his father-in-law from the composition of the *ballets de cour* and for dissuading him from following his experiments in the domain of dramatic music. After the *Ballet de la naissance de Vénus* Lambert refrained from writing for several voices, and contemporary sources give us only airs for solo voice, a genre in which Lully hardly troubled to shine. It is significant that Lambert waited until after his son-in-law's death (1687) to give us the true measure of his art by offering the public two years later a large anthology of airs: a collection in which he unequivocally claimed these pieces, which tradition had buried away among Lully's works.

Besides these three *grands dialogues*, analysed below, four monologues for solo voice might be attributed to Lambert, although some doubt remains regarding such attribution. Two of them, 'Si l'Amour vous soumet à ses loix' (*Le mariage forcé*, 1664, Récit de la Beauté, LWV 20/2) and 'Rochers vous estes sourds, vous n'avez rien de tendre' (*Ballet de la naissance de Vénus*, 1665, LWV 27/32) are attributed to 'Mr Baptiste' by Bénigne de Bacilly, but they are found in the Foucault manuscript, a commercial copy of which we now know five specimens, entitled *Airs de M. Lambert, 75 simples, 50 doubles*; this collection, in all likelihood put together after Lambert's death, contains about fifteen airs of doubtful attribution. 'Ne craignez point le naufrage', Thétis's monologue from the *Ballet des arts* (LWV 18/8) is credited to Lambert by Bacilly. The fourth, 'Dans ces déserts paisibles', from *La grotte de Versailles* (1668, LWV 39/11) is attributed to Lambert only in a large manuscript collection that belonged to Jules Ecorcheville, Henry Prunières and Geneviève Thibault, countess of Chambure (F-Pn: Rés. Vma. ms. 958). With the exception of 'Ne craignez pas le naufrage', all these *récits* have a *ritournelle* with trio and a *double* in diminution – considerations that seem to argue in favor of attribution to Lambert.

This collaboration extends, therefore, over a very short period (from 1663 to 1665) – and we must concede that Lambert was not involved in the composition of a large number of ballets, among them are the *Ballet d'Alcidiane*, the *Ballet de la raillerie*, the *Ballet de l'impatience*, the *Ballet des saisons*, the *Ballet des muses*, the *Ballet de Flore*, etc.

An examination of Lambert's authenticated dialogues seems to be important in so far as comparison can be made with earlier texts. The first, published in 1660, dates in fact from 1641: 'Philis j'arreste enfin mon humeur vagabonde' displays a rigid structure in binary form with reprise wherein the voices alternate simply, then join for the conclusion. Faithful to the rhythmically freer writing in the French style that Etienne Moulinié could have taught him, Lambert used little of that syllabic, note-against-note style, that Lully was to favor. Another dialogue, 'Pour vos beaux yeux, Iris, mon amour est extresme', whose purpose is unknown,[19] places three characters on stage; even if this setting is on a larger scale, here again one finds in it a linearity of dialogue development and a total absence of characterization that make it a concert piece completely devoid of dramatic interest. Much more significant from that point of view seems to be the dialogue of the *Ballet des arts*, which is situated in a new instrumental context: 'After Happiness and Peace which accompany [the shepherds and shepherdesses] throughout have sung a *récit* in dialogue, a chorus of rustic instruments replies.' Referring to the composition of the rustic wind band given by the livret of *Les noces de village*, a ballet danced that same year, one finds employed eight instrumentalists belonging to the Musique de l'Ecurie: four members of the Hotteterre family, as well as Descoteaux, Brunet, Pièche, and Destouches, all flautists, oboists or *musettes de Poitou*. In addition, the instrumental *ritournelle* of nineteen measures which precedes the dialogue possesses its own originality: it is not presented like a simple reproduction of the sung part; the conjunct melodic line and the frequency of dotted notes indicate a concern for its adaptability to instrumental technique. On the other hand, the true ingredients of a dramatic exchange are present here: interweaving of voices, short lines, sometimes in imitation, breaking of the phrase in order to emphasize important words like 'toujours'.[20]

In 1664 and 1665, with the two dialogues of the *Ballet des amours déguisés* and the *Ballet de la naissance de Vénus*, Lambert followed up his pioneering work. The dialogue between Marc-Antoine and Cléopâtre already possesses the dimensions of a great scene of French opera (twenty-five measures of *ritournelle* and one hundred of sung dialogue, repeated once.) The on-stage instrumental group made up of the two characters' slaves, was played by three *petits violons* of the Chambre: Laquièze, Marchand, and La Fontaine. The famous episode to which the dialogue alludes occurs at the moment of the first meeting between the queen of Egypt and Marc-Antoine at Tarsus in Asia Minor: Cléopâtre appears on the river Cydnos, drifting in a sumptuous vessel and surrounded, in the fashion of Venus, by young cupids. The captivated hero then abandons his heart, his person, and his power to her, submitting himself to the maxim, 'To live happily, one must be in love.' In the general construction of the scene, a procedure that was to become dear to Lully can be observed: the insertion of two airs in the dialogue, simple extensions of two of the protagonists' lines (Cléopâtre: 'Vous avez tout quitté' and Marc-Antoine: 'Amour, j'ay fait ceder ma gloire'). Here Lambert made another important innovation, the successful characterization of emotions of the characters by musical formulae. In this instance he employed diminished intervals to manifest doubt (example 1), a chromatic descending bass for an 'Alas!' (example 2), and a vocal structure related to that of a drinking song for the final optimistic effect, based on the predominance of dotted notes (example 3). Lambert also used the contrast of a change of mode, G minor for the

[19] M. Lambert, *Airs* (Paris, 1689), pp. 196–200.
[20] C. Massip, 'Michel Lambert', vol. I, pp. 243–6; *Ballet des Arts Dansé par sa Majesté le 8 janvier 1663* (Paris, R. Ballard, 1663), pp. 4–5.

Example 1

Example 2

Example 3

scene, with one section in G major, which corresponds to Marc-Antoine's air, already cited.

If the dialogue of the *Ballet des amours déguisés* invites us to emphasize possible affinities between Lambert and Lully, that of the three Graces of the *Ballet de la naissance de Vénus* substantiates the disparity that exists between the two temperaments. The quality of this text permits us to abandon the theory that the supplanting of Lambert was due to the unoriginal quality of his music. This ballet, one of the most important of the period 1660–70, includes four vocal episodes among a profusion of dances. The *récit* of Neptune and Thétis, followed by a chorus of Tritons, serves as an introduction to the work; the three episodes that follow are regrouped in the second part. After Lambert's dialogue for the Three Graces and Ariane's complaint 'Rochers vous estes sourds' (by Lambert or by Lully?), Orpheus has a short *récit* by Lully. When reading these pages, one gets the feeling that the two composers belonged to different worlds. In the French-style overture, Lully manipulates a solid five-part counterpoint with extreme ease. His great introductory scene, rigorously constructed in its development, prefigures analogous scenes that will punctuate his operas: Neptune and Thétis speak different languages, the first characterized by a strong tonal and rhythmic foundation and by wide intervals, the second, by a sort of restrained *récit* 'arioso' to which is joined a homophonic chorus of compound rhythm, interspersed with a violin *ritournelle*. The insignificant *récit* by Orpheus – in fact, a quite simply constructed air – seems to be rapidly elaborated to an expressive intensity far beyond the words 'Grand dieu des Enfers, escoutez mes peines', the contrast with the moving plaint of Ariane appearing all the more striking. On the contrary, the dialogue for three characters, written in praise of Henriette d'Angleterre, shows great refinement. The Three Graces, Hilaire Dupuis, Anne de La Barre, and Mademoiselle de Saint-Christophe, (one *bas dessus* and two *dessus*), exchange pleasant, commonplace observations on the qualities of Madame, sister-in-law of the king and Duchess of Orléans, to whom the role of Venus was assigned in this *entrée*. Around verses by Isaac de Benserade, Lambert weaves a simple and airy three-part counterpoint of great melodic quality. Only the breaks and changes of rhythm imposed by the versification or a textual idea requiring emphasis introduce some variety. Like the vocal writing, the distribution of the vocal parts is characteristic of Lambert: the frequent overlappings, inversions and crossings between the two upper parts are found throughout his work. A technique of development that he may have borrowed from Lully appears here; a harmonic progression permits repetition of the phrase 'Ah! qu'elle a bien d'autres grâces'. By his rejection of symmetrical constructions, of the picturesque, of excess, of word by word setting, Lambert establishes himself at opposite poles to the Italian techniques to which he seemed to be modestly conforming in the Marc-Antoine/Cléopâtre dialogue. Did Lully consider this intimist art inadequate for the stage? One might imagine so.

What remains then of 'Lambertism', as it was called by his contemporaries, in Lully's works? If one takes a work like *Cadmus et Hermione*,[21] it is simple to eliminate at once that which owes nothing to Lambert: the instrumental parts, the musical treatment of the recitative, and the vocal scenes for the bass voice, strongly influenced by the drinking song. On the other hand, one must admit that Lully assimilated the techniques of the air to the point of imitation and that, in a sort of skilful collage, he utilized and integrated its expressive possibilities and its ornamentation. Hermione's air, 'Cet aimable séjour' (Act I, scene iii), placed in a scene formed by the juxtaposition of binary airs with reprise or *en rondeau*, is decorated on each cadence of phrase by ornaments *à la* Lambert. Act III, scene v is made up of an *air galant* with *ritournelle*, 'Amour vois quels maux' with the structure AABCC'. Scene i of Act v, which has Cadmus on stage, is another air *en rondeau*, 'Belle Hermione, hélas puis-je être heureux sans vous'. If one examines the dialogues, rather than certain episodes for soloists, one finds next to 'Italian' elements a type of dialogue well tried by Lambert: alternating voices, then homophonic conclusion in thirds (e.g. Act IV, scene vi, dialogue of Cadmus and Hermione).

[21] J.-B. Lully, *Oeuvres complètes, vol. I. Les opéras. Cadmus et Hermione*, H. Prunières (ed.)   (Paris, Ed. de la Revue musicale, 1930; repr. New York, Broude Bros., 1966).

One can understand more clearly, under these conditions, the testimony of
Lecerf de La Viéville: it makes complete sense only if one considers Lully's inter-
preters to have been totally imbued with singing techniques taught by Lambert
– the principal teacher of his time – and especially with the style of the *air galant*,
the predominant vocal genre of the period.

This evidence, belated and posthumous, was given in 1704–6 in the *Comparaison de la musique italienne et de la musique française* and must be considered with
prudence. Lambert appears in the work as an unworthy successor of Lully, who
nevertheless professes a great admiration for his father-in-law:

> His wife was Lambert's daughter, and Lully had great respect for them both. He always
> referred to Lambert as his father-in-law, an indication that he considered it an honor to be
> his son-in-law . . . Ah, he respected him? And, Marquis, did he like his Airs a great deal?
> . . . Yes, very much, he would often sing one of them, and there is especially one old air,
> one of Lambert's least brilliant, that Lully was in the habit of singing: 'Vous qui craignez
> tant que les loups/N'entrent dans votre bergerie etc.' Brunet even told us last year that he,
> as a Page of the Musique du Roi, used to go with the other pages to sing before Lully,
> their Surintendant, and he liked them to sing him Lambert's airs and listened to them
> attentively.[22]

It is, to say the least, curious, that the 'old' air cited by Lecerf appeared anonymously in 1682, through the efforts of Christophe Ballard, in the *XXV Livre
d'airs de differents autheurs* but appears in none of the important Lambert anthologies: only Lecerf's assertion permits its attribution to Lambert. The majority of
musical references to Lambert made by Lecerf are imbued with the same lack of
detail:[23] 'Eh, pourquoi faut-il que mon coeur/Adore une inhumaine?' (II, 40)
has not been traced. 'Beaux yeux de Climene' (III, 27) is found (with no author's
name) in volume III of the *Brunetes*, published by Christophe Ballard in 1703. 'Je
veux me plaindre de vos rigueurs' (III, 78), to words by the Countess of Aische,
is attributed to Le Camus in the *Recueil d'airs sérieux et à boire* by Christophe
Ballard, 1703; in addition, 'Le beau berger Tircis' (III, 96) is sometimes credited
to Le Camus, sometimes to Lambert and to a certain Marquis de Bullion, and
appeared anonymously in the *Brunetes* of 1703. One may conclude from this
consistency of error that Lecerf was particularly acquainted with collections of
contemporary airs and that he troubled himself little with bibliographic plausi-
bility. Why, under these conditions, should one unreservedly accept other
aspects of his testimony?

Lully's admiration for Lambert sometimes took an ambiguous turn: 'Lully
applauded with pleasure others' music when it pleased him. And he constantly
praised old Boesset and Lambert.'[24] Lambert was placed here on the same plane

---

[22] C. Massip, 'Michel Lambert', vol. I, pp. 111–
20; J. L. Lecerf de La Viéville de Freneuse,
*Comparaison de la musique italienne et de la
musique française* (Brussels, F. Foppens, 1704;
repr. Graz, Akademische Druck, 1966); references to this work are indicated in the text
(roman or arabic numerals) or in the notes.
The accounts of the rehearsals of *Le triomphe*
de l'amour (1681) confirm the extremely active role played by Lambert as *maître de la
musique de la chambre*.

[23] C. Massip, 'Michel Lambert', vol. II, pp.
422–4.

[24] Lecerf de la Viéville, *Comparaison*, vol. III,
p. 314.

with a certain Antoine Boesset, who died in 1643, an out-dated composer for
the generation of Lully to which Lambert belonged.

According to Lecerf, Lully made use of his father-in-law for his pedagogic
gifts – Lambert having amply fulfilled the educative role associated with his
functions as *maître de la musique de la chambre*:

[Lully] knowing the other [Lambert] well as the most charming of all singers, sent him all
his actresses so that he could teach them the fine art of singing. . . . Lambert had them
add some ornaments to Lully's recitative from time to time, and the actresses ventured to
essay these embellishments at rehearsals. 'Dear me, ladies', Lully used to say, sometimes
using a less polite term, and rising from his chair, 'there is nothing like that on your page,
so for heaven's sake, no embroidery. My recitative is only for speaking; I want it to be
completely unadorned.'[25]

It is in that last sentence that we see the theme of the underlying conflict
between Lambert and Lully, between singer and dramatist. The 'method' that
Lambert wanted obstinately to teach his singers affected, among other things,
the decoration of the vocal line – unwritten ornamentation, often added on the
initiative of the singer. Indispensable in the *petits airs*, especially in the reprises,
this method might well have detracted from the great recitatives that Lully
wrote, beginning with *Cadmus et Hermione*. Lully also refused to use the technique of the *double*, that ornamental variation of the air that all the composers of
the 1660s, Bacilly, Lambert, Le Camus, d'Ambruis, used:

. . . but when they [the Pages] tried to add the *double* to the *simple*, following the custom
of that time, where it seemed that the *double* was part of the Air . . . Lully stopped the
pages de la musique with a motion of his hand and head. 'That will do', he told them, 'that
will do; save the *double* for my father-in-law.' And he would have had to force himself to
listen to it . . . Lully detested variation, passages, flourishes, and all those precious niceties
with which the Italians are infatuated.[26]

In his contradictory discussion, Lecerf here addresses the question of Lully's
affinity for French and Italian tastes.[27] Ornamentation and the *double* were considered by him to be characteristics of Italian style, while the image that he
wanted to present of Lambert was that of a truly French musician. Lecerf's text
abounds with confusion and repetitiveness. As examples of the latter, we may
cite the two long passages devoted to the question of ornaments and the composition of the *double*. They also show that the subject preoccupied music-lovers
at a time when there was a sudden upsurge of interest in this technique: the
famous collection of *Brunetes ou Petits airs tendres avec les doubles et la basse continue,
meslées de chansons à danser; recueillies et mises en ordre par Christophe Ballard* encompassed three parts, published in 1703, 1704, and 1711, with a few of the
pieces having no less than two or three different *doubles*.

In one excerpt, Lecerf develops Lully's opinions on the use of ornaments:

Didn't Lully enjoy using them and didn't he decorate his music with them? Remember
Isis: 'Il s'est armé du Tonnerre/Mais c'est pour donner la Paix' And Roland: 'Ce n'est

---

[25] Ibid., vol. III, pp. 187–8.   [27] Ibid., vol. II, p. 93.
[26] Ibid., vol. III, pp. 182.

qu'aux plus fameux vainqueurs/Qu'il est permis de porter votre *chaîne.*' And think of a hundred others of that power and length. Lully, replied the Chevalier [i.e. Lecerf] rarely used those grand flourishes [*roulemens*] – no more than three or four times at most in an opera. That certainly shows that he didn't believe it very necessary or advantageous to use them . . . Italian though he was by birth, he had so little taste and talent for writing *doubles* that when he condescended to use any in his works, he had it done by his father-in-law, Lambert: witness the lovely air from *La grotte de Versailles*, 'Dans ces déserts paisibles'.[28]

Lecerf's opinions regarding Lully further offer a reflection of the ideas that were circulating at the beginning of the eighteenth century with reference to the founder of French opera. Despite the reservations that we have expressed regarding the bibliographic validity of Lecerf de La Viéville's references to Lambert's airs, an examination of the *doubles* transcribed in the sources of Lully's ballets prior to 1670 appears strongly to confirm his statements.

Here is a list of those *doubles*: (1) *Ballet de la naissance de Vénus*, 'Rochers vous estes sourds'; (2) *Ballet des muses*, Orpheus' *récit*, 'Trop indiscret amour'; (3) *Le Sicilien*, 'Pauvres amants, quelle erreur'; (4) *George Dandin*, 'Icy l'ombre des ormeaux'; (5) *La grotte de Versailles*, 'Dans ces déserts paisibles'; (6) *Ballet de Flore*, 'Amour veut qu'on suive ses loix' (the air and the *double* were sung by two singers, Mademoiselle de Saint-Christophe and Anne Fonteaux de Cercamanan); (7) *Divertissement de Chambord* (Monsieur de Pourceaugnac), 'A me suivre tous ici votre ardeur'.

All these *doubles*, in particular that of Orpheus' *récit* from the *Ballet des muses*, seem to be very close to Lambert's style as it appeared in the 1660 book of airs. Therefore, it must be concluded that either Lully gave in to the style of the times by assimilating his father-in-law's teachings, or he simply assigned a part of the work to him.

Lambert's 'mania' regarding the *double* was very personal and quite different from that of a Bacilly, for example; his ideas followed three great principles: respect for the prosody, simplicity, and a striving for expressiveness. He therefore avoided flourishes that were excessive in length or frequency and arranged them in a way that would preserve the clarity of the words and the melodic line. We find this same relative simplicity in Lully, at the service of dramatic exigencies.

The stakes of a collaboration that place two such assertive personalities in opposition are doubled. If Lully learned to extract the few stylistic elements that he needed from the mature works of his father-in-law, Michel Lambert did not dismiss the new possibilites that Lully's organizing genius offered him. James Anthony has noted the similarity that exists between 'Ma bergère est tendre et fidéle', an air with *basse continue en chaconne*, dating from 1681, and the air of *Atys* dating from 1676 (Act I, scene iii) 'Peut-on estre insensible aux plus charmans appas?'.[29]

In the field of Lully scholarship, there yet remains an important area to be

---

[28] Ibid., vol. II, p. 23–4.
[29] J. Anthony, *La musique en France à l'époque* *baroque*, 3rd ed. (Paris, Flammarion, 1981), p. 117.

investigated – that of stylistic analysis. It would be desirable for such a study to be undertaken in a 'comparatist' spirit, and for the musical contributions of Lully's contemporaries, like those of Michel Lambert, to be weighed objectively: Lully developed an important part of his language in the *comédies-ballets*, even more so than in the ballets, and thus the years 1664–70 represent a crucial period that must be evaluated in its entirety.

In the case of Lambert and Lully, we find ourselves with an example of a collaboration that has been partially obscured by posterity. The two protagonists symbolize, each in his own way, two types of vocal music that appear to be opposite in concept. Lambert devoted all his creative energies to the air for solo voice, a 'miniaturized' form, according to Anthony's felicitous expression, while Lully personified French musical theater, intellectual and monumental alchemy. However, the links between the two spheres of creation remain: nurtured by the air, the *tragédie en musique* remained submissive to the constraints of that closed form, from which the principles of repetition and development were almost totally absent. Inserted into a dramatic and musical continuum, the air remained for a long time one of the most original elements of French opera and of vocal art. Lully's genius capitalized on Lambert's remarkable gifts – therein lies one of the principal keys to the evolution of Lully's art.

Chronology and evolution of the *grand motet* at the court of Louis XIV: evidence from the *Livres du Roi* and the works of Perrin, the *sous-maîtres* and Lully[1]

LIONEL SAWKINS

Not long after preparations began in 1978 for the first publication of all Lully's motets as part of the new complete edition it became clear that several areas important to the understanding of the development of the *grand motet* in general, and Lully's motets in particular, had received little attention in previous investigations. This essay discusses some of the substantial results of studies since undertaken in three of these areas:

1. Pierre Perrin's involvement in the provision of Latin devotional texts for setting by several composers (including Lully), and his observations on the form and function of music in the French royal chapel;

2. the nature, extent and chronology of the repertory of the chapel during Lully's period at court, as disclosed by the *Livres du Roi* (the books of texts printed each quarter or semester to enable the chapel congregation to follow the words of the *grands motets* and *élévations* sung at the king's daily mass);

3. instrumental scoring practices in the *grands choeurs* of motets by Lully compared with those of the *sous-maîtres* responsible for the composition and direction of music in the chapel.

PERRIN'S LATIN LYRICS

The name of Pierre Perrin has long been familiar to students of opera history as the librettist and entrepreneur of the *Pastorale d'Issy* (1659), and of *Pomone* (1671). However, for much of the decade between these two operatic essays, Perrin was preoccupied with the writing of religious verse, both in Latin and in French, with the specific intention that it be set to music for use in the Chapelle royale. Indeed, the *Lettres patentes* granted to Perrin in 1669 for the Académies d'Opéra make it clear that it was his activity as a court librettist for motets and *élévations* of the Chapelle and for *airs de cour* for the Chambre, together with his post as *Introducteur des Ambassadeurs* for the duc d'Orléans, which persuaded the king to grant the *Lettres patentes*.[2]

[1] This article is a development of a paper given at the 1981 annual meeting of the American Musicological Society, at Boston, Mass., at the invitation of Professor James R. Anthony. Research of sources in Parisian libraries was generously aided by the Maison des Sciences de l'Homme and the British Academy, whose help is gratefully acknowledged.

[2] The complete text of the *Lettres patentes* is reproduced in A. Pougin, *Les vrais créateurs de l'opéra français, Perrin et Cambert* (Paris, 1881), pp. 96–9.

James R. Anthony has drawn attention to the preface of Perrin's *Cantica pro Capella Regis* (Paris, 1665), which sheds much light on contemporary practice in the royal chapel;[3] both this volume and other collections of Perrin's works are examined in detail by Louis Auld in *The Lyric Art of Pierre Perrin*, (3 vols, Henryville, 1986). This monumental study includes, as well as a critical analysis of Perrin's poetry, the original text of the *Epître dédicatoire* and the *Avant-propos* to *Cantica pro Capella Regis*, and the text (together with a translation of the *Avant-propos*) of the *Recueil de Paroles de Musique de Mr. Perrin*.[4]

Perrin's Latin texts for sacred music appear in several manuscripts and publications dating from 1661 to 1666. Table 1 lists these sources (with abbreviated designations henceforth used for ease of reference) and table 2 analyses their contents.

Professor Auld has shown that a total of 152 of the 193 works in Ms fr 2208 were claimed by Perrin to have been set to music by some seventeen composers, whose names Perrin noted beside the relevant texts. However, only 14 of these works are to sacred Latin texts (which Perrin styled 'Cantiques et Chansons

Table 1 *Sources of Perrin's Latin texts for sacred music*

Poësie 1661 = *Les Oeuvres de Poësie. . .* Paris, 1661
Contains two texts for the marriage of Philippe, duc d'Orléans and Henrietta of England

Paroles 1661 = *Paroles de Motet pour le baptême de Monseigneur le Dauphin. . .* Paris, 1661.
Contains text of *Plaude laetare, Gallia*

CASRM = *Cantica a sacelli Regii Musicis. . . Motets chantez pendant la Messe du Roy. . .mis en Musique par T. Gobert, Maistre de Musique de la Chapelle du Roy. . .*
Contains texts of 4 motets and 4 *élévations* for the Mass of the King, and other members of the royal family. All the texts are also included in Ms fr 25460 and CPCR.

Ms fr 25460 (F-Pn) = *Cantiques ou Paroles de Motets Pour la Chappelle du Roy. . .* Probably an early draft for *Cantica pro Capella Regis*, though significantly different from the latter.
Contains a dedication to the king (but no *Avant-propos*) and Latin texts for 39 motets and 12 *élévations*, all except one of the latter being included in CPCR. Probably written in 1661 or 1662

CPCR = *Cantica pro Capella Regis. . .*, Paris, 1665
Contains an *epître dédicatoire* addressed to the king, mentioning settings of Perrin's texts by Lully, Gobert, and Expilly (in his capacity as *Sous-maître*). As Expilly did not take up duties until the July–September quarter, 1664, Perrin must have submitted his MS to the printer after that time. Also contains an extensive *avant-propos* explaining the author's aims and methods.
Contains texts for 50 motets and 12 *élévations*, including all but one of those in Ms fr 25460

Ms fr 2208 (F-Pn) = *Recueil De Paroles de Musique De Mr Perrin. . .Dédié à Monsieur Colbert*
Contains a dedication and an *avant-propos* which continues the discussion in that of CPCR. Contains 29 Latin texts, 27 of which do not appear in CPCR. Marginal notes indicate composers who have set some texts. Completed by summer, 1666

[3] James R. Anthony, *French Baroque Music from Beaujoyeulx to Rameau* (New York, rev. 1978), p. 175. The title-page of Perrin's book is reproduced in Marcelle Benoit, *Versailles et les Musiciens du Roi* (Paris, 1971), p. 59.
[4] The present writer is grateful to Professor Auld for making available substantial sections of his work in advance of publication. With the original texts of these documents now available in his book, citations from them here are given in translations made by the present writer, cross-referenced to Auld's text.

Latines pour l'Eglise'). But a much fuller picture of how often court composers set these *cantiques* by Perrin emerges from a comparison of his collections with the extant musical sources, and especially with the *Livres du Roi*, the motet texts printed for use during the king's mass (discussed later and listed in table 4).

As table 2 shows, most of Perrin's Latin texts are found in Ms fr 25460, CPCR, and Ms fr 2208. There has been some conjecture among scholars as to the date of Ms fr 2208; Prunières suggested 1667, Anthony, more cautiously, gives 'about 1667' (*French Baroque Music*, p. 353), while Isherwood states: 'Released from jail in 1666 [7 April], Perrin had already completed a collection of poems intended for musical settings, which he dedicated and sent to Colbert.' (Robert Isherwood, *Music in the Service of the King*, Cornell, 1976, p. 174). Auld (III, pp. ii, vii) points to the allusion in the *Avant-propos* to 'la feüe Reyne', who had died in January 1666, showing that the foreword (at least) must have been written after that date. That the volume was complete by or during the summer of the same year is clear from one of the *Livres du Roi* (the issue for the last quarter of 1666) (no. 2 in table 4). This *Livre* includes, among 14 texts ascribed to Perrin, 6 from Ms fr 2208, but only 3 of which are said by Perrin to have been set by Dumont. Therefore, the other 3 must have been set by Dumont either without the knowledge of Perrin, which seems unlikely, or else after Perrin had finished writing out this collection. But Dumont's works could not have been finished any later than September, since the texts were included by Ballard in the *Livre* for Dumont's quarter beginning in October. Even allowing Dumont no more than a week per motet, Perrin's collection for Colbert must have been complete little later than July 1666.

As already noted, only 14 musical settings of his Latin lyrics were mentioned by Perrin in Ms fr 2208: 5 by Dumont, 4 by Expilly and 5 by Sablières; these 14 are indicated in table 2 by asterisks (see also table 5, note 4). But table 2 shows that a minimum of 47 of Perrin's Latin texts were set by ten composers, producing 62 works (since more than one composer set some texts). At least 24 of these works are extant (see table 2, note 2). Dumont composed 26 of the 62 settings, with Expilly (13) and Gobert (8) the other composers most prominently represented. Sablières, one of two French composers of Perrin's Latin texts not *sous-maîtres de la Chapelle* (Danielis was the other), is represented by only 5 works in this genre, although he also set some 35 French texts by Perrin. (Auld, II, 171, Table A.) Lully set only 3 of Perrin's Latin texts (*Plaude laetare* and *O Lachrymae* as *grands motets* and *Ave coeli munus supernum* as a *petit motet*). Of the *sous-maîtres* appointed in 1683 (eight years after Perrin's death), Colasse and Minoret set one each, Coupillet and Lalande none. (Table 3 illustrates the succession of *sous-maîtres* for the reign of Louis XIV.) Daniel Danielis (1635–96) set one Perrin text, and 3 settings are attributed to Carissimi (see note 24).

It may be instructive to consider some of Perrin's observations about the chapel music which, with one exception, appear not to have been noticed previously. If some of his claims are naïve, even outrageous, he also provides information not available elsewhere. In his *Epître dédicatoire* addressed to the king in CPCR we read:

Table 2

Perrin, Pierre: Latin texts for sacred music

Text sources (see also notes to table 5)

| Poësies 1661 | | Paroles 1661 | CASRM | | Ms fr 25460 | | CPCR | | Ms fr 2208 | Livres du Roi (see table 4) | | |
m	e		m	e	m	e	m	e		m	e	
						x			x			Agnos pascebat
						x		x				Agnus innocens
					x		x					Alleluia, Christe laudate
			x		x		x					Angele, Regni summe Minister
			x		x		x					Anna, Christi Mater
						x		x				Ante faciem tuam
			x		x		x					Arbor Olivae pacifica
					x		x					Arma fideles
x												Auditi sunt cantores
					x		x					Auditur magnus
					x		x					Audi virgo Regina coeli
				x		x		x				Ave coeli munus supernum
				x		x		x				Comedit homo cibum laethalum
					x		x					Con vallibus in desertis
					x		x					Coronatur imperator
							x					Cracovia diripitur
					x		x		x			Currite, populi
							x					De profundis terrae
									x			Descende coelitus
									x			Dum sanctorum
					x		x					Ecce Gallus cantavit
							x					Ecce qui terram gladio
						x			x		x	Ecce sol illuminat
					x		x		x			Ecce templi vela rumpuntur
					x		x					Ecce triumphat in coelis
					x		x					Echo sacra verbi
						x			x		x	Errate per vallus (colles)
						x				x		Exultat animus
									x			Ferte date lauream
					x		x					Festa solemnis plena
					x		x					Flores, O Gallia
					x		x					Fremite novo fremite plausu
					x		x					Fugite contremiscite
						x			x			Gaudia coeli, gaudia terris
						x			x			In Cymbalis & organo
						x					x	In te Domine credimus
						x					x	Jesu, dulcedo cordium
									x			Jesu morientis
									x			Lugete gentes
					x		x					Margarita pretiosa
					x		x					Magdalena lachrymae
					x		x					Natura languet & desolatur
											x	Non amo te perfido munde
					x		x					O Dilectissime
						x		x			x	O fideles miseremini
									x			O flos convallium
					x		x					O foelicium chorus
									x		x	O fortissime
									x		x	O gloriosa Mariae viscera
						x		x				O gratiae sacramentum
					x		x					O Joannis, O fidelis

Table 2 (*cont.*)

Composers and Sources of attributions								Music extant
Dumont (table 5)	Expilly/ CPCR, Liv. 1	Gobert/ CASRM	Lully (note 2)	Robert/ Liv. 7	Sablières/ 2208	Colasse/ Liv. 17	Minoret (note 2)	
	x							
		x						Gobert ?
		x						
		x						
		x	x					Lully
		x						
	x						x	Minoret
				x	x*			Robert
x*	x*				x*			
x						x		
x*								?Carissimi, Danielis[24]
x								Dumont
	x							
					x*			
x								
x								Dumont
x								Dumont
x								Dumont
x	x							Dumont
x								Dumont
x								
x*								Dumont

Table 2 (*cont.*)

Perrin, Pierre: Latin texts for sacred music

Text sources (see also notes to table 5)

Poësies 1661		Paroles 1661	CASRM		Ms fr 25460		CPCR		Ms fr 2208	Livres du Roi (see table 4)		
m	e		m	e	m	e	m	e		m	e	
					X		X					O lachrymae fideles
									X			O lignum mortis
			X			X		X				O lux mundi quondam celata
					X		X					O Maria, quid obtulisti
						X		X				O Mater Christi
						X				X		O mysterium venerabile
						X						O quam suavia
X						X						O Rex summe Poli
					X		X					O sancte Joseph
									X			O sponsa, quam suavia
									X		X	O summa charitas (O tu quis es)
									X	X		O tremendum judicium
								X				O virgo semper immaculata
										X		Pax aurea
					X		X					Philippus in cruce pendens
					X		X					Plaude coelum, plaude terra
		X										Plaude laetere Gallia
									X			Plaudite, plaudite
			X		X		X					Psallite, plaudite
									X			Pulchra gratiosa
					X		X			X		Pulsate, pulsate tympana
								X				Quae nova mediis
									X			Qualis murmur
			X			X		X			X	Quare tristis es
					X		X			X		Quid cessatis (lenitis)
									X	X		Quid times
									X		X	Regina divina
					X		X					Regum sydus oritur
									X			Salve fidei
									X	X		Salve Maria
									X		X	Salve sancte panis
									X		X	Serva Christe
					X		X			X		Silete venti
									X			Spira, sancte spiritus
						X		X		X	X	Sub umbra noctis profundae
					X		X					Te reducem salutamus
					X		X					Terram perflavit amoris
					X		X					Terra pone moestitiam
									X		X	Te timeo judex terribilis
											X	Tolle sponsa
					X		X					Tuba coeli resonans
						X		X		X		Ubi es Deus meus
									X		X	Usque quo Domine languebit
								X				Ut rosa moriens
									X	X		Velut unda vagabunda
					X		X					Veni, veni mors jucunda
									X	X		Victoria, victoria
1	1	1	4	4	39	12	50	12	29	21	16	(98 texts)

[1] * indicates composer cited by Perrin in Ms fr 2208.
[2] Sources of Dumont's works extant are given in

Table 8, of Robert's in table 9, and of Lully's in Appendix 3. Minoret's *Currite, Populi* is found in

Table 2 (*cont.*)

Dumont (table 5)	Expilly/ CPCR, Liv. 1	Gobert/ CASRM	Lully (note 2)	Robert/ Liv. 7	Sablières/ 2208	Colasse/ Liv. 17	Minoret (note 2)	Music extant
			x					Lully
		x						
x								Dumont
x*								Dumont
x*								
x								
			x					Lully
		x						
x								Dumont
x	x	x						Dumont
	x							
	x*							
x								Dumont
	x*							
x								
x								
	x							
					x*			
x	x							Dumont ?Carissimi[24]
x								Dumont ?Carissimi[24]
x								
	x							
x								
	x*				x*			
x								
26	13	8	3	1	5	1	1	

F-Pn, Rés. F.932. A setting of *Angele, Regni summe Minister* in F-B, Ms 279146, may be   Gobert's. See also notes 5, 24.

[3] m=motet, e=*élévation*.

Table 3 Sous-maîtres of the royal chapel during the reign of Louis XIV (1643–1715)

Year	Events, publications	Jan–Jun / Jan–Mar	Apl–Jun	Jul–Sep	Jul–Dec / Oct–Dec
1643		*Jan–Jun* T. GOBERT (c. 1605–72) (from 1638)			*Jul–Dec* J. VEILLOT (c. 1600–62)
1652	Dumont: *Cantica Sacra*				
1657	Dumont: *Mélanges*				
1660	Gobert: Royal Wedding Music				
1663	1st Versailles Chapel	*Jan–Mar* GOBERT	*Apl–Jun* P. ROBERT (1610–99)	*Jul–Sep* G. EXPILLY (c. 1630–c. 1690)	H. DUMONT (1610–84) · *Oct–Dec* DUMONT
1664	Lully: *Miserere*				
1665	Perrin: CPCR				
1666	Perrin: Ms fr 2208				
1668	Dumont: *Motets a 2 v*	DUMONT		DUMONT	ROBERT
1672	2nd Chapel				
1675	Death of Perrin				
1677	Lully: *Te Deum*				
1681	Dumont: *Motets II, III, IV*				
1682	3rd Chapel				

	Year	N. COUPILLET (c. 1640–c. 1713)	P. COLASSE (1649–1709)	G. MINORET (c. 1650–1717)	M-R de LALANDE (1657–1726)
Lully: *De profundis/D. Irae*	1683				
Lully, Robert: *Motets à 2c*	1684				
Lully: *Quare fremuerunt*	1685				
Dumont: *Motets à 2 c*	1686				
Death of Lully	1687				
Lalande: 27 Motets (VPh) (see table 7)	1689				
Coupillet: resignation	1694	LALANDE			
Colasse: resignation	1704		LALANDE		
Toulouse/Philidor MSS (TPh)	1706				
Great Chapel	1710				
Minoret: resignation	1714			LALANDE	
Death of Louis XIV	1715				

Having taken note that Your Majesty . . . has assembled with much care and success, the most beautiful voices and the best orchestral players of the Kingdom to make up your Chapel Music and [that Your Majesty] has then provided excellent Masters who assuredly render [this music] worthy of you, that is to say, the most beautiful music on Earth, as you are the greatest King, I have desired on my part to contribute those things which alone seem to be lacking, those which are pure gold and uncut stones, for these excellent artists – agreeable objects to serve as models for these inimitable composers – in a word – beautiful texts for these incomparable musicians . . .

We will see in the person of Your Majesty, a new Gallic Hercules, who, by the charms of his music . . . will bind our hearts and ears in golden chains. Such promises . . . will not seem vain and ill-founded, if Your Majesty recalls the success of some of these canticles when they were sung in your chapel; among others, that for the Martyr, which le Sieur Expilly had performed . . . [and] which delighted all your court . . . and then those for Saint Anne and the Virgin Martyr with which he had regaled it during his quarter,[5] [as well as] that which begins *O lachrymae* which le Sieur Lully had given at Versailles, and those which Monsieur Gobert had set to music for Your Majesty and for Monseigneur le Dauphin.[6]   (original text reproduced in Auld, II, pp. 165– 6)

In the *Avant-propos* following, Perrin states that 'the motet is a piece varied with several melodies or musical passages, linked but different [from one another]' (ibid., II, p. 167, para. 1). He also refers to his treatise, called *L'Art Lyrique*, which 'by rules and examples, explains the manner of composing all kinds of words for music'; unfortunately, no copy of this treatise – if it was ever published (or even written) – seems to have survived. Perrin promised it would reveal 'an art hither-to unknown, which has cost me so much study and application, out of which have come these psalms and more than five hundred pieces of lyric poetry, which have been, and are still heard at the Court and elsewhere every day, set to music by all the illustrious musicians of the Kingdom' (ibid., II, p. 168, para. 5).

Of his Latin style, Perrin says he has 'tried to make it elegant and well-constructed, while easy to understand, [with] words and phrases corresponding to our French [ones]'. Although some of Perrin's contemporaries criticized his Latin verse (see below), it is fair to say that it was modelled on the French lyric poetry of his day – the poetic style and structure used by Corneille, for example, and not the models of classical Latin. It was nothing more than contemporary French verses put into Latin, almost word for word, without any pretensions to classical metre. Perrin also states quite frankly that his Latin Canticles 'are written to be sung and not recited' (ibid., II, p. 168, paragraphs 7, 8).

There follows his well-known explanation of 'the length of the *Cantiques* as they are written for the King's mass, at which three are normally sung: a *grand*, a

---

[5] This must refer to 1664 or 1665, since Expilly's quarter was July–September; in Ms fr 25460 and CPCR, each text is assigned to a feast day, and from these headings we find that the text for the Martyr is *Quid cessatis* (*lenitis*), *O tortores*, for Saint Anne, *Festa solemnis plena decoris* and for the Virgin Martyr, *Currite, populi*. The first two of these, together with the 4 texts ascribed to Expilly in Ma fr 2208 and 6 other texts by Perrin

are included in *Livre* 1 (see appendix 1, and tables 2 and 4).

[6] Presumably these are among the works whose texts are contained in CASRM. The music for one, *Angele, Regni summe Minister,* may survive; in a manuscript Recueil in F-B, MS 279146, fos. 36r–41v, there is an anony-mous setting of Perrin's text headed 'Mottet du Roy'.

petit for the elevation, and a *Domine salvum fac Regem*' (ibid., II, p. 169, para. 10). (That '*cantique*' is merely his expression for the text of a *motet* is made clear in the *Avant-propos* to Ms fr 2208 (f. 10r), where he refers to 'Cantiques ou paroles pour des motets'.)

Perrin then makes an extraordinary assertion which seems at odds with his earlier flattering remarks about the king's musicians:

I know that few scholars hear enough music to be able to comprehend the spirit or the letter of my intentions, and the majority of musicians know too little Latin to be able to understand and perform my works well. But we will not always be living in the Dark Ages and the inclination for music witnessed by our great monarch will one day give us Amphions and Orpheuses who will make other discoveries in this unknown territory.

(ibid., II, p. 169, para. 11)

Such a remark hardly seems calculated to win the approval of the *sous-maîtres* (if it came to their attention). Evidently, Perrin was aware that his work had come in for criticism, as he mentions that 'certain critics have raised themselves up against me with much heat, understanding neither the reasons for my works, nor the use to which they are put' (ibid., II, p. 169, para. 13). Some hint of previous trouble with the *sous-maîtres* of the chapel may be contained in the final sentence, where he says that 'the *maîtres* don't now make any more difficulties, and they compose every day to suitable words, particularly for their motets for the elevation' (ibid., II, p. 170).[7]

THE *LIVRES DU ROI*

Only nineteen of these volumes are known to be extant from the reign of Louis XIV (although many more survive from the time of his two successors – the largest collection is today in the Bibliothèque municipale at Versailles).[8] These collections of texts, listed in table 4 are of considerable value to students of both text and music, for several reasons. The extant examples include those for most of Dumont's periods of service as *sous-maître* (table 6), no. 1 of table 4 provides valuable information about the output of Expilly (appendix 1), no. 7 for that of Robert (table 9), no. 17 for that of Colasse (appendix 2), as do nos. 18, 19 for that of Lalande (table 7); as we have seen, they also considerably amplify our knowledge of the extent to which Perrin's verses were set. The character of their title-pages, without designated author, yet often citing one or more composers, and thus occupying an ambiguous position between music and text, has led to their classification in libraries under a wide variety of headings.[9]

[7] For analysis of Perrin's character, aims and achievements, see Auld, particularly: I, pp. 1–25 (preface and chapter I); II, pp. 40–55 (Aesthetics and Rhetoric); II, pp. 159–60 (Latin Lyrics).
[8] F-V, Rés. G. 80–204, 207, 208 (127 volumes 1762–91). Other copies from the same period are in GB-Lbl, Hirsch IV. 1318 (1761); F-B, 60886 (1762); F-Pn, Rés. 1364–75 (12 volumes 1780–92); US-Wc, M2020.

M66 (1784).
[9] The author is grateful to Mlle A. Garrigoux, Mlle J. Linet, M. M. Barthélémy, and Mme L. Colas, respectively librarians at F-V, F-Psg, B-Lc and F-VAL, and to Mme Hélène Charnassé and M. Robert Lutz, for access to their collections, and their ready responses to extensive enquiries; also to Dr Herbert Schneider, of Heidelberg University, who drew his attention to the *livre* at F-VAL.

Table 4 *Extant* Livres du Roi *for the Chapelle royale during the reign of Louis XIV*
(in chronological order)

1	*Motets et élévations de M. Expilly pour le quartier de juillet, aoust et septembre*		1666
2	id.	*de M. Du Mont...*	*octobre, novembre et decembre*	1666
3	id.		*juillet, aoust et septembre*	1670
4	id.		*juillet, aoust et septembre*	1674
5	id.		*janvier, février et mars*	1675
6	id.		*juillet, aoust et septembre*	1677
7	id.	*de M. Robert...*	*avril, mai et juin*	1678
8	id.	*de M. Du Mont...*	*juillet, aoust et septembre*	1678
9	id.		*janvier, février et mars*	1679
10	id.		*juillet, aoust et septembre*	1679
11	id.		*janvier, février et mars*	1680
12	id.		*juillet, aoust et septembre*	1680
13	id.		*janvier, février et mars*	1681
14	id.		*janvier, février et mars*	1682
15	id.		*juillet, aoust et septembre*	1682
16	id.		*janvier, février et mars*	1683
17	*Motets et élévations pour la Chapelle du Roy...Quartier de Avril, May et Juin*		1686
	(includes texts of *motets* by Robert, Lully and Colasse and of *élévations* by Colasse)		
18	id.	*Quartier de Janvier, Février et Mars*		1703
	(includes texts of *motets* by Robert, Lully and Lalande and of *élévations* by Lalande)		
19	id.	*Quartier de Janvier, Février et Mars*		1714
	(includes texts of *motets* by Robert, Lully and Lalande and of *élévations* by Lalande)		

Locations:
  1: F-Pn, Inv. Rés. B.2524
  2: B-Lc, Fonds Terry, Litt.204
  3–6, 8–12, 14–16 (12 vols.): F-Psg, Vm 18
  6 (another copy): F-Psg, Rés. BB 8°, 1592.Inv.1729
  7: Collection Mme Hélène Charnassé
 13: F-Pn, B.7213
 17: F-Psg, Vm 19
 18: F-VAL, Bz 1.100
 19: F-Psg, Rés. △ 16646

Contents:
The texts present in no. 1 are listed in appendix 1, nos. 2–6, 8–16 are listed in table 6, and those in no. 7 in table 9. Those of Colasse's works in no. 17 are listed in appendix 2, and of Lalande's in nos. 18 and 19 in table 7. Nos. 17–19 also contain the texts of the 24 motets by Robert and the 6 by Lully published as *Motets pour la Chapelle du Roy* in 1684, but not those of Dumont, published in 1686.

They were printed in two formats. Plate 1 shows a title-page of a quarto volume; bound in green or red leather and embossed in gold with the royal arms, these were no doubt destined for members of the royal family. Plate 2 shows two examples of the smaller format, simply bound in black and probably intended for the rest of the congregation.

Although Madeleine Garros and Simone Wallon noted most of the *livres* for Dumont in their *Catalogue du fonds musical de la Bibliothèque Sainte-Geneviève de Paris* (Kassel, 1967), the significance of these books seems to have been overlooked. Their importance lies in two particular areas:

1. they show that the number of Dumont's settings of Perrin's texts is considerably greater than that indicated in Perrin's own works. Table 5 demonstrates that no less than twenty-eight such works can be traced, rather than the five which Perrin claimed in Ms fr 2208.

2. they authoritatively establish the date at which each motet entered the repertory of the Chapelle royale, as table 6 shows.

MOTETS
ET
ELEVATIONS
POUR LA CHAPELLE
DU ROY,

Imprimez par Ordre de Sa Majefté.

Quartier de Janvier, Février & Mars 1703.

A PARIS,

De l'Imprimerie de CHRISTOPHE BALLARD,
feul Imprimeur du Roy pour la Mufique.

M. DCCIII.

Plate 1. Title-page for one of the *Livres du Roi* – a quarto volume designed
for the royal family

MOTETS,
ET
ELEVATIONS
DE M. DV MONT.

Pour le quartier d'Octobre,
Nouembre, & Decembre _jour—_
mil six cent soixante-fix. _et fevr—_

MOTETS;
ET
ELEVATIONS
DE M. ROBERT.

Pour le Quartier d'Auril, May,
& Iuin 1678.

A PARIS;
Par Christophe Ballard,
seul Imprimeur du Roy
pour la Musique.

Plates 2a, b. Title-pages of the _Livres du Roi_ in the smaller formats – probably intended
for the congregation

Table 5 *Twenty-six Perrin texts set by Dumont (28 settings – 14 extant)*

Attribution to Perrin					Genre		Attribution to Dumont — Texts				Attribution to Dumont — Music				
F-Pn Ms fr 25460	CPCR	F-Pn Ms fr 2208	Livres du Roi (table 6)		Motets	Elévations	F-Pn Ms fr 2208	1666 Livre	1670 Livre	1674 Livre	1668 Motets	1681 Motets	1686 Motets	F-Pn Rés Vma Ms 572	GB-Lbl Add Ms 24293
		x	x	1 Ecce sol illuminat	x	x									
x	x	x	x	2 Ecce templi vela rimpuntur	x				x						
		x	x	3 Errate per colles		x	x	x							
				Errate per colles	x							x			
	x		x	4 Exultat animus	x			x					x		
		x	x	5 In cymbalis & organo	x			x							
		x	x	6 In te Domine credimus		x		x			x				
			x	7 Jesu dulcedo cordium		x		x				x			
			x	8 Non amo te, perfide		x		x			x				
x	x			9 O fideles miseremini		x					x				
			x	10 O flos convallium	x				x					x	
		x	x	11 O fortissime	x						x				
		x	x	12 O gloriosa Mariae viscera		x	x	x				x			
	x		x	13 O mysterium venerabile	x			x					x		
		x	x	14 O summa charitas (O tu quis es)		x	x	x				x			
		x	x	15 O tremendum judicium	x		x	x	x						
			x	16 Pax aurea	x		x		x	x					
x	x			17 Pulsate, pulsate tympana	x			x					x		
x				18 Quare tristis es		x		x				x			
			x	19 Regina divina		x		x							
				Regina divina	x					x					
	x			20 Salve, sancte panis		x				x					
		x	x	21 Serva Christe		x				x					
x	x	x	x	22 Sub umbra noctis		x			x						x
		x	x	23 Te timeo judex terribilis		x		x			x				
			x	24 Tolle sponsa		x				x					
	x			25 Usque quo Domine languebit		x				x					
		x	x	26 Victoria, victoria	x					x					
5	8	13	21		13	16	5	14	5	7	5	5	3	1	1

Comments:

[1] Six texts (7, 8, 10, 16, 19, 24) are attributed to Perrin in the *livres* but are not found in any of his collections.

[2] Of the twenty-four texts by Perrin in the *livres* three (17, 20, 25) are not attributed to him there.

[3] One text by Perrin (9) does not occur in the *livres* but is found in the 1668 edition of *Motets à 2 voix*.

[4] One text claimed by Perrin in Ms fr 2208 to have been set by Dumont occurs neither in the *livres* not in the extant music (1).

[5] The twenty-six attributions in Perrin's own works concern only twenty different texts.

[6] Twenty of the texts by Perrin in the *livres* do not occur in Ms fr 2208.

Table 6

Motets et Elévation de M. Du Mont. . .(1666–83) (14 volumes) (see also table 4) Contents of each issue extant, showing cumulati
nature of the series; texts are included in the order shown (except for four *élévations* added between 1667 and 1670); volumes fro
1670 onwards commence with alphabetical indices, newly made for each issue. Psalm texts and those by Perrin are identifie
attributions in brackets are not given in the *livres*, but are derived from Perrin's collections (see table 5, note 2)

		Motets			*Elévations*	
Pour le quartier d'octobre,	1	Exultat animus	Perrin	1	O salutaris hostia	
novembre & décembre 1666	2	O mysterium venerabile	Perrin	2	Quam pulchra es	
	3	Ecce templi	Perrin	3	Ave virgo gratiosa	
	4	Exaudiat te	Ps 19	4	Dic mihi o bone Jesu	
	5	Tribulater ego		5	Jesu Rex admirabilis	
	6	Mater Jerusalem		6	Tota pulchra es	
	7	Foelicis Sancti Dei		7	Gloriosissima Maria	
	8	Deus pacis		8	Ne memineris dulcissime	
	9	Te Deum		9	Fuge mundum	
	10	Veni Domine		10	Doleo super te	
	11	Deus patrum meorum		11	Ecce ferculum charitatis	
	12	Exurge Domine		12	O dulcedo amoris	
	13	Domine mi Rex		13	Quid est hoc quod sentio	
	14	Domine in virtute tua	Ps 20 ⎤	14	Quid commisisti	
	15	Omnes gentes	Ps 46 ⎥	15	O quam suavis es o bone Jesu	
	16	Dixit Dominus	Ps 109 ⎥	16	Miserere mei Domine	Ps 50
	17	Beatus vir	Ps 111 ⎥	17	Quare tristis es	Perrin
	18	Laudate pueri	Ps 112 ⎥	18	Sub umbra noctis profundae	Perrin
	19	Credidi propter	Ps 115 ⎥	19	Memorare, o piissima Virgo	
	20	Laetatus sum	Ps 121 ⎥	20	Quis mihi det Domine	
	21	Lauda Jerusalem	Ps 147 ⎦	21	Per foeminam mors	
	22	Memento Domine	Ps 131	22	Paratum cor meum	
	23	Magnificat		23	Venite ad me omnes	
	24	Ave Maris Stella		24	O Gloriosa Mariae viscera	Perrin
	25	O tremendum judicium	Perrin	25	Te timeo, judex terribilis	Perrin
	26	Salve mater		26	In te Domine credimus	Perrin
	27	In cymbalis & organo	Perrin	27	Errate per colles	Perrin
	28	Congratulamini		28	O tu quis es	Perrin
	29	Jubilemus		29	Ego enim accepi	
	30	Vanitas vanitatum		30	Jesu dulcedo cordium	Perrin
				31	Non amo te perfide munde	Perrin
. . .*juillet–septembre 1670*	31	Victoria, victoria	Perrin	32	Peccator ubi es	⎫ Added to head o
	32	Confitebimur	Ps 74	33	O nomen Jesu	⎬ list of *élévations*
	33	Veni Creator		34	Desidero te millies	⎮ by 1670
	34	O aeterna misericors		35	O sponse mi, o lilium	⎭
	35	Pax aurea	Perrin	36	Panis angelicus	
	36	O flos convallium	Perrin	37	Regina divina	Perrin
	37	Benedictus Dominus	Cant. Zach.	38	In lectulo meo	
	38	Pulsate, pulsate tympana	(Perrin)	39	Benedicite Deum	
	39	Confitebor	Ps 110	40	O bone Jesu	
	40	In convertendo	Ps 125			
	41	Miserere	Ps 50			
	42	Domine quid multiplicati	Ps 3			
. . .*juillet–septembre 1674*	43	De profundis	Ps 129	41	Salve sanote panis	(Perrin)
	44	Domine quis habitabit	Ps 14	42	Usque quo Domine languebit	(Perrin)
	45	O fortissime	Perrin	43	Anima Christe	
	46	Sacris solemniis		44	Congregati sunt	
	47	Regina divina	Perrin	45	Adoro te	
	48	Memorare, o piissima Virgo		46	Tolle sponsa	Perrin
	49	Verba mea auribus	Ps 5	47	Serva Christe	Perrin

Table 6 (*cont.*)

	Motets		Elévations	
	50 Nisi Dominus	Ps 126	48 Quam dilecta	Ps 83
	51 Domine, Dominus noster	Ps 8	49 Euge serva bone	
	52 Super flumina Babylonis	Ps 136	50 Media vita in morte	
	53 Errate per colles	Perrin	51 Ad Dominum cum tribularer	Ps 119
	54 Exaltabo te Deus	Ps 144	52 Sancta & immaculata	
			53 Virgo prudentissima	
			54 O praecelsum	
			55 Ad te levavi	Ps 122
			56 Cantate Domino	Ps 95
			57 Jubilate Deo	Ps 99
janvier–mars 1675	55 Ecce iste venit saliens		58 Hodie nobis	
	56 Laudate Dominum	Ps 150		
juillet–septembre 1677	57 Cantemus Domino	Exod. 15	59 Unde tibi	
	58 Beati omnes	Ps 127	60 Quae est ista	
	59 Benedicam Dominum	Ps 33	61 Converte Domine	
	60 Exaudi Deus	Ps 60	62 In lectulo meo	
	61 Dum esset in acubitu		63 O Maria Mater Dei	
			64 Duo Seraphim	
			65 Anima mea	
juillet–septembre 1678	62 Quemadmodum	Ps 41	66 Omne die dic Mariae	
	63 Domine Deus meus dulcedo		67 Nil canitur suavius	
janvier–mars 1679			68 O gloriosa Domino	
juillet–septembre 1679	64 O Dulcissima			
janvier–mars 1680	65 Benedic anima mea Domino		69 Sit gloria Domini	
juillet–septembre 1680	66 Ecce nos tanquam			
janvier–mars 1681			70 Alma redemptoris Mater	
			71 Stella coeli	
janvier–mars 1682	67 Cantate Domino	Ps 95	72 Ave Regina coelorum	
	68 Domini est terra	Ps 23		
juillet–septembre 1682 *janvier–mars 1683*	(No additions)		(No additions)	

Further, the cumulative nature of the books meant that they gradually increased in size with each issue, so that the last three for Dumont's last quarters as *sous-maître* contain more than twice as many works as the earliest of his extant. The printer apparently kept the type set and normally just added the texts of new motets at the back of the book, while rearranging the alphabetical index at the front each time to enable the king and chapel congregation to find their way about the book. (The only exception to this practice occurred some time between 1666 and 1670 when four *élévations* were added to the head of the second section containing these texts.) As nothing was ever removed from these cumulative volumes when new texts were added, they comprised the entire repertory up to the date of each issue, rather than being confined to the actual works to be performed during that quarter.

Thus these *livres* offer clear evidence of chronology of entry into the chapel repertory, and this chronology probably corresponds to the order of composition, at least for those works written after the composer took up his appointment as *sous-maître*. In the case of Lalande, there is corroborative evidence for this view. Fortunately, the two extant *livres* correspond to different points in Lalande's career, the second marking the virtual end of his composition of new motets. Table 7 provides an analysis of their contents; whilst the *livres* are for the first quarters of 1703 and 1714, they are clearly cumulative from Lalande's earliest years as *sous-maître*. A comparison of the lists of dates found in MS 5840 in the Bibliothèque du Muséum Calvet at Avignon (henceforth A5840) with a similar list in the posthumous edition of forty of the composer's motets (H) illustrates that the texts appear in the *livre* in a generally chronological order.

If the dating seems somewhat haphazard in the early part of the list derived from the *livres*, the reasons are not hard to conjecture. To begin with, the first fourteen titles are in alphabetical order, suggesting they formed the contents of the first *livres* to be printed for Lalande's early quarters as *sous-maître*, and represented works composed before he took up his appointment.[10] The dates shown in parentheses almost certainly refer to second settings of these texts; such settings are extant in all cases but four (8, 9, 10, 41). Further, the contents of the Philidor MSS of 1689–90 (VPh) all appear in the upper part of the list. The works numbered 65 onwards are those added in the 1714 *livre*. The discovery of these *livres* adds four *grands motets* and nine *élévations* to the list of known works by Lalande, gives the text of three other motets previously only known by the inclusion of their titles in A5840, and completes the text of four motets of which only fragments of the music survive in a *recueil* compiled in Apt in 1765 (denoted Apt).

For Dumont, a comparison of the contents of the *livres* with those of his published collections discloses new information (table 8). For example, for the *Motets* published in 1668 and 1681 (columns 5, 6), a comparison with the dates of the extant *livres* (column 1) shows that many of these works were already in the chapel repertory before their publication. Of the 1668 collection, 13 of the 30 come into this category, and 28 of the 37 in the 1681 publication had been sung in the chapel before publication. For the *grands motets*, it is clear from table 8 that the 20 motets comprising the posthumous collection of 1686 were a representative collection from at least the two preceding decades, as surmised by Anthony (*French Baroque Music*, p. 176). In total, 109 (more than half) of Dumont's sacred works in Latin had been composed by 1666, just three years after he had taken up his first appointment as *sous-maître*. This is to be expected, as Dumont was fifty-three at the time of his appointment, with a long and distinguished career as composer and performer, and several publications already behind him.

---

[10] Probably, only the first thirteen should be considered as forming this group; the fourteenth, *Veni Creator spiritus*, may be accidentally in sequence alphabetically, since one source of the work (the copy in the private collection of M. R. Lutz, Strasbourg) gives 1684 as its date of composition (the year after Lalande's appointment as *sous-maître* commenced).

Table 7

alande's *grands motets* in order of texts in *Livres du Roi* of 1703 and 1714, showing those included in VPh of 1689–90, and giving omparisons with dating from other sources, and postulated dates of cumulative additions to *livres* 1683 onwards (for quarters when alande was *sous-maître*), together with assigned S (Sawkins) numbers.

VPh = F-V, Ms mus 8–17, *Motets de M. Delalande* (Philidor MSS, 1689–90)
H = *Motets de feu M. De La Lande*, Paris, 1729–33 (engraved by L. Hue)
A5840 = F-A, MS 5840, *Table(s) des motets de feu Mr De la Lande et l'année qu'il les a composés*
Apt = F-Pn, Vm¹ 3123, *Récits et Duo de Msr de La Lande*, 1765 (compiled in Apt)
TPh = F-Pn, Rés. F. 1694–7 (Toulouse-Philidor collection)
V18 = F-V, Ms mus 18, V24 = F-V, Ms mus 24, V25 = F-V, Ms mus 25
Lutz = Manuscript in private collection of M. Robert Lutz, Strasbourg
MR = Musique du Roi, F-Pn, H. 400B

?Date added	S No.	Text	VPh	H	A5840	Comments and explanations of discrepancies
		(contents of 1703 *Livre*)				
t1683	6	Ad te levavi	x		*	*listed undated
	4	Afferte Domino	x		1683	
	7	Audite coeli	x		(1689)	?revision date
	5	Beati quorum	x		1683	
	3	Deitatis majestatem	x		1682	
	1	Dixit Dominus	x		1680	first setting
	8	Ecce, nunc benedicite	x		(1686)	?revision date
	9	Jubilate Deo	x		(1689)	?revision date
	10	Laudate Dominum Ps 116	x		(1686)	?revision date
	2	Magnificat			1681	music lost
	11	Omnes gentes	x		*	*listed undated
	12	Quam dilecta	x		(1686)	?revision date
	13	Super flumina	x		(1687)	?revision date
t1684	14	Veni Creator	x		(1722)	Lutz: 1684
t1685	15	Miserere Ps 56	x		1685	
t1686	16	Deus misereatur	x		1687	?revision date
	17	Domine, Dominus noster			1686	Apt unicum
	18	Laudate pueri	x		1686	
	19	Lauda Jerusalem	x	(1725)	(1725)	?revision date
t1687	20	Deus, Deus meus	x		1685	
	21	Christe, redemptor	x		1690	in VPh by 1689
t1688	22	Cantemus Domino	x		1687	
	23	De profundis	x	1689	1689	?revision date
	24	Exaudi Deus	x		(1719)	?revision date
	25	In convertendo	x	1684	1684	?revised version
	26	Nisi quia Dominus		(1703)	(1703)	?revision date
t1689	27	Miserere Ps 50	x	1687	1687	
	28	Domine non est exaltatum	x		1691	in VPh by 1689
t1690	29	Domine in virtute tua	x	1689	1689	
t1691	30	Deus stetit in synagoga			§	§not listed, music lost
	31	Dies Irae			(1711)	Lutz: 1.mai.1690
	32	Te Deum laudamus	x	1684	1684	?revised version
t1692	33	Deus in adjutorium		1691	1691	
t1693	34	Cantemus Virginem			§	§not listed, music lost
	35	Deus in nomine tuo			1690	Apt unicum
	36	Exaudiat te			1688	music lost
1694	37	Domine quid multiplicati			1691	Apt unicum
	38	Judica me		1693	1693	
1694	39	Beatus vir		1692	1692	
	40	Usquequo Domine		1692	1692	Mercure: oct1692
1695	41	Cum invocarem			(1714)	?rev'n date; Apt unicum
	42	Nisi Dominus		(1704)	1694	?H = revision date

Table 7 (cont.)

?Date added	S No.	Text	VPh	Dates in: H	Dates in: A5840	Comments and explanation of discrepancies
oct1695	43	Dominus regit me		1695	1695	
jan1696	44	Benedictus Ps 143		1695	1695	
oct1696	45	Quemadmodum		1696	1696	
jan1697	46	Laudate Dominum Ps 150			§	§unlisted; V18:rev1697
oct1697	47	Laetatus sum			1693	?this setting lost; cf.78
jan1698	48	Confitebor Ps 137		1697	1697	
	49	Credidi propter		1697	1697	
	50	Eructavit			1697	Lutz: déc1697
oct1698	51	Beati omnes		1698	1698	
	[52	O filii et filiae		1698	1698]	Livres omit[1]
	[53	Regina coeli		1698	1698]	Livres omit[1]
oct1699	54	Deus noster refugium		1699	1699	
	55⟩	Cantate Domino Ps 95			1698	Lutz: déc1698
	56⟩	Confitebor Ps 110		1699	1699	
oct1701	58	Venite exultemus		1700	1700	V25: jan1701
	57	Laudate Dominum Ps 146		1700	1700	V24: mar1700
jan1702	59	Confitebimur		1701	1701	?Dangeau VIII/255
	60	Ad Dominum cum tribularer			§	§not listed, music lost
	61	Magnus Dominus		1702	1701	?added oct1702
oct1702	62	Benedictus Cant. Zach.		1702	1702	
	63	Notus in Judaea		1702	1702	
jan1703	64	Ad te, Domine, clamabo		1703	1703	composed by déc1702
		(additional texts in 1714 Livre)				
avr1704	65	Dominus regnavit		1704	1704	in TPh/1706
	[65a	Domine salvum fac regem]				Livres omit
	66	Exaltabo te, Domine		1704	1704	in TPh/1706
	[66a	Domine salvum fac regem]				Livres omit
	67	Pange lingua gloriosi		1689	1704	?revised version[1]
avr1705	68	Confitemini Domino		1705	1705	in TPh/1706
	69	Verbum supernum prodiens			§	§not listed, music lost
oct1706	70	Quare fremuerunt		1706	1706	Ramillies, mai1706
jan1707	71	Exurgat Deus		1706	1706	
avr1707	72	Cantate Domino Ps 97		1707	1707	
	[73	Dixit Dominus		1708	1708]	2nd setting
avr1709	74	Sacris solemniis		1709	1709	
avr1710	75	Exultate justi		1710	1710	
avr1712	76	Exaltabo te, Deus meus		1712	1712	
jan1714		[no additions]				
		[other works not in livres:]				
	77	Omnes gentes			1721	2nd setting; cf.11
	78	Laetatus sum				?Lalande (MR); cf.47
	79	Conserva me				?Lalande (Apt)

Elévations in order of texts in *Livres du Roi* of 1703 and 1714.
1 Salve caro Salvatoris
2 Jesu quem velatum nunc aspicio
3 O salutaris hostia
4 Ave verum corpus
5 Tantum ergo sacramentum
6 Ignis vivus, dulcis flamma
7 Ad gaudia cordis
8 O bone jesu
9 Properate multitudo

[1] The earlier dating of 67, *Pange linqua* (H gives 1689), if accurate, would suggest it ought to be found in VPh (1689–90), but 2, *Magnificat* and 17, *Dominus Deus noster* were also omitted. Is there a volume missing? Another possible explanation for the omission of 67 (often sung on Palm Sunday) from the 1703 *livre* is the late date of Easter that year (8 April). A similar explanation might be offered for the omission of the Easter antiphons (52, *O filii et filiae* and 53, *Regina coeli*) from both *livres*, since Easter Day fell on 1 April in 1714.

Of these 109 works in the repertory by 1666, 31 were *grands motets*. This suggests that Dumont had been at work in this genre long before his appointment at the royal chapel, and that the orchestral motet was a product neither of the influence of Louis XIV nor of Lully, but rather, a natural evolution of a form already familiar in cathedrals and large churches outside the court. (Isherwood's citation of a 'contemporary' author (ibid., p. 306), implying that the king was responsible for the introduction of the string orchestra into the motet, derives from the *Etat actuel de la musique du Roi . . .* of 1772 – more than a century later. Similarly, the legend, also quoted by Isherwood, that 'Dumont protested that the Council of Trent had forbidden the use of instruments in church music' was long ago discredited by Henri Quittard (*Henry Du Mont*, Paris, 1906, pp. 63–6) who traced its origins to Fontenay (1776), from whence it was repeated by Laborde, Fétis and many others. As for the choral structure, the difference between the *petit choeur* and the *grand choeur* was clearly well-established by the time of Thomas Gobert, *sous-maître* from 1638; in a letter to Constantin Huyghens in 1643, he wrote: 'Le grand choeur, qui est à cinq, est toujours remply de quantité de voix. Aux petits choeurs les voix y sont seules de chaque partie.')[11]

Thus, it now seems unlikely that Dumont wrote in these larger forms only in response to his obligations at the royal chapel, or that he may have used Lully's *Miserere* as a model, as Anthony had earlier suggested before the *Livres du Roi* had been analyzed (ibid. p. 176). Admiring the formal strength, melodic beauty, harmonic resource and rhythmic impulse of works in the 1686 collection, such as *Memorare* and *Super flumina Babylonis*, recently assembled into score and recorded, should one now question the view that 'Dumont's inspiration flagged from time to time under the necessity of filling such a breadth of musical space, for he was essentially a miniaturist' (ibid., p. 178)? We must recall in this connection that Dumont arrived in Paris some years before Lully, with wide experience in Liège and Maastricht behind him, and a thorough grounding in the Italian *basso-continuo* style, all of which must surely have equipped him well to compose *grands motets* without the example of his celebrated contemporary.

Further information about Dumont's output may be derived from table 8. Firstly, the *Livres du Roi* disclose the existence of 62 works of which the music is lost, increasing the number of Dumont's known compositions to Latin texts from 138 to 200.[12] Conversely, 57 of the 138 extant works to Latin texts (mostly from Dumont's earlier publications) do not occur in the chapel *livres*; for example, 29 of the 35 works in the 1652 *Cantica sacra* were never taken into the chapel repertory, nor, with one exception, were those in the 1657 *Mélanges*.

---

[11] Quittard observes, significantly, that neither Brossard, in his *Catalogue* (1724), nor Titon du Tillet (*Le Parnasse françois*, 1732) makes any mention of the 'Council of Trent' story in their quite detailed entries on Dumont. Gobert's letter dated 17 October 1646, is quoted by J. R. Anthony, *La Musique en France à l'époque baroque*, Paris, 1981, p. 213, from W. J. A. Jonckbloet and J. P. N. Land, *Musique et musiciens au XVIIe siècle* (Leyden, 1882), p. ccxvii.

[12] These figures are based on a preliminary survey of sources extant in F-Pn, F-V, F-BO, GB-Lbl and several other libraries, but must be regarded as *minima*, awaiting a more exhaustive enquiry (see note 23).

Table 8

Chronology of Dumont's Latin church music

Livres dates		Elévations and Petits Motets									Grands motets						Overall progressive total
		Cantica Sacra 1652 (35)	Mélanges 1657 (12)	Motets a 2v 1668 (30)	Motets II–IV 1681 (37)	GB-Lbl Add MS 14336	F-Pn Vm 1/1302	Extant	Not extant	Progressive total	Motets a 2 cb 1686 (20)	F-Pn Vm 1/1302	F-Pn Rés Vma ms 572	Extant	Not extant	Progressive total	
1652		Published						35		35							35
1657			Published					11*		46							46
1666	x	1		13	13		1	27	5	78	5	1	1	7	24	31	109
1668				Published				15*		93							124
1670	x	2	1	2	5			5	9	107	5		1	6	6	43	150
1674	x	1			7			7		114	4		1	5	7	55	169
1675	x								1	115	1			1	1	57	172
1677	x	1		2	1			1	3	119	2		3	5		62	181
1678	x				1			1	1	121	1			1	1	64	185

1679	x	1								(121)	1	1		65	186
1680	x				1		1	2		123	1	1	1	67	190
1681	x				Published			6*		129					196
1682	x				2				1	130			2	69	199
1683	(Resignation of Dumont)														
1684	(Death of Dumont)					1		1		131					200
1686											Published				
TOTALS								111	20	131		27	42	69	200
Works in *livres*		6	1	17*	30*			54	18	72		27	42	68	140
Works not in *livres*		29	10*	11*	4*	1	2	57		57					57
Other texts Perrin claimed Dumont had set									2	2			1	1	3
Totals								111	20	131		27	42	69	200

*Does not include works duplicated from earlier collections.

For the manuscript collections, the numbers given are for works unique to each.

But not only Dumont had been writing *grands motets* before his appointment to the chapel, if we accept the evidence of the *livres*. Pierre Robert, too, appears to have done so, perhaps for one of his previous appointments at Senlis, Chartres or Notre Dame de Paris. A long-running dispute at Senlis regarding the use of 'la Simphonie & les Instrumens que l'on a voulu introduire dans leur Eglise aux Leçons des Ténèbres' implies that such instruments were already in use outside Holy Week.[13]

Table 9 lists the contents of the *livre* for Robert's quarter in 1678, toward the end of his career as a *sous-maître*. Like the Lalande *livres*, Robert's begins with a group of texts (26) alphabetically listed, and then proceeds in random order. Thus, once again, as in the *livres* for Lalande, the first group probably represents those composed before Robert's appointment in 1664, while the other 23 were written over the ensuing fourteen years. That the *livre* was assembled in the now familiar fashion of adding texts at the back is also borne out by several tell-tale pieces of information from the printer. For example, a printer's by-line, 'Elevations', at the foot of page 72, shows that at one point in the book's development, the collection of *élévation* texts began on the next page (after the first 35 motet texts). Further, page 82 only contains a few lines of text; the rest of the page is occupied by a rather elegant printer's device, suggesting that the motet texts concluded at this point at a later stage (after the first 40 motet texts); the printer left the page like this even after the subsequent addition of the other 9 texts.

When the selection was made for the collected edition published by Ballard on the king's orders (*Motets pour la Chapelle du Roy*, Paris, 1684), of the 24 chosen from the 50 *grands motets* apparently written by Robert up to this time, 17 were taken from the lower part of the list, and only 7 from the first 26. The contents of this *livre* show that the output of Robert must have included at least 32 more works than previously known, giving totals of 50 *grands motets* and 17 *élévations* rather than the 24 of the former and 11 of the latter, of which the music is extant. Thus a study of the *Livres du Roi* not only considerably widens our knowledge of the number of works composed by the *sous-maîtres*, it is also particularly useful in establishing the chronology of their output.

LULLY AND THE *SOUS-MAÎTRES*

Several events in the years 1683–7 were significant in the history and development of the *grand motet* – the *concours* for new *sous-maîtres* in 1683, the death of the queen later the same year, the publication by Ballard of substantial collections of the motets of the retiring *sous-maîtres* and of Lully in 1684–6, the impact of the prolific young Lalande on the repertory, and the death of Lully in 1687.

The king's decision to retire Dumont and Robert from their posts led to the *concours* to find their successors, an event that attracted much attention and a large field of candidates, of whom four (Colasse, Coupillet, Lalande and Minoret) were eventually chosen in May 1683.[14] Of the new *sous-maîtres*, two

[13] See: *Critique D'un Docteur de Sorbone, sur les deux Lettres de Messieurs Deslyons ancien & de Bragelongne nouveau Doyen de la Cathédrale de* Senlis. . . , Senlis, 1698 (copy in F-Pm, A. 10821[21]).

[14] An account, based on the surviving docu-

(Minoret and Coupillet) were in holy orders, and had been nominated by the Archbishop of Rheims (the *Maître de la Chapelle*) and Robert, one of the retiring *sous-maîtres*, respectively. Lully's protégé, not surprisingly, was his amanuensis, Colasse; it was the king who chose Lalande. For the occasion, Lully composed his *De profundis*, no doubt with the intention of dazzling the shortlisted candidates who were obliged to listen to it after emerging from a week's incarceration during which each had composed a setting of *Beati quorum*; a few weeks later, in August, Lully was able to put his new work to a more appropriate use, when the queen, Marie-Thérèse, died.

In the short time remaining until his own unexpected demise early in 1687, both the appointment of Lalande and the queen's passing were to have more significance for Lully than he could have foreseen. The Chapelle royale was the one area of court music where Lully held no official appointment, such motets as he had composed having been written for official occasions when, by virtue of his post as *surintendant*, he would have directed their performance. (This prerogative of the *surintendant* presented no difficulty during the subsequent long period of Lalande's domination of the court music, since, for much of the time, he held posts both as *surintendant* and *sous-maître*. However, when these duties were assigned to different musicians towards the end of Lalande's life, the supposed privileges of *surintendant* and *sous-maître* became a battleground that sustained hostilities until the Chapelle and Chambre were amalgamated in 1761; the controversy owed much to the intransigent personality of Colin de Blamont, *surintendant*, 1719–60.)[15] But the growing influence on the king of the pious Madame de Maintenon, whom he had secretly married within weeks of the queen's death, and the rising star of the young Lalande as the most talented composer among the *sous-maîtres* combined to cultivate a growing interest in the chapel music on the part of Louis XIV. The same influences must inevitably have undermined the previously-unassailable supremacy of Lully, despite his long friendship with the king.

Lully may even have felt threatened by Lalande in the realm of stage music, for the delay in completion of *Armide* led to the performance at Versailles of Lalande's *Ballet de la jeunesse* in its place, on five occasions during the month commencing 28 January 1686. As a result, *Armide* received its first performance at the Académie royale (15 February 1686), not at the court, and was not seen by the king until some time later. This turn of events can only indicate how high was the king's regard for Lalande, and must have been a source of dismay to the formerly all-powerful *surintendant*.[16]

---

ments, with lists of the musicians who competed, is given by Marcelle Benoit in *Versailles et les musiciens du Roi* (Paris, 1971), pp. 102–8.

[15] See John E. Morby, 'The Great Chapel-Chamber Controversy', *Musical Quarterly*, LVIII (1972), pp. 383–97. The texts of the four principal documents enshrining the controversy are reproduced for the first time as an appendix to L. Sawkins, 'The Brothers Bêche: An Anecdotal History of Court Music', *Recherches sur la musique française classique*, XXIV (1986). (The originals are located in F-Pan, 0¹ 842.)

[16] *Le Mercure de France* (Février, 1686, I, p. 294) reported very favourably on Lalande's work, adding the comment: '. . . peut estre que c'est le premier début des Ouvrages de cette nature qui ait esté d'un aussi bon goust'. For other views of these events, see Lois Rosow, 'Lully's *Armide* at the Paris Opéra: A Performance History, 1686–1766' (unpubl. PhD diss., Brandeis University, 1981), pp. 221–6.

Table 9 Motets *and* Elévations *of Pierre Robert – comparison of sources*

Livre of avril, mai et juin, 1678 (in the order the texts are printed) MOTETS		Page numbers	1684 Edition	Remarks	Modern editions
1	Ave Maris stella	Hymne	'1' (5)			
2	Benedicam Dominum	Ps 33	'3' (7)	23		
3	Cantate Domino	Ps 95	'5' (9)			
4	Cum invocarem	Ps 4	'7' (11)			
5	Conserva me, Domine	Ps 15	13	2		*HC
6	Domine mi, Rex		16			
7	Dominus illuminatio mea	Ps 26	17	13		
8	Deus, Deus meus	Ps 62	21			
9	Deus in nomine tuo	Ps 53	22			
10	Dixit Dominus	Ps109	24			
11	Exultate Deo	Ps 80	26	9		HC
12	Exurgat Deus	Ps 67	28	16		
13	Ego sum panis virus		31			
14	Iudica me Deus	Ps 42	31			
15	In Exitu Israel	Ps113	33	21		
16	Iesu nostra redemptio	Hymne	37			
17	Laudate pueri	Ps112	39			
18	Laetatus sum	Ps121	40			
19	Magnificat	Cantique	42			
20	Memento Domine David	Ps131	44			
21	Pange lingua gloriosi	Hymne	47			
22	Quare fremuerunt	Ps 2	49	11		HC Le Pupitre
23	Regina coeli		52			
24	Te Deum	Hymne	52			
25	Veni Creator spiritus	Hymne	56			
26	Venite adoremus		57			
27	Veniat dilectus meus		58	3		HC
28	Dominus regit me	Ps 22	60	17		
29	Nisi Dominus	Ps126	61	12		
30	Nolite me considerare	Cantique	63	6		HC Costallat
31	Deus noster refugium	Ps 45	64	8		HC Le Pupitre
32	Exultate justi	Ps 32	66	5		HC
33	Christe Redemptor	Hymne	68	24		
34	Cantate Domino	Ps147	69			
35	Cantate Domino	Ps 97	71	14	p. 72: 'Elevations'	
36	Laudate Dominum	Ps146	73	4		HC
37	Dominus regnavit	Ps 96	75	15		
38	Venite exultemus	Ps 94	77			
39	Lauda anima mea	Ps145	79			
40	Ad Dominum cum tribularer	Ps119	81	7	p. 82: (Device)	HC
41	Veni de Libano	Cantique	83			
42	Credidi propter	Ps115	85			
43	Beatus vir	Ps111	86			
44	Bonum est confiteri	Ps 91	88	1		HC
45	Fundamenta eius	Ps 86	90			
46	Exultavit cor meum	Cantique	92	10		HC
47	Ego flos campi	Cantique	95	20		
48	Te decet hymnus	Ps 64	97	18		
49	De profundis	Ps129		19		
	Benedixisti Domine terram	Ps 84		22		

Table 9 (*cont.*)

	ELEVATIONS	*Livre* page (1678)	F-Pn Rés Vmb ms 6 (1688)	Vm¹ 1175 bis	Vm¹ 1176	F-LYm MS 133721
1	Amavit eum Dominus	1	x			
2	Descende caelitus (Perrin)	1	x			
3	Et valde mane	2	x			x
4	Memorare, o piissima	3				
5	O Christe pietas	4				
6	O flamma quae semper luces	4	x			
7	Quid mihi est	6				
8	Splendor aeterna gloriae	7	x		x	x
9	Transfige dulcissime Jesu	8	x			
10	Ovena vitae	9				
11	Sancte spiritus	9	x			x
12	Trade amante	10				
13	Domine quinque talenta	10	x			
14	Euge serve bone	11	x			x
15	O dulcissime Jesu	11				
	Adore te devote		x			
	Memorare dulcissime Jesu			x		

Proposed chronology of Pierre Robert's church music

Motets:

	Livre 1678	1684 edition	Not extant	Totals
1–26	26 (alphabetical)	7	19	26
27–35	9 (to 'Elevations' p. 72)	8	1	9
36–40	5 (to printer's device p. 82)	3	2	5
41–9	9 (to end)	5 (incl. last 4)	4	9
		1		1
	49	24	26	50

Elévations:

Livret 1678	F-Pn Rés. Vmb ms 6 (1688)	Vm¹ 1175bis	Vm¹ 1176	F-LYm MS 133721	Not extant	Totals
9	9		1	4		9
6					6	6
		1				1
	1					1
15	10	1	1	4	6	17

*HC = transcribed by Mme Hélène Charnassé (Private collection)

The composition of three more *grands motets* may have been part of Lully's response to these changing circumstances. *Quare fremuerunt* was first given at *Ténèbres* on Maundy Thursday, 19 April 1685 (when, according to the Marquis de Dangeau, it was 'much praised');[17] the other works were *Notus in Judaea*, and *Exaudiat te, Domine*.[18] All three motets may have been composed at much the same time; they appear together in sequence in four of the five extant collections that include them. Further, they are distinguished from almost all of Lully's earlier *grands motets* (*Plaude laetare* excepted) by their comparative brevity and conciseness although all three are settings of complete psalm texts.[19]

Ballard's publication of the collections of motets of Robert and Lully in 1684 and, posthumously, of Dumont in 1686, a total of 50 motets in as many as nineteen partbooks, was a major undertaking in publishing and as propaganda for the glory of the king's chapel music. Lully included only 6 of his *grands motets* in the publication omitting at least one other composed up to that time, *O Lachrymae* (1661), although 24 by Robert and 20 by Dumont were printed. Of the new *sous-maîtres'* compositions, only Lalande's works were to enjoy similar royal support: 27 of his *grands motets* were handsomely copied by Philidor, Fossard and their assistants and bound in folio in 1689–90. After the death of Lully in 1687, Lalande continued in the king's favour, so that by the time the old monarch died in 1715, the composer held all but one of the principal posts in the court music, and was thus an even greater, if less devious, pluralist than his notorious predecessor.

Earlier in this essay, evidence was presented to suggest that Lully's role in the evolution of the *grand motet* was less significant than that of Dumont. Indeed, comparisons between Lully's occasional forays into the genre and the compositions of the *sous-maîtres* contemporary with him show that, far from being a pioneer, he was, in some respects, less adventurous than the chapel composers; of the various stylistic comparisons possible, and which highlight the differences in their technique, one of the most revealing concerns the manner in which the accompaniment to the voices of the *grand choeur* was disposed.

The variety of practice the *sous-maîtres* employed in scoring their orchestral accompaniments related both to the *dessus* and the inner parts. (The *basse* of the chorus was invariably doubled by the *basse continue*, albeit sometimes in an elaborated form; not until Lalande's late motets, written in the early years of the eighteenth century, are there examples of the vocal *basse* being independent of the *basse continue*.) For the instrumental *dessus*, Robert never employed parts independent from the voices in the *grands choeurs* of his motets, and Lully did so but rarely, and briefly (for example, in his *Miserere*, bars 87–92). But Dumont

---

[17] See Chantal Masson, 'Journal du Marquis de Dangeau', *Recherches sur la musique française classique*, II (1961–2), p. 198.

[18] One source of *Exaudiat* (F-Pn Vm¹ 1048), included in Brossard's collection, contains the ascription 'Authore Dno. Jo. Baptiste de Lully an. 1687'. However, because Lully fell fatally ill as early as 15 January 1687 after his accident a week earlier when conducting his *Te Deum*,

it seems that *Exaudiat* must have been completed earlier than that year.

[19] These three *grands motets*, previously unpublished, form the first volume to appear in Jean-Baptiste Lully, *The Complete Works*, Carl B. Schmidt (general ed.), (New York: Broude Brothers Limited). The editors of this volume are J. Anne Baker, John H. Hajdu, and the present writer.

and Lalande frequently wrote 'independent' *dessus* parts that were often modified octave transpositions upwards of inner vocal parts, usually of the *haute-contre*, though occasionally of the *basse-taille*, the latter sometimes doubled by the orchestral *dessus* two octaves higher.

A selection of Dumont's *grands motets* shows this variety of practice, illustrated in table 10. Some works from early in his career at the Chapelle royale as well as some later ones (those on the chart connected by the double-ended arrow) exhibit similar patterns, illustrating the practice of doubling two of the voice parts by instruments playing an octave higher. The effect is twofold: to create a higher-voiced texture in the orchestra than in the chorus, and to take the second *dessus* in the orchestra frequently above the first – in effect, a descanting trans-posed alto part. This practice of Dumont was modified by Lalande in some of his early works (1680–90), the younger composer sometimes assigning the *haute-contre de violon* (first violas) the role of doubling the choral *dessus* when the single orchestral *dessus* part had independent writing, especially when the latter was doubling the vocal *haute-contre* an octave higher, see plate 3.

But for a number of works in the 1670s, Dumont appears to have used a differ-ent layout (those in the box in table 10), with the choral *basse-taille* now left undoubled (whereas formerly it was doubled an octave higher) and one of the orchestral *dessus* parts freely decorating the ensemble by weaving above and below the other *dessus*, which itself doubles the vocal line.

However, in two other works from the 1670s, both instrumental *dessus* have the same music in the choruses, doubling the choral *dessus*, a practice invariably followed by Robert and Lully, as already noted; one wonders why Dumont did this at some times and not others. However, as these patterns have been derived only from the works named, a study of the remaining motets (which await assembling into score from their sixteen part-books) may well show a clearer trend in Dumont's practice.

In Robert's motets, it is the *basse-taille* which is always doubled by the in-strumental *haute-contre* an octave higher. In 20 of the 24 published motets (those with a five-part accompaniment – the other 4 motets have a six-part orchestra), either the vocal *haute-contre* or the *haute-taille* is left without instrumental dou-bling, as table 10 shows. These scoring patterns appear well-distributed through the complete list of Robert's motets, and thus appear to have no chronological significance.

Scoring consistently for a five-part orchestra of *dessus*, three *parties* and *basse*, Lully's normal practice in his motets was to have all instrumental parts merely doubling the voices at the same pitch, making little use of the octave-doubling patterns (for the inner voice parts) employed by the *sous-maîtres*.[20] But in his last three *grands motets*, apparently written between 1685 and 1687, passages em-

[20] Lully's faithful 'secretary', Colasse, also wrote more elaborate orchestral *dessus* parts in his choruses than his revered master. See, for ex-ample, *Beatus vir*, cited by James R. Anthony, in 'Collasse, Pascal', *The New Grove Dictionary*; also *Enée et Lavinie* (Paris, 1690), pp. 43–5, 149–51 – two of several instances where the woodwind *dessus* are independent of the vocal *dessus*. (The writer is grateful to Graham Sadler for drawing his attention to Colasse's secular practice, and for many other useful comments in the course of preparation of this essay.)

Table 10 *Correspondence of vocal and instrumental scorings in the* grands choeurs *of motets by Dumont, Robert, Lully and Lalande*

[indicated by clefs employed, e.g., G2=G clef on second line]

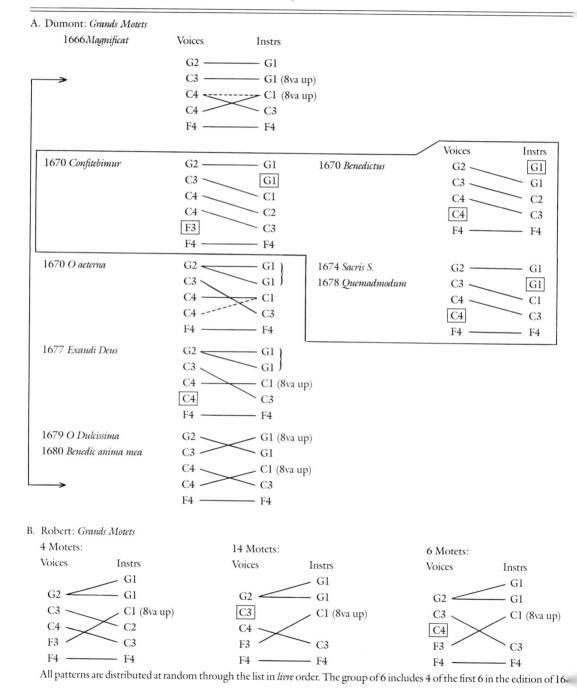

All patterns are distributed at random through the list in *livre* order. The group of 6 includes 4 of the first 6 in the edition of 16.

Table 10 *(cont.)*

Lully: late *Grands Motets*: (*Quare fremuerunt, Notus in Judaea, Exaudiat te Domine*)

Voices	Instrs		Voices	Instrs		Voices	Instrs
G2 —— G1			G2 —— G1			G2 —— G1	
C3 ⨯ C1 (8va up)			C3 ⨯ C1 (8va up)			C3 —— C1	
C4 ⨯ C2			C4 ⨯ C2			C4 —— C2	
F3 ⨯ C3			F3 —— C3			F3 —— C3	
F4 —— F4			F4 —— F4			F4 —— F4	

All patterns are found in all 3 works, the last being the most usual.

Lalande: early *Grands Motets*

1680

Dixit Dominus

Voices	Instrs
G2 —— G1 (decorated)
C3 ⨯ C1 (8va up)
[C4] ⨯ [C2]
F3 ⨯ C3
F4 —— F4

1682

Deitatis majestatem

Voices	Instrs		Voices	Instrs
[G2] —— G1 (8va up)			G2 ⨯ G1 (8va up)
C3 ⨯ C1 (8va up)			C3 ⨯ C1
C4 ⨯ C2			[C4] [C2]
F3 ⨯ [C3]			[F3] [C3]
F4 —— F4			F4 —— F4

1683

Beati quorum

Voices	Instrs
[G2] ⟋ G1 (8va up)
C3 ⟋ C1 (8va up)
C4 ⟋ [C2]
[F3] [C3]
F4 —— F4

As well as other variants of these patterns, there are many passages where the outer vocal and instrumental parts double one another, but the inner parts are independent.

---

dependent parts in the above charts are highlighted: ☐

ploying the patterns used by Dumont and Robert (shown in table 10) occur somewhat more often than in his earlier works. However, these practices may have been the result of the efforts of Lully's faithful Colasse, and others, since extant sources of two of these last three motets exhibit differing versions of both vocal and instrumental inner parts, suggesting that Lully was still content to follow the methods detailed by Lecerf, dictating the outer parts to his *amanuenses* as he composed at the harpsichord, and then leaving it to them to add the vocal and instrumental *parties de remplissage*.[21] The surviving different versions may accordingly be the result of 'realizations' made from the dictated *dessus* and *basse* at different dates by different 'secretaries' (for a table of surviving manuscript sources of Lully's motets, see appendix 3).

Thus, despite the new brevity and the more dramatic portrayal of text that characterize these last of Lully's motets, they stand in contrast to those of Dumont, Robert and Lalande in several ways. Certainly, the older *sous-maîtres* scored their works in a more systematic and methodical fashion. Moreover, Dumont exploited his early training in the Italian style, which shows through in his vivid setting of texts such as *Magnificat* and *Super flumina Babylonis*, somewhat akin to the later psalm settings of Schütz. With great economy of material, Dumont alternates the driving homophony of his choruses decorated with inventive instrumental obbligati, with expressive and reflective passages employing chromatic harmony.

[21] J. L. Lecerf de La Viéville, *Comparaison de la musique italienne et de la musique française*   (Brussels, 1704–6; rptd. 1972), pp. 118–19.

Plate 3. Lalande, *Deitatis majestatem*, 1682

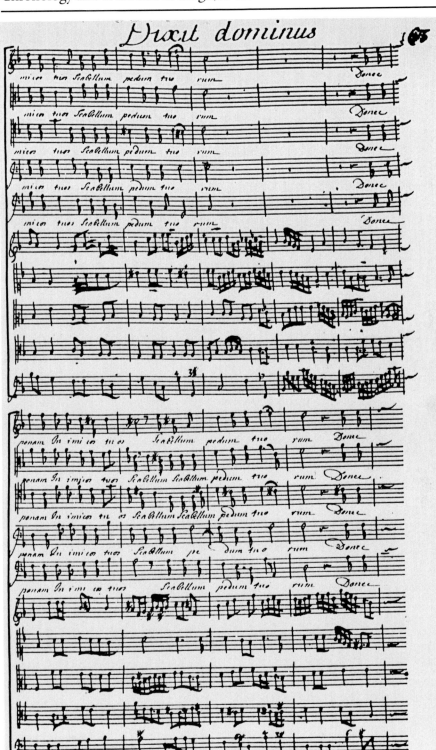

Plate 4. Lalande, *Dixit Dominus*, 1680, his first setting

But it is in the motets of Lalande that these devices are absorbed, elaborated and extended, as even the first collection of twenty-seven motets shows. For the *grands choeurs*, Lalande, while adhering to inherited models in some parts of his earliest motets, was also ready not only to experiment with freer *dessus* parts, but also sometimes to compose the whole orchestral texture without resorting to systematic doubling of the voice parts (as, for example, in his first setting of *Dixit Dominus*, 1680, see plate 4).

Nor was Lalande content always to retain the normal arrangement of *petit choeur* and *grand choeur*, but, possibly taking his cue from the variety of vocal scoring experiments by Robert, could design a canvas of constant variety yet secure structure as in the opening chorus of his *Jubilate Deo*.[22] Thus were both tradition and innovation of the early years of the Sun King's reign absorbed and transformed by Lalande to form what was to prove the most substantial and durable corpus of works in the genre, surviving the composer himself and dominating the repertory of both chapel and concert-room for most of the remaining years of the *ancien régime*.

Appendix 1: *Texts in* Motets et élévations de M. Expilly, pour le quartier de Iuillet, Aoust, & Septembre 1666 *(see table 4)*

Notes. (a) The texts of nos. 14 and 27 by Perrin are among those he describes as *Cantica in elevatione hostiae* in CPCR. This, and the brevity of texts 14–20, suggest that some or all of these 7 texts were set by Expilly as *élévations*, and that the 1664 print of the *Livre* for Expilly's first quarter may have concluded with no. 20.

(b) Similarly, Perrin's mention of nos. 22 and 23 in his preface to CPCR and their performance during Expilly's quarter suggest that, almost certainly, they would have been included in the *Livre* for 1665, and the presence of no. 27 (*Sub umbra noctis profundae*) among the *Cantica in elevatione hostiae* accords with the possibility that the issue for that year only reached this work, with the remaining texts added in 1666. (The heading ELEVATIONS only appears in that issue applying to nos. 36–43.)

(c) No. 19 is not ascribed to Perrin in the *Livre*, but corresponds to the text in Ms fr 2208.

(d) *Quid cessatis, O tortores* appears in this form in Ms fr 25460, and in the *Livre*, but as *Quid lenitis, O tortores* in CPCR.

(e) The motet for the feast of St Anne (*Festa solemnis*), although mentioned in the preface to CPCR as set and performed by Expilly along with nos. 22 and 23, does not appear in the *Livre*. Perhaps it was deleted when other works were added to the book in 1666.

(f) From the *Livre* and CPCR, it is clear that at least 44 sacred works were composed by Expilly, of which 13 were to texts by Perrin.

---

[22] Published by Carus Verlag, Stuttgart, 1985. (Edition 40.081.)

[23] The author is grateful to Mlle Laurence Decobert for locating *Livres* 1 and 13 (table 4), and for several corrections to the tables concerning Dumont. Her *thèse de doctorat* (Paris, Sorbonne), 'Henry Du Mont (1610–1684), Sous-maître de la Chapelle de Louis XIV: contribution à l'étude du grand motet en France' will include transcriptions of all 20 motets which appeared in the 1686 edition.

[24] Since table 2 was drawn up, three of Perrin's texts have been noted in motets attributed to Carissimi in F-Pn, Rés. F. 934b: *Errate per colles*, *Tolle sponsa*, *Sub umbra noctis*. Philidor's Recueil of 1688 (F-Pn, Rés. Vmb ms 6) also attributes the same setting of *Sub umbra noctis* to Carissimi, as well as containing Danielis' setting of *Errate per colles*. Such attributions to Carissimi must remain doubtful until a complete concordance of all sources of the composer's works has been established.

	CPCR	2208	[Motets]	
1			Dixit Dominus	Ps 109
2			Laudate pueri	Ps 112
3			Laetatus sum	Ps 121
4			Nisi Dominus	Ps 126
5			Lauda Jerusalem	Ps 147
6			Ave maris stella	Hymne
7			Magnificat	Cantique
8			Pange lingua gloriosi	Hymne
9			Veni Creator spiritus	Hymne
10			Iste Confessor Domini	Hymne
11			Te Deum laudamus	Hymne
12	x		Silete, venti	Perrin
13			Et ecce terrae motus	
14	x		Ubi es? Deus meus	Perrin
15			Tristis est anima mea	
16			Sub tuum praesidium	
17			Salve Regina	
18			Inviolata integra	
19		x	Salve Maria, caeli delitium	(Perrin)
20			O invictum ducem beatum Zenonem	
21	x		Agnos pascebat	Perrin
22	x		Quid cessatis? O tortores	Perrin
23	x		Currite, populi	Perrin
24			Credidi propter	Ps 115
25			Exaudiat te Dominus	Ps 19
26			Iubilemus & exultemus Domino	
27	x		Sub umbra noctis profundae	Perrin
28			Complaceat tibi Domine	
29			Domine mi rex omnipotens	
30			Ad arma clamabant milites	
31			Ecce egredimur cantantes	
32			Domine, quid multiplicati sunt	Ps 3
33		x	Velut unda vagabunda	Perrin
34		x	Quid times anima	Perrin
35			Litaniae B. Mariae	
			Elévations	
36	x		O fideles miseremini	Perrin
37			O quam dilecta	
38			Quemadmodum	Ps 41 (extr.)
39			Super flumina Babylonis	Ps 136 (extr.)
40			O sacrum convivium	
41			Ecce panis angelorum	
42	x		Quare tristis es	Perrin
43	x		Ecce sol illuminat	Perrin

TABLE
DES MOTETS
DE M. COLLASSE.

Beati quorum remissæ sunt.	page 38
Beatus vir, qui timet.	42
Cantate Domino.	39
Cantate Domino.	41
Cantate Domino canticum.	56
Cantemus Domino.	45
Cum invocarem.	58
Deus in adjutorium.	54
Deus quis similis erit.	44
Domine quid multiplicati.	60
Domini est terra & plenitudo.	49
Dominus illuminatio mea.	47
Ecce in dolore.	56
Exaudiat te Dominus.	35
Exurgat, Deus, & dissipentur.	43
Jubilate Deo omnis terra.	42
Lauda Jerusalem Dominum.	50
Laudate pueri Dominum.	36
Magnificat.	59
Mirabilis es Domine.	40

Appendix 2: Texts of works by Colasse in the *Livres du Roi*, 1686

Omnes Gentes plaudite.   37
O ! Quam dilecta sunt.   54
Pange lingua gloriosi.   52
Quis similis tui in fortibus.   46
Regina cæli lætare.   36
Super flumina Babylonis.   57
Veni Creator Spiritus.   51

TABLE
DES ELEVATIONS.

Ve mundi Domina.   page 1
Ave verum corpus natum.   2
Dilecte Jesu.   6
Ecce templi.   4
Jesu mi benignissime.   1
In tribulationis.   5
Laudem Domini.   2
O bone Jesu.   3
O salutaris hostia.   ibidem.
Suspirat ad te cor.   5
Venite & properate.   2

MOTETS

Appendix 3: Manuscript sources of Lully's motets[1]

P = *Partition* (score) p = *parties* (parts)
* also in Ballard 1684 print
+ issued in OC
‡ formerly GB/T
Bracketed volumes form sets

Column groupings (country / library / shelfmark):
- **B** — Br: MS II 3847
- **BRD** — B (MG): MS 13260, MS 13260/5
- **DDR** — D1: MS 1827-D-1, MS 1827-D-2
- **F** — SW B: 13733; LYm: 133.719, 133.721; Pn & Pc: Vm1 1040, Rés. Vma MS 574, Vm1 1042, Vm1 1043, Vm1 1044, Vm1 1045, Vm1 1046, Vm1 1047, Vm1 1048

	MS II 3847	MS 13260	MS 13260/5	MS 1827-D-1	MS 1827-D-2	13733	133.719	133.721	Vm1 1040	Rés. Vma MS 574	Vm1 1042	Vm1 1043	Vm1 1044	Vm1 1045	Vm1 1046	Vm1 1047	Vm1 1048
12 Grands motets																	
*Benedictus Dominus	P	P		P			P	P	P			P					
*De Profundis+	P	P		P			P	P	P								
*Dies Irae+	P	P		P			P		P								
Domine salvum fac R+	P								P								
Exaudiat te		P							P								
Jubilate																	17p
*Miserere Ps 50+	P	P		P			P	P	P			P	7p				
Notus in Judaea		P							P							17p	
O Lachrymae fideles		P								P	19p						
*Plaude laetare+	P	P		P			P		P								
Quare fremuerunt	P	P							P						18p		
*Te Deum+	P	P		P	P	7p	P		P								
13 Petits motets																	
Anima Christi	P	P				P				P							
Ave coeli munus sup.+	P	P				P				P							
Cor meum eja laetare[2]			4p														
Dixit Dominus	P	P				P				P							
Domine salvum fac R	P	P				P				P							
Exaudi Deus	P																
Iste Sanctus																	
Laudate pueri	P	P				P				P							
Magnificat	P																
O Dulcissime	P	P				P				P							
Omnes gentes+	P	P				P				P							
O Sapientia	P	P				P				P							
Regina coeli[2]	P	P				P				P							
Salve Regina	P	P				P				P							

[1] (Compiled with assistance from John Hajdu Heyer, Catherine Massip, Jean-Michel Nectoux, Carl Schmidt, and Herbert Schneider, whose help is gratefully, acknowledged.)

[2] *Cor meum eja laetare* is a *contrafactum* of *Regina coeli*.

Sigla above columns: ‡ over Rés. F. 1712, Rés. F. 1713, Rés. F. 1714; (P) over Rés. 697; V over Ms mus 6; GB Lbl over Add MS 31559.

Vm¹ 1049	Vm¹ 1050	Vm¹ 1051	Rés. F. 1110 (1, 2)	Vm¹ 1170	Vm¹ 1702	Rés. F. 663	Rés. F. 664	Rés. F. 665	Rés. F. 666	Rés. F. 667	Rés. F. 668	Rés. F. 669	Rés. F. 989	Rés. Vmb ms 6	D 7218-9	‡ Rés. F. 1712	‡ Rés. F. 1713	‡ Rés. F. 1714	(P) Rés. 697	Private collec.	V Ms mus 6	GB Lbl Add MS 31559
			P							P						8p					P	
	P		P						P				P			8p				P	P	
P			P					P					P		P			7p	1p	P	P	P
				P							P					8p					P	
			P																			
			P			P							P				P,P	7p	1p	P		
				P								P				8p					P	
			P										P									
			P															7p	1p	P		
				P							P		P			8p				P	P	
		P	P		P				P						P			7p	1p	P		
				P							P		P	4p				P				
				P							P		P	4p				P				
				P							P		P	4p				P				
											P		P	4p				P				
																		P				
				P							P		P	4p				P				
				P							P		P	4p				P				
				P							P		P	5p				P				
				P							P		P	5p				P				
				P							P		P	4p				P				
				P							P		P	4p				P				

The sources of Lully's *grands motets*

JOHN HAJDU HEYER

Despite his far-reaching power over musical affairs in Louis XIV's court, Jean-Baptiste Lully never held an official position in the Royal Chapel. Nevertheless, throughout his career, or at least from the early 1660s until his death, Lully produced sacred music. By 1664 he had composed the *Miserere*, one of his most respected sacred works: Mme de Sévigné would write that she believed 'no other music to exist in heaven'. Special occasions, for example, the birth of the Dauphin in 1668 (*Plaude, laetare, Gallia*) and the baptism of Lully's eldest son in 1677 (*Te Deum*), brought other motets. At the end of his life it would be during a performance of his *Te Deum* on 8 January 1687, to celebrate the recovery of Louis XIV from surgery, that Lully would strike his foot with the sharp point of his conducting baton, mortally wounding himself. We do not know the circumstances surrounding the genesis of most of the *grands motets* Lully left. The texts of three of them, *Quare fremuerunt gentes*, *Exaudiat te*, and *Notus in Judaea*, and other considerations (see above p. 68) suggest that these works came from Lully's last years, after the important changes that took place following the deaths of the queen and Colbert in 1683, and after Louis XIV came under the influence of the pious Mme de Maintenon.

Because Lully left only a dozen *grands motets* and a slightly larger number of *petits motets*, his output of stage works, ballets and operas, both in quantity and by reputation, has traditionally overshadowed his small corpus of *musique latine*. The motets, however, hold a unique and important position in the context of his oeuvre: Lully's career proceeded from the composition of court ballets in his younger days to the creation of the great *tragédies lyriques* in his later career, but he composed his *grands motets* throughout his mature creative years. This fact lends an importance to the sources of Lully's motets that is disproportionate to the small number of those works for at least two reasons. First, whereas most of Lully's operas (composed between 1672 and 1687) were published soon after composition, and virtually none of the ballets (composed primarily between 1653 and 1671) were published during Lully's lifetime, half of Lully's *grands motets* were published (in 1684) and half have come to us only in manuscripts. Therefore, while the source problems of the operas differ significantly from those of the ballets, the problems of the motet source materials are related to those of both the operas and the ballets: those materials overlap the sources of the other genres both chronologically and in the format of their preservation (manuscripts and published exemplars). Second, because Lully's motets did not hold their popularity, eclipsed as they were by the work of Lalande and others, their manuscript sources probably were produced over a shorter time span than were those of the operas and ballets. The scribes and papers associated with the motets may offer important clues to the chronology of manuscript copies of the operas and ballets. For these reasons this source study of the motets may shed significant light on the sources of Lully's other works.

THE PRINTED SOURCES

No scores of Lully's motets were published during his lifetime. In 1684 Christophe Ballard published six of Lully's motets in seventeen partbooks. An examination of the extant exemplars of those partbooks uncovered no printing variants akin to the stop-press corrections found by Lois Rosow in published exemplars of Lully's *Armide*.[1] The exemplars show neither variation in the impressions made by the movable type, nor corrections of individual notes. Movable typeset would not have been kept standing for a long period of time, and because there is no evidence of a second typesetting, we must assume that the motet partbooks were printed once only, in 1684, and all exemplars originated from that time.

The partbooks contain some obvious errors, particularly in the first of the motets in the collection (*Miserere*, LWV 25). In some exemplars, manuscript corrections of early provenance correct those errors, and of those corrected exemplars, several contain manuscript corrections that date from the seventeenth century (as will be discussed below). The contractual working relationship between Lully and Ballard, which required Lully's approval and certification by means of the entry of his stamp or *paraphe* on exemplars of his *tragédies lyriques* before they could be sold, must not have applied to the motets.[2] There are no stamps or *paraphes* in the extant partbooks like those found in the first editions of Lully operas. But care must have been exercised in the printing of the motet parts, because, on the whole, they do not contain an unusually large number of printing errors. The printing process may have been monitored and checked by the composer or by one or more of his assistants.[3] Table 1 lists all known extant exemplars and identifies those that contain manuscript corrections.[4]

Remarkably, either Ballard misprinted the first four bars at the entrance of the *dessus du petit choeur* in Lully's *Miserere* (see plate 1), or Lully composed a skilful revision of the music after publication. Plates 1 and 2 show the correction in the prints now in Glasgow University (Euing R. b. 11–13) and in the Brussels Conservatory Library (Réf. 15145Z), respectively. The hand appears to be the same in

---

[1] Lois Rosow, 'Lully's *Armide* at the Paris Opéra: A Performance History, 1686–1766' (unpubl. PhD diss., Brandeis University, 1981), pp. 13–29.
[2] Ibid., pp. 8–13.
[3] The *Oeuvres complètes* prepared by Prunières and his associates included half of the motets. Publication was suspended in 1939. It should be noted that many errors in Prunières's

edition of the collected works appear to originate with that edition, and not with the Ballard prints or with faulty manuscript sources.
[4] I am grateful to Lionel Sawkins who provided me with most of the non-RISM listings included here. One known extant exemplar in the André Meyer Collection is not available for examination.

Table 1 *The extant printed sources of Lully's motets*

(Paris: Ballard, 1684)

Library	Call number	Description	Number of parts	Comments
B-Bc	Réf. 15145Z	Complete	17	CORRECTIONS
D(BRD)-W	123 Mus. div	GCh: Ds	1	No corrections
F-Pa	?	HCn	1	Listed in RISM, but not at Pa
F-Pc	Rés. 696	GCh: BTa DsVn 2	3	No corrections
F-Pmeyer	–	Complete	17	Not examined
F-Pn	Rés. Vm.¹ 1039	Complete	17	CORRECTIONS Ex libris Lully
F-Pn	Rés. Vm.¹ 99	Complete	17	No corrections Ex libris Royal Library: Louis XIV
F-Psg	Rés. Vm. 115	Complete	17	No corrections Ex libris Sancta Genovesae Parissientis
F-Psg	Rés. Vm. 117	Complete	17	No corrections Ex libris Le Tellier
F-V	Ms B in 4° 1–11	PCh: Ds 1, Ds 2, HCn, BTa Ds de Vn 1 GCh: BTa BVn, BC (3 ex)	11	No corrections 9 Ex libris Philidor Used for preparation of Toulouse MSS 2 are of other prov.
F-Pm	Rés. 19396	HCnVn	1	No corrections Not in RISM
GB-Ge	R. b. 11–13	Complete	17	CORRECTIONS
US-Wc	M2020 L85. M6P3	PCh: Ds 1	1	No corrections
US-BLl	M1490 L956	PCh: Ds 1, B Ds de Vn 1, QVn	4	CORRECTIONS Not in RISM

Ds=dessus, GCh=Grand Choeur, HCn=haute contre, B=Bass, Ta=Taille   Vn=violin, QVn=quinte de violon, PCh=petit choeur

both exemplars. Another set of partbooks, one partially preserved in the Lilly Library in Bloomington, also shows this hand. Because the presentation exemplars held in Cardinal Le Tellier's library (now the Bibliothèque Ste Geneviève) and in the Royal Library have no corrections, at some point, not immediately upon publication, but well before the stock of printed motets was exhausted, corrections may have been systematically entered by a scribe connected to the Ballard shop or to one of the vendors.

   That most extant exemplars of the 1684 prints contain no corrections is no surprise: exemplars that received the most use, and were corrected for practical reasons, are understandably the ones that would have been discarded when they wore out. The beautifully preserved complete sets at the Bibliothèque Ste Geneviève (Rés. Vm 117) and the Bibliothèque Nationale (Rés. Vm¹ 99), both probably presentation copies given immediately upon publication to Cardinal Maurice Le Tellier (Head of the Royal Chapel) and to Louis XIV respectively, joined those important libraries and would not have been used in performance – thus, it was unnecessary to enter the corrections in them. Even the royal music

Plate 1. J.-B. de Lully: *Motets à deux choeurs* (Paris: Ballard, 1684), *Premier dessus du petit choeur*, p. 1. GB-Ge: R. b. 11–13

librarian Philidor's personal copy, part of which survives today at Versailles, still contained uncorrected errors when he turned to it in 1704 to prepare the motets, including an abridged copy of Lully's lengthy *Te Deum*, for the Count of Toulouse. The blank *collettes* (slips of paper pasted over the original) Philidor used, and some manuscript changes he found necessary to insert in the music in order to shorten the *Te Deum*, remain, in his hand, in this exemplar at Versailles.[5]

Four exemplars, however (F-Pn: Vm[1] 1039, B-Bc: Réf. 15145Z, GB-Ge: Euing R. b. 11–13 and US-BLl: M1490 L956), contain corrections. F-Pn: Vm[1] 1039 draws particular interest because the 17 part-books, bound in leather, each displays Lully's coat of arms on the cover as shown in plate 3. A handwritten note on the title-page of each partbook reads 'donné par Mme. de Lully au P[etits] P[ères] cherubin Augustin deschausée du couvenne de Paris en 1689 pour leur bibliothèque'. The volumes, doubtless from the Lully household, represent a small portion of Lully's personal library that survives, with some other printed scores, in the Bibliothèque Nationale, having come there from the library of the Little Barefoot Fathers. The cropping of several of the corrections at the page edge (for example, some clefs are lost as shown in plate 4) presents strong evidence that

[5] F-V: Ms B in 4° 1–9.

Plate 2. J.-B. de Lully: *Motets à deux choeurs* (Paris: Ballard, 1684), *Premier dessus du petit choeur*, p. 1. B-Bc: Réf. 15145Z

a scribe added these corrections to the prints before binding took place, certainly before 1689 and probably not long after the initial publication. Some of the manuscript additions correct overt errors; others, like the change to the *Miserere* shown in plates 1 and 2, insert material when no obvious need exists.

The hand of the corrections in F-Pn: Vm[1] 1039 clearly differs from that found in the Glasgow, Brussels, and Bloomington sets. Therefore, in the printed sources of Lully's motets we find corrections entered by two scribes. The printed exemplars that contain these corrections present the most authoritative sources for six of Lully's motets, for presumably Ballard published these partbooks with Lully's approval and participation.[6] The direct association of the Vm[1] 1039 partbooks with the Lully household suggests even greater authority for that set and the corrections they contain, but the differences between the several hand-corrected sets are minor.

---

[6] Lois Rosow explains Lully's involvement in the commercial publication of his operas in her dissertation. See Rosow, 'Lully's *Armide*', pp. 8–13.

Plate 3. J.-B. de Lully: *Motets à deux choeurs* (Paris: Ballard, 1684). Cover of partbook with Lully coat of arms for *Premier dessus du petit choeur*: F-Pn: Vm¹ 1039

THE MANUSCRIPT SOURCES

Scholars working to establish an authoritative text for Lully's music[7] confront a monumental problem: the loss of Lully's autograph manuscripts. If we accept the evidence that Lully worked carefully with his publisher, Christophe Ballard, to present his works accurately in print, then for many of the works that were published in or very shortly after Lully's lifetime we may have the most authoritative sources available in the printed exemplars that survive. But for the works that were not published, or published only in the next century, the absence of Lully's autographs presents scholars with the difficult task of determining the most authoritative sources from a large number of late seventeenth- and early eighteenth-century manuscript copies.[8] The early manuscript sources of Lully's

[7] An international group of seventeen scholars is presently at work on a new collected edition of Lully's works for Broude Brothers. See Carl Schmidt, 'A Communication from the Executive Secretary of Broude Brothers' New Lully Edition', *Recherches sur la musique française classique*, XX (1981), pp. 275–6.

[8] Prunières has made a case for some fragments of Lullyian originals, but even if we accept their authenticity, they are of little use. See H. Prunières, 'Lettres et autographes de Lully', *Bulletin français de la société internationale de musique*, VIII/3 (1912). See also H. Prunières, 'Notes musicologiques sur un autographe musical de Lully', *La revue musicale*, X (1928–9), pp. 47–51.

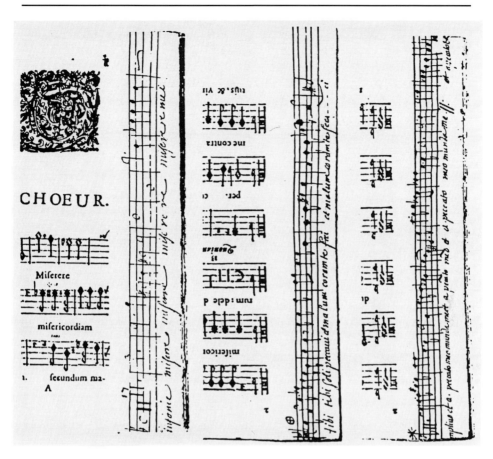

Plate 4. J.-B. de Lully: *Motets à deux choeurs* (Paris: Ballard, 1684). Manuscript
corrections in F-Pn: Vm¹ 1039

motets that have been preserved, therefore, present an important and more complex corpus of material for study than do the early printed sources.

Neither autograph sources nor printed partbooks exist for six motets: *O Lachrymae*, LWV 26; *Quare fremuerunt gentes*, LWV 67; *Domine salvum fac Regem*,
LWV 77/14; *Exaudiat te*, LWV 77/15; *Jubilate Deo*, LWV 77/16; and *Notus in
Judaea*, LWV 77/17. (These motets, the motets Ballard did *not* publish, will
throughout this study be referred to as the 'unpublished motets'.) As Lionel
Sawkins has suggested in this volume, three of Lully's unpublished motets evidently post-date the 1684 Ballard prints: *Notus in Judaea*, *Exaudiat te*, *Dominus*,
and *Quare fremuerunt gentes*. The relationship of these three motets to the manuscript sources merits special attention here because of their presumed origin late in
Lully's career.

Sawkins's appendix 3 (pp. 78–9) identifies the known manuscript sources of
Lully's motets. The present study has determined that many of these manuscript
copies bear only a secondary importance because they simply contain scores that

were prepared from the 1684 printed partbooks.[9] The preservation of certain obvious errors contained in the printed exemplars that appear, in turn, in those manuscript scores strongly supports that conclusion. A study of Sawkins's appendix reveals that the six motets Ballard did *not* print in 1684 survive scattered in the eight volumes of *partitions* and two collections of *parties* as shown in table 2 of

Table 2 *The Manuscript sources of Lully's unpublished grands motets*

P = *partition* (score), p = *parties* (parts)

Lib. Sigla: call no.	Scribe[a]	Contents: LWV 26	67	77/14	77/15	77/16	77/17	Motets from the 1684 partbooks
F-Pn: Rés. F. 669	[Scribe E]		P		P		P	none
F-Pn: Rés. Vma. MS 574	[Dupont]	P	P	P	P		P	none
F-Pn: Vm¹ 1042 } Vm¹ 1045–48 }	[Brossard et al.]	19p	18p		17p		17p	1
F-Pn: Rés. F. 989	[Dupont]		P					4
D(BRD)-B: MS 13260	[Dupont]	P	P		P		P	6
F-Pn: Vm¹ 1170	[Scribe C]		P		P		P	none
F-Pn: Rés. F. 1110^b	[Scribe C]	P				P		6
F-PThibault^c	[Massip C/I]		P		P		P	6
F-Pn: Rés. F. 1712–14 } Rés. F. 697 }	[Philidor l'aîné]		8p		8p		8p	6
B-Br: Ms II 3847	[Scribe A]		P	P				6

[a] None of the manuscripts is actually signed by its scribe.

[b] The call number represents two volumes.

[c] The Thibault collection is in five volumes.

this article.[10] Five of the eight volumes, and both sets of *parties* mix copies of the motets in the 1684 print with the unpublished motets, while three volumes contain unpublished motets exclusively. This study has found that all of the manuscripts of these four 'mixed' collections also prove, upon examination, to hold copies that originated from the Ballard prints, i.e. a scribe either 'scored them up' from the printed partbooks or copied them from scores that had been so prepared.[11] Because *Quare fremuerunt gentes*, dated 1685, appears in all the manuscript collections that hold copies of Lully's unpublished motets, we can conclude that all the manuscript copies of Lully's motets shown in Sawkins's appendix 2 post-date 1684.

[9] Specifically: D(BRD)-B: MS 13260/5; D(DDR)-D1: MS 1827-D-1, MS 1827-D-2; D(DDR)-SW: MUS 3495; F-LYm: 133.719, 133.721; F-Pn: Vm¹ 1040, Vm¹ 1042, Vm¹ 1043, Vm¹ 1049–51, Vm¹ 1702, Rés. F. 663/67, Rés. F. 989, D. 7218–9. F-V: Ms mus 6 and GB-Lbl: Add MS 31559 are reduced scores of secondary importance.

[10] Most of the scribes for the sources of Lully's sacred works remain anonymous. The names and sigla given in table 2 and in this article have evolved from several sources: Massip scribes C and I from C. Massip, *Cantates, Motets, Opéras, Ballets . . . manuscrits de Philidor* a catalogue of the Toulouse–Philidor

Collection prepared for the sale of the collection (Paris, 1978); others are so identified in John Hajdu, 'Recent Findings in the Sources of Lully's Motets', paper read to the *Colloque international sur le grand motet français* (Paris, Sorbonne, 1984), published in the *actes* of the conference: Jean Mongrédien (ed.), *Le grand motet française* (Paris, 1986).

[11] One set, now in the private library of the late Geneviève Thibault, has been unavailable for study, but if the Toulouse–Philidor parts reflect the scores of the collection, these scores also were copied from the printed partbooks. Surprisingly, Philidor did not have access to more reliable originals at that time.

Three volumes, however, contain exclusively motets that are not in the printed partbooks: F-Pn: Rés. Vma. MS 574 (from Brossard's Collection); F-Pn: Rés. F. 669 (a copy that originated in the Royal Library); and F-Pn: Vm¹ 1170 (a copy of unknown provenance). These three volumes require particular attention. The other copies of Lully's unpublished motets will also be discussed below under the rubrics of the various collections to which they belong.

Brossard's collection

Sébastien de Brossard, in the large and important musical library he presented to Louis XV in 1724 for preservation in the Royal Library, provided the largest collection of surviving manuscript sources for Lully's motets. With his royal gift, Brossard included an invaluable *catalogue*, which supplied an inventory of his vast collection with important annotations on the composers and the works contained therein.[12]

Examination of his manuscript copies of the motets that appear in the 1684 printed partbooks establishes that both the parts and scores, copied partly in Brossard's own hand, were transcribed from an *uncorrected* exemplar of the Ballard print. Some obvious errors copied from the prints, and subsequently corrected in another hand, leave no doubt that the printed partbooks served as Brossard's source for those copies.

But Brossard also owned a volume he described in his *Catalogue* as 'Les grands et petits motets non imprimez et en partition de feu Mr. Jean B. de Lully'. He catalogued the pagination and contents of F-Pn: Rés. Vma. MS 574, a collection of Lully's *petits motets* and five *grands motets* in full score, in a single hand.[13] This hand is of considerable interest because it appears in many sources, including F-Pn: Vm⁶ 6, scores of Lully's ballets, also from Brossard's library and two other collections of Lully's motets, D(BRD)-B: MS 13260, and F-Pn: Rés. F. 989. The scribe of the score has been identified as a certain Dupont by means of a signed and dated copy (1694) of Lully's *Airs*, which is located today at Stanford University.[14] This Dupont, who must have been active as a copyist for many years, will be discussed below.

Rés. Vma. MS 574 is undated, but Brossard's library held another manuscript volume in Dupont's hand, a volume of scores of Lully's ballets (now F-Pn: Vm⁶ 6), which evidently was copied at about the same time: the ink is of the same shade of dark brown, and the papers of both volumes hold watermarks in common. Brossard described this ballet volume in his *Catalogue* of 1724 with this note: '. . . ils s'estoient encore plus il y a 40 ans lorsque je le fit copier pour Strasbourg'. The suggested date is before 1684, but could Brossard's memory have failed him? If he ordered the ballets for Strasbourg, it seems to be more

[12] Sébastien de Brossard, *Catalogue*, autograph manuscript (Paris, 1724). Bibliothèque Nationale Vm⁸ 20. Not to be confused with Vm⁸ 21, which is an abridged manuscript copy of Brossard's autograph catalogue.

[13] Brossard may have owned copies of all of

Lully's *grands motets*. The one remaining motet, *Jubilate Deo*, LWV 77/16, appears in only one source, and is, in my estimation, of doubtful authenticity.

[14] Examples of Dupont's hand are reproduced on pp. 84–7, Hajdu, 'Recent Findings'.

likely that he would have done so between 1687 and 1698, his years in that city. Nevertheless, the similarities of the two volumes argue strongly that if the ballets in F-Pn: Vm⁶ 6 were copied in the mid-1680s, the motets in Rés. Vma. MS 574 must have been copied at about the same time. We have no conclusive evidence to refute Brossard's assertion that he ordered the copies around 1684. The presence of a Dupuy watermark (similar to Heawood no. 2988 dated 1694) and the 'Dupont' hand (*c.* 1694) support the seventeenth-century origins for these copies, possibly before 1687, but probably no later than 1694.[15]

Brossard also stated, regarding the ballet volume, that 'C'est tout dire qu'il m'en coûta une pistole pour avoir seulement la communication de l'original sur lequel ils furent copiez'. The source must have been an authoritative one approved by Lully or his heirs. Brossard prepared parts of the unpublished motets with assistance from the same scribes who helped him prepare scores from the 1684 Ballard prints. These associated parts (F-Pn: Vm¹ 1042, Vm¹ 1045–48) appear to have been prepared from the score (Rés. Vma. MS 574), and not vice versa because the parts preserve obvious errors found in the score and introduce additional errors. Errors that occur both in Brossard's score and in his parts indicate that this score was itself probably collated from a set of parts. A copying error on the first page of *Notus in Judaea* in Brossard's score is most logically explained if the scribe were copying from a set of parts: in the *quinte de violon*, in measure three the scribe appears to have jumped ahead to measure seven of the same part, a miscue caused probably because both measures three and seven begin with the same notes. After four incorrectly copied measures of the error the part continues correctly at the beginning of the next system on the page. This error occurs only in Brossard's copy of the motet score. Other errors in the same motet can be similarly explained. The score presents *Notus in Judaea* in 45 pages of manuscript, with fifteen staves to the page, whereas F-Pn: Rés. F. 669, to be discussed below, presents the same music in 22 pages of manuscript, although with twenty staves to the page: the format of Rés. Vma. MS 574, with its many blank staves, displays a much less efficient use of paper. This inefficiency may have resulted from the scribe having had to format the pages during the act of collating the parts. The general lack of good vertical alignment between the parts in this score, too, may have resulted from the 'parts-to-score' process of transcription.

Brossard's statement in his catalogue that he paid a high fee for the delivery of the 'original' presents strong evidence of a direct relationship between one of Lully's original manuscripts and the copy in question. Assuming that permission for use of the original must have come from Lully himself, and in view of the care Lully seems to have exercised in protecting his originals, it would be logical for a set of parts, and not the original autograph score, to have provided the medium of transfer. The obvious errors that appear in Brossard's scores are few,

---

[15] See E. Heawood, *Watermarks, Mainly of the 17th and 18th centuries* (London, 1950; repr. 1957 and 1969). The uses and pitfalls of using watermarks for date identification in music manuscripts are concisely presented in C. Massip, 'Les filigranes: utilisation, lecture et reproduction', *Fontes*, XXVIII/1–2 (1981), pp. 87–93.

and this, too, supports the general notion that this copy may have been just a second generation from the original.

Louis XIV's copy

F-Pn: Rés. F. 669, bound in the Royal Arms of France, contains a hand (Scribe E, see plate 5 and note 10) that indisputably associates itself with Philidor's atelier. Philidor's relationship with this volume is determined by: (1) page numbering in the characteristic hand of Philidor *l'aîné*; (2) the presence of this hand in Philidor-derived ballet copies in Prague (CS-Pnm: II La 11, i.e., Schneider Qu. 38); and (3) the presence of the hand in other copies found in the old Royal Library that Philidor was charged to maintain, including five of Dumont's motets (F-Pn: Rés. F. 927). The hand also appears in a copy of Desmarest's *Didon* (D-Sl: Mss H.B. XVII No. 412) verifying copying activity in or after 1693 (the date of that work), and in F-Pn: Rés. F. 652, another volume of Lully's ballets (Schneider Qu. 11). Schneider has already pointed out that this first volume of what appears to be a Foucault set of Lully's ballets (F-Pn: Rés. F. 652–657) does not appear to originate with the set.[16] The watermarks of F-Pn: Rés. F. 669 bear strong similarities, but are not identical, to watermarks in Philidor *l'aîné's* 1681 copy of Lully's *La révente des habits de ballet* (F-Pn: Rés. F. 530). The marks are of the Richard and Colombier paper-making firms. The Colombier mark, similar to Heawood no. 2432 (dated 1689), has an imperfect concentric circle of approximately 46 mm diameter inside another of approximately 70 mm, between the two circles: B – heart – COLOMBIER – heart. In the center of the inner circle is a cluster of grapes (1/2/3/4/5/6/5/4/3/2). Colombier watermarks of this general type are found in dated manuscripts as early as the 1670s (Vignol's copy of *Alceste* F-V: MS Mus 95, dated 1675) and as late as 1703 (US-STu: Toulouse–Philidor copy of Collasse's *Achille et Polyxène*, 1703). Differences in details in the Colombier and Richard watermarks, in conjunction with a comprehensive study of watermarks in dated manuscripts, could yield more information on the chronology of manuscripts, but this may require an expensive and time-consuming betagraphic study. Would this tell us much more than what we already know? Probably it would not for the motet sources, but possibly it would for the more problematic ballet sources.

The 'St Vallier' collection

F-Pn: Vm¹ 1170 belongs to the most homogeneous collection of Lully's motets, a three-volume set, all in a single hand, under two call numbers in the Bibliothèque National. F-Pc: Rés. F. 1110 in two volumes holds nine motets, including the six motets of the 1684 publication. The companion volume, F-Pn: Vm¹ 1170, contains the presumed last three motets (*Notus in Judaea*,

[16] Herbert Schneider, *Chronologisch-Thematisches Verzeichnis sämtlicher Werke von Jean-Baptiste* *Lully* (Tutzing, Schneider, 1981), p. 6.

Plate 5. J.-B. de Lully: Motets. Manuscript copy in the hand of Scribe E, F-Pn: Rés. F. 669, p. 4

Quare fremuerunt, and *Exaudiat te*) and the *petits motets*. At the top of the first page of music of each of the three volumes is the name 'St Vallier', presumably a one-time owner of the volumes; hence this name is attached to the set. The collection is unique in several respects:

1. It does not identify Lully as the author of the works it contains. Indeed it was once catalogued as work of St Vallier in the Bibliothèque du Conservatoire.
2. Because it holds all the *grands motets* of Lully except for the *Domine Salvum fac Regem*, it is the most complete collection of Lully's *grands motets*.
3. It is the only source of the *Jubilate Deo*, LWV 77/16.
4. It contains unique, and distinctly different versions of *remplissage* for some of the motets. *Quare* and *Exaudiat* have extensive changes from other sources, and *Notus in Judaea* has numerous minor changes. Most of the changes are of an intelligent nature, i.e. they reflect 'improved' voice-leading, or they alter the harmony.

On the surface, the St Vallier collection represents a different branch in the stemma from the majority of the manuscript sources, but the variants in the collections are so extensive that there is no possibility that this collection reflects a more faithful rendering of Lully's original. The six motets of the 1684 print, as they appear in this collection, could have been prepared from a corrected printed copy and then corrected again to include changes in cadential formulae and voice-leading that characterized the St Vallier set, or the collection could have resulted from a separate line that began with the autograph. In either event, while the changes in the St Vallier collection are of some interest, the set appears to be of a later generation than Rés. Vma. MS 574 and Rés. F. 669. Among the considerations that support this are:

1. the presence of a Cusson watermark similar to Heawood no. 693, dated 1732
2. the use of double bars at the end of sections within the motets, a practice that may have been influenced by early eighteenth-century engraving customs
3. the presence of independent *basse de violon* and *basse continue* lines, not found in any other manuscript scores, but provided in the 1684 partbooks
4. a uniform scoring of all the motets in a double-chorus format
5. the presence of a much fuller figured bass than other copies.

Most of these are features that appear to have been influenced by printing practices of the late-seventeenth century. Could this copy have provided the original for the printed edition? This appears not to be the case. The manuscript corrections that appear in the Glasgow and Brussels exemplars appear in the St Vallier versions, but not always in the same way. For example, St Vallier includes the altered opening four measures *premier dessus du petit choeur* of the *Miserere* as a solo in the *grand choeur*. A missing measure in the printed *basse taille* partbook for the *De profundis* appears to have been initially copied as in the Ballard print but subsequently it was corrected. This collection also routinely changes a cadential formula to eliminate certain consecutive fifths, but such fifths are commonly found in Lully's works.[17] Two of the motets, *Exaudiat* and *Quare Fremuerunt*, contain significant alterations in the *remplissage* from that in most other sources. Therefore, evidence suggests that the six printed motets in the St Vallier collection were copied from a clean (uncorrected) exemplar of the 1684 printed partbooks (or a score so prepared), by a scribe who corrected and made alterations to the music as he saw fit. Some alterations, particularly those that address harmonic considerations, appear to take eighteenth-century harmonic practices under consideration.

It may not be possible to determine the source from which the St Vallier scribe copied the unpublished motets. A comparison of variants in *Notus in Judaea* shows some errors in common with both the Royal Library copy (Rés. F. 669) and in the Dupont–Brossard copy (Rés. Vma. MS 574). The variants that these three collections have in common are not significant: they present no case for relating the St Vallier volumes to either Brossard or the Royal Library copy.

The St Vallier scribe, Scribe C, also prepared a reduced score of Lully's *Psyché* (F-RE: Mss 2525) and a full score of *Les fêtes de l'Amour et de Bacchus* (US-BEM: Ms. 448). Scribe C is not found in the Toulouse–Philidor Collection, nor in any known Foucault copies, but he obviously served in a professional capacity, and his work probably exists in other Lully sources.

Philidor's copy for the Count of Toulouse

In the earliest years of the eighteenth century Philidor *l'aîné* and his eldest son prepared a large quantity of Lully's music, including most of the motets, for the Count of Toulouse. The motets were copied in partbooks and in score: the preparation of motet partbooks in 1704 indicates that Ballard's stock of printed partbooks must then have been exhausted. Philidor prepared copies of nine motets, six of which were copied directly from an uncorrected exemplar of the 1684 printed partbooks: Philidor did not include the changes in the *Miserere* shown in plates 1 and 2. The other three motets, Lully's late motets, obviously had to have been copied from a different source. Some evidence supports the notion that Philidor copied directly from the Royal Library copy discussed above, F-Pn: Rés. F. 669. This evidence includes the presence of more common variants for *Notus in Judaea* in the Toulouse–Philidor partbooks with F-Pn: Rés. F. 669 than any other source for that motet, including a lacuna of eleven measures of the continuo part of *Notus in Judaea* in Philidor's copy which exists also in F-Pn: Rés. F. 669. Unfortunately, the scores of the Toulouse–Philidor motets, copied in the hand of Massip C/I, now rest in the estate of the late Geneviève Thibault, which remains unavailable for study.

Dupont's other copies

The Berlin motet copy D(BRD)-B: MS 13260 may have been copied by Dupont

---

[17] Hajdu, 'Recent Findings', p. 78.

at about the same time (i.e. 1694) as the copy of Lully *Airs* (US-STu). Although it shares variants with Brossard's score, the correction of the errors in *Notus in Judaea* (those cited to support the copying of Brossard's score from a set of parts) indicates that the Berlin collection was probably copied from a more accurate score that Dupont came to use sometime later. The Berlin copy shares certain scribal details in common with the 1694 copy of Lully's *Airs*, including a distinctive, more calligraphic upper case L not found in Brossard's Dupont manuscript. The improved appearance of this copy, and its more refined calligraphy, support the assumption that the Berlin motet copy post-dates Brossard's motet volume by a number of years.

We cannot altogether discount the possibility that the Dupont hand may actually represent the work of more than one scribe, for example one for the music and another for the text. The textual handwriting of Rés. Vma. MS 574 appears to be the same as that in the signed copy at Stanford, but it is less refined. A third copy of motets that carries Dupont's hand, F-Pc: Rés. 989, displays the presence of two types of custos, one with an upward gesture, the other downward, indicating the possibility of a studio operation with two or more individuals engaged in the production process, of which Dupont was one. Rés. F. 989 and the Berlin motet copy (MS 13260) and the copy of *Airs* signed by Dupont all appear to be more refined than Brossard's 'Dupont' copies of motets and ballets, and that suggests the probability of a later preparation. The 'Dupont' manuscripts are possibly the work of Pierre Dupont, whose death certificate identified him as a 'marchand de musique'. This Dupont wrote an elementary music treatise, *Principes de musique par demandes et par réponses* (Paris, 1714).

The Brussels collection

A copy in Brussels holds, in addition to the six motets of the Ballard print, two unpublished motets: *Quare fremuerunt gentes* and *Domine salvum fac Regem*. The anonymous scribe of this copy, Scribe A (see plate 6) draws considerable interest because he or she was highly productive, perhaps over a long period of time, having produced important copies of music by Lully and others.[18] The variants in *Quare fremuerunt gentes* support a closer kinship for this copy with those of Dupont than with the others.[19]

In 1983 James R. Anthony identified certain manuscripts for Lully's *Ballet des amours déguisés* that he linked to the copying activities of: (1) the royal copying atelier supervised by Philidor *l'aîné*, and (2) the commercial shop of Henry Foucault, called *Le Règle d'or*.[20] In a subsequent paper I cited evidence that the

[18] Catherine Massip and others have compiled a long list of manuscripts by this scribe.

[19] I am grateful to Lionel Sawkins for providing me with his statistical study of variants in *Quare fremuerunt gentes*.

[20] J. R. Anthony, 'The Music Sources for the *Ballet des amours déguisés*', paper presented to the annual meeting of the American Musicological Society, Louisville, 1983. See also J. R. Anthony, 'Towards a Principal Source for Lully's Court Ballets: Foucault vs Philidor', *Recherches sur la musique française classique*, XXV (1987).

Plate 6. J.-B. de Lully: Motets. Manuscript copy in the hand of Scribe A, B-Br: Ms II 3847

sources for Lully's motet *Notus in Judaea* (LWV 77/17) manifest a similar align-ment, and I suggested that Dupont may have produced copies for Foucault.[21]

We know from Foucault's advertisements that he sold manuscript copies of Lully's motets in the 1690s.[22] The establishment of a definite connection between surviving manuscript copies and Foucault's shop has proven to be more elusive for Lully's motets than for the ballets and operas. Some copies of ballets and operas carry Foucault's advertisements, but no motet copy has yet surfaced that can be directly traced to Foucault's shop. Anthony's 1983 findings, which placed Brossard's copy of Lully's *Ballet des amours déguisés* (today F-Pn: Vm⁶ 6), a score copied by Dupont, in the tradition of ballet copies that stem from other copies associated with Foucault's shop, now establish an indirect association between Dupont and Foucault by virtue of the volume of Lully's motets that Dupont also copied for Brossard (F-Pn: Rés. Vma. MS 574). These two volumes, identically bound, share similar manuscript characteristics: they may have been prepared by Dupont at about the same time. The strong similarities between his two scores suggests that Brossard must have used the same services to secure his copy of the motets as for his copy of Lully's ballets. The kinship in variants that the several motet copies by Dupont share with the Brussels copy of *Quare fremuerunt*, furthermore, links Dupont to Scribe A. Did Dupont and Scribe A both produce manuscripts for Foucault to sell at the Règle d'or? That appears to be likely, but, so far, only indirect evidence supports this conclusion.

The role of the Règle d'or aside, the motet copies associated with Philidor (copies by Philidor, Massip C/I, and Scribe E) and those copies associated with Dupont (Dupont and Scribe A) delineate a copying stemma for most of the motet sources under consideration here. The St Vallier collection, because it holds so many variants, cannot be assigned to either of the traditions with conviction, but it lies closer to Philidor than to Dupont. The differences, as reflected by the number of variants, between the Dupont motet copies and those associated with Philidor appear to be less pronounced than those found in the two ballet traditions described by Anthony. This may have resulted from a closer kinship of the motet copies to their originals because the more limited demand that existed for the motets subjected them to more limited motet copying activity, both in time span and in quantity. One thing is certain: the manuscript copies of Lully's works that have come down to us were derived, directly or indirectly, from Lully's originals. A relatively narrow divergence, as reflected in the number of variants, between the Royal Chapel copy, F-Pn: Rés. F. 669, and Brossard's copy, F-Pn: Rés. Vma. MS 574, may reflect the existence of the identified scribal branches in their initial stages of development. The indirect evidence in this study suggests that one branch includes a copy associated with Sébastien Brossard and a scribe named Dupont, who copied Lully's unpublished motets from an authorized set of original parts. The Royal Librarian Philidor, too, claimed access to originals in Lully's hand, originals that

[21] Hajdu, 'Recent Findings', p. 80.
[22] For example, see the advertisement in the front of the copy of Collasse's *Ballet des saisons* at US-BEm: Case X.

presumably would have been scores.[23] The origins, then, of the note variants
that subsequently led to the identification of (at least) two copying traditions in
the motets and ballets may have initially resulted from that difference in the
original source material: parts and scores (as suggested in table 3). We must hope
for a more complete picture to emerge after further study of the work of Dupont
and the other scribes of the motet sources in the manuscript copies of Lully's
other works.

Table 3 *Hypothetical stemma for the sources of Lully's late motets*

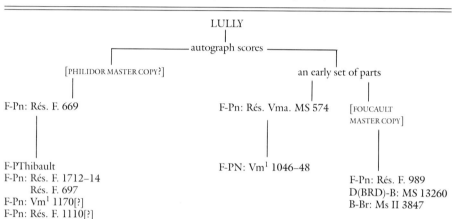

[23] See Anthony's discussion of Philidor and
Fossard's anthology of *Airs Italians* (Paris,
Pierre Ballard, 1695) in 'Towards a Principal

Source for Lully's Court Ballets', *Recherches
sur la musique française classique* XXV (1987).

Some notes on Lully's orchestra*

JÉRÔME DE LA GORCE

Quand la toile se lève et que les sons charmans
D'un innombrable amas de divers instrumens
Forment cette éclatante et grave symphonie
Qui ravit tous les sens par sa noble harmonie,
Et par qui le moins tendre en ce premier moment,
Sent tout son corps ému d'un doux fremissement . . .

Thus wrote Charles Perrault in his poem *Le siècle de Louis le Grand*, published in 1687,[1] to describe the public's emotion at the start of a performance of a Lully opera. The wonder inspired by those first moments as the overture resounded resulted from that 'vast array of diverse instruments' which were playing, as they do today, in a pit before the stage. The orchestra, with its ability to appeal directly to the senses, constituted one of the basic components of French opera of the period. One has only to look at the scores to realize the importance of its role. In addition to accompanying the voices during the *récits*, airs and choruses, it played dance movements in the *divertissements* in each act and was used to convey events in the plot by means of long descriptive passages. Even those contemporaries most hostile to opera recognized the orchestra's qualities; among them, François de Callières could not help but praise the perfection of the 'concerts de violons, de flûtes et de hautbois', going so far as to compare them to those of Italy, where 'la simphonie' was, according to him, 'greatly inferior because of the dearth of instruments'.[2]

Unfortunately, few documents remain today that can help us gauge the richness of the orchestra that Lully directed and made the greatest in Europe. The sparse information in the scores does not adequately convey either its size or the

* I sincerely thank Monsieur Bardet, Conservateur in the Department of Music at the Bibliothèque Nationale, Mademoiselle Marcelle Benoît, and Mademoiselle Monique Rollin, who have generously supplied information necessary for the preparation of this article.

[1] Charles Perrault, *Le siècle de Louis le Grand* (Paris, J.-B. Coignard, 1687), p. 20. 'When the curtain goes up and the charming sounds/Of a vast array of diverse instruments/ Create that striking and solemn symphony/ Which delights every sense with its noble harmony,/And from which even the least sensitive soul at that time/Feels a sweet shudder run through his entire body . . .'

[2] 'beaucoup inférieure par la disette des instrumens'. François de Callières, *Histoire poétique de la guerre nouvellement déclarée entre les Anciens et les Modernes* (Paris, 1688), p. 267.

diversity of its timbres.[3] Other sources, not extensively studied by musicologists, must be consulted in order to gain these insights. Among those sources are livrets published for each series of performances given at the Court at Saint-Germain-en-Laye between 1675 and 1682, and a list of names of the musicians who performed the ballet *Le triomphe de l'amour* at this royal residence in 1681.

The livrets were printed by Christophe Ballard, at the time of the creation and revivals at Saint-Germain of the *tragédies en musique Thésée, Atys, Isis, Cadmus et Hermione, Alceste, Proserpine,* and *Bellérophon*.[4] Distributed somewhat like programs on the occasion of these performances, the livrets do not mention all the names of the performers, especially of the orchestra players stationed in the pit, but they do have the merit of listing very precisely, as they had done previously for other spectacles given at court, all the instrumentalists who played on stage, chosen to appear alongside the singers, and thus to participate in the dramatic action. Costumes were even created for these musicians, as sumptuous as those worn by the singers and the dancers, as several costumes designed by Jean Berain attest (see plates 1 and 2). As early as 1671, during a particularly lavish production of the *tragédie-ballet Psyché*, more than a hundred musicians were utilized during the course of the work, some having two entrances and a change of costume.[5] All the orchestra probably participated in the finale, each member taking his place in the machines that formed 'great shining clouds set on three levels',[6] offering the public a glorious ending of exceptional sumptuousness.

Such effects were possible in *Psyché*, a work in which spoken dialogue alternated with music, but they would have been more difficult to produce in opera, where instrumentalists are called on to play continuously. In addition, there were far fewer musicians on stage when Lully's *tragédies en musique* were being performed. Their numbers varied from nine to twenty-one and tended to diminish over the years. This fact can be substantiated by a study of their names, not only at the time of the first production of *Thésée, Atys, Isis,* and *Proserpine* (see table 1), but also when these works were revived. The number of participants fell from thirty-eight to twenty-nine during the course of various performances of *Thésée* presented between 1675 and 1678 (see table 2).

[3] The present study is limited to these two aspects. Obviously, research should be pursued in other areas, notably in organology. On the important subject of Lully's orchestra consult: Marc Pincherle, 'L'interpretazione orchestrale di Lulli', *L'orchestra* (Florence, G. Barbera, 1954), pp. 139–52; C.-L. Cudworth, 'Baptist's vein-French Orchestral Music and its Influence from 1650 to 1750', *Proceedings of the Royal Musical Association,* LXXXIII (1956–7), pp. 29–47; Jürgen Eppelsheim, *Das Orchester in den Werken Jean-Baptiste Lullys* (Tutzing, Schneider, 1961); Neal Zaslaw, 'When is an Orchestra not an Orchestra?' (*Early Music,* forthcoming).

[4] The operas *Thésée, Atys, Isis,* and *Proserpine* were first performed at Saint-Germain-en-Laye. The original livrets relative to these performances, like those that were printed for the revivals of *Thésée* in 1677, of *Alceste* and *Cadmus et Hermione* in 1678, of *Bellérophon* in 1680, and of *Atys* in 1682, are preserved in the Bibliothèque de l'Opéra in Paris (Liv. 17: R 1 and 2). At the Reserve section of the Imprimés at the Bibliothèque Nationale one may consult the livrets published for the revival of *Alceste* in 1677 (Rés. Yf. 1694), as well as for *Thésée* (Rés. Yf. 2451) and *Atys* (Rés. Yf. 1787) published in 1678.

[5] See the original livret of *Psyché* (Paris, Robert Ballard, 1671).

[6] Robinet, *Lettres en vers à Monsieur,* 24 January 1671, p. 2 (Paris, Bibliothèque Mazarine, Rés. F° 296 A5).

Plate 1. Costume designed by Jean Berain for the flutists on stage, Act I, *Thésée*
(Collection Rothschild, Paris)

Plate 2. From the studio of Jean Berain for the flutists on stage, Act III, *Isis*

The revival of *Atys* in 1682 was the sole exception: that production employed more musicians than for its première in 1676. It seems, according to the *Mercure galant*,[7] that this work was mounted under special circumstances: an effort was being made to impress the Ambassador of Morocco during his visit to the French court, and a great deal of money was also spent on behalf of the Dauphine, who had been unable to attend the opera when it was first performed. Marie-Anne-Christine-Victoire de Bavière had just married the heir to the throne, whose tastes for music and dance she shared. Probably the new royal couple wished to have 'de grands embellissemens' in the form of ballet *entrées* added to the work. In addition, this revival of *Atys*, which marked the end of a series of extravagant performances given at Saint-Germain-en-Laye, does not truly reflect the evolution that has been substantiated by the information gathered for the period after 1682. We find that virtually never again were the instrumentalists, to whom tradition had granted recognition from the time of Lully's first operas, mentioned in the livrets printed for lyric spectacles.[8]

This custom, soon to be abandoned, has the merit of allowing other observations to be made. Firstly, we can see that musicians could appear up to four times in different costumes in the course of a single performance (see table 1). For the most part, they belonged to the *Musique du roi* but could also be recruited from the troupe of the Académie royale de musique[9] that Lully directed in Paris. Some of them were already famous or were to become so shortly, for example, the flutist Descoteaux, the viol players Marin Marais and Theobaldo de Gatti, known as Theobalde, both of whom were to compose several operas. To these names, familiar to musicologists today, should be added those of illustrious families, whose importance has been justly recognized by music history: the Hotteterres and the Philidors, whom the livrets do not always list with enough detail to distinguish between the various brothers or the cousin. The facility with which the members of these families moved from one instrument to another during the same performance (generally from flute to oboe) should not minimize the importance of the role of these musicians, whom Lully brought out of the orchestra pit to add greater contrast depth to certain pages of his scores.

The choice of artists assigned to appear on stage was, in fact, rarely dictated by their reputation but was first and foremost due to the instrument they played. The choice, by no means an arbitrary one, was a response to a notion of instrumental colouring that Lully had already had occasion to follow in other productions. Thus, there is nothing surprising in the fact that flutes figure in sacred or pastoral scenes, or that trumpets, sometimes accompanied by the *timbales*, announce the presence of warriors or of the *Renommées*. Oboes, too, are

[7] *Mercure galant* (Paris, January 1682), pp. 278, 279, 318, 320.
[8] During Louis XIV's reign, only the livrets for *Orontée* (1688), for the *Ballet de Villeneuve Saint-Georges* (1692), for *Psyché* (1703 and 1713), and for *Isis* (1704) still list the names of a few instrumentalists.
[9] Several names, among them that of Theobaldo de Gatti, attest to this fact and confirm the information on this subject yielded by the manuscript catalog of André Danican Philidor, presently located in the Musée Calvet in Avignon (Manuscrit 1201, f° 6 to 8).

Table 1 *Number of entries and names of instrumentalists assigned to play on stage*

	THÉSÉE (1675)	ATYS (1676)	ISIS (1677)	Thésée (1677)	Alceste (1677–8)	Atys (1678)	Cadmus (1678)	Thésée (1678)	PROSERPINE (1680)	Bellérophon (1680)	Atys (1682)
Barberay (Denis): trompette	2	–	1	2	–	–	–	2	–	1?	–
Beaupré (Antoine Pelissier): trompette	–	–	1	–	–	–	–	–	–	–	–
Body (Baudy?): basse de violon	1	–	–	1	–	–	1	–	–	–	–
Bonard (Etienne): guitare	–	–	1	–	–	–	1	–	–	–	–
Bonnet: flûte	–	–	1	–	–	–	–	–	–	–	–
Buchot (François): musette	–	–	–	1	1	–	–	–	–	–	–
Charvilhac (François): trompette	2	–	1	2	–	–	1	2	–	1?	–
Chicaneau: guitare	–	–	–	–	–	–	–	–	–	–	–
Descoteaux (René Pignon): flûte, hautbois	3	1	1	2	2	1	–	3	1	2	2
Destouches (Michel Herbinot dit): flûte	–	–	–	–	–	–	–	–	–	2	1
Du Clos (Jean de Penhalleu dit): flûte, hautbois	2	–	–	–	4	1	1	3	–	–	1
Dufour: flûte	–	–	–	1	–	–	1	–	–	–	–
Dupré (Laurent): théorbe	1	1	–	1	–	1?	–	–	–	–	1
Dupré (Thomas): trompette	2	–	–	2	–	–	–	2	–	1?	–
Favre: dessus de violon	–	–	1	–	–	–	–	–	–	–	–
Grenerin: théorbe	1	1	–	1	?	1?	?	?	–	–	?
Hotteterre (Colin): flûte, hautbois	3	2	–	1	?	?	?	?	–	–	?
Hotteterre (Jean): flûte, hautbois	2	2	1	3	?	?	?	?	–	–	?
Hotteterre (Jeannot): flûte, hautbois, timbales	2	3	1	3	?	?	?	?	–	–	?
Hotteterre (Louis): flûte, hautbois	3	3	2	3	?	?	?	?	–	–	?
Hotteterre (Martin): flûte	1	–	–	2	?	?	–	–	–	–	?
Hotteterre (Nicolas): flûte, hautbois	1	1	2	–	?	–	–	–	–	–	–
Joubert (Pierre): dessus de violon	–	–	2	–	–	–	–	1	–	–	–
La Croix: hautbois	–	–	1	–	2	–	–	–	–	–	–
La Pierre (Paul de): basse de violon	1	–	–	1	–	–	–	–	–	–	–
La Plaine: trompette	2	–	–	2	–	–	–	2	–	1?	1
Le Moyne (Etienne): théorbe	–	1	1	–	–	–	–	–	–	–	–
Lorange (Benigne Guillot dit): trompette	–	1	–	–	–	–	–	–	–	–	1
Marais (Marin): basse de viole	–	–	–	–	1?	1?	1	–	–	–	1
Mayeux (Antoine?): guitare	–	–	–	–	–	–	1	–	–	–	–
Monginot: hautbois	–	–	–	–	–	–	–	–	–	–	1

	38	23	22	32	21	20?	9	29	12	14	26
Pezan: guitare	—	—	—	—	—	—	1	—	—	—	—
Philbert (Philippe Rebellé): flûte, hautbois	3	1	2	—	2	1	—	3	—	—	2
Philidor *l'aîné* (André): flûte, hautbois, cromorne, timbales	2	2	2	1	2?	—	1?	2?	—	2	3
Philidor *cadet* (Jacques): flûte, hautbois, cromorne, timbales	2	2	1	—	—	—	—	1	1	1	3
Pieche *père* (Pierre I): flûte	—	—	2	—	—	—	—	1	—	1	1
Pieche *fils* (Pierre II): flûte	—	—	1	—	—	—	—	2	—	—	1
Pieche *l'aîné* (Joseph): flûte	2	1	—	1	2	—	1	1	1	2	2
Pieche *cadet* (Pierre-Alexandre): flûte	—	—	—	—	—	—	—	—	1	1	—
Plumet (François Arthus dit): cromorne, hautbois	—	1	—	3	2	1	—	2	—	1	1
Rousselet: flûte	—	—	—	—	—	—	—	—	—	—	1
Royer (Claude): hautbois	—	—	—	—	—	—	—	—	—	—	1
Salomon: basse de viole	—	—	—	—	—	—	—	—	—	—	1
Theobalde (Jean Theobaldo de Gatti): viole	—	1	—	—	—	—	—	—	—	—	—
Thoulon (or Toulon) *père*: hautbois	—	—	—	—	—	—	—	—	—	1	1
Thoulon (or Toulon) *fils*: flûte	—	—	—	—	—	—	—	—	1	1	2
Number of instrumentalists[a]	38	23	22	32	21	20?	9	29	12	14	26

[a] These figures reflect all entries in the livrets, including those that mention the number of instrumentalists but not their names.

Table 2 *Instruments assigned to play on stage in the different productions of*
Thésée given at Saint-Germain-en-Laye

	1675	1677	1678
Acte I			
Flûtes	6	6	6
Trompettes	4	4	4
Timbales	2	2	1
Acte IV			
Flûtes	6	6	4
Hautbois	4	–	4
Cromornes	2	–	–
Acte V			
Flûtes	6	6	6
Basses de violon	2	2	–
Théorbes	2	2	–
Trompettes	4	4	4
TOTAL	38	32	29

often mentioned in the livrets. They play military marches or announce the descent of the Zephyrs. But generally they are more suitable for rural tableaux, in which they can blend with the musette, as in the Prologue to *Alceste*. This was not the first time that the latter instrument, called upon to play an expressive role in the operas of the eighteenth century, was supposed to depict the charms of nature. In 1664, for example, during the first day of *Les plaisirs de l'île enchantée*, a group of fourteen instrumentalists preceded the gods Pan and Diana with a 'pleasant harmony of flutes and musettes'.[10]

The winds, often grouped from four to eight during the course of the same *divertissement*, were not the only instruments that Lully reserved for the stage. We also find strings, although in lesser numbers: violins in the Prologue to *Isis*, played by two musicians dressed as Muses, and guitars, which four dancers in African costumes played during the first act of *Cadmus et Hermione*. The latter instruments, whose placement in the pit probably would have seemed strange, must simply have been chosen to supply a note of local color, fulfilling a some-what similar role to that of the mandolins in the second act of Verdi's *Otello*. We find them, in fact, mentioned not only in *Cadmus et Hermione* as portraying oriental characters, but also in the livrets of other spectacles in which Lully had taken part in 1658 and 1667, the *Ballet d'Alcidiane* and the *Pastorale comique*, in which guitarists had appeared dressed as Moors and Egyptians.[11]

Other instrumentalists were probably called upon to play the roles of Dreams

[10] Detail supplied by the original livret (Paris, Robert Ballard, 1664).
[11] The original livret of the *Pastorale comique*

notably mentions Lully among the guitarists costumed as Egyptians.

or to participate in a celestial representation for an apotheosis in the midst of heavenly divinities. These included theorbists, violists, or *basse de violon* players, assigned to realize or double the *basse continue*, to which Lully wanted to give an expressive dimension in *Thésée* and *Atys*.

The composer's interest in the choice of instruments that he wished to feature on stage is also attested to by the different livrets printed at the time of the first performance and revivals of the same opera. By comparing those of *Thésée*, published in 1675, 1677, and 1678 (see table 2), one sees few changes from one series of performances to another. As in *Atys*, the crumhorns, however, quickly disappear in favor of flutes or oboes and will never again be mentioned in the cast lists of Lully operas or revivals after 1676. Conversely, the elimination two years later of the theorbos and *basses de violon* in the last act of *Thésée* should not be interpreted as the sign of an evolution, because Lully employed the former, accompanied by *basses de viole*, until 1682 for performances of *Atys*.

The information recorded in the livrets, important though it may be, unfortunately offers only a fragmentary notion of the orchestra that Lully conducted. In the case of *Le triomphe de l'amour*, however, the information in the livret is complemented by a full list of the instrumentalists who took part in a performance of this work in 1681. Preserved in the Archives nationales,[12] the 'Mémoires du pain, vin, verres et bouteilles', supplied to the various players during the course of the ballet's performances are not unknown to musicologists. André Tessier and Marcelle Benoit[13] have already published the invoices and emphasized their historic interest. Nevertheless, these unique documents, which reveal with remarkable accuracy the conditions under which Lully's works were created during that period, deserve further examination. In particular, the names of the musicians listed in them should be compared with those cited in the livrets. The archival sources are in fact rather vague with regard to the role of each artist and it was therefore advisable to attempt to discover what instruments were hidden behind this impressive list of individuals named by a mere purveyor to the *Menus Plaisirs*.

Certain players are first mentioned with the singers in an initial grouping entitled 'Musitiens'. They were the musicians assigned to double or to realize the *basse continue*:

M. Lemoyne (Etienne Le Moyne), theorbo (or *basse de viole*)[14]
M. Marais (Marin), *basse de viole*
M. Salomon, *basse de viole*
M. Danglebert P. [*père*] (Henri d'Anglebert) (harpsichord)
M. Danglebert *fils* (Jean-Baptiste-Henri d'Anglebert) (harpsichord)
M. Dupré (Laurent), theorbo (or lute)

[12] Paris, Archives nationales, O¹ 2984.
[13] André Tessier, 'Un document sur les répétitions du *Triomphe de l'Amour*', *Actes du congrès d'histoire de l'art organisé par la société de l'histoire de l'art français* (Paris, 1924), pp. 874–93; by the same author, 'Les répétitions du *Triomphe de l'Amour* à Saint-Germain-en-Laye', *La revue musicale* (1 February 1925), pp. 123–31. Marcelle Benoit, *Musiques de cour* (Paris, 1971), pp. 76–7; by the same author, *Versailles et les musiciens du roi* (Paris, Picard, 1971), p. 73.
[14] Information obtained from documents other than livrets has been indicated in parentheses.

M. Itier[15] (Léonard) (lute or *basse de viole*)
M. Pierre[16] (Paul de la Pierre?), *bass de violon* (or lute)?
M. Delabarre (Pierre Chabanceau de La Barre) (lute or theorbo)

Two harpsichords, six *basses de viole*, theorbos, lutes and, apparently, one *basse de violon*, may today seem to be a large continuo. However, if one consults other references of the period, one finds this number of instruments to be no exaggeration. In 1664, sixteen fauns playing flutes and violins in concert with thirty other strings, and six harpsichordists and theorbists[17] had been used for the finale of *La Princesse d'Elide*. It seems that these lavish ensembles, capable of bringing more power and density and indeed more dramatic possibilities to the *récits* that they accompanied, were one of the most characteristic aspects of Lully's performances of his works. François de Callières, in his *Histoire poétique de la guerre nouvellement déclarée entre les Anciens et les Modernes*, published only one year after the composer's death, notes that at the Opéra, the voices are 'almost drowned by the accompaniment of the harpsichords, theorbos and other orchestral instruments, which cause the listener to lose part of the melody and almost all the words being sung'.[18] Callières's work, while very critical, thus confirms the importance of the continuo instruments, whose diversity is evoked in another text, this time anonymous, but also contemporary. The *Entretiens galans* which appeared in 1681 alluded to women in the audience who became so impassioned by operatic music that during the performance they could not restrain themselves from imitating the playing 'of the lute on a hand' or 'of the harpsichord on an arm'.[19] The *basses d'archet*, while not as numerous as they were at the beginning of the eighteenth century,[20] already played a substantial role in doubling the *basse continue*. In *Le bourgeois gentilhomme*, the *maître de musique* advised Monsieur Jourdain to have the voices at his concerts accompanied by a *basse de viole*, a theorbo and a harpsichord.[21] For Lully's operas, this number was

[15] This musician's name is just as often written as 'Ithier'.
[16] André Tessier and Marcelle Benoit have conjectured that this name belonged to one of the Italian singers, who were often called by their first names. However, the name is not mentioned in the original livret of *Le triomphe de l'amour*, nor even in the invoices of the *Menus Plaisirs*, other than in the documents relating to the rehearsals and performances of this ballet, cited here. It is for that reason that I believe it might be a reference to La Pierre, a *basse de violon* player mentioned in the cast-list of *Thésée* by two livrets (in 1675 and 1677).
[17] The original livret lists the names of these six players: d'Anglebert, Richard, Itier, the younger La Barre, Tissu, and Le Moine. Thanks to the invoices of the *Menus Plaisirs*, closely studied by Marcelle Benoit, we know that the first two musicians were harpsichordists and that the others were lutenists and theorbists. It seems therefore that between 1664 and 1681 the composition of the continuo evolved little and we would be tempted today to propose the following instruments for per-

formance of a Lully opera: two harpsichords, two theorbos, two lutes, two *basses de viole* and one to two *basses de violon*. The use of theorbos and lutes in Lully's orchestra is substantiated by the accounts of performances of *Psyché* in 1671 that we have from the Marquis de Saint-Maurice. Marquis de Saint-Maurice, *Lettres sur la Cour de Louis XIV* (Paris, Jean Lemoine, 1912), vol. 2, p. 15.
[18] 'presque entièrement étouffées par l'accompagnement des clavessins, des théorbes et autres instrumens de l'orchestre, qui font perdre à l'auditeur une partie de l'air, et presque toutes les paroles qu'elles chantent'. François de Callières, *Histoire poétique*, p. 264.
[19] *Entretiens galans*, vol. II (Paris, 1681), p. 102.
[20] Based on what is known about the orchestra of the Académie royale de musique in 1704. On this subject, see La Gorce, 'L'Académie royale de musique en 1704, d'après des documents inédits conservés dans les archives notariales', *Revue de musicologie*, LXV/2 (1979), p. 182.
[21] Act II, scene i, *Le bourgeois gentilhomme*, by Molière.

to be doubled at least, with the possibility of adding lutes and a *basse de violon*. The livrets of *Thésée* and *Atys* seem to confirm this fact, just as they also lead us to believe that not all the instrumentalists of the continuo played together all the time. Rather, while they undoubtedly were called upon to accompany vocal ensembles or to perform pages reserved for the orchestra, some of them were probably directed to enter only at certain places in the score, when they were not appearing on stage or in one of the machines.

One question remains regarding the role of these musicians. Did they change from one instrument to another in the course of a single performance? We know that several of them, Dupré, Itier, la Barre, and Le Moyne performed as proficiently on the theorbo as on the lute or viol. However, it seems from the precise details found in the relevant livrets that they were usually assigned only one part. Conversely, according to the same sources, it is clear that matters were different for wind players, who were all listed in the document dealing with rehearsals and performances of *Le triomphe de l'amour* in a second group, reserved for them alone, under the description 'fluttes et aulbois':

M. Philbert (Philippe Rebellé): oboe and flute
M. Thoullon *père*: oboe
M. Descoteaux (also known as René Pignon): flute
M. Royer (Claude): oboe
M. Buchot (François): musette (and oboe)
M. Plumet (known as François Arthus): crumhorn, oboe, and flute
M. Destouches (known as Michel Herbinot): flute
M. Duclos (known as Jean de Penhalleu): oboe and flute
M. Delacroix (or de La Croix): oboe
M. Adeline: ?
M. Ferrier (Claude): bassoon
M. Desjardins (Philippe?): ?
M. Thoullon (Thoulon), *fils*: flute
M. Philidor, L. (André): crumhorn, oboe and flute
M. Philidor, C. (Jacques): flute and *timbales*
M. Monginot: oboe
M. Hotteterre: oboe and flute
M. Pieche *père* (Pierre I): flute
M. Pieche *fils* (Pierre II): flute
M. Pieche, L. (Joseph): flute
M. Pieche, C. (Pierre-Alexandre): flute

Leaving aside two musicians, Adeline and Desjardins, and two others whose roles can be inferred from the invaluable research of Marcelle Benoit,[22] it has been possible with the aid of the livrets to establish precisely what instruments were played by all the artists belonging to this second category. Flutists are in the majority but many of them, five out of twelve, are also oboists. Their importance is readily explained by a reading of the livrets, in which they figure in the greatest numbers, and of the scores. In *Le triomphe de l'amour*, for example, there is a 'prélude pour l'Amour', written entirely for an ensemble consisting of 'tailles

---

[22] Marcelle Benoit, *Musiques de cour*, pp. 76–7.

ou flûtes d'Allemagne', a 'quinte de flûtes', a 'petite basse de flûtes', and a 'grande basse de flûtes'.[23] Lully likes to regroup the instruments of one family or those with tonal affinity, such as oboes, crumhorns and bassoons. In this taste for relatively homogeneous instrumental color are to be found the origins of those famous reed trios that adorn the composer's works.

One must observe, however, in the list reproduced above, that while the oboes are numerous and even seem to rival the flutes, the bassoons ought to be better represented. Because they are not mentioned in the opera livrets, it is not possible to list them, but we have every reason to believe, taking into account the information available regarding the interpretation of musico-dramatic works performed in the time of Louis XIV,[24] that several oboists and flautists were also bassoonists capable of passing from one instrument to the other during the course of a single performance. Despite a few lacunae in our information regarding this second category of musicians, we cannot fail to note their considerable number in relation to the final group, made up of forty-seven strings and including the 'vingt-cinq grands violons du roy'[25] and the 'petits violons du roy', also called the 'violons du cabinet'.

The composition of these two famous ensembles could not be found with the aid of the livrets, which say very little about the stringed instruments. It was necessary to turn to sources that, unfortunately, are of a later date: the *Etats de la France* of 1692 *et seq.*,[26] which nonetheless yielded precise information that enables a serious hypothesis to be put forward. One may in fact state, without great risk of error, that in 1692 the *vingt-cinq grands violons* must have presented the same distribution of the various instruments belonging to that family as in 1681, that is: seven *dessus*, four *hautes-contre*, four *tailles*, two *quintes*, and eight *basses*. This judgment does not rely solely on the fact that the *Etats de la France* of 1692 was published only a few years after Lully's death, but also on indications furnished by Mersenne in 1636,[27] which reveal that there were few changes between these two dates in the composition of the *grands violons du roy* (table 3).

Unfortunately, we do not have as precise information regarding the *violons du cabinet* before 1692. But all indications lead one to believe that few modifications were made in this group, particularly because it later showed great stability in the number of different instruments that it brought together. Its evolution must therefore have been close to that of the *grands violons*, as attested by table 3, which has been compiled with the aid of the *Etats de la France*, up to the beginning of the eighteenth century. One may note therein that after 1636 the *dessus*, and in a smaller proportion the *basses*, tended to increase in numbers, to the

---

[23] Jean-Baptiste Lully, *Le triomphe de l'amour* (Paris, Christophe Ballard, 1681), pp. 200, 201.

[24] See La Gorce, 'L'Académie royale', p. 183.

[25] The 'grands violons du roy' did not always number twenty-five, as is shown in table 3 and as is indicated by the name of 'Vingt-quatre violons' generally given to this instrumental ensemble.

[26] Most issues of the *Etats de la France* are found in the Département des Imprimés of the Bibliothèque Nationale (8° Lc. 25 14). However, other copies preserved in the Bibliothèque historique de la Ville de Paris, have been used to complete this information.

[27] Marin Mersenne, *Harmonie universelle* (Paris, 1636–7), book 4, p. 18.

Table 3 *Evolution of the* grands et des petits violons du roi

	Grands violons					Petits violons		
	1636	1692–4	1699–1702	1708–12	1718	1692–4	1698–1708	1712[a]
Dessus	6	7	9	10	11	7	7	8
Hautes-contre	4	4	3	2	3	2	2	2
Tailles	4	4	4	3	2	3	3	3
Quintes	4	2	2	2	–	2	2	2
Basses	6	8	6	7	8	4	5	5
TOTAL	24	25	24	24	24	18	19	20

[a] Following this date the *Etats de la France* no longer
mention the *petits violons du roi*.

detriment of the intermediate parts, whose diminution is such that it leads to
the elimination of the *quintes* in 1718.[28]

These observations (similar to those already formulated elsewhere with regard
to the orchestra of the Académie royale de musique)[29] permit us to conclude
this study with a question: had the instrumental ensemble conducted by Campra in 1704 at the Opéra in Paris greatly evolved since Lully? The research that we
have just concluded with regard to the court ensemble seems to prove that at the
end of the seventeenth century there were a few changes: a harpsichord and
perhaps even lutes had to be eliminated for the realization of the *basse continue,*
and the sound balance of the strings was somewhat altered by giving less importance and hence less weight to the middle parts.

Between Lully and Campra, a change in taste had taken place. From the first
operas of Colasse, the instrumental soloist emerged from the group with which
he had been closely associated. He took on an independence and mingled thereafter more freely and gracefully with others, holding the public's attention like a
picturesque detail in a Watteau painting. Conversely, in the fashion of the great
decorative compositions of a Charles Le Brun, Lully's operatic music had drawn
upon powerful effects of contrast, opposing groups of instruments of the same
family, each of which was capable of offering clearer, more homogeneous colors.
This concept, inherited from the Renaissance, had the virtue of calling for varied
timbres, a notion whose expressive possibilities were to be developed by the
Florentine's successors. The concept also called for a large orchestra – the one
that Lully conducted at Saint-Germain-en-Laye had no less than seventy-seven
musicians, of which twenty-one were winds, a number equal to nearly one-half

[28] This suppression therefore took place at court
well before its counterpart in the orchestra of
the Opéra observed over the period between
1719 and 1738.

[29] In addition to the article cited in n. 20 on
L'Académie royale de musique in 1704, I have
also presented a paper (Société française de
Musicologie, July 1986) on the evolution of
the Opéra de Paris orchestra from the beginning of the eighteenth century to the death of
Rameau.

of the strings. 'To be successful, one needs to have twenty harpsichords and one hundred violins', wrote La Fontaine humorously in his famous *Epître à M. de Nyert*,[30] in which he painted a very critical portrait of Lully. However, it is thanks to this obsession with grandeur and magnificence – closely paralleled in other artistic creations in the first half of the personal reign of Louis XIV – that for more than a century French opera preserved the importance of the instrumental dimension, thereby conferring on itself one of its most original attributes.

[30] Jean de La Fontaine, *Oeuvres diverses* (Paris, Gallimard, 1958), p. 618.

The Amsterdam editions of Lully's orchestral suites

HERBERT SCHNEIDER

Lully's main influence outside France stems far less from the conception of his operas together with Quinault's libretti than from his orchestral practice and the instrumental music of his operas. Leaving aside the ballets and *divertissements*, the important position of the instrumental element in opera is the most striking difference between Italian and French music theater of the baroque era. In Lully's case, the instrumental pieces are essential in conveying meaning. As a rule, it is in his *ritournelles* and preludes that Lully places the affective emphases, presents the principal ideas and gives the signals needed for the understanding of the ensuing vocal passages: these vocal passages concentrate on the correct declamation and certain musical elements which heighten expressiveness in the vocal part itself, but the vocal movements include the principal musical ideas to a far lesser extent than they do in Italian opera.

Lully's instrumental music, moreover, was seen by his contemporaries and by later generations as powerfully expressive. With it the essential musical pronouncements of early French opera were secured and assimilated by the people. While the spread of Lully's vocal and instrumental music in the form of the vocal *Gebrauchsmusik*, hence as secular and sacred parody, was restricted predominantly to France and to a lesser extent also to Canada and the French-speaking Netherlands, the influence of the instrumental music extended to all of central and northern Europe. The question of the extent to which it also left behind traces in Italy cannot yet be answered exactly, but research should take up this question.

Manuscript collections give some information about the knowledge of Lully's instrumental music in and out of France, but the suites printed in Amsterdam by Heus, Pointel, and Roger are far more significant.[1] The designation 'Ouverture' for the orchestral suite apparently goes back to Roger, who entitled his editions of the suites 'Ouverture avec tous les airs'. These opera suites in orchestral settings, and the earlier, unpublished suites from ballets and *comédie-ballets*, represent the beginning of the history of the orchestral suite, which is to be understood as a French counterpart to the Italian concerto, and was understood as such by baroque composers right through to Bach, Handel, and Telemann.

---

[1] See H. Schneider, *Chronologisch-Thematisches Verzeichnis sämtlicher Werke von Jean-Baptiste Lully (LWV)* (Tutzing, 1981) and the chapter 'Opernsuiten in orchestraler und kammer-musikalischer Ausführung' in *Die Rezeption der Opern Lullys im Frankreich des Ancien Régime* (Tutzing, 1982), pp. 123–56.

French copies of suites excerpted from stage works exist, both for the Lully orchestra with five-part string setting, and for the reduced score, that is the 'trio-setting', but only a few prints of such suites exist in France: Ballard published, for example, only the *Symphonies de la tragédie de Didon* of Henry Desmarets (1693), the *Symphonies* by Pierre Gautier (1707), and the *Symphonies du ballet des ages* of André Campra (1718), all in reduced score (i.e. only the *dessus* and bass of the five-part pieces are given, but the trio movements remain unchanged). French orchestral suites in manuscript are presented in five parts, with wind instrument entries simply indicated verbally. At the same time there are separate parts for certain instruments, for example, bassoon or marine trumpet. The only so-called 'commercial' French suite copies – published by Foucault and dated 1708 and 1716 – are designated for the trio setting, as are those mentioned in Boivin's catalogue of 1730[2] (*Dessus & Basse en deux volumes*). The French manuscript copies of suites by Lully or other composers, which exist in numerous libraries of Europe and North America, are, as a rule, notated in the same clefs as in the printed *partitions générales*. Conversely, the splendid manuscript copy *Recueil des symphonies de Mr. de Lully* in the Lobkowitz collection, now in the possession of Národní Muzeum in Prague, shows diverging instrumentation for two *dessus* in g2[3] clefs, one viola in c3 clef (which is musically identical to none of Lully's three inner parts), and bass.

Of the first prints of original suites, George Muffat's *Florilegium primum* and Johann Caspar Ferdinand Fischer's *Journal du Printemps* (both 1695) are scored for a five-part string ensemble and several wind instruments. They contain three viola parts: the first, notated in c1, corresponds to the Italian violetta and should, according to Muffat, be replaced by a violin only when absolutely necessary. The other two violas are notated with c3 for the *taille* and c4 for the *quinte*. This instrumentation, according to Muffat, corresponds to German and Italian practice, but in actuality five-part writing in Venetian opera had been abandoned after Cavalli. Even in France five-part string writing was not always the sole practice, for in 1665 Ballard published *Pièces de violon*, including six movements by Lully for Corneille's *Oedipe*, for four strings, and Charpentier composed *David et Jonathas* (1688) for the same scoring. In Ecorcheville's edition of the *Manuscrit de Cassel*[4] the first four suites and movements 4–7 of the fifth suite show the three inner parts in the same clefs as in Lully, while all the other pieces contain only two inner parts (c1, c3, some movements in suites 15, 16, and 18 have c1 and c2) in an overall four-part orchestra setting. The orchestra suites that come from the French court chapel in Hanover also follow this practice.[5] These orchestral suites are now in the Hessischen Landesbibliothek in Darmstadt (Ms 1227).

[2] See C. Hopkinson, *A Dictionary of Parisian Music Publishers 1700–1950* (London, 1954), p. 14.
[3] Clefs are abbreviated throughout the article as follows: g1=g clef on the lowest line, g2=g clef on the second line, c1=c clef on the first line, c2=c clef on the second line, etc.
[4] J. Ecorcheville, *Vingt suites d'orchestre du XVIIe siècle français* (Berlin/Paris, 1906).
[5] See H. Schneider, 'Unbekannte Handschriften der Hofkapelle in Hannover', in *Aufklärungen: Studien zur deutsch-französischen Musikgeschichte im 18. Jahrhundert*, vol. II, W. Birtel and Chr.-H. Mahling (eds.) (Heidelberg, 1986), pp. 181–4.

The European significance of the French orchestral suite can be gathered from the publications of Amsterdam publishers between 1682 and 1715. All collections appear in printed partbooks; Heus, Pointel, and Roger concentrate primarily on Lully, although they also published some suites of Desmarets, Campra, and Stuck for violin and bass only. The following suites from stage works of Lully appeared in Amsterdam:

Publisher	Stage work	Date	Number of movements
Heus	Cadmus et Hermione	1682	22
Heus	Persée	1682	29
Heus	Phaëton	1683	28
Heus	Amadis	1684	22
Pointel	Amadis	(1687)	22
Pointel	Le triomphe de l'amour[6]	(1687)	32
(Pointel?)	Le temple de la paix	(1687–1700)	18
Pointel	Les fêtes de l'Amour et de Bacchus	(1684–1700)	22
Pointel	Psyché	(1684–1700)	28
Pointel	Cadmus et Hermione	(1684–1700)	20
Pointel	Alceste	(1684–1700)	23
Pointel	Phaëton	(1684–1700)	32
Roger	Phaëton	(1697)	32
Roger	Bellérophon	(1700)	22
Roger	Isis	(1700)	24
Roger	Amadis	(1702)	26
Roger	Cadmus et Hermione	(1702)	22
Roger	Persée	(1702)	29
Roger	Proserpine	(1702)	21
Roger	Le temple de la paix	(1703)	18
Roger	Atys	(1704)	18
Roger	Roland	(1704)	19
Roger	Psyché	(1705)	17
Roger	Acis et Galathée	(1708–12)	22
Roger	Armide	(1708–12)	31
Roger	Alceste	(1709–12)	24

The publication of the suites extends for a period of approximately thirty years, until twenty-five years after Lully's death, but the suites could still be purchased long after this time. As Samuel Pogue observes,[7] Roger's editions could be acquired in Rotterdam, London, Cologne, Berlin, Liège, Leipzig, Halle, Brussels, and Hamburg from his agents there. What alterations to the structure of the music were undertaken and to what extent the original instrumentation was changed will be examined below, thereby critically examining Pogue's statement, 'the firm's music books were carefully edited and beautifully printed from copperplate engravings; they were valued for their quality'.[8] Examples of title-pages are shown in plates 1 (by Pointel) and 2 (by Heus) of the *Amadis* suite. Only the

---

[6] The title-page of this suite also contains an indication of an address for Pointel, 'Au Rosier'.

[7] S. F. Pogue, 'Roger' in *The New Grove Dictionary*, XVI, p. 100.
[8] Ibid., p. 99.

Plate 1. Title-page from the Pointel edition of the *Amadis* suite

first of Roger's publications, the *Phaëton* suite still shows a note pattern in which as many pieces as possible are reproduced in the smallest space possible, thus making the music difficult to read and unclear. From *Bellérophon* onwards the engraving quality, readability, and layout are of an excellent standard, but all of the title-pages are plain and unadorned.

All these Amsterdam suite publications are in a four-part orchestral setting. The original violin part employs a g2 clef and is performed by the *premier dessus*. The original *haute-contre* part is written in the same clef and is taken by the *second dessus*, while the *taille* is the only one of the parts in a c clef (c2, but in the *Proserpine* suite in c3). The *quinte* is lacking, with one exception: in the *taille* of the *Amadis* suite the *quinte* line appears for a single movement, the 'Ouverture' (c3 clef). This *Amadis* suite presents an especially problematic case in other respects. The *premier dessus* and the *taille* parts agree neither in the order of movements nor in the designation of some pieces. The *dessus* part contains twenty-two pieces, but the *taille* lacks the trios (nos. 4, 19, and 20 in the *dessus*) because the lowest voice (which in the original is performed by the inner parts) is entrusted to the bass by a transfer to the lower octave. Added, in comparison to the *dessus*, are a minuet in F major, a gavotte in A major and a *bourée* in G Major,

Plate 2. Title-page from the Heus edition of the *Amadis* suite

as well as the *dessus* and bass part of a 'Variation du Menuet' (= 'Suivons l'amour', LWV 63/12) (example 1). It is to be assumed that both parts of the *Amadis* suite belong to different editions (the *taille* belongs to a later one).

Example 1

The bass part is labeled '*basse continue*' only once, in Roger's *Bellérophon* suite, but its figured bass symbols are lacking as in other printings. If one considers that the number of players for both violins was equal or nearly so, and that the *quinte* is entirely missing, then it becomes clear that the characteristic sound of the French orchestra was abandoned in favor of an approximation of the prevailing

Italian scoring practices. The indications for wind instruments, decisive for the sonority, are sporadic and often contradict Lylly's original scoring. Heus's editions give no indications of the participation of the wind instruments, those of Pointel only through the titles of the pieces, for example, 'air des trompettes'. In seven suites of Roger (*Atys*, *Roland*, *Cadmus et Hermione*, *Isis*, *Le temple de la paix*, *Acis et Galathée*, and *Persée*) there are no winds at all. In the rest of them winds appear only in a few pieces, while in two movements from *Proserpine*, the original oboes are replaced by flutes. *Bellérophon*, *Proserpine*, *Amadis*, and *Psyché* offer occasional indications of instrumentation with trumpets through titles, but usually without specifying the alternation of strings and trumpets in the parts. If the Amsterdam suites were the only sources of Lully's music, we would know nothing about the use of mutes.

Among the general alterations of the original printings we find that Roger,[9] but not Heus and Pointel, replaces 2 and $\mathbb{C}$ with C. This means that Roger's tempo indications, on the basis of the time signatures, are slower than in Lully. This also carries important consequences for the accentuation within the measures and phrases, and leads by a strict interpretation of the indicated meter to a sluggishness that is foreign to the music of Lully. The consequences are especially dramatic when, as in the first 'Air des Sorciers' from *Bellérophon*, in addition to the change of meter from 2 to C the original tempo indication 'vite' is also lacking. In general, one observes that the tempo indications are absent about as often as they are given, and that there are cases such as the *Amadis* suite of Pointel, where only the *taille* part contains the addition of 'vite'. Roger also departs from the original printings in matters of phrasing and the disposition of repeat signs, but the alterations generally appear to be entirely logical and consistent. Especially, both parts of binary movements as well as shorter *préludes* are provided with repeat marks. Pieces in the minor end with *tierces de picardie* in several suites, which is unusual in French printings of the Lully epoch. One surely sees here the influence of Italian music. This influence is noticeable also in the posthumous printing of the *Atys* score in Paris in which the same phenomenon appears. The renaming of many pieces seems problematic, as for example, when 'Vous ne devez plus attendre' from *Amadis* (LWV 63/36, a movement with 6|5+6+4+5+6+4) measures or 'Coeurs accablés' (LWV 63/58, 8|4+6+3 measures) are designated as minuets in spite of a structure that is atypical of the minuet. There is little need to discuss the many other more or less insignificant variants in the reading, articulation, ornamentation, etc., of the Amsterdam suites, because they do not manifest systematic changes that reveal any fixed conception. There are numerous similar well-known examples, also in abundant measure, in the many manuscript scores of Lully's stage works. More interesting are the really decisive interventions, which will be summarized systematically below.

---

[9] Only the suite from *Le temple de la paix* and our music example 8 are exceptions.

1. THE TREATMENT OF THE TRIO MOVEMENTS

In the Amsterdam suites there are several ways of dealing with those trio move-ments in which the original bass part was played by the inner parts. Often the lowest part is assigned to the bass by transposing it down an octave, with the problematic consequence for the sound that the interval between the two *dessus* and the bass becomes as much as two octaves or more. In the 'Prélude' (LWV 63/34) from Roger's *Amadis* suite, this gap is bridged through the inser-tion of a new *taille* part, which often doubles the bass (example 2).

Example 2

The *taille* is inserted more skillfully into 'Vous ne devez plus attendre' (*Amadis* Act II, scene vii), originally a three-part movement for semichorus (example 3).
The duet 'Il est temps que l'amour' from *Proserpine* (LWV 58/11), which Lully

set for two female voices (g1, c1) and continuo, shows how inconsistently the trio movements are treated. In Roger's version, where it is transposed from G to B flat major, the *second dessus*, interestingly, does not play. The *taille* is missing in this movement.[10] The upper part contains a series of variants. Finally, Lully cadences in measure 12 on the supertonic, while in Roger the close in this measure occurs on the secondary dominant to the submediant.

Example 3

Lully

Roger

The treatment of the *taille* in the trio passages of the Chaconne[11] in the *Amadis* suite is not dealt with as consistently by Roger as by Pointel, who routinely transposes the *taille* down an octave to the bass. On the other hand, in the first two trio pieces this part is played in the Roger edition both in the original position and also in the bass at the lower octave. In the remaining trio passages he proceeds as Pointel does (example 4).

In the Chaconne of *Cadmus et Hermione* Lully uses the upper parts plus bass in the first (m. 33) and sixth trio (m. 118) and the *taille* or *quinte* supplies the bass line in the remainder. Roger has the *taille* perform the original bass part in the third trio passage (m. 69) but also inserts a new bass part. In the fourth trio passage (m. 85) both *taille* and bass are practically newly composed. In both cases the contrast between tutti and trio sections is eliminated (example 5).

The instruction in the 1682 printed score of *Persée* 'Les Hautes-Contre & Les Quintes jouent la Basse dans les Triots' is not observed in Roger's *Persée* suite because the bass alone performs the lowest part. On the other hand the bass doubles the *taille* at the lower octave in all trio parts of the Chaconne in the *Phaëton* suite. The instrumentation of the trio pieces in the Passacaille of the *Armide* suite is changed with a thoroughly positive result: Lully specifies two

[10] The *taille* part has come down to us incomplete. It ends with movement no. 17 of the suite.

[11] The bass part of this lengthy chaconne is the

only one of the parts to end with a repeat sign, and even a first ending for the repetition of the entire piece.

Example 4

flutes and *basse continue* for the trio while in Roger the original setting is replaced by a second setting with oboes, bassoons, and continuo in which the lowest part is entrusted to the bass in the lower octave. Finally, the *taille* alone performs the bass part in the corresponding sections in Roger's version of the Chaconne of *Le temple de la paix*.

Example 5

Example 5 (*cont.*)

2. REWORKINGS OF THE AIRS WITH
CONTINUO ACCOMPANIMENT

In the Amsterdam suites the original airs with continuo accompaniment that were especially popular are reworked for the four part string texture. In the process, alterations in the melodic line and, to a greater extent, in the bass line commonly occur. The harmonic interpretation of the melody, which is changed in measures 4 and 5 of 'Que l'amour est doux à suivre' (LWV 58/14), is richer in the Amsterdam suite than in the original (example 6).

Example 6

Example 6 (*cont.*)

In the air 'C'est la saison d'aimer' from *Alceste* (LWV 50/85)[12] the bass is trans-posed down by an octave in the first section. Changes occur in the vocal line that are comparable to improvised ornamentation and there are several part crossings with the *second dessus*, obscuring Lully's melodic line (example 7).

The solo couplets of the chorus 'Suivons Armide' (LWV 71/27), which are accompanied only by *basse continue*, are re-worked in Roger's version into a four-part texture. The dissonant harmonies and progressions that follow here from a faulty *taille* part, however, indicate that this suite would hardly have been per-formed in this version.

Example 7

[12] 'Jeunes coeurs' (LWV 50/31) is also re-worked as a four-part movement.

3 . ALTERATIONS TO FORM AND STRUCTURE

In the movement 'Les Combattants' (LWV 50/41), which Roger labels as a 'Rondeau', a measure is inserted in the refrain that expands the ten-measure phrase to eleven measures (example 8).

Example 8

Lully

Roger

Lully's well-planned harmonic structure:

```
Measure : 3+1 | 1   1   1    1   1   1
Harmony: I  V | I    V  I  V    I V I V I
```

is changed by Roger to:

```
Measure : 3+1 | 1   1   1    1   1   1   1
Harmony: I  V | I    V  I  V    I V I V I V I.
```

Lully's harmonic rhythm, which becomes increasingly more dense right up to the end through the concentration of repetitions of the tonic-dominant progression, is robbed of its effect through the second repetition of the progression.

Also in *Alceste* there is a minuet (LWV 50/14) in the prologue with a ternary form:

```
8+12 | 4+5 | 8+12
a  b  |  c  | a b
```

In Roger the 'a' is left out in the repetition, thereby breaking the symmetry. Moreover, the flute part of the middle section is given to the oboes in this movement.

The editor of the 'Bruit de trompettes' (LWV 58/4) finds a thoroughly acceptable formal solution. The first section, which consists of 1+4 measures (fanfare+antecedent phrase) and 1+6 measures (fanfare+consequent phrase, expanded through a hemiola and the cadence to the dominant), is repeated in the orchestral suite just as is the normally formed (4+4 measures) second section, in contrast with the original, which prescribes no repetitions. In addition the rhythm is sharpened:

Lully: ♩ ♫♫ ♩   Roger: ♩. ♫♫♩

In other *préludes*, as in LWV 58/82 (which Roger labels as an 'Air'), the editor forgoes the repetition of the A portion of the A-B-A form of the original. The instrumental introduction to 'Dans un piège fatal' (LWV 63/29) from *Amadis* is transcribed as a 'Prélude' without the meter change to 3/2 in the first entry of the vocal part, and the whole piece concludes at the second entry of the vocal part. A tempo change to '*vite*' directly after the conclusion of the initial vocal entry mentioned above is new, but musically justifiable.

The examples given for alterations in the structure of single movements show that here, too, significant deliberations were undertaken which led to convincing musical solutions.

4. THE TREATMENT OF FUGATO MOVEMENTS

The reduction of the five-part texture to four parts had the result that, as a rule, in the second section of the overtures the imitative entrance in the fourth part is lacking. This occurs also in the following example from *Armide* (LWV 71/35) in which the tempo indication as well as the indication of 'Sourdines', is absent. As in numerous other suite movements in Roger's publications, new part crossings between second and first *dessus* appear here that are avoided by Lully (example 9).

5. REDUCED SCORING AND RECOMPOSITION

The reduction from five-part to three-part texture is especially striking in the *Armide* suite, where it occurs in the 'Rondeau' and in four *préludes*. Part crossings precipitate extensive changes in the melody of the *Rondeau* (LWV 71/26). The second *dessus* is patched together from portions of the original *haute-contre* and *quinte*. Whereas in Lully the entire *Rondeau* is to be played in the five-part texture, in Roger the refrain is set for four parts and the couplets for three.

A characteristic example of new composition occurs in the last *prélude* from *Armide* (LWV 71/69) in which the five-part string texture is reduced to a trio for two violins and bass. The second *dessus* is entirely new and independent up to measure 9, thereafter it corresponds closely to the original *haute-contre* part.

Example 9

Example 10

Upon examination, however, the second *dessus* is based upon the tenth measure of the *premier dessus*, which again testifies to the skill of the anonymous editor. This movement is among those in which the structure of the Lullian composition is altered in the most thoroughgoing way.

An accumulation of alterations may be observed in the last example, the 'Sommeil d'Atys' (LWV 53/54). The Amsterdam version changes the meter from 2 to ₵, reduces the five-part texture to four parts, and omits the highly expressive sixteenth-note ornament in the *taille* and *haute-contre*, which lent a note of the sinister to the peace of the slumber – together with the slurs, the indication of the mutes for the strings, the flute scoring in the trio movement, and finally the figuring for the thoroughbass instruments.

Example 11

The most important results from this study can be summarized as follows: apparently the rhythmic–metric conception of Lully's music was already misunderstood, outside France, at least, at the beginning of the eighteenth century, as the changes from the 2 and ¢ metric signs to the **C** sign testify. Bach and Handel still notated the slow part of their overtures in the C meter. With the exception of the *Amadis* suite, Roger leaves out the ornamentation that appeared in the original editions. The adaptation of the orchestral texture to the four-part Italian

Example 12

string configuration frequently led to the composition of a new second violin part. The contrast of five-part and three-part textures in the French orchestra is often standardized to the universal four-part style, or, as in Bach, transformed to the contrast of four-part and trio settings, whereby the trio is scored with the *taille* or with the bass, or, as so often the case in the Italian opera until Handel, with both. The general standard of accuracy in regard to the original version is not very high. Also, the indications of the instrumentation are generally quite fragmentary. Because the French orchestra, as a large ensemble with all that implies, was scarcely available anywhere outside Paris, the revision of the suites became a necessity for the publishers in order to make them playable by the commonly available ensembles. For that reason the instrumentation was seen as a secondary consideration, and was therefore not exactly fixed. However, this negligence stands in contrast to the growing interest in instrumental sonorities on the part of composers in France and elsewhere.

We can no longer determine with any certainty who the editors were. The alterations in the pieces were made for differing reasons and led to results of varying quality. The later the suites were edited, the greater were the alterations in the structure. Doubtless, Italian influence on the revisions was significant.

Parnassus revisited: the musical vantage point of Titon du Tillet

JULIE ANNE SADIE

Cineri gloria datur

THE MAN AND HIS MONUMENT

Évrard Titon du Tillet (1677–1762)[1] was a man of culture and intellect who sought above all to win the approbation of his king. When in 1712 he suddenly found himself divested of court connections, he set about solving his predicament in a remarkable way. A man of independent means, he would have been well suited to a life of leisure, given his love of literature and the arts; he spoke several languages fluently and played the bass viol 'passablement'. Instead, he chose to devote himself to the erection of a colossal monument glorifying the departed poets and musicians of the Louis XIV era.[2] Today Titon du Tillet is remembered not so much by the monument as by the anecdotes he published concerning the lives of the poets and musicians he honoured.[3]

Monument-building ran in the Titon family: in 1701 his father, made wealthy by his lucrative appointment as a director general in charge of royal armaments,

[1] The principal biographical sources for Titon du Tillet, in addition to his own writings (see note 3), are:
M. Duboullay, 'Éloge de M. Titon du Tillet (1763)', *Précis analytique des travaux de l'Académie royale de Rouen*, vol. III (1761–70; Rouen, 1817), pp. 256–8;
[Élie Fréron], 'Lettre XII. Mort de M. Titon du Tillet', *L'Année littéraire*, X (1763), pp. 265–77;
Anon., 'Lettre écrite de la Nouvelle-Orléans dans la Louisiane, à M. de la Place, auteur du Mercure à Paris. Par M. F***, sur feu M. Titon du Tillet', *Mercure de France* (May 1764), pp. 54–62 (letter dated 28 August 1763);
Weis, 'Titon de Tillet (Évrard)', *Biographie universelle ancien et moderne*, vol. XLI (Paris, 1865), pp. 608–9;
André Girodie, 'Les Titons, amateurs d'art, et le "Parnasse Français"', *Bulletin de la Société de l'histoire de l'art français* (1928), pp. 60–77;
Judith Colton, *The Parnasse François. Titon du Tillet and the origins of the monument to*

genius (New Haven, 1979).
[2] The principal sources for the iconography associated with the Parnasse François, in addition to Titon's own writings (see note 3), are:
Marc Furcy-Raynaud, *Inventaire des sculptures exécutées au xviiie siècle pour la Direction des Bâtiments du Roi* [Archives de l'art français, n.s. vol. XIV] (Paris, 1927), pp. 235–8;
Gaston Brière, 'Le Parnasse Français', *Beaux-Arts*, VI (1928), pp. 265–8;
'Le Parnasse Français', *Bulletin de la Société de l'histoire de l'art français* (1928), pp. 77–84;
A. P. de Mirimonde, *L'Iconographie musicale sous les Rois Bourbons* vol. I (Paris, 1975), pp. 75–6;
Colton, *The Parnasse François.*
[3] Évrard Titon du Tillet, *Description du Parnasse François* (Paris, 1727);
Le Parnasse François (Paris, 1732); supplements published in 1743 and 1755;
Essais sur les honneurs et sur les monumens accordés aux illustres sçavans pendant la suite des siècles (Paris, 1734);
Description du Parnasse François (Paris, 1760).

Plate 1. Nicolas de Largillière, portrait of Évrard Titon du Tillet, 1736

had presented Louis XIV with an equestrian statue cast in the newly invented medium, cast steel (*acier fondu*); because of its novelty, the statue was given a place in the *petits appartements* of Versailles. Even before then Évrard's older brother, a royal and civic procurator and counsel, had gained popular notoriety by helping to erect royal statues in Paris at Place des Victoires, the Hôtel de Ville and Place de Vendôme. Clearly Titon du Tillet felt that he too must find ways to honour the king who had so generously endowed his family.[4] He effectively abandoned military and legal careers in order to make himself known at court and, still only twenty, he purchased the position of *maître d'hôtel* to the Duchess of Burgundy, with the reasonable expectation that one day she would be queen.[5]

His plans for a literary–musical Parnassus began to take shape. While at court, he consulted Nicolas Boileau Despréaux and Jean-Baptiste Rousseau, among

[4] The family pursuit ultimately cost Titon's great-nephew, Titon de Villotran, his head; he was guillotined on 26 *prairial* of the second year (Girodie, 'Le Titons', p. 77). Titonville, the family mansion in Paris at 31, rue de Montreuil, was ransacked in 1789 (Colton, *The PF*, pp. 17–18; see also plate 10).

[5] Marie-Adelaïde of Savoy was the great-niece of Louis XIV, the wife of his grandson and the mother of Louis XV (whose birth Titon witnessed).

others connected with the royal academies, from whom he hoped to gain support, and in 1708 he commissioned a 7 1/2-foot high bronze model of the monument from the sculptor Louis Garnier. But the measles epidemic of 1712 altered the course of events, taking both the duke and duchess; with them went any hope of royal support for the monument. Titon left Versailles for Paris, purchased the nominal post of *commissaire provincial des guerres* and pursued other avenues of patronage. He lived comfortably in the Faubourg Saint-Antoine and was able to travel extensively in France as well as to Italy, Switzerland, Germany, Holland and England; he amassed a large library and an art collection, in part by commissioning paintings, sculpture and prints, but his heavy losses in the 1720 fall of John Law's Regency banking system meant that he could never realise the Parnasse François at his own expense.[6]

There was an established tradition of Parnassian and Apollonian iconography, with which Titon was familiar, in seventeenth-century Italy and France. He also knew the Félibien descriptions and the Le Pautre engravings of the 1668 *fête* at Versailles (in which Jean-Baptiste Lully took a major role) and Girardon's Versailles sculptures in the Grotto of Thétis, which embody important precedents for the Parnasse François.[7] With this background he designed a neo-Greek sculpture of a mountain on which statuettes, 11 inches to 18 inches tall, were placed at different hierarchical stations around it. Louis XIV appears at the top as Apollo with Pegasus. Eight French poets and one musician (Lully), carefully modelled on genuine likenesses, represent the nine Muses. Three poetesses serve as the Graces, with the people of Paris as the Nymph of the Seine and an assortment of putti portraying genius by means of wings and flames rising from their heads.[8]

The Muses' statuettes represent facets of poetry; in particular, that of Lully, supporting a medallion of Philippe Quinault, symbolizes verse set to music.[9] Other medallions, including those for Elisabeth-Claude Jacquet de la Guerre, Michel-Richard de Lalande and Marin Marais, hang from trees or are supported by the putti. Lully stands at the base of the third side of the monument, a scroll in his right hand, listening intently to the 'concert de Parnasse'. Garnier completed the statuettes in 1718 and three years later they were assembled on the mountain. Confident that royal support would be forthcoming, Titon had two medallions struck: the first displayed his own profile on one side with the Parnasse François on the obverse; the second, an enormous medallion two feet in diameter, commemorated Louis XIV. Early in 1723 he commissioned from

[6] Alfred Cobban, *A History of Modern France*, vol. I (Harmondsworth, 1984), pp. 22–6.
[7] Colton, *The PF*, pp. 65–89.
[8] Colton, *The PF*, pp. 1–11, 58–63, 113–14.
[9] Photographs of the mountain and the statuettes appear in Colton, *The PF*, plates 5–8, 13–25, 43–5, 48; an isolated photo of the Lully statuette is included in Marcelle Benoit, *Versailles et les musiciens du Roi. Étude institutionnelle et sociale (1661–1733)* (Paris, 1971), plate 33. Audran's engraving of 1723, shown in plate 2, presents Lully on Louis XIV's left.

Most of the engravings show Lully to Louis XIV's right, as shown both on the model and in Tardieu's 1730 engraving in plate 3.

It is interesting to note that as early as 1687 Elisabeth-Claude Jacquet [de la Guerre] was proposed as a tenth Muse on Parnassus in an *Epigramme* addressed to her by R. T. S. de Menerville; it is included in her early book of harpsichord pieces and reproduced in facsimile in the Le Pupitre edition of La Guerre's two collections, edited by Carol Henry Bates.

Nicolas de Poilly a painting of the Parnassus, *en grisaille*, after which Jean Audran made an engraving (see plate 2).[10]

Although Titon eagerly hoped to acquire a royal patron, he was obliged to wait until Louis XV came of age. On 30 August 1723, Titon was finally granted an audience with the king, to whom he presented the Poilly painting and an Audran print; the bronze model was refused. If Titon had hoped thus to gain support for the monument, he must have been keenly disappointed, for in his zeal to measure up to his father and brother, he had failed to assess the changes in the political climate at court. The hesitant young king was understandably more interested in inaugurating a new era than in dwelling on the past. Titon was then forced to consider if by acquiring the post of *fermier générale* he might underwrite the expense after all, but a carefully timed gift of a Parnassus print to the philistinic minister of finance proved to be in vain.

Meanwhile, Titon had calculated that at least two million *livres* would be needed to finance the monument. Unbowed, he embarked upon an extended publicity campaign, printing his *Description du Parnasse François* in 1727, commissioning from the *ciseleur* Simon Curé a series of medallions depicting distinguished poets and musicians[11] and distributing them along with the paintings, prints and, occasionally, portraits of himself to lesser and foreign royalty such as Frederick of Prussia, to the academies in Paris and elsewhere, and to influential intellectuals. The *Mercure de France*, the *Journal des scavans* and the Jesuit *Journal de Trévoux* carried many articles referring to the monument.[12] Titon encouraged his many literary friends to write letters of support and laudatory verses, which he then included in his own published works.[13]

Having set all of this in motion, he immersed himself in the task of augmenting and updating the *Description*. The result, produced in 1732, was a handsome folio volume of 660 pages, entitled *Le Parnasse François*,[14] to which he added a new print by Nicolas Henri Tardieu (see plate 3) and several pages of engraved reproductions of the medallions by Louis Crépy which ultimately included at least six that honoured musicians – Lully (see plate 4), La Guerre, Marais, Lalande, Campra, and Destouches. He envisaged, distributed around the monument, scrolls that would be inscribed with the names of the less eminent poets and musicians; he listed their names in the *Parnasse François* and increased their number in subsequent editions. To lend historical perspective to the

---

[10] The painting and the print are reproduced in Colton, *The PF*, plates 26–7 along with later prints commissioned by Titon (see plates 28, 38, 39–40, 42, 46–7); see also Mirimonde, *L'iconographie musicale*, vol. 1, plate 46.

[11] A photograph of the Marais medallion appears in John Huskinson's '"Les ordinaires de la Musique du Roi": Michel de la Barre, Marin Marais et les Hotteterres d'après un tableau du début du xviiie siècle', *Recherches sur la musique française classique*, XVII (1977), p. 22 (fig. 4).

[12] Even after Titon's death Fréron remarked that 'it [the Parnasse François] is widely known,

whether from himself or by the descriptions one encounters in an infinitude of "papiers publiques" and "ouvrages particuliers"' ('Mort', p. 267).

[13] These letters – among them a 'Lettre d'un Habitant du Parnasse à Monsieur Titon du Tillet' – and verses appear primarily in the 1743 supplement and the 1760 *Description*, although verses are also included in the biographical entries of the 1732 *Parnasse François* and its 1755 supplement.

[14] A facsimile edition has been published by Slatkine (Geneva, 1971) that includes the 1743 supplement.

Plate 2. Jean Audran, engraving of the Parnasse François after Nicolas de Poilly, 1723

Plate 3. Nicolas Henri Tardieu, engraving of the Parnasse François, after Jean Audran, 1730 (from *Le Parnasse François*, 1732)

Plate 4. Alexandre Maisonneuve, engraving of the Lully medallion (from the *Description du Parnasse François*, 1760)

project he published a volume of *Essais sur les honneurs et sur les monumens accordés aux illustres sçavans* two years later. Titon commissioned another engraving of the monument from Dominique Sornique. He also ordered a portrait of himself, painted by his friend Nicolas de Largillière in 1736 (see plate 1); it was used for Gilles Edme Petit's engraving the following year.

The appearance of the first chapters of Voltaire's *Siècle de Louis XIV* late in 1739 seems to have rekindled Titon's efforts.[15] He greatly admired Voltaire and was undoubtedly heartened by his efforts to interpret the reign of Louis XIV as one of the high points of civilization.[16] However, their correspondence reveals that they did not see eye to eye on the merits of Rousseau and others already ensconced on Parnassus, not to mention the relevance of creating such a monument.[17] Undaunted, Titon commissioned another painting by Jacques de Lajoüe and in 1757 an engraving by Alexandre Maisonneuve of the Parnassus in a wooded setting, enlarged by a terrace to accommodate the figure of Rousseau (see plate 5).[18] He devoted twenty pages to Rousseau, illustrating the entry (in certain copies) with an engraved portrait by Étienne Desrochers, the only portrait in the 1743 supplement. All the while Titon hoped Voltaire might have a change of heart and agree to the striking of a medallion with his likeness, the first step to Parnassus. Near the end of Titon's life, reconciliation did take place in time for him to commission from Augustin Pajou a statuette of Voltaire, along with those of the departed Rousseau and Prosper de Crébillon; he preferred to waive his cardinal rule for inclusion rather than risk omitting from the Parnasse François the supreme French genius of the era.

As late as 1755, when the second supplement appeared, Titon was still expressing the hope that some way might be found of erecting the monument 'sur une Monticule agréable', whether in Paris or Versailles. He considered the courtyard of the Louvre, the ground separating the Tuilleries and the Champs Élysées (now the Place de la Concorde) and one of the *bosquets* in the gardens of Versailles before rejecting them in favour of the more spacious Étoile, beyond the orange groves, at the far end of the Champs Élysées, now occupied by Napoleon's Arc de Triomphe. There the giant monument, projected as 60 feet high 'en forme Pyramidale', with statues 8–10 feet tall on the four faces and encircled by a reflecting pool 160 feet in circumference, would be visible from all over Paris and the surrounding countryside. Titon envisaged trees and shrubs lining the knoll and surrounding plain, irrigated by waterfalls and canals originating in the central bronze where the nymph would preside over her Castalian fountain.

[15] Titon quotes from Voltaire's earliest version, the *Essai sur le siècle de Louis XIV*, which was suppressed by royal decree (1743: p. 829).

[16] Earlier, in 1732, Titon saluted Charles Perrault, upon whose *Hommes illustres qui ont paru en France ce siècle* (Paris, 1696–1700) he leaned heavily: 'his zeal for the glory of France and for celebrating the reign of Louis XIV was apparent in all of his works, whether in prose or verse' (p. 497).

[17] Colton, *The PF*, pp. 41–2, 161–71. At much the same time (1752) that Titon was suffering at the hands of Voltaire he was receiving the approbation of another historian and pamphleteer, La Font de Saint-Yenne, who wrote that no one had done as much as Titon du Tillet to revive interest in the cultural achievements of the Louis XIV era (see Colton, pp. 43, 105–6; La Font has Colbert's ghost lament the lack of funds for the erection of the Parnasse).

[18] See Marianne Roland Michel, *Lajoüe et l'art rocaille* (Paris, 1984), pp. 25, 198, 343–5.

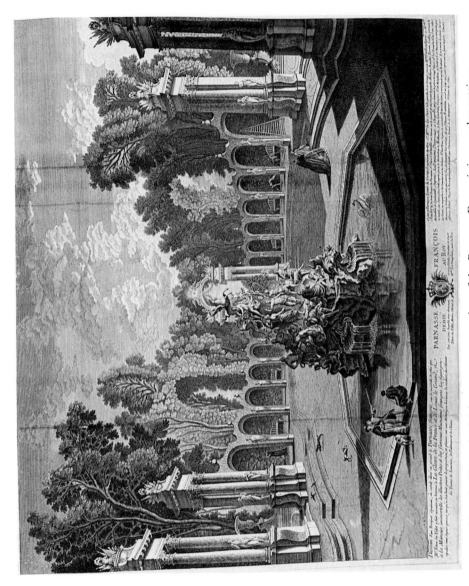

Plate 5. Alexandre Maisonneuve, engraving of the Parnasse François in a garden setting,
after Jacques de Lajoüe

It was to be a place of pilgrimage and inspiration for poets and musicians from all over the world.

Titon was justly anxious about how his work might be continued after his death.[19] Over the years he had nurtured many talented young writers, offering hospitality for extended periods. There had been a steady stream of foreign visitors who, from 1749, called on him to view the bronze in the 'Sallon du Parnasse' at Titonville. But in return for the paintings and prints, medallions and books – the 'présens Parnassiques' – from which he never sought to gain personally, he received letters of congratulations and an array of gold medals, sumptuously bound books and, on one occasion, cinnamon-sugared almonds from a duchess. No one offered financial support for the monument.

The provincial and foreign academies applauded his efforts and his erudition: at least twenty-eight invited him to take up membership. In 1727 he was given a lukewarm reception by the Académie française, in spite of his friendship with a number of well-placed members; according to his nephew, Titon was 'trop philosophe' to prepare the ground properly.[20] Far from offering him membership, their only gesture was the temporary comfort of a *fauteuil d'académicien honoraire* during the meeting he attended, a crumb of respect he nevertheless cherished. He would have been deeply distressed to know that on his death in December 1762 the *Mercure de France* failed to print the customary *éloge* honouring his life, after having publicized his work over the past five decades. Outraged by this snub, an anonymous person, who had been treated kindly by Titon, rectified the situation by writing an open letter to the editor, which was published in the May 1764 issue.[21]

A final volume, a new *Description du Parnasse François*, containing excerpts from the most recent accounts and verses written about Titon and the monument, had appeared in 1760, just two years before his death. When Titon's nephew inherited the model, he fittingly commissioned a final statuette of his uncle. That arranged, he made a last effort to present the model to Louis XV. After decades of indifference, the king acceded, the nephew received a pension and Titon du Tillet's Parnasse François was admitted to the royal art collection in 1766.[22]

Titon always hoped that it might find a permanent home at Versailles in the Salon de la Paix; he even designed a second, complementary monument, a Temple de Victoire (never executed) for the Salon de la Guerre at the opposite end of the Galerie des Glaces. But we can be glad that at the time of the Revolu-

---

[19] Always an optimist, Titon believed that 'il faut toujours vivre dans l'espérance' (1743, p. 684); certainly he would have viewed with interest and pleasure the appearance of Claude-François Lambert's *Histoire littéraire du règne de Louis XIV* in 1751 and Pierre-Louis d'Aquin de Château-Lyon's *Siècle Littéraire de Louis XV, ou lettres sur les hommes célèbres* in 1753. D'Aquin, however, clearly distanced himself from Titon in his opening remarks (I/x), believing that enough had been written about the dead and that it was time to acknowledge the achievements of the living, the true 'ornament and glory of the nation'; elsewhere he makes reference to the *Parnasse François* (I/51).

[20] Brière, *Beaux-Arts*, p. 268.

[21] See note 1.

[22] See André Linzeler, 'L'Entrée du Parnasse Français [*sic*] à la Bibliothèque Royale', *Bulletin de la Société de l'histoire de l'art français* (1929), pp. 151–3.

tion the bronze had been removed to the relative safety of the Bibliothèque du Roi in the Rue du Richelieu where it was exhibited at the entrance to the Galerie Mazarine until 1926. When Versailles was restored, the bronze was returned where it can be seen today in the Galerie des Grands Ecuries.

THE MONUMENT *EN PROSE*

Although Titon wrote his books to publicize the monument, he was very much aware that the lives of many French poets and all musicians, excepting only Lully's, had never before been surveyed.[23] In the 1727 *Description* he accords seven musicians biographical entries, rewriting them for inclusion in the 1732 *Parnasse François*. To these he adds two dozen single and group entries on musicians recently deceased, mentioning numerous distinguished royal and aristocratic amateurs and listing the members of a hypothetical 'Orchestre de Parnasse'.[24] In the 1743 supplement of just over one hundred pages (thereafter bound with copies of the 1732 edition and numbered continuously), Titon devotes nine entries to musicians, among them François Couperin, though even more are referred to in the section devoted to actors and actresses of the Comédie and the Opéra: these were singers, among whom Marthe Le Rochois is treated at length. The 1755 supplement includes over a dozen entries on musicians, important among them André Campra and Louis-Nicolas Clérambault. For Jean-Philippe Rameau, as for Voltaire, Titon was by this time prepared to amend his rules. Although Rameau was to outlive Titon by two years, a medal honouring him was ordered to be struck and a place found on Parnassus.[25] For all his effusive praise of Lully, his taste had, to a certain extent, moved with the times so that by 1760 he could describe Rameau as 'the wisest and most brilliant of celebrated musicians, living or dead', a sentiment echoing those of Voltaire and D'Aquin.[26]

In choosing his Parnassians Titon knew that he would never please everyone and, inevitably, he received petitions from poets' and musicians' relatives and friends. Those of less importance would be accommodated among the amateurs, on a scroll or along the alleys extending in all directions from the 'rond de l'Étoile', according to the merits of his or her talents. Titon modestly positioned himself 'au rang des admirateurs', where he could seek out those responsible for

---

[23] Charles Bouvet, one of the first music historians to realize the value of Titon's work, published two articles:
'A propos de l'Arc de Triomphe de l'Etoile (Titon du Tillet)', *Bulletin de la Société historique et archéologique des viiie et xviie arrondissements de Paris*, n.s., II (1921), pp. 81–90;
'Titon du Tillet, 1677–1762', *Bulletin de la Société historique et archéologique des viiie et xviie arrondissements de Paris*, n.s., II (1922), pp. 163–78.
[24] 1732: pp. 43–4; Titon elaborated on the 'Orchestre de Parnasse' in 1743: pp. 674–7

and 1760: II/16.
[25] In Titon's entry on the librettist Pellegrin (1755: p. 25) he expresses the hope that Rameau and François Colin de Blamont will delay the moment when they take their places on Parnassus.
[26] 1760: I/47–8; Voltaire (*Le siècle de Louis XIV*, vol. II (Berlin, 1751), p. 295) wrote that Rameau enchanted the ears and Lully the spirit, but the profundity of Rameau's harmony elevated him above all others; D'Aquin (*Siècle littéraire*, I/iii–iv, 20, 51–88) devoted an entire chapter to Rameau.

the most significant achievements of the era, which ultimately encompassed most of the *ancien régime*.

Titon's love of books equalled his passion for works of art. He was familiar with the writings and some of the music of most of those about whom he wrote. His knowledge of French printers, including the Ballards, and contemporary editions was formidable. He was a careful reader of journals, the *Mercure de France* and his friend Élie Fréron's *Année littéraire*, whence he collected obituaries. Sometimes he quoted from them, sometimes he summarized. Whenever appropriate he included *éloges en vers* in the biographical entries and, increasingly with an eye towards his own immortality, the verses referring to Parnassus and to himself. In Lully's 1732 entry we find mention of Couperin's extended programmatic chamber piece, the *Apothéose . . . de Lulli* (1725), which is set in the Elysian Fields and on Parnassus.[27]

Not only does Titon present the reader with a 'list of authors and books from which I have taken the greatest part of the memoirs' at the beginning of the 1732 edition;[28] he also includes bibliographies in the entries themselves, particularly those of the poets. These contain references not only to volumes of obituaries[29] and lexicographical works,[30] but also to collections of verse, memoirs and monographs. His entries on poetesses make reference to a particularly rich biographical literature.[31] For the musicians there were no reference works and few printed texts to rely upon; Titon himself produced the first, followed by D'Aquin and Ancelet, whose *Observations sur la musique, les musiciens et les instrumens* was published in Amsterdam in 1757.

The coverage of musicians in the *Parnasse François* varies in length from a few lines to several pages, depending on the availability of sources. Lully is accorded nine folio pages, Lalande five, Marais three-and-a-half; each is based on different source materials. In Lully's case, Titon relies upon popular anecdotes and a Ballard catalogue, avoiding any reference to the criticisms of Guichard, La Fontaine and Saint-Évremond.[32] For Lalande, Titon turned to the *Mercure* obituary and the writings of Alexandre Tannevot and François Colin de Blamont in the posthumous 1729 edition of Lalande's *grand motets*. Nevertheless, Titon's years at court enabled him to witness and later to report occasions like the departure of the Duke of Anjou (Louis XIV's grandson) for Spain in 1700, when Louis XIV

[27] Couperin had already published, in 1724, the *Parnasse ou l'Apothéose de Corelli*; other composers were composing Parnassic works, among them Blamont, who in 1729 produced a *pastiche* entitled *Ballet du Parnasse* (performed on the Cour de Marbre at Versailles to celebrate the birth of the dauphin), Campra, whose 1735 opera *Achille et Déidamie* begins with a prologue set on Parnassus, and Mondonville, whose *ballet-héroïque* of 1749 is entitled *Le carnaval du Parnasse* (text by Fuzelier).

[28] 1732: pp. 93–8.

[29] Titon consulted collections of *éloges* by Scevole de Sainte Marthe (1633), Perrault (1696 and 1700), Baillet (1723), and Teissier (1715).

[30] His primary lexicographical tools were the monumental Moreri *Dictionnaire* (1725), Bayle's *Dictionnaire historique et critique* (1720), and the Pellisson/Olivet *Histoire de l'Académie Française* (1730).

[31] For his many entries on poetesses, Titon consulted Hilarion de Coste's *Les éloges et vies des reynes, princesses, dames et damoiselles* [sic] *illustres* (1630), Abbé Ménage's *Histoire de la vie des Dames Philosophes* (1693), Guyonet de Vertron's *La Nouvelle Pandore, ou les femmes illustres du siècle de Louis le Grand* (1698), and Brantome's *Vies des Dames galantes* (1710).

[32] See Robert M. Isherwood, *Music in the Service of the King* (Ithaca, 1973), pp. 201–2, 242–4.

and his court were reduced to tears by the beauty of a Lalande motet, *Beati omnes* (1698). For Marais, Titon appears to have drawn almost exclusively on personal knowledge: the character and uniqueness of the anecdotes – such as the occasion on which Marais eavesdropped on Sainte Colombe, practising his viol in a tree house – are too intimate to be other than from a friend. In 1709 Titon would probably have had a hand in organizing the subsequent performance *chez* les Bourgognes of a concert of *pièces de violes* given before the king by four of Marais's twenty children, three playing and the fourth turning pages.[33]

Titon lacked printed sources for many of his contemporaries. To rectify this he sought the assistance of the relatives and friends of the persons concerned, many of whom were already among his acquaintances. Thus he gained access to unpublished music in the hands of the relatives of Charpentier, Marais, Marchand, Bernier, Moreau, Royer, and Calvière. He expressed his hope that some of these works might soon be engraved, and from time to time he contemplated publishing the manuscript poems and music of the inhabitants of his Parnassus in a series of volumes under the title 'Concerts du Parnasse'.[34]

Ever the raconteur, Titon particularly relished the opportunity to include hitherto unpublished anecdotes. These remain the greatest strength of the *Parnasse François*. Often he was writing about departed friends:[35] the poets Rousseau, Lainez (whose name, Titon advises, is pronounced 'Laisne')[36] and Marie de Louvencourt, and the musicians Dandrieu and Marais. He and Rousseau became acquainted at Fontainebleau in the autumn of 1703; Titon fondly recalled the occasions on which they were serenaded while they dined by Marie Chappe, Jeanne Moreau and Louise Couperin – 'Syrennes & Virtuoses de la Musique de Roi'. He found Lainez a delightful companion at table and in conversation, and marvelled how he was always at work in the Bibliothèque du Roi by 8 am! He considered Mlle Louvencourt (who wrote cantata texts for Clérambault, sang and played the theorbo) one of the most accomplished women of her day. He actually called Dandrieu his friend and dared to compare his music with that of Couperin. The detail with which he reported on the last years of Marais's life, mentioning where he retired and how he occupied himself with gardening and occasional teaching in the centre of Paris, betokens a long-standing friendship, probably based on Titon's own interest in viol playing.

Many of Titon's anecdotes inevitably involve royal patronage. The Lalande entry is particularly well stocked in this regard, although the important anecdotes originate elsewhere.[37] Bernier, having been appointed *maître de musique* at the Sainte Chapelle by the regent, the Duke of Orléans, was denied the usual lodgings because he was married (to a daughter of Marais); the duke averted the

---

[33] The duke's *maître de musique* was Jean Matho (1755: p. 34).

[34] 1732: pp. 550, 562–3, 649; 1743: p. 831.

[35] Titon counted among his *convives* (companions at table) the poets Lainez, Fontenelle, Rousseau, Vanière, and Abbé des Fontaines.

[36] In his biographical entry on Lainez, Voltaire (*Le Siècle de Louis XIV*, vol. II (Paris, 1966), p. 238) makes reference to 'a man who had

taken the trouble and expense to erect a bronze of his own design, covered in statues *en relief* of poets and musicians', without naming Titon.

[37] 1732: pp. 613–14; see Norbert Dufourcq, *Notes et références pour servir à une histoire de Michel Richard Delalande (1657–1726)* (Paris, 1957).

crisis by transferring Bernier to the Chapelle du Roi. Among the most entertain-
ing anecdotes is the vivid account of Lully's acquisition of a position as *secrétaire
du roi* in 1681: Lully took advantage of a propitious moment, after his successful
appearance in *Le bourgeois gentilhomme* at Saint-Germain-en-Laye, to petition the
king to make him a *secrétaire*. Louis XIV, characteristically charmed by an act of
audacity, gave his approval. The other *secrétaires*, led by the Marquis of Louvois,
disputed the appointment, but were mocked by Lully, who was secure in the
king's grace. The ceremony took place without incident and the other *secrétaires*
(in their long black coats and beaver hats) were Lully's guests at a banquet and a
performance of *Le triomphe de l'amour*.[38]

For all the favours bestowed upon musicians, Louis XIV could also mete out
discipline, particularly in matters of morality. Desmarets fell foul of the king
in this regard. According to Titon (whose source was Destouches), Lully had
thwarted an early attempt by Desmarets to go abroad to study the Italian style by
convincing the king that Desmarets had too fine a command of the French style
to risk outside influences. Swayed by Lully's argument, the king ordered him to
remain in France. In 1699 the restless Desmarets, who was by then a widower,
was condemned to death for eloping with a young girl. He escaped with her to
Brussels, and from there to Spain where, thanks to the intercession of the Duke
of Burgundy, he served the new king, ending up in the service of the Duke of
Lorraine. After several years Desmarets's friends attempted to get him reinstated
at Versailles by performing his music anonymously at the king's mass. The king
had not heard his music for many years, but recognized it at once. In spite of his
friends' pleas – Jean Matho's in particular – the king was adamant; the regent,
however, granted Desmarets a pardon in 1722.[39]

To perform at an *appartement* or *chez* Madame de Maintenon usually meant
royal acknowledgement, money, and position.[40] When the fifteen-year-old
Elisabeth-Claude Jacquet played for the king, she was made a ward of Madame
de Montespan so that she might regularly entertain the king and members of the
court. Titon recounts a rags-to-riches tale of one enterprising provincial musician, Jean-Baptiste Moreau, who managed to gain *entrée* into the highest reaches
of court society by insinuating himself at the *toilette* of the dauphine, whom he
took 'par la manche' and then sang an air. When news of the incident reached the
king, he demanded first that Moreau should perform for him two days later and
that he compose music for a *divertissement* at Marly in two months' time. Titon's
own distaste for such unorthodox behaviour is evident from his approving
remarks about another provincial musician, the composer and viol player Salo-

---

[38] The scenario of the anecdote – Lully's elevation, the patronage of a god-like figure, dis-
sent among Lully's contemporaries, divine
intercession or pardon, celebration and reconciliation – has certain parallels in the satirical essay of Nodot (MS, F-Pa, 1687; reproduced in 'Le triomphe de Lully aux
Champs-Elysées', *La Revue musicale*, VI/2
(1925), pp. 89–106) and in the narrative of
Couperin's *Concert instrumental sous le titre*

*d'Apothéose composé à la mémoire immortelle de
l'incomparable Monsieur de Lulli* (1725).
[39] 1743: pp. 755–8; for a fuller account, see
James R. Anthony, 'Desmarets, Henry', *The
New Grove Dictionary of Music and Musicians*,
vol. V (London, 1980), pp. 390–2.
[40] 1732: pp. 615 (Lalande's daughters), 627
(Marais's sons); 1743: pp. 665 (Couperin's
daughter), 796 (Marie Antier); 1755: p. 57
(Clérambault).

mon: 'He hadn't at all the air of a *petit-maître* or of those musicians who attend the ladies' *toilettes* and the gentlemens' *levers* in order to gain support for their works'.

In Destouches' entry and elsewhere, Titon digresses with varying degrees of authority on the French reception of Italian music. The king, he says, took little pleasure in the sonatas performed by Italian violinists, though other writers report that at this time he enjoyed the performances of Italian music when given by French string players.[41] Titon unhesitatingly proclaims Lambert the first singer in France to popularize solo vocal music – so perfect was his intonation, so elegant his expression and so thrilling his ornamented *reprises* – though were it not for his teacher, Pierre de Nyert, Lambert would never have gained a command of the Italian style.[42]

Without wishing to distance himself from the followers of Lully, Titon makes clear his own interest and enjoyment of Italian music, acquired in 1719 while travelling in Italy and since pursued in Paris at the *hôtels* of Messieurs Crozat, Gaudion and Duhallay, and at the 'théâtres d'opéra'.[43] He recalls with great pleasure an evening of chamber music in 1742 at Fontainebleau *chez* Madame and Mlle Duhallay (excellent harpsichordists themselves) in which the French violinists Guignon and Canavas performed with Geminiani; Canavas *l'aîné* played the cello and the Prince of Ardore, Ambassador of the King of the Two Sicilies, the harpsichord.[44]

Other Italian musicians Titon claims to have heard include the violinists Vivaldi and Somis, the cellists Bononcini, Perroni, and Stuck, and the singers Bernacchi, Farinelli, Faustina, and Cuzzoni. He credits the Duke of Orléans, the Count of Toulouse, and the financier Pierre Crozat with importing Italian musicians to join the violinists Anet and Duval and the bass players Forqueray, Marchand, and La Ferté, who were already performing Italian music in Paris. Titon cites other French musicians known for their command of the Italian style, among them the violinist Quentin, the flautist Blavet, the viol players Roland Marais and Caix d'Hervelois and the harpsichordists Rameau, Daquin, and Duphly. The main difference Titon notes between French and Italian musicians was that, with the exception of Stuck, the Italians never performed French music.

Titon believed, as Le Cerf did, that the Italians could learn from the success of French opera, 'le grand chef-d'oeuvre de la musique', observing that one went away from an Italian opera feeling content but 'grave & pensif', whereas after a French opera one could smile and feel satisfied.[45] Of the Italians, he particularly admired the way that Corelli, Gasparini,[46] Scarlatti, and Tartini – including among them Handel and Le Clerc (presumably Jean-Marie Leclair *l'aîné*) –

[41] See the November 1701 and 1703 issues of the *Mercure galant*.
[42] 1732: pp. 221, 280.
[43] 1743: pp. 677, 755n, liii; 1755: pp. 47–8, 55; see also 1755: p. 39.
[44] 1743: p. 755n; for the Duke of Luynes's account of the evening (22 April 1742), see Dufourcq, *La musique à la cour de Louis XIV et*

de Louis XV d'après les mémoires de Sourches et Luynes, 1681–1758 (Paris, 1970), p. 74.
[45] 1743: p. 756n.
[46] See 1732: p. 396, in which Titon enthuses about his Italian sojourn and, in particular, the performances he attended of Gasparini's *Bajazet*.

avoided 'barbarisms', 'the crags and precipices of the Alps and the Apennines'. Not surprisingly, his favourite French composers were Lully, Campra, Destouches, Lalande, Couperin, and Rameau, the last of whom he admits is 'un peu Italienisé'.

Though his own taste had modified with the times, Titon continued to call Lully 'le Prince des Musiciens', the Italian father of 'la belle musique française'. That his airs were enduring was evident from the way people sang them in the palaces, bourgeois homes and in the street: Titon relates a charming anecdote about Lully's stopping his carriage on the Pont Neuf and elsewhere to instruct itinerant singers and violinists on the proper tempos for his airs.

Many of the musicians entered in the *Parnasse François* owe their places to their connections with Lully. His best pupils, Collasse and Lalouette,[47] were employed to complete the inner parts of his scores and Marais – whom Lully highly esteemed – 'pour battre la mesure' at performances of his operas and other works. Gatti immigrated to France after hearing extracts of Lully's operas in Florence, taking up a place among the *basses de violons* in the Académie Royale de Musique. The harpsichordist Mlle Certain was an 'amie de Lully', known for her immaculate performances of symphonies from Lully's operas. Titon repeats Tannevot's bitter anecdote about Lully's dashing Lalande's aspirations to be an Académie violinist.[48] Cambert preferred exile in England to humiliation by Lully, while Lambert had the dubious honour of being buried in the same tomb as his son-in-law.

Throughout his writings, Titon takes an interest in the circumstances surrounding the deaths of his designated poets and musicians. Lully is quoted on his deathbed; the oboist Du Noyers died in 1720 when an artery was severed during a 'precautionary bleeding';[49] Pierre Gautier, whom Titon describes as Lully's contemporary, drowned when his ship sank in sight of port. Titon appears to have attended the extraordinary memorial service for Mlle Le Rochois, in November 1728, which took place at Notre Dame des Victoires: the church was filled to capacity and the Académie orchestra, led by Campra, was ready to begin when they were interrupted by a messenger from the Archbishop of Paris, informing them that permission for the service had been withheld; everyone was obliged to quit the tribune and crowd into the chapel (where Lully is entombed) to hear a *De profundis* sung in *fauxbourdon*.

Because Titon was seeking above all to publicize the proposed monument, he wrote neither a history[50] nor a comprehensive dictionary of French poets and musicians. He scrupulously documented his articles: his aural sources, as we have seen, generally emerge within the text. He made claims in good faith which have since been qualified or disproved; nevertheless, for many of the slighter figures he remains the only source. He preferred to ignore the seamier side of the

---

[47] 1732: p. 628; Titon makes no mention of Lully's dismissal of Lalouette for having boasted of composing the best bits of *Isis* (1677); see William Hays and Eric Mulard, 'Lallouette [*sic*], Jean', The *New Grove Dictionary*, vol. x, p. 386.

[48] 1732: pp. 612–13; Dufourcq, *Notes et références*, p. 149.
[49] 1743: p. 675n.
[50] However, at the end of the 1743 supplement, Titon does offer a survey of music from ancient times to the present (pp. xvi–liii).

lives like those of Louis Marchand and Antoine Forqueray (if he was even aware of such things) and to concentrate instead on the qualities that made them worthy of places on Parnassus.[51] Indeed, he speaks with admiration of Marchand's triumph over the injury of his left arm in about 1725, amazing everyone with his performances using only his right hand and the pedals.

It was not Titon's intention to be comprehensive, though he did attempt to be chronological. Some musicians, Charpentier in particular, are given extremely short shrift.[52] Occasionally several musicians are crowded into a single entry because, the aging Titon confesses, he did not know enough, or have sufficient energy to gather information for separate treatment; the index (see appendix) reveals how many are tucked away in other people's entries. Treatises on singing and playing, like those of Montéclair and Couperin, are not mentioned; in fact, Titon seems entirely to have dissociated theory from practice in his deliberations.

Although La Guerre is the only *musicienne* to be allocated a medallion and a separate entry, we learn that several eminent poetesses were also accomplished musicians, among them Marie de Louvencourt and Elisabeth-Sophie Chéron.[53] The musical attainments of some women, such as Mlle Marais and Marguerite-Antoinette Couperin, are mentioned in their fathers' entries while others appear in their husbands'; singers, comedians and dancers, male and female, are surveyed in the 1743 supplement. The collective article on lady harpsichordists is appended to La Guerre's entry.[54]

Titon's penchant for anecdote and deftness at the thumbnail sketch endear him to scholars of French music in search of the human face of a composer. Charpentier seemed to him to be 'one of the wisest and most hard-working musicians of his time', whose music, when performed, always succeeded. Equally interesting are his many revelations about who knew whom and, very often, when. His own pursuit of the viol lends weight to the many references to viol players. His familiarity with the theatre and opera houses is everywhere evident; the enthusiastic description of the tempest scene in Marais's *Alcione* offers but one example. Titon's observation that Couperin's chamber music was known throughout France and abroad reflects the wider realm he claims to have experienced. He identifies one of Couperin's lost cantatas, *Ariane abandonnée par Thésée*, not in Couperin's entry but in that of its librettist, Antoine La Fosse; a number of other works – Pierre Robert's *Pièces de symphonie en partition*, Marais's *Concerts de violon & de viole* for the Elector of Bavaria and Montéclair's *Messe de Requiem* – are known to have existed only through Titon's references.

---

[51] Titon rarely indulges in criticism, though he does admit that Destouches' songs can become a little monotonous (1755: p. 56).

[52] Benoit (*Versailles*, p. 395) decries Titon's neglect of Charpentier and the fact that a medal was never struck in his honour. Patricia Ranum ('A Sweet Servitude. A Musician's Life at the Court of Mlle de Guise', *Early Music*, xv/3 (1987), p. 357, n8) suggests that Titon may have based the Charpentier entry on conversations with Thomas Corneille,

Charpentier's collaborator at the Comédie Française and the brother of Titon's close friend Pierre Corneille.

[53] Chéron's self-portrait, in which she holds music of her own composition, hangs in the Musée Magnin, Dijon.

[54] 1732: pp. 626–7; see the author's essay, '*Musiciennes* of the Ancien Régime', in Jane Bowers and Judith Tick (eds.), *Women Making Music* (Urbana, 1986), p. 191.

Fréron affectionately sums up in verse Titon's untiring commitment to honouring the genius of the poets and musicians of his era and thereby ensuring his own immortality:

PARNASSE

TITON, par des travaux solides & durables,
Tes mains ont consacré les talens honorables;
Ton Parnasse François sur le bronze exalté,
Faisant passer ta gloire à la posterité,
Parmi tant de Héros, enfans de l'harmonie,
Présentera ton zèle ainsi que leur génie.[55]

[55] 'TITON, by sound and enduring works,/Your hands have consecrated honorable talents;/ Your Parnasse François extolled in bronze,/ Enabling your glory to pass into posterity,/ Among so many heroes, harmony's children,/ Will represent your zeal as well as their genius.' 'Lettre x', *L'Année littéraire*, VII (1755), p. 217, quoted by Titon in 1760: II/23.

An index of the musicians mentioned in the Parnassian works of Titon du Tillet

COMPILED BY
JULIE ANNE SADIE

GUIDE TO THE INDEX

1.a. Only musicians of the late sixteenth to the eighteenth centuries are indexed. References to musicians in the Scriptures or antiquity – Moses, David, Solomon, Orpheus, Homer, Sapho, Anacreon, etc. – are *not* indexed; Titon refers to them in his 'Remarques sur la musique' (1743: pp. xvi–xxviii). Similarly, early musical kings of France – among them Charlemagne, Louis VII and Charles VI – are omitted; they are mentioned in the 'Remarques sur la poesie et la musique françoises et sur nos spectacles' (1743: pp. xxix–liii).

b. The labels – amateur, violinist, composer – reflect the emphasis Titon himself placed on the entrants' musical attainment.

2. Names are entered in a standard modern spelling. In the course of the supplements, Titon employs more than one spelling for many names as well as soubriquets – usually first names; these are placed in square brackets in the main entries and cross-referred.

3. Titon's successive publications are identified by their year of publication:
   1727 – *Description du Parnasse François*
   1732 – *Le Parnasse François*
   1743 – *Suite du Parnasse François*
   1755 – *Second supplément du Parnasse François*
   1760 – *Description du Parnasse François*

4.a. Page numbers are often followed by parenthesized names: these identify the entry in which the reference appears.

b. Page numbers in italics indicate main entries in Titon's works.

c. References to footnotes are indicated by 'n'.

5. The 1732, 1743 and 1760 publications contain more than one series of pagination.

a. Two systems are used for the medallions: the Crépy engravings are in capitalized Roman numerals (I–XIII), the Maisonneuve in Arabic numbers ('1–3'), which are inserted in copies of the 1732 and 1760 publications.

b. Pages 833–8 of the 1743 supplement are *not* numbered; references to those pages are given in square brackets.

c. The historical essays at the end of the 1743 supplement are paginated in lower-case Roman numerals.

d. The two pages of the 'liste chronologique' of the 1755 supplement are not numbered.

e. The 1760 *Description* is the most complicated, with three series of pagination, in addition to those of the engravings: for the preliminary section, the 'Première Partie' (I) and the 'Seconde Partie' (II).

Adélaïde de France – royal amateur
  1760: 33
Alarius: *see* Verloge, Hilaire
Alessandro [Prince of Ardore, Ambassador
    to the King of the Two Sicilies in France]
    – harpsichordist
  1743: 755–6n (Desmarets)
Anet, Jean Baptiste [Batiste, Baptiste] –
    violinist
  1732: 43, 396 (Lully)
  1743: 756n (Desmarets)
  1760: II/16
Antier, Marie – singer
  1732: 43
  1743: *796–8*
  1760: II/16
Antonio: *see* Guido, Giovanni Antonio
Aubert, Jacques – violinist
  1755: 68 (Fuselier)
  1760: 27
Aubigny [Maupin], Mlle d' – singer
  1732: 43
  1743: 795
  1760: II/16
Babelon, Claude – trumpeter and drummer
  1743: 675
Baïf, Jean Antoine – amateur
  1732: 136, 138, 148, *159–61*, 162, 174,
    192
  1743: xlii–xliii
Balthazarini: *see* Beaujoyeulx [Beau-Joyeux],
    Baltazar de
Baptiste: *see* Anet, Jean Baptiste
Barbarini – female singer
  1743: 756n (Desmarets)
Batiste: *see* Anet, Jean Baptiste
Batistin: *see* Stuck [Stuk], Jean-Baptiste
Baumavielle [Beaumaviel] – opera actor
  1732: 43, 395 (Lully)
  1743: 797
  1760: II/15
Beaujoyeulx [Beau-Joyeux], Baltazar
    [Balthazarini] de – musical director
  1743: xlii

(?)Beaupère [La Plante, Mme de], Jacqueline
    – harpsichordist
  1732: 40, *636–7*
  1743: 675n
  1760: 33
Belleville *le cadet*, J. – bassoonist
  1732: 43
  1760: II/16
Bernachi [Bernacchi], Antonio Maria –
    castrato
  1743: 755n (Desmarets)
Bernier, Nicolas – composer
  1732: 627 (Marais)
  1743: 676, *678–80*, 828n
  1755: 67 (Fuselier)
  1760: 27
Bertin, de la Dové, Thomas – composer
  1755: Liste chronologique, 24 (Pellegrin), *84*
  1760: 27
Besozzi, Alessandro – oboist
  1743: 755n (Desmarets)
Besozzi, Antonio – oboist
  1743: 755n (Desmarets)
Blamont, François Colin de – composer
  1732: 616 (Lalande)
  1743: 705n (Mouret)
  1755: 25 (Pellegrin), 68 (Fuselier)
Blavet, Michel – flautist
  1732: 44
  1743: 756n (Desmarets)
  1755: 83 (La Barre)
  1760: II/16
Blois, Mlle de [Françoise Marie de Bourbon
    Duchess of Orleans] – royal amateur
  1732: 613 (Lalande)
Boësset, Jean-Baptiste – composer
  1732: 366 (Mme de Villedieu), 392
    (Lambert)
  1743: li
Boësset *le fils* – composer
  1732: 392 (Lambert)
Boismortier, Joseph Bodin de – composer
  1755: 75–6 (La Bruere)
  1760: 27

Boivin [Boyvin], Jacques – organist
1727: 222
1732: *401, 404*
1743: 674, lii
Bononcini, Giovanni – cellist
1743: 755n (Desmarets)
Boquet [Bocquet], Charles – lutenist
1732: 405 (the Gaultiers)
Bordoni, Faustina – singer
1743: 755n (Desmarets)
Borosini, Francesco – singer
1743: 755n (Desmarets)
Bourgeois, Thomas-Louis – composer
1743: 670 (Louvencourt)
1755: Liste chronologique, *59*, 68
(Fuselier)
1760: 27
Bousset, Jean Baptiste Drouard de – composer
1732: 38, *603–5*
1743: 671 (Rochebrune)
1760: 27
Bouvard, François – composer
1755: 84 (Bertin)
Brassc, Marquis de: *see* Brissac, Charles
Timoléon Louis de Cossé, Duke of
Brissac [Brassc, Marquis de], Charles
Timoléon Louis de Cossé, Duke of –
amateur
1760: 32–3
Broschi [Farinelli], Carlo – castrato
1743: 755n (Desmarets)
Brossard, Sébastien de – scholar
1732: 39, *652–3*
1760: 27
Buononcini: *see* Bononcini, Giovanni
Caix ?d'Hervelois, Louis de – viol player
1743: 756n (Desmarets)
Calvière, Guillaume-Antoine – organist
1755: Liste chronologique, *79–80*
1760: 27, ɪɪ/16
Cambert, Robert – composer
1727: 224 (Lully)
1732: 38, 385 (Perrin), *387–8*,
395 (Lully)
1743: xlix, l, li, lii
1760: 27
Campra, André – composer
1732: 26, xi (medallion)
1743: 676, 704 and 705n (Mouret), 756n
and 759 (Desmarets), 790 and 793 (Le
Rochois), lxviii
1755: *19–21*, 26 (Pellegrin), 43 (Danchet),
54 (Destouches), 68 (Fuselier)
1760: 22, 48, xi (medallion), ɪɪ/15, 45, 53
Canavas *l'aîné*, Jean-Baptiste – cellist
1743: 755n (Desmarets)

Canavas *le cadet*, Joseph – violinist
1743: 755n (Desmarets)
Canavas – female singer
1743: 756n (Desmarets)
Carissimi, Giacomo – composer
1727: 144 (Charpentier)
1732: 490 (Charpentier)
Cavalieri, Emilio de' – composer
1743: xliii n
Certain [Certin], Marie Françoise –
harpsichordist
1732: 40, *636–7*
1743: 675n
1760: 33
Chambonnières, Jacques Champion de –
organist
1732: 38, *401–2*, 637 (Certin)
1743: 674, lii
1760: 27
Chanlo, Mme de – singer
1727: 222 (Lambert)
1732: 391 (Lambert)
Chaperon, François – organist
1732: 612 (Lalande)
Chappe [Chape], Marie – singer
1743: 734 (Rousseau)
1760: 33
Charles IX – royal amateur
1743: xlii
Charpentier, Marc-Antoine – composer
1727: 11, 43, 94, *144–6*
1732: 38, 381 (Th. Corneille), *490–1*
1743: 678 (Bernier), 828n
1755: 19 (Campra)
1760: 27
Chassé [Chassée] – singer
1743: 800
1760: ɪɪ/15–16
Chatillon – violinist
1732: 43
1760: ɪɪ/16
Chéron le Hay, Elisabeth-Sophie – amateur
1727: 94, *148–50*
1732: 459 (Mme des Houlières), *540–1*,
634–5 (Boutard)
1760: 25
Chevalier, Mlle: *see* Fesch, Marie-Jeanne
Clérambault [Clairambault], Louis-Nicolas
– organist
1743: 663 (Moreau), 670 (Louvencourt),
671 (Rochebrune), 680 (Bernier)
1755: Liste chronologique, 57
1760: 27
Cochinat [Cochinar], François Jérôme –
trumpeter
1732: 44

Cochinat [Cochinar] (*cont.*)
  1743: 675
  1760: II/16
Collasse, Pascal – composer
  1727: 11, 43, 94, *150–1*
  1732: 38, 396 and 400 (Lully), *518*, 543
    (Pic), 586 (Campistron)
  1743: 752 (Rousseau), 754 (Desmarets)
  1760: 27
Corelli, Arcangelo – composer
  1732: 396 (Lully)
  1743: 709 (Dandrieu), 756n (Desmarets)
Couperin, Charles – organist
  1732: *401–3*
  1743: 664 (Fr. Couperin)
Couperin, François – composer
  1732: 43, 396–7 (Lully), *401–3*, 513 (La
    Fosse), 566 (Ferrand)
  1743: *664–6*, 674n, 708 (Dandrieu), 756n
    (Desmarets), lii
  1755: 80 (Calvière)
  1760: 27, II/16
Couperin, Louis – composer
  1727: 222 (Lambert)
  1732: 38, *401–3*, 637 (Certin)
  1743: lii
Couperin, Marguerite-Antoinette –
  harpsichordist
  1743: 665–6 (Fr. Couperin), 734
    (Rousseau)
Couperin, [Marguerite-] Louise – singer
  1732: 403 (Fr. Couperin)
  1743: 664 (Moreau), 665 (Fr. Couperin)
Couperin, Marie-Anne – organist
  1743: 665 (Fr. Couperin)
Cury [Lalande, Mme de], Marie-Louise de –
  viol player
  1732: 615 (Lalande)
Cuzzoni [Cozzoni], Francesca – singer
  1743: 755n (Desmarets)
D'Agincourt [Dagincour], François –
  organist
  1755: 79–80 (Calvière)
Dandrieu, Jean-François – composer
  1743: 663 (Moreau), *708–10*
  1760: 27
Dandrieu, Jeanne-Françoise – harpsichordist
  1743: 664 (Moreau), 709–10 (Dandrieu)
  1760: 33
Daquin, Louis-Claude – organist
  1743: 756n (Desmarets)
  1755: 80 (Calvière)
  1760: II/16
Deniau – viol player
  1743: 664 (Moreau)
Descoteaux [Decoteaux], René-Pignon –

flautist
  1732: 43
  1743: 675
  1760: II/16
Desjardins, ?Jean Hannés or ?Philippe
  Annet – oboist
  1743: 676
Desmarets, Henri – composer
  1732: 396 (Lully), 563 (Sainctonge)
  1743: 752 (Rousseau), *754–9*
  1755: 20 (Campra), 24 (Pellegrin), 33–4
    (Matho), 55 (Destouches)
  1760: 27
Desmarets, Leopold – amateur
  1743: 758 (Desmarets, H.)
Desmatins – female singer
  1732: 43
  1743: 791, 795
  1760: II/16
Des Planes [Deplane]: *see* Piani, Giovanni
  Antonio
Destouches, André Cardinal – composer
  1732: xii (medallion), 615 (Lalande)
  1743: 704 and 705n (Mouret), 755–6n
    (Desmarets), 790, lxvi, lxxiv–lxxv
  1755: Liste chronologique, *53–6*
  1760: 23, xii (medallion), II/15, 43, 50
Dubois [Forqueray, Mme], Marie-Rose –
  harpsichordist
  1755: 60 (Forqueray)
Dubois, ?Pierre – bassoonist
  1732: 43
  1743: 675
  1760: II/16
Du Buisson, ?Jacques – singer
  1732: 392 (Lambert)
Dubut [Du But], Louis – lutenist
  1732: 405 (the Gaultiers)
  1743: lii
Dufaut [Du Fau], François – lutenist
  1732: 405 (the Gaultiers)
Du Flitz – harpsichordist
  1743: 756n (Desmarets)
Du Fresny, Charles Rivière – amateur
  1732: *594–9*
Du Hallay [Du Hallai], Mme –
  harpsichordist
  1743: 755–6n [also Mlle Du Hallay]
    (Desmarets)
  1760: 33
Dumeni – singer
  1732: 43, 395 (Lully)
  1743: 799
  1760: II/15
Du Mont, Henry [Henri] – composer
  1732: 38, *388–9*

1743: li
1760: 27
Du Noyer – oboist
  1732: 43
  1743: 675
  1760: II/16
Duomieni – amateur guitarist
  1755: 54 (Destouches)
Dupuy, Hilaire – female singer
  1727: 222 (Lambert)
  1732: 40, 391 (Lambert)
  1743: 795
  1760: 33
Du Tartre, Jean-Baptiste – composer
  1755: Liste chronologique, 84
Duval, François – violinist
  1732: 43
  1743: 675, 676, 756n (Desmarets)
  1760: II/16
Falco – amateur lutenist
  1732: 406 (the Gaultiers)
Farinelli: see Broschi, Carlo
Faustina: see Bordoni, Faustina
Favre, Antoine – violinist
  1732: 43
  1743: 675, 676
  1760: II/16
Fel, Marie – singer
  1743: 800
  1760: II/16
Fesch, Marie-Jeanne [Mlle Chevalier] –
  singer
  1743: 800
  1755: 78 (Royer)
  1760: II/16
Forqueray [Fourcray], Antoine – viol player
  1732: 44
  1743: 756n (Desmarets)
  1755: Liste chronologique, 59–60
  1760: 27, II/16
Forqueray le fils, Jean-Baptiste Antoine –
  viol player
  1755: 60
Forqueray, Mme: see Dubois Marie-Rose
Francoeur, François – violinist
  1755: 76 (La Bruere), 83 (Rebel)
Gallot, Jacques – lutenist
  1732: 405 (the Gaultiers)
Garnier, Gabriel – organist
  1732: 43, 401, 404
  1743: 674
  1760: II/16
Garron [Garon], Jacques – ordinaire
  1743: 679 (Bernier)
Gasparini, Francesco – composer
  1732: 396 (Lully)

1743: 756n (Desmarets)
Gatti [Theobal, Théobalde], Theobaldo de
  – basse de violon player
  1732: 39, 621
  1760: 27
Gaultier, Denis – lutenist
  1732: 38, 44, 405–6
  1743: 674n, lii
  1760: 27, II/16
Gaultier, Ennemond – lutenist
  1732: 38, 44, 405–6
  1743: 674n, lii
  1760: 27, II/16
Gaumay – composer
  1732: 628 (Lalouette)
Gautier, Pierre – composer
  1727: 11, 43, 94, 180–1
  1732: 38, 477, 573 (Vergier)
  1743: li–lii
  1760: 27
Geminiani, Francesco – violinist
  1743: 755n (Desmarets)
Gervais – maître de musique (Senlis
  Cathedral)
  1743: 756–7 (Desmarets)
Gervais, Charles-Hubert – composer
  1732: 599 (La Font)
  1743: 680 (Bernier)
  1755: Liste chronologique, 19
  1760: 27
Gillier, Jean Claude – basse de violon player
  1732: 610 (D'Ancourt)
  1743: 697–8
Girault – female singer
  1743: xlix n
Goupillet, Nicolas – maître de musique
  1743: 754–5 (Desmarets)
Gregorio – oboist
  1743: 755n (Desmarets)
Grenet, François-Lupien – composer
  1760: 27
Guido [Antonio], Giovanni Antonio –
  violinist
  1743: 756n (Desmarets)
Guignon, Jean Pierre – violinist
  1743: 755n (Desmarets)
  1760: II/16
Guillery – composer
  1732: 628 (Lalouette)
Guyot, Mlle – harpsichordist
  1732: 40, 636–7
  1743: 675
  1760: 33
Handel, George Frideric – composer
  1743: 756n (Desmarets)
Hilaire, Dem.: see Dupuy, Hilaire

Hotteterre, ?Nicolas or ?Louis – flautist
1743: 675, 676
Houssu, Antoine – organist
1732: 43, *404* [also nephew]
1743: 674
1760: II/16
Jacquet, Mlle: *see* La Guerre, Elisabeth Claude
Jacquet de
Jélyotte [Jéliote, Jélyote], Pierre – singer
1743: 756n (Desmarets), 800
1760: II/16
Josquin [Jossien des Prez] – composer
1743: xxxvii–xxxviii
Journet, Fanchon – singer
1732: 43
1743: 795, 798
1760: II/16
La Barre, Anne de – singer
1743: xlix n
La Barre, Michel de – flautist
1732: 43
1755: Liste chronologique, *83*
1760: 27, II/16
Lacoste [La Coste], Louis de – composer
1732: 543 (Pic)
1755: Liste chronologique, 25 (Pellegrin),
84
1760: 27
La Croix, François de – *maître de musique*
1732: 628 (Lalouette)
1743: 679–80 (Bernier)
La Faveur – female singer
1743: xlix
La Ferté, Charles François Grégoire de –
basse de violon player
1732: 43
1743: 756n (Desmarets)
1760: II/16
La Guerre, Elisabeth Claude Jacquet de –
composer
1732: xi (medallion), 35, 62, *635–6*, 656
(La Motte)
1743: 675n, lxv, lxxiv
1760: 22, xi (medallion), II/43, 50
La Guerre, Marin de – organist
1732: 635 (La Guerre, E. C. J. de)
La Jousselinière, René Boudier de – amateur
lutenist
1732: *588–92*
Lalande, Anne de: *see* Rebel, Anne
Lalande, Jeanne – singer
1732: 614–15 (Lalande, M. de)
1760: 33
Lalande, Michel Richard de – composer
1727: 7, 43–4, 94 (name handwritten in

GB: Lbl: 1161.e.5), *219–21*
1732: ix (medallion), 35, 62, *612–16*
1743: 676, 754 and 756n (Desmarets),
lxv, lxxiv
1755: 56 (Destouches)
1760: 22, 48n, ix (medallion), II/43, 49
Lalande, Marie Anne – singer
1732: 614–15 (Lalande, M. de)
1760: 33
Lalande, Marie-Louise de: *see* Cury, Marie-
Louise de
Lalouette, Jean-François – composer
1732: 38, 396 (Lully), *628*
1743: 680 (Bernier)
1760: 27
Lambert, Michel – singer
1727: 11, 43, 95, 126–7 (Benserade),
221–3, 227 (Lully)
1732: 38, 280 (Boisrobert), *390–2*, 401
(Lully), 433 (Benserade), 529 (Lainez)
1743: 795, li, lii
1755: 26 (Pellegrin)
1760: 27
La Milette, de – female singer
1743: 756n (Desmarets)
La Plante, Mme de: *see* (?)Beaupère,
Jacqueline
La Tremouille, Charles-Armand-René,
Duke of – amateur composer
1743: 828
1760: 32
Le Bègue, Nicolas-Antoine – organist
1727: 222 (Lambert)
1732: *401, 404*
1743: 674, lii
Le Camus, Sébastien – composer
1732: 392 (Lambert)
1743: li
Leclair *l'aîné*, Jean Marie – violinist
1743: 756n (Desmarets)
Le Clerc: ?*see* Leclair *l'aîné*, Jean Marie
Le Froid – female singer
1727: 222 (Lambert)
1732: 40, 391 (Lambert)
1743: 795, [838]
1760: 33
Le Maure, Catherine-Nicole – singer
1743: 704 (Mouret), 796, 797
1760: II/16
Le Moine, Étienne – lutenist
1732: 44
1743: 675
1760: II/16
Le Page ?Jacques – singer
1743: 800

Le Rochois, Marthe [Marie] – opera actress
  1732: 40, 43, 395 (Lully)
  1743: *790–5, 796–9*
  1760: 33, ɪɪ/16
Louis XIII – royal amateur
  1743: 828, xliii
  1760: 32
Louvencourt, Marie de – amateur
  1732: *550*
  1743: *670*
  1760: 25
Lucas – flautist
  1743: 675
Lully, Jean – composer
  1732: 401 (Lully, J.-B.)
Lully, Jean-Baptiste – composer
  1727: 3, 5, 15–17, 40–1, 43, 44–6, 61,
    78, 80, 89, 95, 106, 110, 151
    (Collasse), 179 (La Fontaine), 221
    (Lambert), *223–7*, 286 (Quinault)
  1732: Épitre, 9, 14, 20, 22, 30–1,
    (medallion in Slatkine reprint: '3'), 35,
    43, 46–7, 60–1, 63, 64, 73, 85, 86, 318
    (Molière), 381 (Th. Corneille), 385
    (Perrin), 388 (Cambert), 391 (Lambert),
    393–401, 408 (Quinault) 435 (La Fond),
    464 (La Fontaine), 477 (Gautier), 518
    (Collasse), 573 (Vergier), 586 (Campis-
    tron), 612 (Lalande), 621 (Gatti), 625
    (Marais), 628 (Lalouette), 637 (Certin)
  1743: 676, 705n (Mouret), 709
    (Dandrieu), 755–6n (Desmarets), 789,
    790 and 793 (Le Rochois), 795, 797,
    821, [838], xxv–xxvi, xliv n, xlix n, l–li,
    lvi, lxviii, lxxvii
  1755: Avertissement, 20–1 (Campra),
    26 (Pellegrin), 33–4 (Matho),
    43 (Danchet), 55 (Destouches)
  1760: 22, 47–8, ɪ/4, 18, 19, '3' (medal-
    lion), ɪɪ/15, 20, 34, 45, 52, 62, 72
Lully, Jean-Louis – composer
  1732: 401 (Lully, J.-B.)
Lully *l'aîné*, Louis – composer
  1732: 401 (Lully), 586 (Campistron), 625
    (Marais)
Madin, Henri – composer
  1755: Liste chronologique, *21–2*
Mallet – Intendant de la Musique des Etats
    de Languedoc
  1743: 662 (Moreau)
Mangeon, Étienne – violinist
  1743: 756n (Desmarets)
Marais, Marin – viol player
  1732: ix (medallion), 35, 44, 62–3, 396
    (Lully), 586 (Campistron), *624–7*
  1743: 678, lxv, lxxiv

  1760: 22, ix (medallion), ɪɪ/16, 43, 49
Marais, Mlle [?Radegonde Angélique,
    ?Marie Madeleine, ?Anne Marie] – viol
    player
  1732: 627 (Marais, M.)
Marais, Roland – viol player
  1743: 756n (Desmarets)
Marchand, ?Jean-Baptiste – *basse de violon*
    player
  1732: 43
  1743: 675, 756n (Desmarets)
  1760: ɪɪ/16
Marchand, Jean Louis – organist
  1732: 39, 43, 401, *404*, 637 (Certin),
    658–60
  1743: 674–5, lii
  1755: 54n (Destouches)
  1760: 27, ɪɪ/16
Marchand, Joseph – violinist
  1743: 675
Mascitti, Michele – violinist
  1743: 756n (Desmarets)
Matho, Jean – composer
  1743: 757 (Desmarets)
  1755: Liste chronologique, *33–4*, 68
    (Fuselier), 79 (Royer)
  1760: 27
Maupin: *see* Aubigny [Maupin] Mlle d'
Mellin de Saint Gelais: *see* Saint Gelais,
    Mellin de
Ménétou, Françoise-Charlotte de – composer
  1755: 11 (La Ferté, Le Chevalier de)
Ménétrier, Claude-François – writer on
    music
  1743: xli–xlii
Michel: *see* Mascitti, Michele
Minoret, Guillaume – composer
  1732: 38, *561*
  1743: 754 (Desmarets)
  1760: 27
Mollier, Louis de – composer
  1732: 392 (Lambert)
Mondonville, Jean-Joseph Cassanea de –
    composer
  68 (Fuselier)
Montalan – organist
  1732: 318 (Molière)
Montéclair, Michel Pignolet de – composer
  1743: 663 (Moreau, J.-B.), *696–7*
  1755: 24–5 (Pellegrin)
  1760: 27
Moreau, Fanchon – singer
  1732: 43
  1743: 791 (Le Rochois), 795
  1760: ɪɪ/16
Moreau, Jean-Baptiste – composer

Moreau, Jean-Baptiste (*cont.*)
  1727: 198 (Lainez)
  1732: 525–6, 529 (Lainez)
  1743: *661–4*, 696 (Montéclair)
  1760: 27
Moreau, Jeanne – singer
  1743: 734 (Rousseau)
Moreau [Deniau, Mme], Marie-Claude –
  singer
  1743: 664 (Moreau, J.-B.)
Morin, Jean Baptiste – composer
  1743: 680 (Bernier)
  1755: Liste chronologique, *84*
Moulinié, Etienne – composer
  1732: 392 (Lambert)
Mouret, Jean-Joseph – composer
  1732: 599 (La Font)
  1743: 677, *703–6*, 756n (Desmarets)
  1755: 68 (Fuselier), 73 (Destouches,
    P. N.)
  1760: 27
Mouton, Charles – lutenist
  1732: 405 (the Gaultiers)
  1743: lii
Muraire – singer
  1732: 43
  1743: 800
  1760: ɪɪ/15
Nantes, Mlle de – royal amateur
  1732: 613 (Lalande)
Niel, Jean Baptiste – composer
  1755: 68 (Fuselier)
Noailles, Mlle de – royal amateur
  1732: 613 (Lalande)
Novelles – female singer
  1743: 677
Pélissier, Marie – singer
  1743: 704 (Mouret), 797
  1760: ɪɪ/16
Penon, Mme – harpsichordist
  1732: 40, 636–7
  1743: 675n
  1760: 33
Perroni [Perone], Guiseppe Maria – cellist
  1743: 755n (Desmarets)
Petit ?François – violinist
  1743: 756n (Desmarets)
Pétouille [Petouville], François – composer
  1732: 628 (Lalouette)
Philibert: *see* Rebillé, Philibert
Philidor, André – bassoonist
  1743: 675
Philidor *le fils*, André – oboist
  1743: 675
Philidor, François – oboist
  1743: 675, 676–7
Philidor, Jean Danican – trumpeter

1743: 675
  1760: ɪɪ/16
Philidor, Pierre Danican – oboist
  1732: 43
  1743: 675, 676
  1760: ɪɪ/16
Philippe, Duke of Orléans – royal amateur
  composer
  1727: 145 (Charpentier)
  1743: 678–80 (Bernier), 756n, 828
  1760: 32
Piani [Deplane, Des Planes], Giovanni
  Antonio – violinist
  1743: 756n (Desmarets)
Piroye, Charles – organist
  1732: 404
Quentin, Jean-Baptiste – violinist
  1743: 756n (Desmarets)
Quinault, Jean-Baptiste – composer
  1755: 68 (Fuselier)
Rameau, Jean-Philippe – composer
  1743: 705n (Mouret), 756n (Desmarets)
  1755: 25 (Pellegrin), 31 (Autreau), 68
    (Fuselier), 76 (La Bruere)
  1760: 47–8, ɪɪ/15
Rebel [Lalande, Mme de], Anne – singer
  1732: 614–15 (Lalande, M.-R. de)
Rebel [Rebelle], Jean-Féry [Ferri] – violinist
  1732: 43
  1755: Liste chronologique, 76 (La
    Bruere), *83*
  1760: 27, ɪɪ/16
Rebillé, Philibert – flautist
  1727: 213–14 (Lainez)
  1732: 43
  1743: 675
  1760: ɪɪ/16
Richard, François – composer
  1732: 392 (Lambert)
Robert, Pierre – composer
  1732: 38, *392–3*
  1743: li
Romanina – female singer
  1743: 755n (Desmarets)
Royer, Joseph-Nicolas-Pancrace – composer
  1755: Liste chronologique, *78–9*
  1760: 27
Saint-Christophle, Mlle de – singer
  1732: 40, 395 (Lully)
  1743: 795
  1760: 33
Sainte Colombe – viol player
  1732: 624–5 [also two daughters] (Marais)
Saint Gelais, Mellin de – amateur
  1732: *123–4*
Salomon, Joseph-François – viol player
  1732: 39, *658*

1755: 23 (La Roque)
1760: 27
Scarlatti [Scarlati], ?Alessandro – composer
  1743: 756n (Desmarets)
Senallié, Jean-Baptiste – violinist
  1743: *673–4*, 675, 816n
  1760: 27
Sicard, Jean – composer
  1732: 392 (Lambert)
Somis [Vanloo, Mme], Anne-Antoinette-
  Christine – singer
  1743: 756n (Desmarets)
Somis, Giovanni Battista – violinist
  1743: 755n (Desmarets)
Stuck [Stuk], Jean-Baptiste [Batistin] –
  composer
  1743: 705n, 755–6n (Desmarets)
  1755: 69 (Jolly)
  1760: 27
Taillard *l'aîné*, Pierre-Évrard – flautist
  1743: 756n (Desmarets)
Tartini, Giuseppe – composer
  1743: 756n (Desmarets)
Théobalde [Theobal]: *see* Gatti, Theobaldo
  de
Thevenard, Gabriel – singer
  1732: 43
  1743: 797–9
  1760: II/15
Thomelin [Tomelin], Jacques – organist

1727: 222 (Lambert)
1732: 43, *401*, *403–4*
1743: 674, lii
1760: II/16
Tribou – singer
  1743: 800
  1760: II/16
Valentiné, Louis Bertin de – amateur
  1755: *39–41*
  1760: 30
Vanloo: *see* Somis, Anne-Antoinette-
  Christine
Verloge [Alarius], Hilaire – viol player
  1755: 34 (Matho)
Verrières, Henri Cahagne de – amateur viol
  player
  1755: Liste chronologique, *76–8*
  1760: 25
Victoire de France – royal amateur
  1760: 33
Villeneuve, André-Jacques – composer
  1755: 25 (Pellegrin)
Villeneuve, Mlle de – singer
  1732: 280 (Boisrobert)
Visée [Visé], Robert de – lutenist
  1732: 44
  1743: 675
  1760: II/16
Vivaldi, Antonio – composer
  1743: 755n (Desmarets)

The residences of Monsieur de Lully:
a west side story

MARCELLE BENOIT

Does a parallel exist between the destinies of Louis XIV and Lully? While one must keep things in proportion, these two individuals – the powerful despot and the artistic genius – seem to have more than one trait in common, in their behavior as in their work: absolutism, greatness, nobility and correctness of form, reason, taste, a certain selfish bent, a certain coldness . . .

Like his master, Lully was an avid builder; this involvement implied not only his need for a certain lifestyle or the usefulness of a good investment; he attached the symbolic value of 'appearances' to this endeavor (one might equate it with our concept of 'snob appeal'). This *bourgeois-gentilhomme*, proud but (unlike M. Jourdain) not vain, considered the location of his residence, whether in town or in the country, to be of some importance. This gifted upstart thus gained a footing on the social ladder, at the risk of provoking jealousy in worthy but less fortunate fellow artists and the condescending smiles from genuine nobles, ensconced in their family *hôtels*.

Before following the composer to some of his residences, we must first describe the geographic development of Paris in the second half of the seventeenth century.

MONSIEUR DE LULLY IN TOWN

The Palais-Royal quarter

Should an astral significance be accorded to the westward-tending movements of capital cities or is there an inescapable attraction in the East towards the West (quite appropriate under the reign of a *Roi-Soleil*) as recorded in the annals of long-lasting civilizations? Do climatic factors explain this progression, or does it result from more immediate social considerations?[1] All these tendencies are probably interrelated.

Paris was no exception to the rule. The city stretched out along the right bank of the Seine, beyond the Louvre, the Tuileries with its vast gardens, even beyond the Porte Saint-Honoré. La butte des moulins was covered with dwellings.

---

[1] Edmond Radet, *Lully, homme d'affaires, propriétaire et musicien* (Paris, Librairie de l'Art, 1891), p. 7.

[This] artificial hill, crowned with mills, [was] formed in 1536 at the southwest corner of the present-day Rue des Petits-Champs and Rue Sainte-Anne by the piling up of rubble from the fortification works undertaken that year when, after Carlos V [of Spain] had invaded Picardie, François I planned to reinforce the enclave of Charles V; the hill was levelled from 1667 to 1677 by Villedo, its soil used to fill the marshy ground on the Mathurin farm. Thus, it had lasted for almost a century and a half. After that, the Rue des Moulins could be extended northward to the Rue des Petits-Champs.[2]

The Saint-Roch quarter became important. As the mills disappeared around Palais-Cardinal (Richelieu's palace, the future Palais-Royal), roads and streets were laid out: Rue Traversière (our Rue Molière) and the Rue Sainte-Anne (in honor of Anne of Austria). At the corner of Rue Richelieu and Rue des Petits-Champs, the Palais-Mazarin was built (now the Bibliothèque Nationale). Around it, prestigious residences were constructed: the *hôtels* of Colbert, Coislin, Louvois, Lyonne, and Ventadour. It became the quarter of aristocracy and finance. Such crowning glories as the Place des Victoires (1685) and the Place Louis-le-Grand (1686, the future Place Vendôme) were soon to be added.

If Michel Lambert, because of his in-laws (the Dupuis), remained attached for a long period of time to the Bel-Air quarter of the village of Vaugirard, several events caused him to decide to leave it: the death of his wife (1642), his presumed duties as *chantre* in the *Musique royale* (1645) and shortly thereafter, as *maître de la musique de la chambre* (1661). This situation inspired him to cross the Seine and return to the heart of the capital. From 1657 to 1664, he resided in a house located in the Rue Notre-Dame-des-Victoires, opposite the Augustins Déchaussés monks, known as the Petits-Pères, with Hilaire Dupuis, his sister-in-law, a royal singer, and Claude Marchand, canon of Saint-Etienne de Dreux (d. 1661), his protector.[3]

Lully had just married Madelaine Lambert (on 14 July 1662 in Saint-Germain-en-Laye), only daughter of Michel, through whom he obtained the right to the office of *maître de la musique de la chambre*. Jean-Baptiste and Madelaine at first settled in the quarter known as Petits-Pères, on the Rue Notre-Dame-des-Victoires in the parish of Saint-Eustache, near Michel Lambert and Hilaire Dupuis (1662). Then for three years, from 1664 to 1667, they lived on the Rue Neuve-Saint-Thomas, next to the church cloister, in a house that belonged to the canons of the royal collegiate church of Saint-Thomas du Louvre. This house comprised 'two courtyards, a stable, kitchen, small hall, carriage entrance and drive, with an exit through the courtyard, formerly a cemetery, belonging to the said church, two floors above the said premises, with bedrooms, garrets, and attics above' at an annual rent of 1050 *livres*.[4] The musician's handsome signature sprawls quite unabashedly across the lease, somewhat overshadowing those of the seven canons (see plate 1).

The household moved next (1667) to the Rue Travercine (our present-day

[2] Jacques Hillairet, *Dictionnaire historique des rues de Paris* (Editions de Minuit: 1963, 2 vol., supplement by Jacques Hillairet and Pascal Payen-Appenzeller, 1972), vol. II, p. 168.

[3] Catherine Massip, 'Michel Lambert (1610–1696): Contribution à l'histoire de la monodie en France' (unpubl. diss., doctorat d'état, Paris-IV Sorbonne, 1985), pp. 49–50.
[4] C. Massip, 'M. Lambert', p. 104.

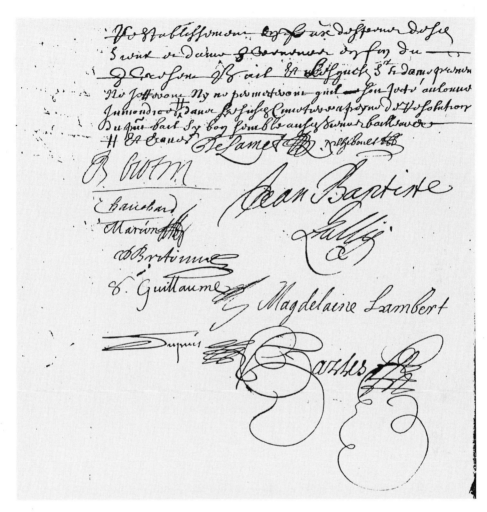

Plate 1. Lully's signature at the bottom of the lease for the Rue-Neuve-Saint-Thomas,
6 June 1664

Rue Molière) into a house that overlooked Saint-Roch parish, rented for four
years from Pierre de Franciny, royal butler and councillor (without doubt related to Nicolas de Francine, who would marry one of Lully's daughters). The
house was comprised of 'a double-sized main building with carriage entrance on
its front side . . . a driveway with carriage house, stable, four cellars, a mezzanine used as a kitchen, a hall, bedroom, and dressing room, two floors above
this level, with garrets and loft above, and outbuildings' at an annual rent of
800 *livres*.[5]

[5] Ibid.

From now on, the real estate operations of the surintendant would be based on three closely related objectives: family, career, and money. In the 1670s, Lully, still very close to his father-in-law, made decisions that were both favorable to Lambert's career, which was at a standstill (he was nearing sixty), and to his own, which was blossoming. The time had arrived to build more spaciously, more luxuriously, and more profitably. The musician wanted a residence to his specifications and to his taste, one that would be beautiful and functional. He would have it built according to his own plans.

He began to realize this ambitious project with the purchase on 28 May 1670 of a plot of 78 *toises*[6] and, on the following 13 June of another plot of 30 *toises* adjoining the first, situated at the corner of Rue Sainte-Anne and Rue Neuve-des-Petits-Champs. These building sites belonged to two royal councillors who lived nearby in the Rue de Richelieu: Prosper Bauyn d'Angervilliers,[7] Maître de la Chambre aux Deniers de sa Majesté [Royal Finances], and Paul Mascranny, seigneur de La Verrière, Maître des Eaux et Forêts in the Department of Normandy. Sold at 210 *livres* per *toise*, the plots cost the musician 22,680 *livres*. At this juncture (14 December), his friend and collaborator, Molière, loaned him 11,000 *livres*, nearly one-half the price of the land (a sum that Lully was to return to the actor's widow). The Italian contractor, Jean-Baptiste Predo (or Predot) proposed a fixed price of 45,000 *livres* for the construction of the buildings. But the architect, Daniel Gittard, one of the eight architects of the Académie, was to design the facade.[8] The only entrance, on the Rue Sainte-Anne, was crowned by a bas-relief of musical instruments.[9]

Not content with this space, Lully enlarged it by buying another 72 *toises* from the same owners (on 30 December 1674), for the price of 12,000 *livres*, with one-half down and the balance to be paid six months later. To help him in this new acquisition, Lambert loaned his son-in-law 1200 *livres*[10] 'to cover urgent business expenses'. This statement was no exaggeration, for Lully had only two years earlier (1672) dealt with Perrin regarding the *privilège de l'Opéra* under the form of an annual pension, and he had also recently paid for his lands and paid his contractors for constructing the buildings (1670–1, 1674).

Lully brought the family clan together again in the *hôtel* on the Rue Sainte-Anne, giving a home to his wife, their six children, his father-in-law Lambert, the latter's sister-in-law, Hilaire Dupuis, and servants. He also welcomed, on a permanent basis, a page of *la Musique royale* and several musicians for the rehearsals of works that he was presenting at court and at the Académie royale de musique.

[6] *Toise*: a measure of length equal, in Paris, to 1.949 meters. [Translator's note: a 'toise'= 6 1/2 feet.]
[7] 'Could this Bauyn d'Angervilliers be the owner of the famous manuscript which bears his arms?' asks Catherine Massip, not unreasonably. See Massip, 'M. Lambert', p. 105.
[8] Radet, *Lully*, p. 49ff. H. Prunières, *La Vie illustre et libertine de Jean-Baptiste Lully* (Paris, Plon, 1929), p. 105. C. Massip, 'M. Lambert', p. 106. Jacques Hillairet, *Dictionnaire*, vol. II,

p. 263. These parcels of land are among the group of plots on the butte Saint-Roch belonging to a real estate partnership established in 1668, whose members included the Villedo brothers and Pierre Le Maistre, architects.
[9] The entrance on the Rue Neuve-des-Petits-Champs dates only from the eighteenth century.
[10] C. Massip, 'M. Lambert', p. 106.

The parts of the building that he did not use, on the Rue Neuve-des-Petits-Champs, were rented out to important people; on the ground floor and mezzanine, to shopkeepers (a shoemaker and a wine-merchant).[11] Plates 2 and 3 show this residence, which stands today at the corner of the Rue Sainte-Anne and the Rue des Petits-Champs. The profits realized from rents must have inspired the composer to increase his investments in the quarter. On 24 September 1674 he bought, yet again from Prosper Bauyn, another building site on Rue Royale, 6 *toises* wide and 12 *toises* deep, for the sum of 12,000 *livres*. The building, completed in February 1676, consisted of 12 meters of facade, with five windows, three floors, and an attic (see plate 4). He rented it to Jean Arnault, *conseiller du roi* (1676), Jacques de Manse, *conseiller du roi* (1677), the Marquis de la Popelinière, seigneur d'Arvaux (1680), and to Armand Deschamps, Vicomte de Marsilly (1682) among others.[12]

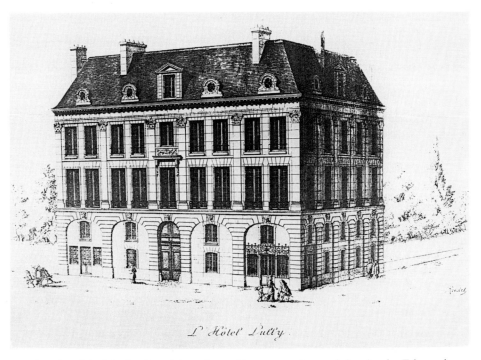

L' Hôtel Lully.

Plate 2. L'hôtel Lully, Rue Sainte-Anne. Reconstruction and drawing by Edmond Radet in *Lully, homme d'affaires, propriétaire et musicien*

[11] Radet, *Lully*, p. 55.
[12] Ibid., p. 38–9. The building is situated at what is now 10 Rue des Moulins.

Plate 3. L'hôtel Lully, Rue Sainte-Anne; detail of the facade. Present-day condition

By 1684 Lully had amassed considerable real estate holdings in Paris: Edmond Radet noted in an *Etat de partition de la ville et des faubourgs de Paris* of 1 January 1684[13] on the subject of the Palais-Royal quarter:

Rue Royale
No. 842 M. Lully's house, occupied by several tenants.[14]

Rue Neuve-des-Petits-Champs
No. 844 M. Lully's house, occupied by several tenants.[15]
No. 845 Another house owned by M. de Lully, occupied by several tenants.[16]

Rue Sainte-Anne
No. 847 M. Lully's house, occupied by several tenants.[17]

In this developing quarter, a plot in front of Lully's house on the Rue Sainte-Anne was still vacant. In 1674 it became the site of an event which certain people used to advantage in order to arouse feelings against the composer. According to Prunières, the surintendant:

[13] Radet, *Lully*, p. 36.
[14] Radet adds: Rue Royale, 'formerly "des Moulins". This is the house that is today No. 10, Rue des Moulins.'
[15] Radet adds: 'Today No. 47'.
[16] Radet adds: 'Today No. 45 and at the corner of Rue Sainte-Anne. This is the hotel Lully.'
[17] Radet adds: 'Today No. 43'.

Plate 4. The house built by Lully on Rue Royale in 1676; present-day condition;
now 10 Rue des Moulins

wished to celebrate the conquest of the Franche-Comté by a fireworks display in front of his house. By a stroke of bad luck, heavy rain fell during the day and in the evening; the fireworks would not ignite. On the facade of the house, a display had been erected to represent the gallic cockerel and the Austrian lion. The cockerel was supposed to set fire to the lion's tail but it turned around on itself and the rockets misfired. As a result of this mishap, the following ditty was composed:

> Quitte, Baptiste, le caprice
> D'entreprendre mal à propos
> De faire des feux d'artifice
> Tu n'es bon qu'au feu de fagots . . .[18]

This verse, an allusion to the Florentine's morals, seems to have been the work of Henri Guichard, an individual of questionable character.

Mlle Hilaire left the *hôtel* Lully at the end of 1677 to go into retreat at the Nouvelles Catholiques on the Rue Sainte-Anne, where she was to die in December 1709. Lambert ended his days in his son-in-law's home, the latter allowing him the use of an apartment in which he was to die on 27 June 1696, at the age of eighty-five. After the surintendant's death, the *hôtel* Lully was jointly owned by his heirs as part of his estate, until the death of his widow (1720).

If the walls of the house could speak, they would evoke the finest years of Lully's career, and the most eventful ones, too: much work to do, much money to spend, many enemies to fight, and a great deal of music to compose. These events can be summarized: the purchase of the *privilège de l'Opéra* from Perrin, the difficulties in registering this privilege, the cabal and lawsuits which ensued as a result of it; Colbert's support; the partnership with Vigarani and Quinault; the outfitting of the theater on the Rue de Vaugirard opposite the Jardin du Luxembourg; the falling-out with Molière; illness; the Chausson affair and royal indignation; Molière's death; taking over the direction of the Salle du Palais-Royal; the success of *Cadmus et Hermione*; the Guichard trial, the hostility of the *devots*; the singers' rehearsals, their vocal coaching with Lambert; the collaborations with Lalouette and Colasse; the disagreement with La Fontaine; Quinault's disgrace; illness once again; competition from the talented Lorenzani; Vigarani's resignation in favor of Berain; the success of *Le triomphe de l'amour*; the obtainment of *lettres de noblesse* and the problems involved in their confirmation . . .

Lully's home quickly became an annexe of the Palais-Royal. The building, erected under the name of Palais-Cardinal by Richelieu in 1629, was given by His Eminence to the king, hence the name 'Palais-Royal'. It was in 1692, after Lully's death, that Louis XIV gave it to his brother, the duc d'Orléans, *in apanage*, that is, for his exclusive use during his lifetime but to revert to the crown after his death.

Richelieu had a private theater built by Lemercier in 1637. Located in the right wing of the palace, on the front of the building, it extended the length of an extremely dark cul-de-sac (on the site of the present-day Rue de Valois). When Molière installed himself there with his troupe in 1661, he had an entrance made on the Rue Saint-Honoré. At his death, the theater passed to Lully, who had the

[18] H. Prunières, *La Vie de Lully*, p. 161. Jacques Hillairet, *Dictionnaire*, vol. II, p. 490.

actors relegated to the Salle de la Bouteille, a bit further away. He proceeded to have the roof and the stage raised and the basement redesigned for better use of the stage machinery.[19]

The proximity of the composer's residence would make his task simpler. For a decade, men and ideas moved between the Rue Sainte-Anne and the Rue Saint-Honoré, a circumstance which contributed to one of the finest periods in French opera – from *Cadmus et Hermione* to *Acis et Galathée*.

The faubourg of La Ville-l'Evêque

Perhaps the time came for Lully to step back from the bustle and intrigues of the city (the 'rumeurs souterraines', as Couperin was to term them). There was also the added excuse of age: the composer was nearly fifty. Of course, the Palais-Royal would remain the nerve center of creation for opera, but by coach, distances are not very great.

In fact, Paris continued to spread out towards the west, by a sort of attraction towards the new capital or, rather, the new seat of government, Versailles, where the court was installed in 1682:

The western part of the city became fashionable, while the Marais was to remain, until the Revolution, a quarter inhabited by families of noble blood but modest means. . . . In the new neighborhoods of the west, *hôtels* were being built, one after another, and in the Faubourg Saint-Germain, as in the Faubourg Saint-Honoré, there were practically no craftsmen and only a few shops and markets. The inhabitants of the *hôtels* traded in merchandise themselves or sent their servants to buy vast quantities of provisions at les Halles. They themselves bought frills and flounces, porcelain or books in the old workshops of the Palais or in the shops which were beginning to appear along the Rue du Faubourg Saint-Honoré. The Pont Royal, begun in 1685 at the instigation of Louvois, and the first stone bridge to span the Seine that did not use an island in its center for support, linked these new western quarters. The Tuileries gardens, newly enlarged and redesigned, the Cours la Reine and the Esplanade des Invalides surrounded the area's mansions with trees and flower beds.[20]

Pursuing his westward progress along the axis of the Rue Saint-Honoré, Lully went beyond the faubourg's gate and discovered a vast area of land belonging to the bishopric of Paris (*villa episcopi*), with farming and cultivation, where there was a small shrine dedicated to Sainte Madeleine. Around 1659, Mlle de Montpensier laid the first stone of a new church bearing the same dedication, on the foundation of the old chapel's ruins (now the site of the Blvd Malesherbes, in front of the Rue de l'Arcade).[21] Perhaps Lully recalled the time when he had

[19] Jean Cordey, 'Lully installé l'Opéra dans le théâtre de Molière. La décoration de la salle (1673)', *Bulletin de la Société de l'Histoire de l'Art Français* (1950).

[20] Orest Ranum, *Les Parisiens du XVIIe siècle* (Paris, Armand-Colin, 1973), p. 333.

[21] Albert Dauzat and Fernand Bournon, *Paris et ses environs* (Paris, Larousse, 1925), p. 86. 'A century later, its restoration was ordered

once more on a piece of land situated a bit further to the east, facing the Rue Royale and the Place Louis XV [future Place de la Concorde], whose creation was decided at the same time. The first stone of the Madeleine church, rededicated for the fourth time, was placed by Louis XV on 3 April 1764.' The old church that Lully knew was not destroyed until the beginning of the Revolution.

served the princess, whom he left in 1652, when the Grande Mademoiselle re-
belled against the king.

The surintendant's project was realized in two stages: first, by the acquisition
on 5 October 1682 from Félix du Verger, officer of the Grande Écurie, of a house
and garden at 'la Ville l'Evesque lès Paris' of 605 *toises*, for the price of 6640 *livres*,
into which he moved at the end of 1683. The second stage of his plan was the
purchase on 29 February 1684, from Pierre Gillot, Procureur au Parlement, of

a house and garden surrounded by a wall, covering an entire *arpent*,[22] located at what is
known as la Ville l'Evesque lès Paris . . . for an annual payment of twenty *livres* to the
benefice of la Ville l'Evesque and, in addition, the sum of 4000 *livres*.

Lully retained one of the houses on these two adjoining pieces of land and on
the other he had a building constructed with a frontage of nearly 20 meters.[23]

The great new residence, in which he lived at the edge of the Rue de la
Madeleine, rose three stories high and 'was extended by means of two wings
facing one another across the courtyard. The farther ends of the wings were
joined by a low building which contained the stables and carriage house and
marked the boundary of the courtyard. Next to it was a garden with an
orangery.[24]

Radet furnishes us with the details of the layout of the house, taken from the
inventory following Lully's death:

Court, kitchen, servants' hall, pantry, small downstairs room giving onto the garden
and part of the right wing of said house, office, stables, grand salon facing the courtyard,
large bedroom adjacent to the salon, small adjoining bedroom, antechamber in the right
wing, large bedroom in the said right wing, bedroom on the second floor with view of the
street, which is the room of the said widow, bedroom of Monsieur François [read:
Francine], bedroom serving as wardrobe for the said widow, bedroom on said second
floor in the right wing, another bedroom adjoining, which is the one in which Monsieur
de Lully died, bedroom on the third floor with view of the street, another bedroom in
the passage which connects one wing of the house to the other, small bedroom next to
that of the deceased, storeroom, study at the end of the right wing of the said house
on the first floor with view of the court and garden, antechamber with its entry off the
great staircase on the left side, with view of the street, large bedroom adjoining, another
bedroom in the said left wing. . . .[25]

A closer reading by Jean Cordey[26] of the same inventory offers us interesting
details about this house and those who lived in it. Here are some of those details:

In the grand salon of the first floor: a marble table on sculpted wooden legs,
decorated with golden figures; two almost identical pedestal tables; a large
mirror; a bed with tall posts and on the mantlepiece a decoration of nine small
Delftware pieces.

---

[22] *Arpent*: An old agrarian measure divided into 100 *perches* and variable according to different locales (from 35 to 50 *ares*). *Are*: a unit of measure for agrarian land equal to the area of a square of 10 meters or a square decameter.

[23] Radet, *Lully*, pp. 39–41.

[24] Jean Cordey, 'Lully d'après l'inventaire de ses biens', *Revue de musicologie*, XXXVII (July 1955),

pp. 78–83.

[25] Radet, *Lully*, p. 41.

[26] All the descriptive information which follows was taken from Cordey, pp. 78–83. A complete study of the inventory made after Lully's death, with analysis and annotations, remains yet to be done.

In Lully's bedroom on the second floor: the bed has tall oak posts, topped with four spheres decorated with tassels; all the bed furnishings are in red and golden yellow damask; near the bed, a walnut desk; two armchairs and four chairs covered in Turkish-style upholstery; a table with a cloth of the same material; the walls decorated with seven Flemish tapestries.

In the adjoining bedroom: a harpsichord

whose case is of fir resting on its walnut base of three wreathed columns.

On the same floor were Madame Lully's quarters where there is scarcely anything worth mentioning apart from several small religious paintings and engravings, as well as the bedroom of her son-in-law, Francini, decorated with six paintings on canvas of shepherds, ploughing scenes, and animals.

In the salon of the left wing: three small-figured Audenarde tapestries and two Gobelins, one depicting a hunt and the other a bacchanal, in a sculpted and gilded wooden frame; four paintings depicting the four seasons; a harpsichord painted in the 'façon de la Chine'.

In the storage room: a pastoral Audenarde tapestry in nine panels, estimated at 1000 *livres*; a Gobelins in four parts, depicting a bacchanal, valued at 1500 *livres*; various hangings of Venetian silk brocade and Luccan damask; a 'lit d'ange en impérial' with low gilded wooden posts, estimated value of 1000 *livres*.

At the very top of Lully's house and rising above the roof was a *donjon* (this was the name given to a small structure, installed, according to the *Encyclopédie*, 'to enjoy a beautiful view'). It consisted of a single bedroom whose walls were covered in silk brocade, as was the furniture. This is where Colasse, who collaborated with Lully on the orchestration of his last operas, used to stay.

At the far end of the house, beyond the court, the carriage house and the stables, was the garden with its orangery. In earthenware vases grew pink laurel, stands of myrrh, Spanish jasmine, and in planters, orange trees, pomegranate trees with double flowers and fruit, and even two fig trees.

All of this evokes the lifestyle, not to mention the sumptuous wardrobe, silverware, pearls, and diamonds. An estate of more than 800,000 *livres*!

The large and small houses, as well as a third, newly described, and the garden, were left to Lully's children, who multiplied the repurchases and the exchanges of shares. The entire fortune finally came into the hands of Antoine Bourot de Valroche, one of His Majesty's Fermiers Généraux, and Jean Maurice de Casaubon, former official receiver of the Compagnie des Indes. From the second half of the eighteenth century onwards, following other changes and radical transformations of the property and the quarter, it becomes difficult to recognize the aspect and character of the residence described above (today merged with the buildings at nos. 28 and 30 of the Rue Boissy-d'Anglas, see plate 5).[27]

The final five years, a brief but luxurious period in the surintendant's life, saw Lully leaving his father-in-law Lambert in the house on the Rue Sainte-Anne to move to la Ville-l'Evêque with his wife, his children, his son-in-law Nicolas de

---

[27] Paul Jarry, 'Lully at la Ville l'Evêque. No. 30, Rue Boissy-d'Anglas', *Bulletin de la société de l'histoire de Paris et de l'île-de-France*, 61st year (1943), pp. 103–7. Jacques Hillairet, *Dictionnaire*, vol. I, pp. 208–9.

Plate 5. Vestiges of Lully's house on the Rue de la Madeleine in la Ville-l'Evêque,
incorporated into an eighteenth-century building. Present-day condition;
now 28–30 Rue Boissy-d'Anglas

Francine (who would help him with the administration of the Académie royale de musique before taking over its direction), his student and secretary, Pascal Colasse, tucked away in his 'donjon', a page of the *Musique royale*, and servants.

This period was full of events: *Phaëton*, the death of the queen and of Colbert; the ousting of Lorenzani; the competition for control of the Royal Chapel in the face of Delalande's ascendancy (1683); the success of *Amadis*; the marriage of Lully's daughter to Nicolas de Francine (1684); *Roland*; the renewed outbreak of libertinism; Mlle Certain, the affair of the page Brunet; the royal disfavor (1685); the Dauphin's friendship; the masterpiece *Armide*; reconciliation with La Fontaine, collaboration with Racine; the triumph of Le Rochois, Desmatins, Saint-Christophle, Fanchon Moreau, Dumesnil and Beaumavielle, *Acis et Galatée* at the Château d'Anet, home of the duc de Vendôme (1686); the king's fistula operation; Lully's *Te Deum* at the Feuillants; the surintendant's gangrene, his 'conversion', and his death.

MONSIEUR DE LULLY IN THE COUNTRY

The village of Puteaux

As we have seen above, the years 1670–5 weighed heavily on the lives of Lully and his father-in-law Lambert: the move from house to house, the construction of buildings on the Rue Sainte-Anne, the settling in of the entire family in a rapidly-developing quarter, the conversion of the new Salle du Palais-Royal, the establishment of the opera troupe, the completion of the first operas, rehearsals, the journeys to the court – all of that entailed responsibility and overwork that were to be compensated by a few moments of calm and relaxation in the country.

Practical considerations must not be overlooked, and the retreat was to be chosen with an eye towards other activities. Since, apart from Fontainebleau, the court seemed to prefer the residences at Saint-Germain-en-Laye and Versailles, Lambert and Lully must have looked westward to find shelter from the stresses of the city, as well as from the excitement and pressures of the royal *fêtes*.

Our musicians set their hearts on Puteaux, midway between the Palais-Royal and the châteaux of Saint-Germain, in the second loop of the Seine, near Suresnes (see plate 6). The abbey of Saint-Germain-des-Prés were 'lords, protectors, founders, and patrons' of the church and parish of Suresnes and its annexe, Puteaux. The abbey of Saint-Denis also had the right to collect taxes from the nobility of Puteaux.

According to a map of the mid-seventeenth century (see plate 7),[28] the village consisted of about sixty dwellings along the river, encircling a small sixteenth-century church (which still stands). Tradition has it that the Lullys' property corresponded to the present-day addresses of 58–60 Rue Voltaire,[29] at the time a large open space with fields, cultivated areas, and streams descending to the Seine along a path leading to a large house topped with a dovecote and facing a church.

---

[28] Archives nationales; série N. III Seine, 345.
[29] Georges Weill (ed.), *La Perspective de la Défense*   *dans l'art et l'histoire* (Nanterre, 1983), p. 39.

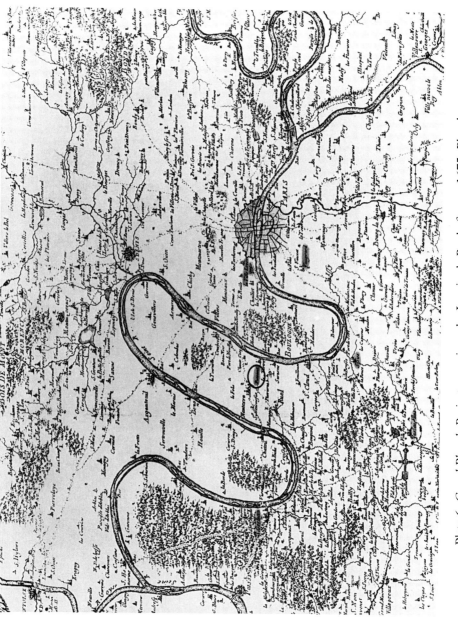

Plate 6. *Grand Plan de Paris et ses environs*, by Jouvin de Rochefort, *c.* 1675. Planche IX, 'Les environs de Paris'. From east to west: la Ville-l'Evêque and Vaugirard; Puteaux and Sèvres; Saint-Germain-en-Laye, and Versailles

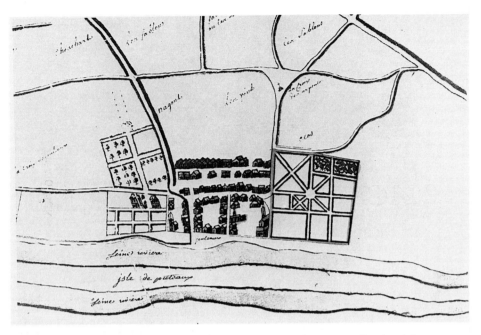

Plate 7. The village of Puteaux in the seventeenth century. On the right,
the sixteenth-century church; facing on the right,
the presumed house of Lambert and Lully.
(Archives nationales, N III Seine, 345, detail)

This property seems to correspond to the layout recorded by the notary with
reference to the residence acquired by Lambert, Lully, and Hilaire Dupuis, each
a one-third owner, on 11 October 1675. Here is the description of the property,
according to the bill of sale:

A house with carriage entrance situated in the village of Puteaux, near Paris, on the main
street of the said village, consisting of a main building to the left of the entrance and leading down to the carriage entrance; a large hall, an adjoining pantry,[30] a kitchen, two
floors of bedrooms and sitting rooms with lofts above; a chapel and study above it; a staircase under construction; to the right of the entrance, a long row of buildings leading
down to a wine press, complete with utensils, a vat and two chablis; next, a cellar in which
are three large vats; a stable, carriage house, cow barn with small courtyard and dairy;
a pigeon house at the far end, complete with pigeons and under which is a conservatory;
at the top level of this row of buildings are two bedrooms, the remainder being
storerooms; a large court in the center of this property; a garden at the back with approximately a *demy arpent* planted with fruit trees, vines, and grass; at the back of the garden is
another building, on whose lower floor are two rooms, in one of which is a billiard table
covered with green cloth and dust cover, six billiard games having two balls each; a small
pathway between the two rooms leading down to the bank of the Seine; large open arcade
above and other outlying buildings; the entire property covered in tile and slate. . . .[31]

[30] 'Depense' [pantry]: 'Room in a house, an
establishment, etc. where one stores food
provisions or carries out tasks associated with
said room.' (*Larousse de la langue Française*
(1977).)
[31] Quoted by Massip, 'M. Lambert', pp. 107–8.

For all of this, the buyers paid 7000 *livres* for the house, the garden, and the river bank reserved for the parish of Puteaux; 1000 *livres* for the 'furniture and miscellaneous'; 250 *livres* for other furniture in one of the bedrooms; 300 *livres* for interest; 120 *livres* 'pour la chaisne et pot de vin'.

The musician's presence brought honor to the village. Consequently, in 1685, he and his daughter were chosen to christen a bell consecrated in the parish church.

On the 24th day of the said month of March a bell was blessed at the church of Notre Dame in Pitié, Puteaux, by Maitre Charles Caron, priest, curate in charge of Suresne and its adjoined chapel. The bell was named Jean Baptiste Louise by Monsieur Jean Baptiste Lully esquire, *secrétaire* to the King's household and royal house of France, *intendant* of his music. The christener was Caterine Madelaine de Lully, wife of Monsieur de Francine, butler to the King; the above have signed this document together with the said priest.

Lully   C. M. Lully[32]

Mlle Hilaire did not enjoy her stay in Puteaux very long for, as we have seen, she retired to the Nouvelles Catholiques on the Rue Sainte-Anne at the end of 1677. She then gave over her part of the house to Lully, who became the owner of two-thirds of the estate. He continued to live there with his father-in-law, but that did not prevent him from acquiring yet another country residence.

The village of Sèvres

More than one mystery remains regarding Lully's country house located in the village of Sèvres (often called 'Sèves' at that time) which was in the first loop of the Seine on the left bank of the river. Everyone is in agreement regarding the acquisition of this house, without, however, giving the date thereof, nor its exact location or description. We have been unable to find a trace of the surintendant's name in the titles to the property in the seigniory of Sèvres.[33] Radet identifies this residence as 'the old château called "la Diarme"';[34] Prunières considered it to be 'a small country house where he [Lully] used to sleep when the court was at Versailles'.[35] Historians refer to it as 'la Guyarde'. Should one link it to that 'little house on the hillside called "Château Guillard"', which later (1760) would belong to the Parisian banker Antoine Léonard Guldiman;[36] or to the 'large house with gardens known as "la Gaillarde"' that Jean François Verdun owned in 1754?[37] It seems that the latter identification is the correct one.

In a well-documented work, Mariette Portet,[38] while maintaining the usual reservations regarding the location of this house, gives us numerous historic and descriptive details about the property:

[32] Archives municipales Puteaux, Registres paroissiaux, Notre-Dame de Pilié, 1685. I am grateful to Mlle A. Chabot, Archiviste, for alerting us to this act.
[33] Archives nationales, o¹ 3865, 3866, 3867.
[34] Radet, *Lully*, p. 43. Is it possible that *la Diarme* is a misreading of *la Guiarde*? Did Radet really see the pavilion whose picture is

reproduced here, when he assures us that, of Lully's residence 'nothing remains today but an outbuilding of no interest'?
[35] H. Prunières, *La Vie de Lully*, p. 214.
[36] Archives nationales, O¹ 1 3866⁶, pièce 5.
[37] Ibid., O¹ 3867⁷, pièce 39.
[38] Mariette Portet, *Sèvres en Ile-de-France* (Paris, La Nef de Paris Editions, 1963), pp. 125–7.

Among the beautiful residences of the seventeenth century . . . one offers a very special interest for the history of Sèvres, because the manufacture of porcelain would eventually take over the estate. . . . This property was somewhat outside of the village, on a bad road that linked Sèvres to Meudon, on the side of the hill overlooking the valley; it was La Guyarde, and tradition has it that it was the country house of Lully, without, however, there being any proof to support this claim; the theory is quite plausible, because if his post of Surintendant de la Musique de la Chambre tied him to Versailles, Lully had a great deal to do as well, during a certain period, at the Rue de Vaugirard in Paris, where he had a theater in 1672.

. . . Lully's name is linked to the only vestige that remains of this fine property, 'La Guyarde': a pavilion 'in the form of a square, roofed with slate', built on a terrace, accessible by two sets of stone stairs; this pavilion was first known as 'La Chapelle'; a billiard game[39] was to be set up in it, as well as an ice-house. At that time, it was roofed with tiles. Later, it was called 'the Opéra'. Today, it is designated the 'Pavillon Lulli'.[40] This small structure, miraculously preserved, standing out against a background of greenery that has remained unchanged for three hundred years, in the most charming intimacy, still inspires dreams in those fortunate enough to enter it. [See plates 8 and 9].

The property was quite extensive and adjoined to the east a glass-works and the road leading from Sèvres to Bellevue; on the west it bordered the Petit-Moulin, which belonged to the Archbishop of Paris, and the property known as the Petit-Château; to the north, after crossing the Sèvres-Meudon road, the valley deepened; a wide stone staircase decorated with marble vases followed its descent; the Marivel stream was crossed by means of a small bridge; a sandy path between the flower beds led to a second set of stairs which in turn led up the opposite bank, the garden being enclosed by a beautiful gate on the edge of the Versailles road. . . . Finally, to the south, the property was bordered by a long wall which followed the direction of the Plaine Perdue, stretching to the Rue des Fontaines.

La Guyarde had two main buildings separated by a paved court; its gardens climbed the hillside above a terrace embellished by niches and arcades. It seems that a lawyer, a monsieur Courtin, succeeded Lully as owner of the property; next, it was divided among his children and grandchildren until 1700, when a Pierry Bory, esquire, conseiller et secrétaire du roi, took over the estate . . .[41]

The choice of Sèvres is explained by the importance accorded to Versailles in the 1680s, as well as by the proximity of the château and park at Saint-Cloud, where Monsieur, the king's brother, settled, appropriating a number of neighboring properties for his use. There were several ferries near Sèvres that were used for crossing the Seine (one of them dating from 1650) so that the young king, hunting on the plains of Grenelle, Auteuil, and Boulogne, could pursue his journey to Meudon with his retinue and in a carriage drawn by six horses.[42] Between the Faubourg Saint-Honoré and Versailles, Sèvres represented a necessary and restful retreat for Lully.

---

[39] Is it one of those that François de Mez left for Lambert and Lully in their home in Puteaux in 1675?

[40] This pavilion is situated today in the gardens of the Centre international d'études pédagogiques in Sèvres.

[41] The estate was to pass through several more hands before falling to Jean François Verdun de Montchiroux, for the sum of 18,000 *livres* (1754). Madame de Pompadour would have the Royal Manufacture of Porcelaine transferred from Vincennes, set up on the property, in order to give the domain more prestige: still this attraction towards the West, in the direction of Versailles.

[42] Archives nationales, O[1] 3866.

Plate 8. Le Pavillion Lully at Sèvres, before restoration (Christian Decamos, 1985. General inventory, Société de Propriété Artistique des Dessins et Modèles)

Plate 9. Le Pavillon Lully at Sèvres. Panoramic view. Present-day condition

The unattainable

Striking out yet again to the west, beyond even Saint-Germain-en-Laye and Versailles, the composer finally set his sights on the estate of Grignon, to the north of Neauphle-le-Château, on the Gally brook.

'One cannot help but admire Lully's unending insolence', wrote one of the prospering composer's contemporaries, M. Cabart de Villeneuve, in 1682. 'The first President wished to acquire Grignon and offered 40,000 *livres* for it. The violin [player] made a bid of 60,000 *livres*, which is very good for the creditors; but truly, is it proper for a mere dancer (*baladin*) to have the temerity to own such lands, someone who has loaded himself down with a great number of children but has also discovered how to please the greatest King in the world! A man of this quality has greater wealth than the prime ministers of the other princes of Europe!'[43]

This was too much: outbid, Lully was obliged to renounce his grandiose plan.

MONSIEUR DE LULLY AT COURT

Even though he had failed to acquire the Grignon estate, Lully must have felt somewhat at home in the royal residences that he frequented all year, whether he was lodged in a wing of the château or in the city.

[43] A. Jal, *Dictionnaire critique de biographie et d'histoire*, 2nd ed. (1872), after the Abbé de Dangeau; quoted by Radet, *Lully*, p. 43.

Vincennes, the Louvre, and Fontainebleau stood for the past. At Fontaine-bleau, the sojourns coincided with the hunting season, autumn. Balls and *divertissements* were presented as relaxation after the many hours spent in the saddle. The musicians were probably lodged at the château.

Saint-Germain-en-Laye

Saint-Germain represented the present: on the one hand, a Château-Vieux, rebuilt on the ruins of a medieval castle by François I, with its buttresses, turrets, balustraded terraces, its gothic-vaulted halls, its vast chapel – the entire estate facing the forest; on the other hand, a few steps away, overlooking the Seine, a Château-Neuf, planned in 1594 by Henri IV, around the country house of Henri II. Terraces extended down to the river, filled with grottos that were animated by hydraulic machinery. Louis XIII, who often hunted here, died in this house; Louis XIV was born here. He took refuge at the Château-Vieux during the Fronde, went back to Paris from 1649 to 1661, then became interested once again in Saint-Germain, whose châteaux he had restored by Le Vau, Hardouin-Mansart, and Le Brun. The Château-Neuf was improved: its flower beds redesigned by Le Nôtre from 1663 onwards, the terrace repositioned at the edge of the forest (1669–73), the grottos and their machinery refurbished in 1674.[44]

Lully lived life to the full during these twenty prestigious years of the two palaces, years which saw baptisms and princely weddings, plays and *divertissements*. The Château-Vieux had a *salle de fêtes* in which were presented, among others: *La Princesse d'Elide* (1669), *Les amants magnifiques* (1670), *Cadmus et Hermione* (1674), *Thésée* (1675), *Atys* (1676), *Isis* (1677), *Alceste* (1678), *Bellérophon* (1680), *Proserpine* (1680), and *Le triomphe de l'amour* (1681), apotheosis of the *ballet de cour* and the Saint-Germain festivities.

Where did Lully stay during the preparations of these spectacles? No trace of a lease in his name at the host residence exists in the records of the period kept by the notary of Saint-Germain.[45] And Puteaux or Sèvres seem very far away for him to have returned there every night. Probably some apartment in one of the châteaux was assigned to him.

At the age of forty-four, the king grew tired of Saint-Germain-en-Laye and thought only of enlarging and embellishing Versailles. The surintendant would follow his master there.

[44] G. Lacour-Gayet, *Le Château de Saint-Germain-en-Laye* (Paris, Calmann-Lévy, 1935), p. 171, cites the itineraries followed by Parisians going to Saint-Germain. By water: Meudon, Bellevue, Bois de Boulogne, Ile Saint-Denis, Argenteuil, Ile de Crossy, La Malmaison, Bougival, Louveciennes, Marly, Le Pecq; access up to the château by the terraces. By road in carriages: Neuilly, Nanterre, Rueil, La Malmaison, Bougival, Marly, Saint-Germain-en-Laye.

[45] Catherine Massip, 'Musique et Musiciens à Saint-Germain-en-Laye (1651–1683)', *Recherches*, XVI (1976).

Versailles

Versailles was to be the future. Laye to the north, Yveline to the west, Josas to the south; the forest of Meudon nearby, the towns of Chaville, Viroflay, Porchefontaine, Montreuil, and Clagny: these are some of the places that Lully knew, and some of the roads that he travelled extensively.

But the edict to establish Versailles as a city dated only from 1671. The large private *hôtels* built by courtiers, functionaries, businessmen, and merchants did not appear until long after Lully's death. Between 1682 and 1687, the château, continually under construction, did not offer sufficient furnished buildings for the surintendant to find an apartment worthy of him. As part of his post, he was given modest official lodgings in the Grande Ecurie, newly erected by Hardouin-Mansart:[46] two rooms, a bedroom and a kitchen; two fir tables, twelve chairs 'en perroquet', an armchair, a high four-poster bed with hangings of brown material and multicolored fringes. On the walls, six Flemish tapestries, three oil paintings, 'one portraying a woman stepping out of her bath, the other, [a woman] in Egyptian costume, playing a tambourine. . . . Also, a painting of the Virgin'; a mirror. Radet[47] assures us that the inventory of these items required a valuation by 'Monsieur Jean-Baptiste Berain, Dessinateur Ordinaire du Cabinet du Roy, residing in the Galleries du Louvre', the surintendant's collaborator.

The first Versailles period seemed far away – the days of collaboration with Molière for *L'impromptu de Versailles* (1663) and *Les plaisirs de l'île enchantée* (1664). When the great era of Versailles began, there was still no formal theater at the château, but there were splendid areas in the salons, the marble courtyard, the equestrian ring in the Grande Ecurie, in the thickets – natural or adapted settings to serve the needs of the play, the ballet, the *divertissement*, or the opera. Lully, at the zenith of his career, inaugurated this brilliant series of spectacles by producing (in alternation with the Palais-Royal or in preview performances) *Persée* (1682), *Phaëton* (1683), and *Amadis* (1685).

At Rue Sainte-Anne, at la Ville-l'Evêque, at Puteaux and Sèvres, Lully reigned as master. At Saint-Germain-en-Laye, at Versailles, even at Saint-Cloud, with Monsieur (the king's brother and his neighbor at Sèvres) as his host, at Palais-Royal, at the Tuileries, at Chambord, Vaux-le-Vicomte, Anet, Beauregard, he reigned as guest. Palace life – lived at many different châteaux – could not fail to have an influence on the man's personality; he was ambitious, certainly, but compelled by his duties and his entourage to lead an ostentatious existence. A musical architect, he projected onto his own lifestyle a glimpse of the majesty of the sovereign he served. His widow and father-in-law were to retain this aristocratic posture; they would perpetuate this preoccupation with grandeur at the time when Lully was to return to the house of the Father.

---

[46] Cordey, p. 81.   [47] Radet, *Lully*, pp. 35–6.

MONSIEUR DE LULLY IN HIS FINAL ABODE

On 22 March 1687, Monsieur de Lully died, at the end of a life of hard work, adventure, creativity, of contacts with the highest-born – the king, courtiers, ministers – as well as with the lowest: actors, comedians, musicians, dancers.

After the requiem mass at his parish church, La Madeleine, the musician's remains were laid to rest at the Petits-Pères, according to his wishes.

Private chapels, with their vaults under tombstones, were very much in vogue during the whole of the seventeenth century. In prestigious churches, such as Saint-Paul, Saint-Gervais, and Saint-Eustache, their price (negotiable with the churchwardens) was as high as that of an estate or town house. They were never granted in perpetuity and, in medieval churches, they had been rechristened and redecorated on average every two hundred years. For example, it appears that the chapels of Saint-Gervais were all resold at the end of the sixteenth and in the seventeenth centuries to families that had recently grown rich through financial dealings. On the other hand, those of Saint-Eustache became the private preserve of princes of the blood or of new peers of France.[48]

On 5 May 1688, the musician's widow 'requested and obtained the ownership of a chapel . . . on the right side, the fourth one from the entry portal or the third from the chancel . . . It is at present the chapel of the Seven Sorrows and was formerly the chapel of Saint John the Baptist, Lully's patron saint.'[49]

The original drawing of the tomb[50] allowed Radet to give us a detailed description of this funerary monument, entrusted to the sculptor Michel Cotton, and crowned by a bust, reputedly the work of Antoine Coysevox (but today attributed to Gaspard Collignon):

. . . at a height of approximately two meters above a black and white marble flagstone floor rose a wide marble entablature. It was supported by six consoles and a death's head crowned with a wreath, framed in bat-wings and flanked on each side by a cartouche of Lully's coat of arms. All these ornaments were in gilded bronze. In the center of the entablature stood a black marble table with a gold-lettered inscription. On the table, which functioned as a base, rested the actual mausoleum, in black and white marble, with several gilded bronze decorations. On both sides of the sarcophagus were seated two white marble figures of women in attitudes of grief and mourning. The left figure, representing 'la Musique légère', has placed her gilded bronze lyre at her feet, while the right figure, 'la Musique dramatique', holds a gilded bronze trumpet in a gesture of abandon. On top of the sarcophagus, two small figures of grieving spirits, in white marble, sit beneath Lully's bust, which dominates the entire memorial. The background against which the monument was displayed was in dark stucco and the arch which framed it was decorated on top by a heavy stucco curtain that was being raised by a bronze skeleton of Death.[51]

Plate 10 shows the tomb in its present state.

[48] O. Ranum, *Les Parisiens*, p. 221.
[49] Radet, *Lully*, p. 60.
[50] Bibliothèque Nationale, Cabinet des Estampes, collection Gaignières.
[51] Radet, *Lully*, p. 61. The sanctuary was desecrated during the Revolution, its art objects pillaged. All that remains of Lully's tomb, reinstated in the chapel of Saint John the Evangelist in 1817, are the cenotaph, the two mourning spirits, and the weeping women, with Lully's bust surmounting the emplacement. Opposite the bust is 'a medallion in white marble haut-relief, depicting Lully surrounded by a garland, without attribution and of no great worth'.

Plate 10. Vestiges of Lully's mausoleum at Petits-Pères
(now Notre-Dame-des-Victoires); present-day condition

In the place where passions are finally calmed, Lully was to be joined by
Jean Louis, his son (15 December 1688); by Michel Lambert, his father-in-law
(28 June 1696); by Catherine Madeleine, his daughter, wife of Jean Nicolas de
Francine (3 January 1703); by Madelaine Lambert, his widow (5 May 1720);
by Louis, another son (2 April 1734); by Louis André, his grandson (22 July
1735); and by the abbot Jean-Baptiste, his third son (10 March 1743).[52]

In this way the family clan was preserved, reunited *post mortem* in this privileged
place in Paris, a stone's throw from the Louvre and the Palais-Royal, whence
could be heard the echos of the immortal operas.

BIBLIOGRAPHY

This article has used as its basis the work of Edmond Radet, architect and music
lover, who almost a century ago, in a book that has become extremely rare,
succeeded in assembling important documentation regarding certain houses
built or inhabited by Lully.

In addition, the fine thesis (unpublished) by Catherine Massip offers new and
precise details regarding the joint residences of Lambert and Lully. I am

[52] Radet, *Lully*, p. 63.

extremely grateful to her for having permitted us to use the fruits of her research on this subject.

Finally, it must not be forgotten that in 1961 Ariane Ducrot devoted her thesis at the École des Chartes to Lully's biography. Because the author has never wished to publish this text (which, moreover, is not available for consultation), this article could not offer the reader the benefit of her findings in this domain.

Sources

Archives nationales, series N, Cartes et Plans
Archives nationales, series O^1, Maison du Roi
Archives nationales, Minutier central
Archives municipales de Puteaux, Registres paroissiaux
Inventaire général des Monuments et Richesses artistiques de la France. Paris, Grand Palais
Plan de Gomboust, 1653
Plan Jouvin de Rochefort, *c.* 1675
Plan de Blondel, 1676
Plan de Turgot, 1739

The geographical spread of Lully's operas during the late seventeenth and early eighteenth centuries: new evidence from the livrets

CARL B. SCHMIDT

Throughout his lengthy reign (1661–1715) Louis XIV systematically exploited cultural events as a means of focusing attention on the French court. Under his munificent patronage dramatists like Jean-Baptiste Poquelin Molière, Isaac de Benserade, and Philippe Quinault, composers like Jean-Baptiste Lully and Michel-Richard de Lalande plus countless artists, theatrical designers and performers of every description, produced a steady flow of entertainments. These entertainments ranged from relatively unpretentious *ballets de cour* to sophisticated *tragédies lyriques* that utilized the full spectrum of available stage machinery and lavish costumes, not to mention singers, dancers and orchestral musicians – in the aggregate often numbering more than one hundred. Virtually all were first performed in the Île-de-France orbit of Paris – Versailles, Fontainebleau, and Saint-Germain-en-Laye. But Lully's works generated sufficient interest to be performed in the provinces and, more gradually, elsewhere in Europe.[1] This interest continued well into the eighteenth century under the auspices of the Académie Royale de Musique and its two chief later patrons, Louis XV and Louis XVI.

As the legacy of a resplendent period of French culture, Lully's music, particularly his *tragédies lyriques*, has drawn much attention. Not surprisingly, though, that attention has centered on productions at court or by the Académie Royale de Musique, while performances in the French provinces, Germany, Belgium, and Holland have received far less scrutiny. James Anthony, in his important study *French Baroque Music from Beaujoyeulx to Rameau*, was obliged to summarize the cities and dates suggested by Alfred Loewenberg for lack of newer, more authoritative information.[2] During 1981 and 1982, this situation began to change with the publication of significant new data by Herbert Schneider, who added substantially to our knowledge of performance in the French provincial academies of music from 1688 to 1750 through his own investigation and

---

[1] Lists of Île-de-France performances appear in DucrotR and La GorceO. All short-form bibliographical references are given in full at the end of the chapter under the rubric 'Bibliography of Secondary Literature Cited'. Information is presented in both narrative and tabular forms for performances in the French provinces and the Low Countries; performances in Germany, England, and Spain are shown only in table 6 found at the end of the text.

[2] AnthonyF, p. 109. Anthony's statement that 'The Geographical spread of Lully's operas in the closing years of the seventeenth century is remarkable considering the relative lack of mobility of opera at the time' has provided the inspiration for this essay.

by drawing together research of Léon Vallas, Jeanne Cheilan-Cambolin and others.[3] Now, in the shadow of the three hundredth anniversary of Lully's death, it is appropriate to re-examine Lully's non-Parisian operatic performances and to provide a new chronology according to which the dissemination of his music across Europe can be viewed.

Paradoxically, the task of providing such a chronology appears both well-focused and rather diffuse: focused, because it singles out one aspect of Lully performance that helps us to assess his larger reputation as a composer; and diffuse, because the research required to compile this chronology involves a seventy-five-year period plus a plethora of different cities and countries. Archival material documenting these performances is generally exceedingly scarce, if not entirely lacking, and the only 'new' documentation provided here comes from two main areas: (1) livrets (contemporaneous printed librettos) published in conjunction with performances, and (2) secondary sources that have not yet been channeled into the mainstream of Lully research. Future archival studies will, no doubt, modify this sketch of performances, but the findings of this study result from an exhaustive effort to locate livrets that add to the canon of known Lully performances. These livrets have been discovered in the course of preparing a 'Catalogue raisonné of the Literary Sources for the *Tragédies Lyriques* of Jean-Baptiste Lully',[4] intended to complement Herbert Schneider's monumental thematic catalogue.[5] The problem of locating exemplars remains substantial: livrets were not always printed for a given performance and even when they were, press runs were often exceedingly small. But used in tandem, the combination of newly-discovered livrets and overlooked secondary sources permits us to make at least a preliminary reassessment of the remarkable geographical spread of Lully's *tragédies lyriques* that began during the 1680s and lasted well into the eighteenth century.

Before Lully's death on 22 March 1687, the 'rayonnement' of his works, as Borrel so aptly put it, took place primarily south of Paris, predominantly in Marseille and Lyon, where the necessary privileges to produce *tragédies lyriques* had been granted.[6] From these centers, musicians travelled to Toulon, Avignon, Arles, Montpellier, Grenoble, Chalon, Aix-en-Province, and Dijon introducing stage works by Lully and others. As the exclusive owner of the royal privilege to produce *tragédies lyriques*, Lully (and later his heirs) sold to regional impressarios the rights to perform and publish both the music and the literary texts of Lully's works, thereby keeping relatively strict control over performances. After Lully's death, however, a wider distribution appears. Within French territory performances took place in Rennes and Vitré (1689–?) to the west, Rouen (1689–95) and Lille (1718–47) to the north, at the court of the Duke of Lorraine in Lunéville and Nancy (1706–17) or Metz (*c.* 1730) to the east, and later in Dijon (1729–32) and Strasbourg (1732–6). Outside French territory, productions were almost exclusively limited to what are now Germany, Holland, and Bel-

---

[3] See SchneiderR, VallasL and CheilanC.
[4] To be published by The Broude Trust for the Publication of Musicological Editions, New York City.
[5] See SchneiderC.
[6] See BorrelJ, p. 95.

gium. The earliest predominantly took place in Germany with performances in Regensburg (1683), Wolfenbüttel (1685–1719), Ansbach (performance dates unknown, but before 1686), Darmstadt (1687), Hamburg (1689–95), Stuttgart (1698), and Bonn (between 1719 and 1723). Additional performances were given in Brussels (1682–1741), Antwerp (1682), Amsterdam (1687–1718?), Ghent (1679 (doubtful)–1698), and The Hague (1701–18(?)). Isolated performances have also been postulated or documented in London (1686), Modena (1687), Rome (1690), Madrid (1693), and Mantua (1696(?)).

MARSEILLE, TOULON, AVIGNON, ARLES, MONTPELLIER, GRENOBLE, CHALON, AIX-EN-PROVINCE

On 8 July 1684 Lully agreed to a six-year contract with Pierre Gautier of Marseille granting permission 'to establish an academy of music in the city of Marseille in Provence' to perform *tragédies lyriques* by Lully or others in Marseille.[7] The contract also granted temporary rights to perform in various unnamed provincial cities. Lully jealously guarded his prerogative to sell such rights as an *Act Royal* signed by the king and Colbert (his minister of finance) on 17 August 1684 attests. The *Act* begins 'ORDONNANCE, Portant défenses d'établir des Opera dans le Royaume, sans la permission du sieur DE LULLY' and after reminding its readers of strictures laid down against French and Italian comedians in March 1672, goes on to detail the penalties applicable to those who might break it.[8] Gautier, once he had formed a troupe, produced his own *Le triomphe de la paix* on 28 January 1685, and we know that Charles Brebion was paid to print two hundred copies of the livret.[9] In 1686 Gautier and his troupe performed Lully's *Phaëton* and *Armide* followed by *Atys* and *Bellérophon* during 1687 (see table 1). Acknowledging the lead of peripatetic Italian troupes of a half century earlier and of contemporary French *Troupes de comédiens*, Gautier led his company to Avignon during the summer of 1687 before bankruptcy forced him to sell his assets and leave for Lyon.[10] Between 1687 and 1693, years that are poorly documented, we at least know that the company added *Amadis* and *Le triomphe de l'amour* to its repertory. Also during 1693, Jacques Gautier, Pierre's brother, took over directorship of the Marseille company, which widened its performance radius in 1695 to include Aix-en-Provence and Toulon (spring and summer) and again in 1696 to include Aix (May), Avignon (October), Arles (November), and Montpellier (December). From 1697 to 1734 sporadic performances of Lully's music continued in Marseille under a long succession of theatrical entrepreneurs.

Unfortunately, only two Lully livrets have surfaced from this early period of provincial activity. The first, for *Armide* (Avignon: L. Lemolt, 1687), was already known to Jean Robert in 1965, but the second, for *Persée* (Marseille: Pierre Mesnier, 1697), had gone unnoticed.[11] *Persée*, so the title-page proclaims,

---

[7] See CheilanC, pp. 82–4. To save space the most thorough documentation of secondary sources here occurs in the tables.
[8] This printed royal act is found in F-Pn (F 23614(199)).
[9] See CheilanC, p. 86.
[10] Concerning one such Italian travelling opera company see BianconiF. A general survey of French *comédiens* is found in MongrédienD.
[11] See RobertC, p. 313.

Table 1 *Performances in and around Marseille*

* These tables are primarily devoted to Lully's *tragédies lyriques* plus *Acis et Galatée*. Other stage works, when known, have been included in square brackets [ ]. Angle brackets < > denote works, the performance of which is doubtful. An attempt has been made to list all the non-Paris orbit stage productions which took place before the Revolution; some are amply documented while others receive but the scantest notice. It is hoped that the listings here will stimulate new archival research and further interest in locating livrets.

** Numbers in this column refer to my forthcoming book titled *A Catalogue Raisonné of the Literary Sources for the Tragédies Lyriques of Jean-Baptiste Lully – Lully Livret Catalogue – (LLC)* (New York, The Broude Trust for the Publication of Musicological Editions). Except where noted, all known copies of the livret have been listed. Standard RISM sigla have been used.

Date	City	Work performed*	Livret**	Bibliography and Remarks
1680	< Marseille	*Bellérophon* >		AnthonyL, p. 326 (according to the F-Po 'Journal de l'Opéra' this was performed 'without machines' at the Château d'If. I have been unable to corroborate this from any other source)
1685	Marseille	?		SchneiderR, p. 356
	Caen	Unspecified prologues		CarlezM, p. 22; BorrelJ, p. 98; SchneiderR, p. 356
1686	Marseille	[*Le triomphe de l'amour*]		CheilanC, pp. 99, 140 & 475; SchneiderR, pp. 70 & 356
29 Sept.?	Marseille	*Phaéton*		CheilanC, pp. 100–1, 475; SchneiderR, pp. 70 & 356
	< Marseille	*Armide* >		CheilanC, p. 475; SchneiderR, pp. 70 & 356
1687 July–Aug.	Avignon	*Phaéton*		LoewenbergA, col. 73; CheilanC, p. 107; SchneiderR, pp. 70 & 356
Sept.–Dec.	Avignon	*Armide*	13–5ᵃ	LoewenbergA, col. 79; CheilanC, pp. 102 & 107; SchneiderR, pp. 70 & 356; RobertC, pp. 304–13 (including a facsimile of the title-page opposite p. 308)
1688	Marseille	*Atys*		CheilanC, pp. 113, 114–17 & 475; SchneiderR, pp. 70 & 356
	Avignon	*Bellérophon*		CheilanC, pp. 117 & 475; SchneiderR, p. 356
	Marseille	*Bellérophon*		SchneiderR, p. 356
1689 Feb.	Marseille	*Atys*		LoewenbergA, col. 59; CheilanC, pp. 124–5 & 475; SchneiderR, pp. 70 & 356
	Marseille	*Amadis*		CheilanC, pp. 127–8
	< Marseille	*Atys* >		SchneiderR, p. 356 (error for *Amadis*)
1690?	Toulouse	*Phaéton*	10–41ᵇ	GrosPQ, p. 782
1692	Marseille	[*Le triomphe de l'amour*]		CheilanC, pp. 140 & 475; SchneiderR, pp. 71 & 356
1694	Marseille	*Armide*	13–14ᶜ	
	Marseille	*Roland*	12–15ᵈ	
1695 Oct./Nov.	Marseille	*Alceste*		CheilanC, pp. 165 & 475 (prepared but maybe not performed); SchneiderR, p. 356

Table 1 (*cont.*)

Date	City	Work performed*	Livret**	Bibliography and Remarks
1696	Marseille	*Alceste*		CheilanC, p. 166; SchneiderR, pp. 71 & 356
	Avignon	?		CheilanC, p. 170 ('Sur la fin du mois d'octobre 1696 l'opéra de Marseille, qui était à Avignon vint à Arles où il demeura environ un mois, et après avoir joué quatre ou cinq comédies en musique il alla à Montpellier où les Etats du Languedoc étaient assemblés'.)
Oct.–Nov.?	Arles	?		CheilanC, p. 170; SchneiderR, p. 356 (referring to CheilanC, p. 170 says 'vier oder fünf Opern Lullys')
Nov.?	Montpellier	?		CheilanC, p. 170
1697	Marseille	*Persée*	9–15ᶜ	CheilanC, pp. 176 & 475; SchneiderR, pp. 71 & 356
1699	Marseille	*Proserpine*		CheilanC, pp. 192 & 475; SchneiderR, pp. 71 & 356
1700	Marseille	*Proserpine*		CheilanC, p. 194; SchneiderR, p. 71
	Marseille	*Alceste?*		CheilanC, pp. 194 & 198; SchneiderR, pp. 71 & 356 (troupe from Lyon)
1701 7 & 9 March	Marseille	*Isis*		FabreR, pp. 298–9; LoewenbergA, col. 60; CheilanC, pp. 199 & 475; SchneiderR, p. 356
10 & 12 March	Marseille	*Armide*		FabreR, p. 299; LoewenbergA, col. 80; CheilanC, pp. 199, 201–2 & 475; SchneiderR, p. 356
9 April	Marseille	*Phaëton*		CheilanC, p. 202; SchneiderR, p. 356
	Marseille	[*Le carnaval*]		CheilanC, p. 475; SchneiderR, p. 356
1704	Marseille	[*Le carnaval*]		CheilanC, p. 214; SchneiderR, p. 356
	Marseille	*Bellérophon*		SchneiderR, p. 356
1714 29 Oct.	Marseille	*Phaëton*		FabreR, p. 300 (prologue only); CheilanC, p. 475; SchneiderR, p. 357
1720 17 May	Marseille	*Phaëton*		LoewenbergA, col. 73 (concert); CheilanC, pp. 314 & 475 (first four acts only); SchneiderR, p. 357
	Marseille	*Thésée*		CheilanC, p. 314 (fragment of prologue only)
1723	Marseille	*Alceste*		CheilanC, p. 344; SchneiderR, p. 357
1727	Marseille	*Alceste*		CheilanC, p. 344; SchneiderR, p. 357
1734	Marseille	*Psyché*		CheilanC, p. 407; SchneiderR, pp. 71 & 357

ᵃ Livret published in Avignon: L. Lemolt, 1687. Copy in F-A (8° 3.859ⁿᵒ· ⁶). Not listed in SchneiderC.

ᵇ Gros incorrectly dates this livret as 1680, but places it in a chronological list of livrets between 1688 and 1698. No copy has been located.

ᶜ Livret published in Marseille: Pierre Mesnier, 1694. Listed in GrosPQ, p. 782, but no copy has been located.

ᵈ Livret published in Marseille: Pierre Mesnier, 1694. Listed in GrosPQ, p. 781, but no copy has been located.

ᵉ Livret published in Marseille: Pierre Mesnier, 1697. Copy in F-A (8° 3.859ⁿᵒ· ⁵). Not listed in SchneiderC.

was 'REPRESENTE'E Par L'ACADEMIE ROYALE de Marseille'. Unlike many Parisian livrets, these two make no mention of the singers and dancers responsible for the performance. They provide only the literary text in unabridged form, with no reference to either Quinault or Lully. Etienne Gros, who made the first systematic study of Quinault's literary output, cites editions of two further works: one of *Roland* (Marseille: P. Mesnier, 1694 (in-4°)) and another of *Phaëton* (Toulouse: J.-J. Boudé, 1680 (in 4°)). *Phaëton* must be misdated because it appears in a chronological list between livrets assigned to 1689 and 1698.[12] Gros's list of sources has proven to be quite reliable, notwithstanding a few minor printing errors, and he had access to the sizeable collection assembled by Auguste Rondel, most if not all of which now rests in the Paris Bibliothèque de l'Arsenal. For Lyon, however, a substantially larger number of printed livrets exist, livrets that assist us in documenting Lully performances unknown to Vallas and his successors.

LYON

Just four years after granting a privilege for operatic productions in Marseille, Lully's heirs issued a second privilege permitting establishment of the Académie Royale de Musique de Lyon. Beginning in 1688 this three-year privilege awarded, for the sum of £2000, performance rights for those *tragédies lyriques* that had already premièred in Paris.[13] Pierre Gautier of the Marseille academy soon replaced the first leader of this company, Pierre Delacroix, a dancer from the Marseille company. Gautier produced *Bellérophon* and *Phaëton* before the first opera house was destroyed by fire in late 1688, but over the next decade the company persevered (see table 2). After a period in the private residence of the governor of Lyon, the issuance of a nine-year privilege to Nicolas Le Vasseur, granted in 1690 by Lully's heir Nicolas Francine, led to a move to new quarters in the Place Bellecour. Most of the privileges granted during this decade extended also to other cities; at various times including Marseille, Aix, Montpellier, Grenoble, Dijon, Chalon, Avignon, Toulouse and Bordeaux.

Before the turn of the century Lully's *tragédies lyriques* constituted a major portion of the Lyonnaise repertory. Many Lully productions can be documented through the careful archival research of Léon Vallas, but even Vallas acknowledged gaps in the sources that prevented full disclosure of the repertory performed.[14] Of the twenty-one productions (of 11 different *tragédies lyriques*) that can be documented before 1700, livrets have been recovered for sixteen, half of which were previously unrecorded. Two livrets, for example, help us establish repertory for a time period about which Vallas woefully remarked 'Nul docu-

---

[12] See GrosPQ, pp. 781–2. Although I have been unable to locate these two livrets, there is no reason to doubt that Gros saw them. From a slightly later period, I have located the livret for a 'PROLOGUE REPRESENTE' PAR L'ACADE-MIE ROYALE DE MUSIQUE DE MARSEILLE' set to music by André Campra (Marseille, La Veuve d'Henry Brebion & Jean-Pierre Brebion,

1716). This livret names five singers. See F-Pn (Rés. Yf. 2367). N.B.: Original orthography and accent usage have been retained in all quoted material in this article.
[13] A facsimile of this 'Traité pour l'opera de Lion' is printed in CatTS, p. 43.
[14] Much of the information summarized here is documented in VallasL.

Table 2 *Performances in Lyon*

Date	Work performed	Livret	Bibliography and Remarks
1688 *3 or 7 Jan. plus Dec.*	Phaëton	10 –12[a]	VallasL, pp. 28 & 503; LoewenbergA, col. 73; CheilanC, p. 123; SchneiderR, p. 356; CatTS, pp. 23 & 31
April–20 June	Bellérophon		VallasL, p. 31; LoewenbergA, col. 67; CheilanC, p. 123; SchneiderR, p. 356; CatTS, pp. 23 & 31
	< Atys >		SchneiderR, pp. 70 & 356 (date in CheilanC, p. 123 is 1689)
1689 *Jan. & Feb.*	Phaëton	10–14[b]	VallasL, p. 31
15 Feb.	Armide	13–8[c] 13–9[d]	VallasL, pp. 29 & 31; CheilanC, p. 123;
			LoewenbergA, col. 79; CatTS, pp. 23 & 31
7 Aug.	Atys		VallasL, p. 31; LoewenbergA, col. 59; CheilanC, p. 123; CatTS, pp. 23 & 31
1690	[Idylle sur la paix]	?[e]	SchneiderR, p. 356
1691	Thésée	3–24[f]	SchneiderR, p. 356
	Cadmus et Hermione	1–17[g]	
1692	Roland	12–10[h]	SchneiderR, p. 356
	Thésée	3–25[i] 3–26[j]	VallasL, p. 503; LoewenbergA, col. 56;
			SchneiderR, p. 356
1694	Proserpine	8–19[k]	SchneiderC, p. 356
1695	Alceste		VallasL, p. 51, CatTS, pp. 23 & 33
	Persée		VallasL, pp. 51 & 504; CatTS, pp. 23 & 33
1696	Alceste	2–20[l]	LoewenbergA, col. 53; SchneiderR, p. 356
winter 1696/7	Persée	9–14[m]	LoewenbergA, col. 73; SchneiderR, p. 356
	[Le temple de la paix]		VallasL, p. 51 (indicates a livret was published by T. Amaulry); SchneiderC, p. 356
1698	Isis	5–18[n]	
	Psyché	6–14[o]	SchneiderR, p. 356
	Phaëton	10–19[p]	SchneiderR, p. 356
	Armide	13–16.1[q] 13–16.2[r]	BorrelJ, p. 98; LoewenbergA, col. 79;
			SchneiderR, p. 356
	< Proserpine >		SchneiderR, p. 356
1699	Alceste	2–22[s]	VallasL, p. 504; LoewenbergA; CheilanC, p. 475; SchneiderR, p. 356
	Armide		CheilanC, p. 475; SchneiderR, p. 356
	Phaëton	10–21[t]	
1701 *9 April*	Phaëton		VallasL, p. 60; CheilanC, p. 475; SchneiderR, p. 356
1704	Bellérophon		VallasL, pp. 75–6; CheilanC, p. 477
1710	Acis et Galatée		SchneiderR, p. 357
	Amadis		SchneiderR, p. 357
	Atys		SchneiderR, p. 357
	Phaëton		SchneiderR, p. 357
1715 *21 Aug.*	Acis et Galatée		BorrelJ, p. 98 (1 act only); SchneiderR, p. 357
1730 *26 & 29 April*	Armide		LoewenbergA, col. 79; CheilanC, p. 479; SchneiderR, p. 357
	Alceste	2–32[u]	SchneiderR, p. 357

Table 2 (*cont.*)

Date	Work performed	Livret	Bibliography and Remarks
1740	*Roland*	12–30[v]	VallasL, pp. 231 & 506; CatTS, p. 23 (listed under the title *Renaud*); SchneiderR, p. 357
1741	*Thésée*	3–44[w]	VallasL, pp. 253 & 507; SchneiderR, p. 357
	Armide		VallasL, p. 235; SchneiderR, p. 357
	Atys		VallasL, p. 235; SchneiderR, p. 357
1742	*Armide*	13–31[x]	VallasL, p. 507; CatTS, p. 40
Dec.	*Atys*	4–45[y]	VallasL, p. 507, LoewenbergA, col. 59; SchneiderR, p. 357; CatTS, p. 40
1743	*Atys*		VallasL, p. 507; see under 1742 above
1745 19 Feb.	*Thésée*		VallasL, p. 236
1749 through 1 Jan. 1750	*Roland*	12–23[z]	VallasL, p. 247; SchneiderR, p. 357
	Atys		SchneiderR, 357
Dec.	*Thésée*	3–47[aa]	VallasL, p. 247 & 508; SchneiderR, p. 357; CatTS, p. 41
1750 March	*Armide*	13–36[bb]	VallasL, pp. 248 & 509; SchneiderR, p. 357

[a] Livret published in Lyon: Thomas Amaulry, 1688. Copy in F-LYm (360.806); for a facsimile of the title-page see CatTS, p. 42. Listed in SchneiderC, p. 388.

[b] Livret published in Lyon: Thomas Amaulry, 1689. Copy in F-Pn (8° Yth. 14055). Listed in SchneiderC, p. 388.

[c] Livret published in Lyon or possibly Amsterdam: 'Suivant la copie imprimée à Paris', 1689. Not listed in SchneiderC.

[d] Livret published in Lyon or possibly Amsterdam: 'Suivant la copie imprimée à Paris', 1689. Listed in SchneiderC, p. 465. Livrets 13–8 and 13–9 represent editions which have been completely reset.

[e] SchneiderR, p. 356 indicates that a libretto was published, but none is cited in SchneiderC, p. 449.

[f] Livret published in Lyon: Thomas Amaulry, 1691. Copy in F-Pa (Ro. 8528). Listed in SchneiderC, p. 246. Some performers from a Parisian production are named in the interior of the livret.

[g] Livret published in Lyon: Thomas Amaulry, 1691. Copy in I-Vgc. Not listed in SchneiderC.

[h] Livret published in Lyon: Thomas Amaulry, 1692. Copies in F-Pa (Ro. 8521) and GB-Mr (842.49Q42 18 Sp. Coll.). Listed in SchneiderC, p. 428.

[i] Livret published in Lyon: Thomas Amaulry, 1692. Copy in F-LYm (360.805). A few performers from the Parisian performance listed in note *j* are also given in this livret. Not listed in SchneiderC.

[j] Livret published in Lyon: Thomas Amaulry, 1692. Copies in D-brd:Hs (5 in MS $\frac{368}{3}$: 1) and I-Bu (A.V.Tab.I B III Vol. 7[1] n. 1). The performers listed are those from the Paris: Christophe Ballard, 1677 livret. Listed in

SchneiderC, p. 246. Livrets 3–25 and 3–26 represent editions which have been completely reset.

[k] Livret published in Lyon: François Roux, 1694. Copies in D-brd:Hs (3 in MS $\frac{368}{3}$: 2), I:Vgc (Collezione Rolandi LULLY A-Z) and US-PHu (FC65Qu422.680p 1694). Listed in SchneiderC, p. 332.

[l] Livret published in Lyon: Thomas Amaulry, 1696. Copy in F-Po (Liv. 18[R6(2)). Not listed in SchneiderC.

[m] Livret published in Lyon: Thomas Amaulry, 1696. Copies in C-Ou (PQ1881.P4 1696), F-LYm (120.150) incomplete and PL-Kj (Mus.Ant. T76; formerly in D-brd:B).

[n] Livret published in Lyon: Thomas Amaulry, 1698. Copies in C-Ou (PQ1881.I 8 1698 Coll. Spec.) and D-brd:Hs (1 in MS 3: 2). Not listed in SchneiderC.

[o] Livret published in Lyon: Thomas Amaulry, 1698. Copies in D-brd:Hs (2 in MS $\frac{368}{3}$: 1) and F-Pa (Ro. 1429). Listed in SchneiderC, p. 310 (date misprinted as 1678).

[p] Livret published in Lyon: Thomas Amaulry, 1698. Copy in D-brd:Hs (6 in MS $\frac{368}{3}$: 2). Listed in SchneiderC, p. 388.

[q] Livret published in Lyon: Thomas Amaulry, 1698. Copy in F-Pn (8° Yth. 1194). Listed in SchneiderC, p. 465.

[r] Livret published in Lyon: Thomas Amaulry, 1698. Copies in F-Pa (Ro. 8510), Pla gorce and I-Bu (A.V.Tab. I G. III Vol. 34,4). Not listed in SchneiderC. Livrets 13–16.1 and 13–16.2 contain different title-pages, but the contents have not been completely reset.

[s] Livret published in Lyon: André Molin, 1699. Copy in F-LYm (804.301). Listed in SchneiderC, p. 225.

[t] Livret published in Lyon: André Molin, 1699. Copies in I-Vgc (Collezione Rolandi LULLY A-Z)

ment musical ne nous est parvenue des années 1690 et 1691.'[15] Livrets were printed for *Thésée* and *Cadmus et Hermione* during 1691, both which premiered in Lyon that year. Other productions, such as those for *Alceste* and *Persée* during 1696, have been established through documents by Vallas, but no livrets for these performances had previously been located.

The right to print livrets in Lyon belonged to Thomas Amaulry, whose shop printed the majority of livrets between 1688 and 1700. On two occasions, however, Amaulry ceded his right to other printers: during 1694 it passed to François Roux and during 1699 to André Molin.[16] All Lyonnaise livrets of this period display duodecimo format (similar to the countless Amsterdam editions) and present the original texts with virtually no alterations. Few, though, provide information about the actual performances. Unfortunately, not one name of a singer or dancer appears in these livrets, nor do they mention an actual performance date.

Between 1701 and 1715 Lully's *tragédies lyriques* continued to see occasional performances in Lyon, but not with their earlier regularity. Extant archival evidence and the remaining printed livrets show clearly that, when the theater was busy at all, taste ran to the music of Destouches rather than to that of the more venerable Lully. Even for the few Lully works that were performed, no livrets (if any were printed) have come to light. The years from 1716 to 1729 appear barren of Lully works altogether.[17] During 1730 both *Armide* and *Alceste* were performed, but another decade passed before the next Lully performance. Lully's music enjoyed a final renaissance in the decade from 1740 to 1750, which saw *Atys* mounted four times, *Armide* and *Thésée* three times each and *Roland* twice. Extant livrets for about half of these productions provide full lists of the performance personnel. Those published from 1740 to 1744 occur as single

---

[15] VallasL, p. 43.
[16] These privileges, to be published in my forthcoming livret catalogue, are found in livrets for *Proserpine* (LLC 8–19) and *Phaëton* (LLC 10–21).
[17] For general information about the inclusion of Lully's music in eighteenth-century concerts see CizeronV.

Notes to Table 2 (*cont.*)

and US-BAu (PH3737.C58S7 1695 Special Collection). Not listed in SchneiderC.
" Livret published in Lyon: Antoine Olyer (printed by Jean Baptiste Roland), 1730. Performers listed (plus the dancers for the 1677 Paris production). Copies in F-DO (B.M. Dole 3887) and Pa (Ro. 8503). Listed in SchneiderC, p. 225.
ᵛ Livret published in Lyon: Aymé Delaroche, 1740. Performers listed. Copies in F-Pa (Ro. 1031.(8)) and Pn (Cons. X. 1212 [vol. 2(7)]). SchneiderC, p. 429 lists a copy in F-LYm, which cannot be located.
ʷ Livret published in Lyon: Aymé Delaroche, 1741. Performers listed. Copy in F-Pa (Ro. 1032). I have been unable to trace the copy listed as in the 'Bibl. Palais des Arts' (see VallasL, p. 507). Listed in SchneiderC, p. 247.
ˣ Livret published in Lyon: Aymé Delaroche, 1742.

Performers listed. Copies in F-LYm (116.224), Pa (Ro. 1032.(4)), (Ro. 1033.(6)), TLm (Conservatoire 3067 (1)) and US-Wc (ML48.S5760a). Listed in SchneiderC, p. 465.
ʸ Livret published in Lyon: Aymé Delaroche, 1743. Performers listed. Copies in F-LYm (116.225), Pa (Ro. 1033.(1)), TLm (Conservatoire 3067 (8)) and US-Wc (ML48.S5761ᵃ). Listed in SchneiderC, p. 269.
ᶻ Livret published in Lyon: Rigollet, 1749. Performers listed. Copy in F-LYm (359.301). Listed in SchneiderC, p. 429.
ᵃᵃ Livret published in Lyon: Rigollet, 1749. Performers listed. Copies in F-LYm (359.344) and Pa (Ro. 8530). Listed in SchneiderC, p. 247.
ᵇᵇ Livret published in Lyon: Rigollet, 1750. Performers listed. Copies in F-LYm (313.291) and Pa (Ro. 8511). Listed in SchneiderC, p. 465.

volumes and in *recueils factices* (collections of separately paginated livrets each with individual title-pages and sometimes also with a collective title-page) presented to Monseigneur le duc de Villeroy commemorating the re-establishment of opera in Lyon (beginning with Montéclair's *Jephté* in April of 1739). Because these livrets have been well-known for years, we need not dwell on them here. After *Thésée* in March 1750 Lully's star was eclipsed by those of Philidor, Gluck, Grétry and others: thus a cycle extending more than sixty years came to a close.

PERFORMANCES ELSEWHERE IN THE FRENCH PROVINCES

In his article on the founding of an académie de musique in Rouen during the reign of Louis XIV, Jérôme de La Gorce mentions numerous privileges granting rights to establish opera companies (or académies de musique) in a variety of French cities.[18] To those cities already named, La Gorce cites acts relative to Rennes, La Rochelle, Toul, Metz, Verdun, Strasbourg, Nantes, Vannes, Toulon, Arles, and Nîmes. Privileges, though generally granted for specific cities, sometimes covered regions such as Flandre, la Bourgogne, or le Dauphine. Although relatively little systematic study has yet been done by theater historians on early operatic activity in many of these cities or regions, livrets and secondary literature have yielded enough information to show that Lully figured prominently in their musical activity. Livrets presently exist, or can be shown to have existed, for Lully performances in Rennes (and neighboring Vitré), Rouen, Lunéville, Nancy, Metz, Lille, Dijon, and Strasbourg: none has yet been found for La Rochelle, Toul, Verdun, Nantes, Vannes, Toulon, or Nîmes.[19]

Rennes

Despite its tradition of ballet performances that dates as early as 1671, no musical history for the city of Rennes during the reign of *le Roi-Soleil* has yet been published.[20] Livrets for more than a dozen pre-1700 ballets performed at 'le théâtre du college de Rennes de la Compagnie de Iesus' exist, the largest concentration of which dates from the decade 1690–1700.[21] This same decade saw the establishment of an 'academye royalle de musique ou opera,' for which 'nostre bien aimé Louis de Golard Sr du Mesny, musicien de l'academye royalle' received the '*lettres patentes*' early in 1689.[22] As with other such privileges, this

[18] I am deeply grateful to Monsieur La Gorce for his generosity in providing me with a typescript of his important essay (see La GorceA) and for permitting me to see Lully livrets in his private collection.
[19] Although no Lully livrets are known to have been published in Montpellier, DesgravesR, p. 180, no. 723 lists the following livret in F-MOv (30552): 'L'Europe galante ballet en musique représentée par l'Académie royale de musique. – *On la vend a Montpelier, a l'entrée de* la porte de l'Academie royale de musique, par Honoré Pech, 1700.' For additional information concerning provincial privileges for Lille, Bordeaux, La Rochelle, and others granted in 1720 see BenoitD, p. 237.
[20] For a general introduction to Rennes in this period see MeyerH.
[21] See RonsinR for the present location of these ballet livrets.
[22] This document is published in BourligueuxD, pp. 195–6.

one makes specific reference to 'Les representations des opera Composez par le feu Sr de Lully'. Though we know little about the precise repertory performed in Brittany, three Lully livrets exist documenting performances there (see table 3). *Atys*, performed in late October or early November 1689, represents a special case. It was not, as might be suspected, the first fruits of the new 'Academye', but rather a production imported from Paris by the same Du Mesny who had negotiated the privilege. Du Mesny dedicated the performance, given in neighboring Vitré, to Monseigneur le Mareschal d'Estrée. A new prologue, composed especially for the occasion by Pascal Collasse, replaced Lully's original. The title-page for the published livret, the only one for a Lully *tragédie lyrique* that advertises the prologue to the exclusion of the *tragédie* itself, begins: 'PROLOGUE MIS EN MUSIQUE Par Monsieur COLLASSE, Maistre de Musique de la Chapelle du Roy. . . .'

The shop of Philippes Le Sainct in Rennes printed livrets for two other Lully works, *Acis et Galatée* and *Cadmus et Hermione*, suggesting their performance there. Unfortunately, neither livret is dated, nor has archival information yet established when the performances took place. The choice of *Cadmus* is unusual: only performances at The Hague (1680) and Lyon (1691) are known to have been given outside the Île de France.

Rouen

The year 1689 also saw the founding of an académie de musique in Rouen.[23] La Gorce discovered three livrets for Lully performances and documented a fourth production for which no livret is known. Aided by secondary sources, he established Lully's *Phaëton* as the first work to be staged by the new académie. Through a printed livret he added a totally unknown montage titled *Les fragmens du triomphe de l'amour et des plaisirs de Versailles* to the Lully canon. We know of no subsequent Lully performances until 1692 when the company performed *Atys*, which had gained popularity in both Marseille and Lyon. La Gorce also located a livret for *Roland*, performed in 1693 and Schneider found another for *Proserpine* (1695). To these can be added a sixth livret for *Amadis*, which was apparently performed in 1693 along with *Roland*. No further Lully livrets published in Rouen are known, but others may await discovery. Print runs for these livrets were probably exceedingly small; in any case, only six exemplars of five Lully livrets known to have been published there survive.[24]

Lunéville – Nancy – Metz

The remaining provincial staged performances of Lully's *tragédies*, all from the eighteenth century, are located in four distinct geographical areas: (1) Lorraine (Nancy, Lunéville, Metz), Lille, Dijon, and Strasbourg. Printed livrets docu-

[23] For a general introduction to Rouen in this period see PeriauxH.
[24] SchneiderR, p. 32 indicates that Christophe Ballard printed 2150 livrets for *Ballet de la jeunesse* in 1685 and that 1050 were printed for its 1718 revival. See note 9 for a press run in Lyon of only 200 exemplars. Very little information is known about the size of press runs for livrets in the provinces or the Low Countries.

Table 3 *Performances elsewhere in the French provinces (by city)*

Date	City	Work performed	Livret	Bibliography and Remarks
1689 Oct./Nov.?	Vitré	*Atys*	4–19[a]	SchneiderR, pp. 73 & 356. New prologue (author unknown) set to music by Pascal Collasse. 'APOLLON PAROIST DANS la Gloire tel que les Poëtes & les Peintres le representent la teste couronnée de Lauriers & la Lire à la main. Plus bas sont la Nymphe de la Seine qui represente toute la France, & la Nymphe de la Loire qui represente la Bretagne. Elles sont accompagnées de Tritons & de Nayades'. Production coordinated by Louis de Golard Du Mesny
N.D.	Rennes	*Acis et Galatée*	14–26[b]	
N.D.	Rennes	*Cadmus et Hermione*	1–32[c]	SchneiderR, p. 356
1689	Rouen	*Phaëton*		La GorceA
	Rouen	[*Les fragmens du triomphe de l'amour et des plaisirs de Versailles*]	Yes[d]	La GorceA
1692	Rouen	*Atys*	4–21[e]	La GorceA
1693	Rouen	*Roland*	12–13[f]	La GorceA
	Rouen	*Amadis*	11–15[g]	
1695	Rouen	*Proserpine*	8–20[h]	SchneiderR, p. 356; La GorceA
1706	Lunéville	*Acis et Galatée*	Yes[i]	BorrelJ, p. 98; AntoineH, p. 123; SchneiderR, p. 356
1708 5 & 9 Feb.	Lunéville	*Thésée*	3–35[j]	BorrelJ, p. 98; AntoineH, pp. 128 & 134; SchneiderR, p. 357. Production mounted by Henri Desmarest
	Lunéville	[*Le bourgeois gentilhomme*]	Yes[k]	BorrelJ, p. 98; AntoineH, p. 130
1709 7 & 14 Feb.	Lunéville	*Amadis*	11–27[l]	BorrelJ, p. 98; AntoineH, p. 130; SchneiderR, p. 357
August	Lunéville	[*Les fêtes de l'Amour et de Bacchus*]	Yes[m]	AntoineH, p. 130; SchneiderR, p. 357
1710 15 Nov.	Lunéville	*Armide*	13–24[n]	AntoineH, p. 130; SchneiderR, p. 357. New prologue by Desmarest
1717 Carnaval	Nancy	[*Le bourgeois gentilhomme*]	Yes[o]	BorrelJ, p. 98; AntoineH, p. 136
Carnaval	Nancy	[*Monsieur de Pourceaugnac*]		AntoineH, p. 136
1730	Metz	*Atys*	4–41[p]	
N.D.	Metz	*Atys*	4–52[q]	
N.D.	Metz	*Alceste*	2–41[r]	
N.D.	Metz	*Armide*	13–44[s]	
N.D.	Metz	*Roland*	12–40[t]	
N.D.	Metz	*Thésée*	3–55[u]	

Table 3 (*cont.*)

Date	City	Work performed	Livret	Bibliography and Remarks
1718	Lille	*Phaëton*	10–30[v]	LefebvreM, I, 216; LoewenbergA, col. 73
	Lille	*Thésée*	3–38[w]	LefebvreM, I, 218; LoewenbergA, col. 56
1720	Lille	*Alceste*	2–29[x]	LefebvreM, I, 216; LoewenbergA, col. 53
1720?	Lille	*Atys*	4–53[y]	LefebvreM, I, 216; LoewenbergA, col. 59
N.D.	Lille	*Roland*	12–39[z]	LefebvreM, I, 218; LoewenbergA, col. 76
N.D.	Lille	[*Les fêtes de l'Amour et de Bacchus*]	Yes[aa]	LefebvreM, I, 217
1729	Dijon	*Isis*	5–26[bb]	
	Dijon	*Amadis*	11–31[cc]	
1730?	Dijon	*Thésée*	3–42[dd]	SchneiderR, pp. 74 & 357 under the date 1740
1732	Dijon	*Phaëton*	10–34[ee]	
1732	Strasbourg	*Isis*	5–28[ff]	SchneiderR, pp. 74 & 357
1736	Strasbourg	*Bellérophon*	7– 27[gg]	

[a] Livret published in Paris: Christophe Ballard, 1689. Copy in F-RE (15138). Listed in SchneiderC, p. 269.

[b] Livret published in Rennes: Philippes le Sainct, N.D. Copy in F-Po (Liv.17[84; this copy is incomplete). Not listed in SchneiderC.

[c] Livret published in Rennes: Philippes le Sainct, N.D. Copy in US-Wc (ML48.L84P83 1699). Listed in SchneiderC, p. 209.

[d] Livret published in [Rouen]: Jean-Baptiste Besongne, 1689. Copy in F-Pn (Rés. Yf. 2128). La Gorce explains that this work was a montage of scenes from Lully's *Le carnaval* and *Le triomphe de l'amour*. Not listed in SchneiderC.

[e] Livret published in Rouen: Jean-Baptiste Besongne, 1692. Copy in F-R (O. 600 a). Not listed in SchneiderC.

[f] Livret published in [Rouen]: Jean-Baptiste Besongne, 1693. Copy in F-R (O. 600 b). Not listed in SchneiderC.

[g] Livret published in Rouen: Jean-Baptiste Besongne, 1693. Copies in F-Lm (22323) and V (Holmes E 72). Not listed in SchneiderC.

[h] Livret published in Rouen: Jean-Baptiste Besongne, 1695. Copy in F-Pa (Ro. 1051). Listed in SchneiderC, p. 332.

[i] Livret published in Nancy: Barbier, 1706. According to FavierC, p. 554 a copy was in F-NAm. Not listed in SchneiderC.

[j] Livret published in Nancy: Paul Barbier, 1708. Lists performers. Copy in F-NAm (98 030 (24)). Not listed in SchneiderC.

[k] Livret cited in AntoineH as published by Jean-Louis Bouchard. Copy in F-NAm (80 209[19]). Not listed in SchneiderC.

[l] Livret published in Lunéville: Jean-Louis Bouchard, 1709. Lists performers. Copy in F-NAm (80.326[7]). Not listed in SchneiderC.

[m] Livret cited in AntoineH as published by Jean-Louis Bouchard. Copy in F-NAm (702 034[11]). Not listed in SchneiderC.

[n] Livret published in Lunéville: Jean-Louis Bouchard, 1710. Lists performers. Copy in F-NAm (275 440). Not listed in SchneiderC.

[o] Livret cited in AntoineH as published by Charlot and Deschamps, 1717. Copy in F-NAm (80.177[21]). Not listed in SchneiderC.

[p] Livret published in Metz: La Veuve Brice Antoine, 1730. Copy in F-MZ (P1751). Not listed in SchneiderC.

[q] Livret published in Metz: Jean Antoine, N.D. Copy in F-NAm (Réserve 11.167f). Not listed in SchneiderC.

[r] Livret published in Metz: Jean Antoine, N.D. Copy in F-NAm (Réserve 11.167c). Not listed in SchneiderC.

[s] Livret published in Metz: Jean Antoine, N.D. Copy in F-NAm (Réserve 11.167b). Not listed in SchneiderC.

[t] Livret published in Metz: Jean Antoine, N.D. Copy in F-NAm (Réserve 11.167e). Not listed in SchneiderC.

[u] Livret published in Metz: La Veuve Brice Antoine. Copy in F-MZ (P1751). Not listed in SchneiderC.

[v] Livret published in Lille: François Malte, 1718. Lists performers. The copy formerly in F-DOU was destroyed in World War II. LhottéT, pp. 38–9 gives a full list of the performers and DanchinL, I, 267, no. 1085 describes the livret. Not listed in SchneiderC.

[w] Livret published in Lille: Charles-Maurice

ment virtually all these, even if, as in the case of Lille, not one can now be located. Unquestionably the greatest interest in Lully's stage works was exhibited in the Lorraine, where Léopold Ier. Duke of Lorraine and of Bar (1697–1729), possessed a large palace in Lunéville. Gradually, with the encouragement of Duchess Elisabeth-Charlotte, Léopold became an active patron of the arts in the opening decades of the eighteenth century.

As early as 1700 Destouches' opera *Marthésie* appeared in Nancy, with choreography by Claude-Marc Magny, a member of the Parisian Académie royale de danse and 'maître à danser' of the duchess. In 1706, Magny was also responsible for producing Lully's *Acis et Galatée* in Lunéville (where the court had transferred in 1702). Apparently, after the model of Versailles, Magny utilized members of the court in his *corps de ballet*. But the real vogue of Lully came after the duke employed Henry Desmarets to be his *surintendant de la musique* in April of 1707.[25] During each of the next two years Desmarets (along with Charles-Antoine Royer de Marainville, *surintendant des Plaisirs*, and the dancer Magny) mounted a pair of Lully works: *Thésée* and *Le bourgeois gentilhomme* in 1708; *Amadis* and *Les fêtes de l'Amour et de Bacchus* in 1709. Finally, in 1710, the team produced *Armide*, Lully's last completed *tragédie lyrique*, for which Desmarets had written a new prologue. Michel Antoine has suggested that the duchess, who may have wished to revive the very spectacles she had known during her youth at the court of Louis XIV, may have prompted the choice of repertory.[26]

Between 1711 and 1716 no further Lully works are known to have been performed and evidence suggests that the court adopted a more fiscally restrained position toward theatrical entertainments than had been exhibited during the

[25] See AntoineH.   [26] AntoineH, p. 131.

Notes to Table 3 (*cont.*)

Cramé, 1718. LefebvreH, I, 218 lists a copy in a 'private collection', which I have been unable to locate, and DanchinL, I, 257, no. 1027 describes the livret. Not listed in SchneiderC.

[x] Livret published in Lille: François Malte?, N.D. LefebvreH, I, 216 lists a copy in a 'private collection', which I have been unable to locate, and DanchinL, I, 268, no. 1098 describes the livret. Not listed in SchneiderC.

[y] Livret published in Lille: François Malte, N.D. Lists performers. The copy formerly in F-DOU which was destroyed in World War II. LhottéT, pp. 39–40 gives a full list of the performers and DanchinL, I, 267, no. 1087 describes the livret. Not listed in SchneiderC.

[z] Livret published in Lille: François Malte, N.D. LefebvreH, I, 218 lists a copy in a 'private collection', which I have been unable to locate, and DanchinL, I, 268, no. 1093 describes the livret. Not listed in SchneiderC.

[aa] Livret published in Lille: François Malte, N.D. LefebvreH, I, 218 lists a copy in a 'private collection', which I have been unable to locate, and DanchinL, I, no. 1092 describes the livret. Not listed in SchneiderC.

[bb] Livret published in Dijon: Arnauld-Jean-Baptiste Augé, 1729. Copy in F-Pa (Ro. 1415). Not listed in SchneiderC.

[cc] Livret published in Dijon: Arnauld-Jean-Baptiste Augé, 1729. Copy in F-Pa (Ro. 1415). Permission to print granted on 3 Dec. 1729. Not listed in SchneiderC.

[dd] Livret published in Dijon: Arnauld-Jean-Baptiste Augé, 1740 [*sic?*]. The permission to publish (livret p. 63) was granted on 4 Feb. 1730 and since the Academy of Music in Dijon existed between 1725 and 1738 it is likely that 1740 should read 1730. Copies in F-Dm (Fonds Delmasse no. 1385) and Pa (Ro. 8529). Listed in SchneiderC, p. 247 under the date 1740.

[ee] Livret published in Dijon: Arnauld-Jean-Baptiste Augé, 1732. Copy in F-Dm (Fonds Delmasse no. 1381). Not listed in SchneiderC.

[ff] Livret published in Strasbourg: Jean-François Le Roux, 1732. Copy in D-brd:DS (41/1265(6)). Listed in SchneiderC, p. 292.

[gg] Livret published in Strasbourg: Jean-François Le Roux, 1736. Copy in DK-Kk (75[iv], 164 4°). Not listed in SchneiderC.

vogue of Lully. The last pair of Lully works produced under Desmarets's supervision were modest *comédies ballets* rather than *tragédies*. The 'Opéra de Nancy' (constructed by Francesco Bibiena between 1708 and 1709) presented *Le bourgeois gentilhomme* and *Monsieur de Pourceaugnac* during the Carnival of 1717.

No theatrical history of Metz – the last of our triumvirate of cities in the Lorraine – has yet been written, and published materials concerning opera there are scarce. Gilbert Rose, in a recent article on eighteenth-century musical life in Metz, indicates that the first mention of music in a theatrical context dates from 1667, but concerns only itinerant musicians.[27] La Gorce locates a '*Consession de privilège*, valable pour Toul, Metz, Verdun et Strasbourg' dating from 4 April 1699, and Rose adds that Guillaume Paisible, *maître de musique* at the cathedral, was granted permission to perform *opéra* regularly.[28] Rose makes clear that material does exist to help write a history of eighteenth-century opera in Metz and he tantalizes us with the remark 'Mais tous les opéras créés à Paris de LULLY à GLUCK furent ensuite repris à Metz . . .', but his article is too brief to undertake such a task.[29]

Our search for livrets suggests that Metz indeed had an active interest in Lully's music. Six of them, each extant in but a single copy, remain for five Lully *tragédies* including *Atys* (2), *Alceste*, *Armide*, *Roland*, and *Thésée*. Four, all published by Jean Antoine, bear no date, while one of the two others published by La Veuve Brice Antoine dates from 1730. None mentions actual performances, nor lists any performers. Those published by Jean Antoine, however, do name Lully and Quinault as composer and librettist respectively. Because all of these livrets were readily available in Amsterdam editions, not to mention literary reprints of Quinault's *oeuvre*, it is likely that they document performances, but confirmation of actual performance dates must await future archival research.

Lille

Just when interest in Lully's music ebbed in Lunéville and Nancy, the flow began again to the north in Lille, due largely, no doubt, to the peace that returned Lille to France in 1713. Thanks to the indefatigable research on theater history in Lille carried out by Léon Lefebvre before World War II, we have a vivid picture of opera there from its inception in 1698.[30] Lefebvre, one of the first to demonstrate the value of livrets in establishing repertory when corroborating documents are lacking, devoted great attention to the tentative beginnings in terms of management and available theaters. Altogether Lefebvre located seventeen different livrets for operas given in Lille between 1718 and 1725, the period Lully's music was performed, including works by Lully (6), Campra (2), Berton (2), Destouches (2), Desmarets (1), Lacoste (1), Mouret (1), Collasse (1), and

---

[27] See RoseV, p. 57.
[28] See La GorceA and RoseV, p. 57.
[29] See RoseV, p. 58.
[30] See LefebvreH. BenoitD, p. 234 prints notice of a privilege granted to Joseph Garnier 'de faire représenter l'Opéra dans la ville de Lille pendant trois années consécutives, à dater du 1er février 1718, moyennant la somme de 1500 livres par an payable à la caisse de l'Académie royale de Musique de Paris, de trois mois en trois mois'.

Campra/Desmarets (1).[31] Were it not for the work of Lefebvre and Gustav Lhotte (another Lille theater historian), knowledge of Lully performances in Lille would be all but nonexistent.[32] Of the seventeen livrets they uncovered, four of Lully's livrets belonged to a private collector and two to the library at Douai. The private collector's identity has never been ascertained and the Douai livrets were destroyed in World War II. We do know that some livrets from this period, among them *Phaëton* and *Atys*, name the performers. Once again a familiar problem surfaces in many of these livrets, because most, including three for Lully's operas, are undated. All must have been published before 1720 when François Malte ceased activity as a printer.[33] Without access to the sources, however, little more can be said.

Dijon and Strasbourg

Finally, newly discovered livrets present evidence of more activity in Dijon and Strasbourg than previously known: for Dijon we know of four productions (1729–32) and for Strasbourg, two (1732, 1736). Only one Lully production in each city had previously been recorded and the additions permit some basic conclusions to be drawn. Though little has been written about it, Craig Wright notes that an academy of music was active in Dijon between 1725 and 1738.[34] Apparently our four Dijon livrets document performances given under the auspices of this academy despite a livret for *Thésée* that carries '1740' on its title-page. This date must be a misprint for '1730' because the permission (on p. 63 of the livret) reads '*PERmis d'imprimer. A Dijon, ce 4. Fevrier 1730. Signé* BAUDOT.' As with livrets published in most provincial cities (except, for example, late editions from Lyon), these do not exhibit the often heavy suppression of lines prevalent in many later Parisian livrets for Lully revivals.

The Strasbourg livrets exhibit neither reverence for the original text nor, by extrapolation, for the original music. The title page of each proclaims 'DIVERTISSE-MENT *EXECUTÉ* A L'ACADEMIE DE MUSIQUE DE STRASBOURG' thereby immediately dispensing with the notion that readers are about to encounter the standard reprint of a *tragédie lyrique*. In fact, each play has been heavily cut eliminating the prologue entirely and reducing the drama proper from five to three acts. This reduction has been accomplished at its most drastic level by excising entire scenes and, in the case of *Bellérophon*, Act IV in its entirety. Without the scores it is difficult to say much more than that the length has been dramatically shortened, the size of the cast reduced, and the original structure of the plot simplified. Clearly the requirements of the Académie de Musique de Strasbourg (founded in 1730 or 1731) differed vastly from those satisfied by Lully and his librettists; modesty was the goal, whether motivated by taste, financial considerations, or both.[35]

---

[31] Listed in LefebvreH, pp. 216–18.
[32] LhotteT, pp. 38–41 prints cast lists for *Phaëton*, *Atys*, and *L'Europe galante* (Lille, François Malte, n.d.).
[33] See DanchinL, vol. I, 266.

[34] See WrightD, p. 475.
[35] HappelS, p. 200 gives 1730 while LivetH, p. 445 gives 1731. For a general introduction to Strasbourg see LivetH.

Although the appearance of printed livrets argues against the hypothesis, the very active concert series the Académie is known to have had suggests the possibility that Lully's works were never actually staged there.[36]

PERFORMANCES IN LA HAYE AND AMSTERDAM

Dutch interest in Lully's music and in the literary legacy of Quinault and his successors at the Académie Royale de Musique in Paris manifested itself during the 1680s, maintaining its vitality into the second decade of the eighteenth century. Several points corroborate this view: (1) the wealth of Amsterdam editions of livrets numbering more than one hundred for works set by Lully alone; (2) the appearance of many books of airs or instrumental excerpts from his stage works (even including several complete operas) issued from 1682 on by Jean Philip Heus, Antoine Pointel, Estienne Roger, and others; and (3) productions of the *tragédies lyriques* that can be documented from archival sources, livrets, or both.[37] Space here precludes a discussion of these materials in the integrated manner they merit, so I will focus almost exclusively on the final point, the livrets.

Earlier this century Jan Fransen wrote an excellent history of opera in Holland from its inception through the eighteenth century.[38] Fransen's extensive work in Dutch archives established that late in 1680 Dirk Strijker (Theodoro Strijker) opened a permanent theater in Amsterdam, and subsequently, in May 1683, the Prince of Orange granted Augustin Fleury permission to perform an opera at The Hague. Strijker began with an Italian opera *Le Fatiche d'Ercole per Deianira* (music by Pietro Andrea Ziani, originally performed in Venice, 1662) and though the first opera given in The Hague is unknown, it was probably French because the town fathers (Bourgmestres de La Haye) authorized performances to be given by a 'bande françoise de musiciens et d'opéristes'. In any case, no Lully work can be documented in either city with certainty until the 1686–7 season by which time Strijker's troupe had disappeared and been replaced by 'l'opéra néerlandais de Buiksloot [a town near Amsterdam]', directed by David Lingelbach and J. Koenerding. According to Fransen, they rented the Théâtre National d'Amsterdam for the second half of their season. Lully's music figured prominently during 1687 with multiple performances of *Amadis*, *Cadmus et Hermione*, and *Atys* (see table 4). Apparently the management also intended to present *Roland*, but could not due to the lack of trained singers. Livrets for all four were printed in Dutch translation.[39]

Lully's 'presence' in the 1688 Amsterdam season remained strong, for it in-

[36] For a summary of concert performances of Lully operas see SchneiderR, pp. 64–8. A performance (staged or concert?) of *Acis et Galatée* is mentioned in DestrangesT, p. 23 as having been given in Nantes (n.d.) and Lionel Sawkins and Albert Cohen have both informed me of probable eighteenth-century performances of Lully in Bordeaux.

[37] A full description of these Amsterdam contrafactions, issued as single volumes or in *recueils factices*, will appear in my forthcoming livret catalogue. For listings of Dutch editions of Lully's music see WalkerD and SchneiderC.

[38] See FransenC. The following discussion draws heavily on his archival research.

[39] See LoewenbergE, pp. 229–30.

Table 4 *Performances in La Haye (The Hague) and Amsterdam*

Date	City	Work performed	Livret	Bibliography and Remarks
1677	< La Haye	*Isis* >		FransenC, pp. 161–2; it would be entirely exceptional for a performance to have been given outside of Paris during the year of creation
1686	Amsterdam	*Roland*	12–6[a]	LoewenbergA, col. 76; LoewenbergE, p. 230 states that 'Arendsz adapted his [Dutch] version to the original music, but for the lack of trained Dutch singers it could not be performed'
1686 or 1687?	< Amsterdam	*Phaëton* >		CampistronA, p. 14 (Prunières claims to have seen a livret translated into Dutch by T. Arendsz)
1687	Amsterdam	*Amadis*	11–7[b]	FransenC, pp. 20 & 170 (cites 19 performances); LoewenbergA, col. 75
	Amsterdam	*Cadmus et Hermione*	1–10[c]	FransenC, pp. 20 & 170 (cites 20 performances); LoewenbergA, col. 52
	Amsterdam	*Atys*		FransenC, p. 170 (cites 11 performances); LoewenbergA, col. 59 (perf. The Hague)
1688	Amsterdam	[*Les fêtes de l'Amour et de Bacchus*]		FransenC, pp. 171–2 (cites 7 performances)
21 Aug.– 14 Sept.	Amsterdam	*Persée*		FransenC, pp. 171–2 (7 performances); LoewenbergA, col. 73 (perf. The Hague)
15 Sept.– 18 Sept.	Amsterdam	*Proserpine*		FransenC, pp. 171–2 (3 performances); LoewenbergA, col. 69 (perf. The Hague)
1701–2?	La Haye	*Armide?*		FransenC, pp. 202, 204, 206, 208, & 210; LoewenbergA, col. 80 (1701)
	La Haye	*Atys?*		FransenC, pp. 208 & 210
	La Haye	*Thésée*		FransenC, pp. 202 & 210; LoewenbergA, col. 56 (1701)
1703	La Haye	*Proserpine*	8–25[d]	LoewenbergA, col. 69. Contains an entirely new prologue for 'L'Enchanteur, Troupe de Genies de sa suite' (scene i) and 'La Paix & sa suite' (scene ii)
	La Haye	*Thésée*	3–32[e]	Contains an entirely new prologue now set in 'les Environs de la Haye'
1704	La Haye	*Amadis*	11–24[f]	many lines of text have been changed, but all have a scansion which would permit the retention of Lully's original music
1710 15 Dec.	La Haye	*Phaëton*		FransenC, p. 228; LoewenbergA, col. 73
1718?	La Haye	*Phaëton*		FransenC, p. 256
	La Haye	*Atys*		FransenC, p. 256

Table 4 (*cont.*)

Date	City	Work performed	Livret	Bibliography and Remarks
1723	Amsterdam	*Atys en Sangarida*	4–37[g]	GrosPQ, p. 788 ('Imité de Quinault par G. F. Domis'). The livret prints three substitute 'Airs' composed by a Monsieur Nozeman

[a] Livret published in Amsterdam: Albert Magnus, 1686 [in Dutch]. A number of copies known including F-Pn (8° Yth. 69576). Listed in SchneiderC, p. 428.
[b] Livret published in Amsterdam: Albert Magnus, 1687 [in Dutch]. A number of copies known including US-NYp (NHLpr 122). Listed in SchneiderC, p. 410.
[c] Livret published in Amsterdam: Albert Magnus, 1687 [in Dutch]. Copies in B-Gu (Acc. 6249), F-Pn (Yth 67513 and 69570) and US-NYp (NHLpr 122). Listed in SchneiderC, p. 209.
[d] Livret published in Amsterdam: Henri Schelte, 1703. Copy in NL-DHgm (3 K 116). Published in 4° rather than the 12° common in Amsterdam contrafactions. Not listed in SchneiderC.
[e] Livret published in Amsterdam: Henri Schelte, 1703. Copies in D-brd:W (Lm 4° Kapsel 1 (8)) and US-Wc (ML50.2T45L92 1703). See note d concerning size. Not listed in SchneiderC.
[f] Livret published in Amsterdam: Henri Schelte, 1704. Partial cast list given. Copy in D-brd:BFb (3 in B-St 97). Listed in SchneiderC, p. 410. See note d concerning size.
[g] Livret published in Amsterdam: Erfg. van J. Lescailje, 1723 [in Dutch]. Copies in B-As (C 27594); F-Pn (Yth. 67226, 67227 and 67228); and US-Cn (PT5605.A4A72 1687). Not listed in SchneiderC.

cluded *Les fêtes de l'Amour et de Bacchus* (July), *Persée* (Aug.–Sept.) and *Proserpine* (Sept.). These performances, known solely from theater documents, apparently conclude Lully activity until the opening years of the eighteenth century. By that time the itinerant troupes of French comedians, so indigenous to Europe during the seventeenth century, noticeably began to give way to more stable enterprises. Thus, in Holland, late in 1700, the town fathers of The Hague awarded Gérard Schott (a Hamburg native already experienced at operatic production there) a privilege to produce operas. Fransen thoroughly discusses the intrigues and tribulations of Schott's first few years, and suggests that Schott included *Armide, Atys,* and *Thésée* in his repertory for the years 1701–2. Fransen, however, was unable to establish any further Lully performances there until 1710, but with the discovery of livrets for *Proserpine* and *Thésée* (1703), and *Amadis* (1704) this picture changes significantly.

Almost all livrets published in Amsterdam for Lully's stage works served a literary function and were not intended to accompany any actual performance. Printed in duodecimo format, the vast majority are inscribed 'Suivant la copie imprimée à Paris' and were issued by Abraham Wolfgang, Antoine Schelte, les Héritiers d'Antoine Schelte, Henri Schelte or claim no publisher. Performers, if mentioned, duplicate those given by Christophe Ballard in Parisian editions, texts (complete with prologue) appear uncut, and no new material has been added. The livrets for *Proserpine, Thésée,* and *Amadis,* however, were published by Henri Schelte in quarto format. Uncharacteristically, the texts have undergone revision; *Proserpine* and *Thésée* both contain new prologues while some lines in *Amadis* have been eliminated. The livret for *Amadis* also names more than a

dozen singers and dancers who took part in the production thus adding significantly to our meager knowledge of the Amsterdam company at this time.[40]

The remaining three Lully performances given at The Hague are known solely
from fragmentary accounts: no livrets remain for *Phaëton* (1710 and 1718(?)) or
for *Atys* (1718?). Holland's romance with Lully was to be carried on only in a few
final printings of livrets intended for the literary minded.[41] The Dutch flirtation
with staging his *tragédies lyriques*, unlike that of the French, whose reverence led
to revivals throughout the eighteenth century, had run its course after thirty
years. Theater impresarios then looked more to living composers for repertory.

PERFORMANCES IN BRUSSELS, ANVERS (ANTWERP), AND GAND (GHENT)

Clearly one of the strongest bastions of Lully performance outside France existed
in Brussels. From 1682 until 1741 no less than thirty-six productions of a broad
spectrum of works can be documented with relative certainty. *Isis*, *Proserpine*,
and *Achille et Polixène* are not known to have been performed, and Borrel's
mention of two productions of *Psyché* is sufficiently suspect to add that work to
the list, but Brussels clearly experienced most of Lully's *tragédies lyriques*.[42] Henri
Liebrecht, whose work has generally been overlooked by Lully bibliographers,
deserves credit for most of our knowledge about operatic performances in Brussels.[43] Liebrecht, a fastidious researcher like Fransen, found numerous archival
documents, memoires, journal accounts, and other materials relating to opera in
Brussels. His work uncovered a wealth of Lully performances, but he stopped
short of making a systematic attempt to find livrets outside of Brussels that
might aid his cause by signalling still other performances. Few Lully livrets for
Brussels performances actually remain there today. The largest single cache
known is in the Forschungsbibliothek Gotha (German Democratic Republic)
while a smaller group remain in Graz, Austria at the Universitätsbibliothek.[44]
Others are widely scattered and few are presently known from more than one or
two exemplars. Brussels performances spawned a regular history of printing
livrets that continued until 1725 at least, so other livrets will probably surface as
bibliographers continue their travail. Our investigation has yielded livrets for
seventeen Brussels productions, only three of which had previously been known
to Lully scholarship.

Performances of Lully's *tragédies* given outside the Île de France during the

---

[40] The exchange of performers within the
provinces or between Paris and the provinces
can be established through theater documents and from cast lists indexed in my forthcoming book on Lully livrets. Some of the
same performers can also be found working
between Amsterdam, Lille, Brussels, and The
Hague.

[41] *Recueils factices* of livrets including Lully's
tragédies lyriques continued to be printed in
Amsterdam as late as 1753 when a mul-

tivolume set containing works from the
reigns of Louis XIV and XV was printed by
Abraham Wolfgang.

[42] See BorrelJ, p. 99.

[43] See LiebrechtH.

[44] I particularly wish to thank Dr Helmut Claus
of the Forschungsbibliothek Gotha for his
many kindnesses in promptly supplying
information and microfilms over the past
nine years.

composer's lifetime are of the greatest rarity. Liebrecht's reference to a performance in May 1682 of Lully's *Thésée* for the arrival ('incognito') of Madame la
princesse d'Orange, therefore, demands more than passing interest (see table 5).[45]
A livret for the occasion has been located in Halle at the Universitätsbibliothek
of the Martin-Luther-Universität (German Democratic Republic). This livret,
which confirms that *Thésée* was '*Représentée par l'Académie Royale de Musique, ce* 18.
May, pour l'heureuse arrivée de son Altesse royale, MADAME LA PRINCESSE D'ORANGE',
bears no place of publication or name of publisher. It does, however, contain a
new prologue and is the only known Brussels livret to list any of the performers.
But this early production of *Thésée*, along with *Persée* (1682) and *Cadmus et
Hermione* (1683?), occurred at a time when French and Italian operas shared the
stage in Brussels: it was not until more than a decade later that Lully's *tragédies*
saw steady production.

Brussels, like many provincial French cities during the closing years of the
seventeenth century, experienced regular changes both in its operatic director-
ships and in the buildings in which operatic activity took place. On 1 November
1694, when Giovanni Paolo Bombarda and the composer Pietro Andrea Fiocco
signed a three-year contract to rent the Théâtre du Quai au Foin, a significant
new direction was forged. Fiocco immediately installed a repertory of *tragédies*
exclusively by Lully, writing new prologues for some honoring the Elector of
Bavaria.[46] Of the nine Lully *tragédies* mounted by Fiocco in this three-year
period (1695–7), we now know of *Atys*, performed in 1695, only through a
newly-discovered livret. According to an agreement between Joseph Joannis
(an agent for Bombarda) and an official in Ghent, Bombarda also extended his
activity to Ghent, giving twelve performances of *Thésée* there in the late spring of
1698.[47] Bombarda, who bore responsibility for the next phase of opera in Brussels, had a strong influence on opera there until his death in 1712. Following a
devastating attack on the city in August of 1695, which saw much of its center
destroyed by fire, Bombarda built a new theater on some of the cleared land.
Dubbed 'Grand Théâtre sur la Monnoie', the théâtre opened late in 1700 with
a performance of *Atys* (no livret known).[48] Almost immediately Bombarda
encountered many difficulties, some of which were not eased until 1704 when
Maximilien (l'Electeur de Bavière) changed the status of the opera to that of
'Académie de Musique' and appointed Fiocco to direct the orchestra. Most of
Bombarda's repertory remains unknown except for productions of *Alceste* during
late 1705 and early 1706 (cited only in the Brussels gazette *Relations véritables*),
Acis et Galatée in November 1705, and *Roland* (1706). A newly discovered livret
still located in Brussels drew our attention to that performance of *Roland*.

When Bombarda's privilege expired during 1706 a new one was granted to

---

[45] See LiebrechtH, pp. 29 and 98–100.
[46] For information concerning Fiocco see
StellfeldF.
[47] The document is printed in ClaeysH,
pp. 45–6. Bombarda's involvement, if any,
with *L'Europe galante* (see FaberH, vol. I, p. 65
and vol. IV, p. 292 who cites a livret printed in

Gand: Les Héritiers de Maximilien Graet,
1706) or *Phaëton*, 1708 has not been
determined.
[48] Considerable information about this theater,
in addition to that supplied by LiebrechtH,
appears in IsnardonT (see particularly p. 6ff.)
and FaberH, vols. I and IV.

Table 5 *Performances in Brussels, Anvers (Antwerp), and Gand (Ghent)*

Date	Title	Livret	Bibliography and Remarks
All performances in Brussels			
1682 18 May	Thésée	3–11[a]	LiebrechtH, pp. 29 & 98–100. New prologue (author and composer unknown) for 'LA GLOIRE, LA VERTU, & LE PLAISIR en habit de Pelerin'. Performed for the arrival of Madame la princesse d'Orange
11 Nov.	Persée		FaberH, I, 71–2; LiebrechtH, 29 & 98–100; LoewenbergA, col. 73
1683?	Cadmus et Hermione		LiebrechtH, pp. 99–100 (performed?)
1685 6 Nov.	<Persée>		LoewenbergA, col. 73
1695 20 Jan.	Amadis	11–17.1[b] 11–17.2[c]	FaberH, I, 74; LiebrechtH, pp. 31 & 104; LoewenbergA, col. 75; New prologue (author unknown) set to music by Pietro Antonio Fiocco and described in the livret as 'LE TRIOMPHE DE L'AMOUR, PROLOGUE D'AMADIS, Fait au sujet des Noces de Son Altesse Electorale de Baviere, & de la Serenissime Princesse Roiale de Pologne'
21 Jan.	Armide		LiebrechtH, p. 103; LoewenbergA, cols. 79–80 (20 Jan.). New prologue set to music by P. A. Fiocco
	Atys	4–25[d]	
11 Nov.	Acis et Galatée	14–10.1[e] 14–10.2[f]	FaberH, I, 74; IsnardonT, p. 17; LiebrechtH, p. 104; LoewenbergA, col. 81 (7 Nov.). New prologue (author unknown) set to music by P. A. Fiocco. The stage directions indicate that 'Le Theatre represent un Bois, avec un Campement, & au fond on void le Chateau de Naumur assiegé'.
28 Nov.	<Amadis>		IsnardonT, p. 17
1696 24 Jan. + 14 & 28 Oct.	Phaëton	10–40[g]	LiebrechtH, pp. 31 & 104; LoewenbergA, col. 73
8 Nov.	Bellérophon	7–19[h]	FaberH, I, 74; IsnardonT, p. 17; LiebrechtH, pp. 31, & 103–4; LoewenbergA, col. 67. New prologue (author unknown) set to music by P. A. Fiocco. The stage directions indicate that 'La Scene est dans les Campagnes voisines de la Ville de Troye Capitale de la Phrigie'.
	<Psyché>		BorrelJ, p. 99
1697 9 April, 1 Aug. & Oct.	Armide	13–15[i]	LiebrechtH, pp. 104 & 109 (indicates nine performances in Oct.)
6 Aug.	Amadis		LiebrechtH, p. 104
10 Nov. & 31 Dec.	Thésée		FaberH, I, 75 (*Relations véritables*: 'avec la première représentation du nouveau prologue fait au sujet de la paix, dont la musique est de la composition du fameux s[r] Fiocco [author of text unknown]'); IsnardonT, p. 17 (31 Dec. only); LiebrechtH, p. 104; LoewenbergA, col. 56
1700 17 Oct.	Atys		FaberH, I, 77 (from an account of 19 Oct.: 'Dimanche au soir, S.A.S. donna aux Altesses Electrices de Brandenbourg et de Brunswick-Lunenbourg le divertissement d'une répétition de l'opera d'*Atis*, au grand théâtre'.)
19 Nov.	Atys		LiebrechtH, p. 31 ('une representation d'*Atys* qu'on y celebre la nouvelle de l'acceptation du testament de Charles II par Louis XIV'); LoewenbergA, col. 59; AntoineH, p. 89

Table 5 (*cont.*)

Date	Title	Livret	Bibliography and Remarks
23 Nov.	*Atys*		FaberH, I, 77; IsnardonT, p. 17
1705 11 July & 11 Nov.	*Acis et Galatée*		FaberH, I, 81 (*Relations véritables*: 'Le 11 (juillet) jour de naissance de S.A.E. on fit dans l'église ducale de Caubergue une Messe solemnelle. . .Les Ministres, et les Seigneurs et Dames de la Cour se trouverent à cette fonction en habits de fête, et furent le soir au grand theatre voir l'opéra d'*Acis et Galatée*, qui fut representé par l'Academie Roïale de Musique, à l'occasion de cette fête'); IsnardonT, p. 6 (11 July); LiebrechtH, p. 31 (11 Nov. 'jour anniversaire de l'Electeur'). I have been been unable to resolve the discrepancy in dates
12 Oct. & 19 Dec.	*Alceste*		FaberH, I, 81; LiebrechtH, p. 31 & 131 (12 Oct. 'pour la fête de l'Electeur'); Liebrecht also notes two performances several days after 11 Nov.: 'pour la fête du Roi Philippe V, une représentation d'*Alceste* mit tout Bruxelles en émoi; une seconde audition fut donnée lors de l'arrivée à Bruxelles de l'Archevêque de Cologne'; IsnardonT, p. 6 & 17 (19 Dec. only); LoewenbergA, col. 53
1706 16 Feb.	*Alceste*		FaberH, I, 93 ('jour du mardi-gras'); IsnardonT, p. 12; LiebrechtH, p. 131
28 Dec.	*Persée*		FaberH, I, 93; IsnardonT, p. 13 (vague reference); LiebrechtH, p. 134; LoewenbergA, col. 73; concerning a possible livret see under 1707 below
	Roland	12–20[j]	
1707 14 Nov.	*Bellérophon*		LiebrechtH, p. 134; LoewenbergA, col. 67 mistakenly dates this performance one year later
	Persée	9–21[k]	this livret may belong with the 28 Dec. 1706 performance listed above
1708	*Armide*	13–23[l]	LiebrechtH, p. 135 (date probably 1708)
	[*Le bourgeois gentilhomme*]		LiebrechtH, p. 135
	[*Georges Dandin* (= *Le grand divertissement royal de Versailles*)]		LiebrechtH, p. 135
	< *Psyché* >		BorrelJ, p. 99
1709 4 & 14 or 15 Oct.	*Amadis*	11–26[m]	FaberH, I, 93 (4 & 15 Oct.: attended by 'le prince Eugène de Savoie, qui venait de revenir de l'armée, à Bruxelles'); IsnardonT, p. 13 (4 & 15 Oct.); LiebrechtH, p. 136 (4 & 14 Oct.); LoewenbergA, col. 75
1713 1 Jan.	*Thésée*	3–36[n]	FaberH, I, 97; IsnardonT, p. 14; LiebrechtH, p. 140; LoewenbergA, col. 56. New prologue (author and composer both unknown)
1721 21 Nov.	*Roland*	12–25[o]	IsnardonT, p. 17; LiebrechtH, p. 146; FransenC, p. 266; LoewenbergA, col. 76
1722	*Armide*	13–28[p]	
1724 12 Nov.	*Roland*		FaberH, I, 97; LiebrechtH, p. 147; FransenC, p. 266
1725 1 Jan.	*Alceste*	2–30[q]	FaberH, IV, 14; LiebrechtH, p. 147; FransenC, p. 266; LoewenbergA, col. 53
4 Nov.	[*Le bourgeois gentilhomme*]		FaberH, I, 103 & IV, 14; LiebrechtH, pp. 149–50

Table 5 (*cont.*)

Date	Title	Livret	Bibliography and Remarks
1726 9 & 11 Oct.	*Roland*		FaberH, I, 104 (11 Oct. only); LiebrechtH, p. 150 (9 Oct. only, the first spectacle attended by 'S.A.S. l'Archiduchesse Marie-Elisabeth d'Autriche, la nouvelle Gouvernante des Pays-Bas')
10 & 12 Nov.	*Armide*		FaberH, I, 104 (12 Nov. only); LiebrechtH, p. 151 (10 Nov. only)
1727 Jan.	*Alceste*		LiebrechtH. p. 151
1734 Nov.	*Cadmus et Hermione*		LoewenbergA, col. 82 (in Flemish)
1741	*Roland*		LiebrechtH, p. 169
	Atys		LiebrechtH, p. 169
All performances in Gand (Ghent)			
1679	*< Cadmus et Hermione >*		MercierM, I, 230 (noted without further documentation)
1698 June	*Thésée*		LoewenbergA, col. 56
1708	*Phaëton*	10–25[r]	FaberH, I, 65 and IV, 292; ClaeysH, II, 44–6
Performance in Anvers (Antwerp)			
1682	*Proserpine*		BorrelJ, p. 99; LoewenbergA, col. 69

[a] Livret published in [Brusselle]: N.Pub., 1682. Nine members of the cast listed. Copy in D-ddr: HAu (D1 4649 (D1 1650)). Not listed in SchneiderC.

[b] Livret published in Brusselle: N.Pub., 1695. Copy in D-ddr: GO1 (Poes. 8° 597(2)). Not listed in SchneiderC.

[c] Livret published in Brusselle: N.Pub., 1695. Copy in F-Pa (Ra[11] 47). Gives the date as 20 Jan., which is not given in LLC 11–17.1. SchneiderC, p. 410, refers only to Gros' listing of the livret.

[d] Livret published in Brusselle: N.Pub., 1695. Copies in D:brd-Mth (R 389) and D-ddr:GO1 (Poes. 8° 597(3)). Listed in SchneiderC, p. 169.

[e] Livret published in Brusselle: N.Pub., 1695. Copies in D-ddr:GO1 (Poes. 8° 597(1)); F-Pa (Ra[11] 48), PL-Wu (ObceXVII–4°–16°–2254) and possibly CS-Pk. Not listed in SchneiderC.

[f] Livret published in Brusselle: N.Pub., N.D. Copy in D-ddr:GO1 (Poes. 8° 727). Except for the omission of the date, this copy is identical to that listed in note *e* above. Not listed in SchneiderC.

[g] Livret published in Brusselle: N.Pub, N.D. Copy in D-brd:W (Lm Sammelbd 114(2)) and possibly CS-Pr. Not listed in SchneiderC.

[h] Livret published in Brusselle: N.Pub., 1696. Copy in D-ddr:GO1 (Poes. 8° 879(2)). Not listed in SchneiderC.

[i] Livret published in Brusselle: N.Pub., 1697. Copy in D-ddr:GO1 (Poes. 8° 879(3)). Not listed in SchneiderC.

[j] Livret published in Brusselle: N.Pub., 1706. Copy in B-Br (III.91.623A Mus.). Not listed in SchneiderC.

[k] Livret published in Brusselle: François Foppens, 1707. Copy in B-Gu (B.L. 6218). Not listed in SchneiderC.

[l] Livret published in Brusselle: N.Pub., 1708. Copy in B-Br (VI. 5548 A.L.P.). Not listed in SchneiderC.

[m] Livret published in Brusselle: N.Pub., 1709. Copy in US-PHschmidt. Not listed in SchneiderC.

[n] Livret published in Brusselle: N.Pub., 1713. The sole known copy in F-Pmeyer has been unavailable for study. Listed in SchneiderC, p. 246.

[o] Livret published in Brusselle: N.Pub., 1721. I
Copy in A-Gu (29204). Not listed in SchneiderC.

[p] Livret published in Brusselle: N.Pub., 1721. I
Copy in A-Gu (29204). Not listed in SchneiderC.

[q] Livret published in Brusselle: N.Pub., 1725. I
Copies in A-Gu (29204) and US-Cu (PQ1881.A65 1725 Rare). Not listed in SchneiderC.

[r] Livret published in Gand: Les Héritiers de Maximilien Graet, 1708. Copy in B-Gu (G 1230). Not listed in SchneiderC.

Joseph de Pestel, whose tenure lasted until October of 1708 when financial difficulties forced him to relinquish his authority. De Pestel's repertory, better documented than that of his predecessor, shows a heavy bias toward Lully's music. Beginning with *Persée* (December 1706), de Pestel also produced *Bellérophon* (November 1707), *Armide* (1708) and two works from other genres, *Le bourgeois gentilhomme* and *Georges Dandin*. At present only livrets for *Persée* and *Armide* have been located, both in the duodecimo format ubiquitous to the Low Countries.

The last owner of the privilege who paid homage to the long tradition of Lully performances in Brussels was Francesco-Paolo d'Angelis. D'Angelis produced *Amadis* in 1709 (known both from documentary accounts and a livret which recently came on the market for sale), but after that no other Lully performances are documented before 1721 except for one of *Thésée* on New Year's Day 1713.[49] In the interim extant printed livrets document an influx of works by Destouches and Campra before the theater entered a period characterized by Liebrecht as 'extremely confused'.[50] Political problems in Brussels coupled with Bombarda's death, assorted intrigues, and attempts to seize theater assets (costumes, etc.) – not to mention a developing taste for the work of other composers – all led to a decline in Lully performances. Between 1721 and 1741 only eleven productions of six Lully works are known to have been given. The last confirmed Lully livret published was *Alceste* in 1725. Again in Brussels, Lully's stage works formed the portal through which eighteenth-century opera entered.

Lully's *tragédies lyriques*, created in a span of fifteen years, proved to be remarkably resilient until well into the eighteenth century. His immediate posthumous reputation rested on these works, and because of them the name 'Lully' remained on the tongues of countless opera enthusiasts for many decades. In actuality Lully's operas knew few boundaries, either geographical or chronological. Though in some cases the facts have remained elusive for centuries, a systematic attempt at recovering Lully livrets and a re-examination of secondary literature have made possible a fresh look at the geographical spread of Lully's *tragédies*. The tables that accompany this article list more than two hundred productions with newly discovered livrets for almost half of them. There can be no doubt that the spread was more far-reaching than previously thought and that in cities like Brussels and Lyon it was more extensive. There can also be no doubt that during Lully's lifetime and in the decades immediately following his death, rights to perform his music and to create new académies de musique were carefully controlled by royal privilege. Possessed of a personality and temperament that made him easy prey to his enemies, Lully nevertheless created entertainments that outlasted even the most vocal critics and that introduced Europe to a taste of French culture from the court of Louis XIV.

[49] This livret, offered for sale by H. Baron (London) and listed as item 61 in his catalogue no. 124 titled *French Opera Performed & Published Prior to 1760*, was purchased by the author.
[50] See LiebrechtH, p. 139.

Table 6 *Performances in Germany, England, and Italy*

Date	City	Work performed	Livret	Bibliography and Remarks
1683	Regenspurg	*Isis*	5–9[a]	
1685	Wolffenbüttel	*Proserpine*	8–10[b]	LoewenbergA, col. 69; BrockpählerH, p. 89
1686 Aug.	Wolffenbüttel	*Psyché*	6–5[c]	LoewenbergA, col. 64; BrockpählerH, p. 89
1687 19 Aug.	Wolffenbüttel	*Thésée*	3–14[d] 3–15[e]	LoewenbergA, col. 56; BrockpählerH, p. 89 The prologue has been rewritten, but still retains some of the original lines and accommodates Lully's music. The place has been changed from Versailles so that 'Le Théâtre represente la Ville de Venise du costé de la Place de St. Marc avec la Mer, au delà de la quelle on void dans l'enfoncement un Ciel remply d'Amours, de Graces, de Plaisirs & de jeux.'
1719	Wolffenbüttel	*Psyché*	6–22[f]	Reduced to 3 acts and it is uncertain if Lully's music was used
Before 1686	Ansbach	*Cadmus et Hermione*		BrockpählerH, p. 34
Before 1686	Ansbach	*Thésée*		BrockpählerH, p. 34
Before 1686	Ansbach	*Isis*		BrockpählerH, p. 35
Before 1686	Ansbach	*Psyché*		BrockpählerH, p. 35
Before 1686	Ansbach	*Bellérophon*		BrockpählerH, p. 35
Before 1686	Ansbach	*Proserpine*		BrockpählerH, p. 35
Before 1686	Ansbach	*Roland*		BrockpählerH, p. 35
Before 1686	Ansbach	[*Le triomphe de l'amour*]		BrockpählerH, p. 35
Before 1686	Ansbach	*Alceste*		BrockpählerH, p. 36
Before 1686	Ansbach	*Atys*		BrockpählerH, p. 36
1687	Darmstadt	*Acis et Galatée*		BrockpählerH, p. 127
1689 Dec.	Hamburg	*Acis et Galatée*	14–27[g]	BorrelJ, p. 100; LoewenbergA, col. 81; BrockpählerH, p. 201. The location of the prologue has been changed so that 'Le Théâtre Represente les Environs de la ville d'Hambourg'.
1692 Dec.	Hamburg	*Achille et Polixène*	15–9[h]	BorrelJ, 100; LoewenbergA, col. 83; BrockpählerH, p. 202
1695	Hamburg	*Acis und Galatée*	14–11[i]	BorrelJ, p. 100; LoewenbergA, col. 81
1698	Stuttgart	*Acis und Galatée*	14–12[j]	BorrelJ, p. 100; LoewenbergA, col. 81; BrockpählerH, p. 127
1719–23?	Bonn	*Alceste*		BrockpählerH, p. 82
1687	Modena	*Psyché*		LoewenbergA, col. 64 (French with Italian interpolations)
1690	Rome	*Armida*	13–10[k]	TorrefrancaP, 191–7
1686 11 March	London	*Cadmus et Hermione?*		LS, I, 341 & 346–7. Performed by a company of French actors

BIBLIOGRAPHY OF SECONDARY LITERATURE CITED

AnthonyF   Anthony, James R. *French Baroque Music from Beaujoyeulx to Rameau*, rev. ed. (New York, W. W. Norton and Co., 1978)

AnthonyL   Anthony, James R., 'Lully, Jean-Baptiste', *The New Grove Dictionary of Music and Musicians*, Stanley Sadie (ed.), vol. XI (London, Macmillan, 1980), pp. 314–29

AntoineH   Antoine, Michel, *Henri Desmarest (1661–1741) biographie critique*, La Vie musicale en France sous les rois Bourbons, vol. X, (Paris, A. and J. Picard, 1965)

BenoitD   Benoit, Marcelle and Norbert Dufourcq, 'Documents du minutier central. Musiciens français du XVIIIe siècle', *Recherches sur la musique française classique*, IX (1969), pp. 216–38

BianconiF   Bianconi, Lorenzo and Thomas Walker, 'Dalla *Finta pazza* alla *Veremonda*: storie di Febiarmonici', *Rivista italiana di musicologia*, X (1975), pp. 379–454

BorrelJ   Borrel, Eugène, *Jean-Baptiste Lully: Le Cadre. La Vie. L'Oeuvre. La Personalité. Le Rayonnement. Les Oeuvres. Bibliographie* (Paris, Colombier, 1949)

BourligueuxD   Bourligueux, Guy, 'Document: Académie Royale de Musique en Bretagne', *Recherches sur la musique française classique*, X (1970), pp. 195–6

BrockpählerH   Brockpähler, Renate, *Handbuch zur Geschichte der Barockoper in Deutschland* (Emsdetten/Westf., Lechte, [1964])

CarlezM   Carlez, Jules, *La Musique à Caen de 1066 à 1848* (Caen, F. Le Blanc-Hardel, 1876; rpt. Geneva, Minkoff, 1974)

Notes to Table 6

[a] Livret printed in Regensburg: Paul Dalnsteinern, 1683. Copy in D-brd:US. Listed in SchneiderC, p. 292.

[b] Livret printed in Wolffenbüttel: Caspar Jean Bismarck, 1685. Performers listed. Copies in D-brd:W (Textb. 394 and Textb. 727 (1)). SchneiderC, p. 332 lists a copy in D-brd:KNu, which I have been unable to confirm.

[c] Livret printed in Wolffenbüttel: Caspar Jean Bismarck, 1686. Performers listed. Copies in D-brd:BS (Brosch. I 20.557), HVl (Op. 8,14) and W (Gräflich Schulenburgische Bibliothek Km 2 (4)). GuibertB, 2nd suppl., pp. 13–15 lists two further copies in unspecified private collections. Listed in SchneiderC, p. 310.

[d] Livret printed in Wolffenbüttel: Caspar Jean Bismarck, 1687. Performers listed. Copy in D-brd:W (Textb. 385). SchneiderC, p. 246 lists a copy in D-brd:HVl, which I have been unable to confirm.

[e] German synopsis only printed in Wolffenbüttel: Caspar Johann Biszmarck, 1687. Performers listed, except for the prologue. Copy in D-brd:W (Textb. 385). SchneiderC, p. 246 lists a copy in D-brd:HVl, which I have been unable to confirm.

[f] Livret printed in Wolffenbüttel: Christian Bartsch, 1719 [in German]. Copy in D-brd:DS (Op. 1,84). Listed in SchneiderC, p. 310.

[g] Livret printed in [Hamburg?]: N.Pub., N.D. [French text with German synopsis]. Copies in A-Wn (4362-B); D-brd:B (33 in: Mus.T 1 R), Hs (35 in MS $\frac{639}{3}$: 3), HVl (Op. 11,1) and US-Uu (x782.12C685 no. 1 Rare Book Room). Listed in SchneiderC, p. 482.

[h] Livret printed in [Hamburg?]: N.Pub., 1692 [French and German texts]. Copies in A-Wn (625.346-A.Th and 4204-B); D-brd:B (43 in Mus.T 1 R), Hs (46 in MS $\frac{639}{3}$: 3). Listed in SchneiderC, p. 494.

[i] Livret printed in Hamburg: N.Pub., 1695 [in German]. Copies in A-Wn (4220-B); D-brd:B (19 in: Mus.T 2 R and 1 in: Mus.T. 17R), Hs (68 in MS $\frac{639}{3}$: 5). Listed in SchneiderC, p. 482.

[j] Livret printed in Stuttgart: Paul Treuen, 1698 [in German]. Copy in US-Wc (ML4.S5757). Not listed in SchneiderC.

[k] Livret printed in Rome: Angelo Bernabò, 1690 [in Italian]. A number of copies known including US-Wc (ML48.S5779). Facsimile of title-page in TorrefrancaP. Listed in SchneiderC, p. 465.

CatTS	*Trois siècles d'opéra à Lyon de l'Académie royale de Musique à l'opéra-nouveau* (Lyon, Association des amis de la bibliothèque municipale de Lyon, 1982)
CheilanC	Cheilan-Cambolin, Jeanne, 'Un Aspect de la vie musicale à Marseille au XVIIe siècle: cinquante ans d'opéra 1685–1739' (Diss. Univ. d'Aix, 1972)
CizeronV	Cizeron, Janine, 'La Vie musicale à Lyon au XVIIIe siècle', *Musique et société: La Vie musicale en province aux XVIIIe, XIXe et XXe siècles*, Actes des Journées d'Etudes de la Société Française de Musicologie (Rennes, Lices-Rennes, 1981), pp. 83–9
ClaeysH	Claeys, Prosper, *Histoire du Théâtre à Gand*, 3 vols. (Gand, J. Vuylsteke, 1892)
DanchinL	Danchin, Fernand, *Les Imprimés lillois: Répertoire bibliographique de 1594 à 1815*, 3 vols. (Lille, Emile Raoust, 1926–31)
DesgravesR	Desgraves, Louis, *Repertoire bibliographique des livres imprimés en France au XVIIe siècle*, VII Biblioteca bibliographica aureliana, XCV (Baden-Baden, Valentin Koerner, 1983)
DestrangesT	Destranges, Etienne, *Le Théâtre à Nantes depuis ses origines jusqu'à nos jours: 1430–1901* (Paris, Fischbacher, 1902)
DucrotR	Ducrot, Ariane, 'Les Représentations de l'Académie Royale de Musique à Paris au temps de Louis XIV (1671–1715)', *Recherches sur la musique française classique*, X (1970), pp. 19–55
FaberH	Faber, Frédéric, *Histoire du théâtre français en belgique depuis son origine jusqu'à nos jours d'après des documents inédits reposant aux archives générales du royaume*, 5 vols. (Brussels, Fr. J. Olivier, 1878–80)
FabreR	Fabre, Augustin, *Les Rues de Marseille*, 5 vols. (Marseille, E. Camoin, 1867–9)
FavierC	Favier, J[ustin], *Catalogue des livres et documents imprimés du fonds Lorrain de la bibliothèque municipale de Nancy* (Nancy, A. Crépin-Leblond, 1898)
FransenC	Fransen, J[an], *Les Comediens français en hollande au XVIIe et au XVIIIe siècles* (Paris, Honoré Champion, 1925)
GrosPQ	Gros, Etienne, *Philippe Quinault: sa vie et son oeuvre* (Paris, Edouard Champion, 1926; rpt. Geneva: Slatkine, 1970)
GuibertB	Guibert, A[lbert]-J[ean], *Bibliographie des oeuvres de Molière publiées au XVIIe siècle*, 2 vols. (Paris, CNRS, 1977 (rpt. of the 1961 ed. with the supplements of 1965 and 1973))
HappelS	Happel, Jean, 'Strasbourg', *The new Grove dictionary of music and musicians*, Stanley Sadie (ed.), vol. XVIII (London, Macmillan, 1980), pp. 198–201
IsnardonT	Isnardon, Jacques, *Le Théâtre de la Monnaie depuis sa fondation jusqu'à nos jours* (Brussels, Schott frères, 1890)
La GorceA	La Gorce, Jérôme de, 'Une Académie de Musique en province au temps du Roi-Soleil: l'opéra de Rouen', Unpub. paper delivered in Strasbourg, France at the 1980 meetings of the International Musicological Society
La GorceO	La Gorce, Jérôme de, 'L'Opéra française à la cour de Louis XIV', *Revue de la Société d'histoire du théâtre*, XXXV (1983), pp. 387–401
LefebvreH	Lefebvre, Léon, *Histoire du théâtre de Lille de ses origines à nos jours*, 5 vols. (Lille, Lefebvre-Ducrocq, 1901–7)
LhotteT	Lhotte, Gustave, *Le Théâtre à Lille avant la révolution* (Lille, L. Danel, 1881)

LiebrechtH   Liebrecht, Henri, *Histoire du théâtre français à Bruxelles aux XVIIᵉ et au XVIIIᵉ siècle* (Paris, Edouard Champion, 1923)

LivetH   Livet, Georges and Francis Rapp, (eds.), *Strasbourg de la Guerre de trente ans à Napoléon 1618–1815*, vol. III of *Histoire de Strasbourg des origines à nos jours* (Strasbourg, 1981)

LoewenbergA   Loewenberg, Alfred, *Annals of opera, 1597–1940*, 3rd ed. (Totowa, New Jersey, 1978)

LoewenbergE   Loewenberg, Alfred, 'Early Dutch librettos and plays with music in the British Museum', *The journal of documentation*, II (1946–7), pp. 210–37

LS   *The London stage 1600–1800. Pt. I 1660–1700*, William Van Lennep (ed.) (Carbondale, Ill., Southern Illinois University Press, 1965)

MercierM   Mercier, Philippe, 'La Musique au Théâtre: Bruxelles-Liège', vol. I of *La Musique en Wallonie et à Bruxelles*, Robert Wangermée and Philippe Mercier (eds.) (n.p., La Renaissance du livre, 1980)

MeyerH   Meyer, Jean, (ed.), *Histoire de Rennes* (Toulouse, Edouard Privat, 1972)

MongrédienD   Mongrédien, Georges, *Dictionnaire biographique des comédiens français du XVIIᵉ siècle suivi d'un inventaire des troupes (1590–1710) d'après des documents inédits* (Paris, CNRS, 1961)

PeriauxH   Periaux, Nicétas, *Histoire sommaire et chronologique de la ville de Rouen de ses monuments, de ses institutions, de ses personnages célèbres, etc. jusqu'à la fin du XVIIIᵉ siècle* (Brionne, Le Portulan, 1970)

RobertC   Robert, Jean, 'Comédiens, musiciens et opéras à Avignon (1610–1715)', *Revue d'histoire du théâtre*, XVII (1965), pp. 275–323

RonsinR   Ronsin, Albert, *Repertoire bibliographique des livres imprimés en France aux XVIIᵉ siècle*, X, Bibliotheca bibliographica aureliana, XCVIII (Baden-Baden, Valentin Koerner, 1984)

RoseV   Rose, Gilbert 'La Vie musicale à Metz au XVIIIᵉ siècle', in *Musique et société: La Vie musicale en province aux XVIIIᵉ, XIXᵉ et XXᵉ siècles*, Actes des Journées d'Etudes de la Société Française de Musicologie (Rennes, Lices-Rennes, 1981), pp. 51–61

SchneiderC   Schneider, Herbert, *Chronologisch-thematisches Verzeichnis sämtlicher Werke von Jean-Baptiste Lully* (LWV) (Tutzing, Hans Schneider, 1981)

SchneiderR   Schneider, Herbert, *Die Rezeption der Opern Lullys im Frankreich des Ancien Regime*, Mainzer Studien zur Musikwissenschaft, vol. XVI, Hellmut Federhofer (ed.) (Tutzing, Hans Schneider, 1982)

StellfeldF   Stellfeld, Christiane, *Les Fiocco. Une Famille de musiciens belges aux XVIIᵉ et XVIIIᵉ siècles* (Brussels, Palais des Académies, 1941)

TaveneauxH   Taveneaux, René, *Histoire de Nancy* (Toulouse, Edouard Privat, 1978)

TorrefrancaP   Torrefranca, Fausto, 'La Prima opera francese in italia? (L'Armida di Lulli, Roma 1690)', in *Festschrift für Johannes Wolf zu seinem sechzigsten Geburtstage*. Walter Lott *et al.* (eds.) (Berlin, Martin Breslauer, 1929), pp. 191–7

VallasL   Vallas, Léon, *Un Siècle de musique et de théâtre à Lyon (1688–1789)* (Lyon, P. Masson, 1932; rpt. Geneva, Minkoff [1971])

WalkerD   Walker, Thomas, 'Due apocrifi corelliani', *Nuovissimi studi corelliani: atti del terzo congresso internazionale (Fusignano, 4–7 settembre 1980)*, Quaderni della Rivista italiana di musicologa, vol. VII (Florence, Leo S. Olschki, 1982), pp. 381–401

WrightD   Wright, Craig, 'Dijon', *The New Grove Dictionary of Music and Musicians*, Stanley Sadie (ed.), vol. V (London, Macmillan, 1980), pp. 474–6

How eighteenth-century Parisians heard Lully's operas: the case of *Armide*'s fourth act

LOIS ROSOW

The libretto that Philippe Quinault wrote for Lully's opera *Armide* has received few public airings in modern times. In 1983, however, both Lully's setting (1686) and that of Gluck (1777) became available in commercial recordings for the first time; in addition, another production of Gluck's version, unrelated to the recorded one, occurred that same year. Yet only one of these three productions presented the complete text; in the other two, Act IV was entirely omitted.[1] I do not mean to quarrel with the directors, who evidently had practical reasons for abridging the text, but merely to point out the ironic difference between their handling of these operas and eighteenth-century practice: while the weakness of Act IV is indeed a persistent theme in early commentaries on Lully's *Armide*, eighteenth-century directors dealt with the problem not by eliminating the act but by trying to fix it, sometimes lavishing more attention on it than on any other portion of the opera. This study examines the reception and treatment of Lully's Act IV in seventeenth- and eighteenth-century Paris, and places that treatment within the context of broader historical considerations.

An overview of the plot (omitting the allegorical prologue in praise of Louis XIV) reveals the anomalous nature of Act IV:

The story is taken from Torquato Tasso's epic *Gerusalemme liberata* and occurs at the time of the First Crusade. In *Act I* the beautiful sorceress Armide, niece of the king of Damascus, is introduced. She has used a combination of her womanly charms and her power over the demons of the Underworld to capture almost all the Crusaders in the camp of Godefroy; the valiant knight Renaud, however, has eluded her. A messenger brings word that Renaud has singlehandedly freed the captive knights, and Armide vows revenge. In *Act II* demons, following Armide's instructions, disguise themselves under pleasant exteriors and lull Renaud to sleep in a bucolic setting; Armide stands over him, dagger in hand, but is overcome with love for him and cannot kill him. She decides to punish him by making him love her ('Let him love me by my sorcery so that, if possible, I might hate him') and orders the demons to transport them to a faraway desert, where she will be able to hide her weakness and shame. In *Act III* Armide, unable to hate

[1] Lully, *Armide*, soloists and Ensemble Vocal et Instrumental de la Chapelle Royalle, conducted by Philippe Herreweghe, Erato STU 715302. The omission of Act IV is clear from the liner notes; however, numerous small, arbitrary cuts distort the remaining acts, and these go unmentioned. The recording of Gluck's *Armide*, directed by Richard Hickox, includes all five acts: EMI, SLS 1077513. Performances of Gluck's version without Act IV, directed by Alan Curtis, occurred at the University of California, Berkeley, on 20 and 22 January 1983.

Renaud, is nonetheless too ashamed to enjoy their relationship: she needed the help of magic to win his love, whereas he, by his own charms, was able to prevent her vengeance. Armide calls to Hatred to save her from Love; Hatred, followed by an army of hateful passions, attempts to do so, but is eventually stopped by Armide herself ('No, it is not possible to remove my love without breaking my heart'). In *Act IV* Ubalde and the Danish knight, Crusaders from the camp of Godefroy, make their way through the desert in search of Renaud. Armide has taken precautions against such a search by filling the desert with traps: the two knights must cope first with monsters, then with the distractions of seductive women (apparently the girlfriends they left at home but actually demons in disguise). Fortunately, they are armed with a magic scepter, and of course they have each other: Ubalde is able to drag the Danish knight away from his apparent lover, and vice versa. *Act V* takes place in the beautiful magical palace that Armide's demons have created for her in the desert. She and Renaud sing of their love, then she unwisely leaves him alone for awhile. Ubalde and the Danish knight discover Renaud and break the magic spell. Armide returns in time to find Renaud leaving; though he expresses pity for her, he is firm in his renunciation of Love in favor of Glory and Duty. Armide, alone, flies into a rage then descends into despair; she orders the demons to destroy the magical palace and, with it, her fatal love.

While the other acts are dominated by Armide and Renaud, Act IV is populated entirely by minor characters making their first appearances; furthermore, even though the moral tone of Act IV, in which the two knights admonish each other to beware of the trouble caused by love, prepares Renaud's eventual renunciation of his love for Armide, the actual events in Act IV are merely incidental to the plot. To a modern audience the respite from the main story-line after Armide's climactic rejection of Hatred might seem a welcome chance to catch one's breath (not to mention a chance for the lead singer to catch hers); we might reasonably expect Quinault's contemporaries – schooled in the French classical tragedy and continually rationalizing opera's routine departures from the unities[2] – to have felt differently.

If Quinault's contemporaries talked about the problems of Act IV, unfortunately their words are lost to us. Eighteenth-century critics tell us more: there are the well-known pamphlets of Lecerf de la Viéville as well as a series of critiques occasioned by the 1724–5 Paris revival of *Armide*, and these contain a few relevant comments. 'Quinault', wrote Lecerf in 1705, 'was excessively bare and sterile here. He ought to have provided some action . . .'[3] One of the later critics claimed that Act IV was '. . . too moral, and this is not what is sought in entertainments'.[4] Another, however, listed the 'morality' of Act IV among its positive qualities: 'This fourth Act has never succeeded, [for] it is considered false

---

[2] The attitude persisted in the eighteenth century: 'Le Miraculeux ou le Surnaturel qui règne dans tout l'Opéra autorise aussi le changement de Scène, puisque la machine peut transporter en un moment les acteurs d'un bout de la terre à l'autre'. Abbé (Jean) Terrasson, *Dissertation critique sur l'Iliade d'Homère*, 2 vols. (Paris, Fournier, 1715), vol. I, p. 208.

[3] (Jean-Laurent Lecerf de la Viéville), *Comparaison de la musique italienne et de la musique française*, part 2 (Brussels, 1705), republished in (Jacques Bonnet and Pierre Bourdelot), *Histoire de la musique et de ses effets*, 4 vols. (Amsterdam, 1725; reprint ed., Graz, Akademische Druck-u. Verlagsanstalt, 1966), vol. III, p. 13. Lecerf's remarks are paraphrased, but without citation, in *Le Mercure de France*, November 1724 (repr. ed., Geneva, Slatkine, 1968), pp. 2454–6.

[4] *Mercure*, May 1725 (repr. ed., Geneva, Slatkine, 1968), p. 922.

[*postiche*]; however, to consider it by itself, and without regard to what precedes and what follows, it seems to me very pretty and very moral'.[5] Despite his sympathy for Act IV, this last critic was sufficiently offended by its departure from the main story-line ('what precedes and what follows') to suggest the virtual elimination of its contents; in his proposed revision of the libretto, Ubalde and the Danish knight would make their first appearance during Act V, at which point '. . . they would expose in four lines whence, how, and why they came; they would break Renaud's enchantment, and the Piece would end as it ends'.[6]

The critics generally agreed that the repetitive action at its end was the weakest aspect of this troublesome act: first the Danish knight is tempted by Lucinde (or what appears to be Lucinde), then Ubalde receives the same treatment from Melisse. In each case, the unaffected knight makes the apparition disappear and offers a brief sermon on the need to avoid temptation. Table 1 shows the location of these analogous plot developments within the scene structure. Eighteenth-century commentary ranged from politely negative – 'a bit too much uniformity'[7] – to harshly reproachful: 'cold repetition, a game [that is] only appropriate to Comedy and that one must cut, despite the artistry of Lully's Songs'.[8] As this comment indicates, the librettist rather than the composer received the blame; in actuality, an examination of these scenes[9] shows that neither Quinault nor Lully was guilty of 'cold repetition'.

Table 1 *Correspondence in plot between scenes ii–iii and scene iv*

	Dan. knight & Lucinde	Ubalde & Melisse
Attempted seduction of Danish knight begins with songs and dances by rustic folk (*divertissement*)	scene ii, first part	–
Seduction of each knight is attempted by his lover, over protests of the other knight, who eventually causes the woman to disappear	scene ii, second part	scene iv, first part
Deceived knight looks for his lover but is brought to his senses by his companion	scene iii	scene iv, second part

Each episode of attempted seduction (scene ii, second part; scene iv, first part) is dominated by the lovers, while the remaining knight interjects only a few verses of protest. Despite the general parallelism of action, the two episodes

[5] *Mercure*, December 1724 (repr. ed., Geneva, Slatkine, 1968), p. 2815.
[6] Ibid., p. 2821.
[7] Ibid., p. 2816.
[8] Lecerf de la Viéville, *Comparaison*, as in Bonnet/Bourdelot vol. III, p. 13.
[9] See the full score of *Armide* (Paris, Christophe Ballard, 1686), in a facsimile edition (*French Opera in the Seventeenth and Eighteenth Centuries*, vol. VI: forthcoming from Pendragon Press, New York); the reduced score (Paris, de Baussen, 1710; repr. eds., Paris, Ballard, 1713, 1718, 1725); or the modern piano-vocal score, Théodore de Lajarte (ed.) (Paris, Michaelis, n.d.; repr. ed., New York, Broude, 1971).

differ completely in formal structure (division into airs, duets, and recitatives), and the second pair of lovers repeats no words or music sung by the first. Lully and Quinault limited repetition to three brief comments by the unaffected knights: 'Non, ce n'est qu'un charme trompeur/Dont il faut garder vostre coeur', 'Fuyez, fuyez faites-vous violence', and 'Est-ce là cette fermeté/Dont vous vous estes tant vanté?' In the first and third of these, both music and words recur literally; in the second, 'Fuyez, fuyez faites-vous violence', context required that the two occurrences of the verse receive somewhat different musical settings (compare examples 1 and 2):[10] Ubalde's version descends to a relatively weak cadence,

Example 1 Excerpt from scene ii, second part (bc omitted)

Example 2 Excerpt from scene iv, first part (bc omitted)

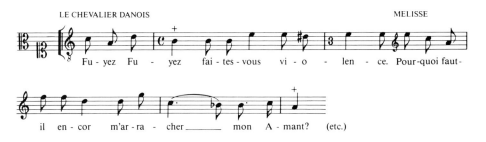

after which the Danish knight responds directly to the remark with a series of three verses that begin on rising scale degrees; the Danish knight's version rises to a much stronger cadence (with the root approached from both the dominant and the leading tone in the voice part), which provides a firm sense of closure before an extended *récitatif mesuré* for Melisse. The episodes that follow the disappearance of Lucinde and Melisse (scene iii; scene iv, second part) involve a similarly small amount of recurrence: Lully did use the identical instrumental prelude to announce the beginning of the new episode in each case; however, the two conversations between the knights, though they express equivalent senti-

---

[10] Examples 1, 2, 4, and 10a are taken from the printed score of 1686. All other musical examples come from the part-set F-Po: Mat.18.[27(1–206) (see appendix). Verbal quotations from *Armide* within the text of this article follow the spellings of those same musical sources: the printed score for quotations from the 1686 version, Mat.18.[27(1–206) for later versions.

ments, are musically independent and are bound together by only one instance of verbal recurrence: 'Ce que l'Amour a de charmant/N'est qu'un funeste enchantement'.

Clearly the few instances of textual agreement between Lucinde's scenes and Melisse's scene represent a deliberate effort to enhance the irony of the parallel situations. This compositional device was handled particularly well in the latter portion of scene iv: Ubalde, hearing the very words of warning that he himself addressed to the Danish knight earlier, joins in; they repeat those words in a brief duet, then end the scene in complete agreement regarding their goals and future behavior. Early audiences might have been more inclined to perceive the differences between the episodes of Lucinde and Melisse – and to appreciate the subtlety with which textual recurrences were introduced – if they had been more sympathetic to Act IV as a whole and less impatient to return to the protagonists, Armide and Renaud.

For almost a century after Lully's death, his operas remained staples in the repertory of the Académie royale de musique (the Paris Opéra); during any given season premières of new works shared the Académie calendar with revivals of old ones by Lully and others.[11] *Armide* was in the repertory from 1686 to 1766. Though little is known of the seventeenth-century production schedule, various sources mention isolated performances in 1686, 1687, 1688, 1692, and 1697; in the eighteenth century, productions occurred in 1703, 1713–14, 1724–5, 1746–8 (with performance runs in January–March 1746, February–March 1747, and March 1748), and 1761–6 (with runs in November–March 1761–2, December–February 1764–5, and March 1766).[12] Fortunately we have a substantial number of musical sources reflecting most of these productions (see appendix); these, along with the published librettos, make it possible to examine the revisions introduced into *Armide* during the course of its eighty-year history.

When an old opera was revived, those in charge of the production did not hesitate to alter the score and libretto in any way they thought likely to ensure financial success.[13] After 1750 such textual emendations were usually quite extensive, for reasons to be discussed below, but before then they tended to be relatively small in number and modest in scope. The handling of *Armide* up until 1748

[11] William Weber, in '*La musique ancienne* in the Waning of the Ancien Régime' *Journal of Modern History*, LVI (1984), pp. 58–88, proposes a political explanation for the French emphasis on a repertory of old works.

[12] For the seventeenth century, Chantal Masson, 'Journal du Marquis de Dangeau: 1684–1720: Extraits concernant la vie musicale à la Cour', *Recherches sur la musique française classique*, II (1961–2), pp. 200–1, 205; *Le Mercure galant* (January 1687), pp. 186–7; (François and Claude) Parfaict, *Dictionnaire des théâtres de Paris*, 7 vols. (Paris, Lambert, 1756), vol. I, p. 303; (Evrard Titon du Tillet), *Supplement du Parnasse françois, jusqu'en 1743* (n.p., n.d.), p. 792. The eighteenth-century

dates appear in numerous announcements and reviews in *Mercure*, as well as dated librettos from 1703, 1713, 1714, 1724, 1746, and 1761.

[13] See Herbert Schneider, *Die Rezeption der Opern Lullys im Frankreich des Ancien régime* (Tutzing, Hans Schneider, 1982), pp. 75–122; and Lois Rosow, 'Lully's *Armide* at the Paris Opéra: a Performance History, 1686–1766' (unpubl. PhD diss., Brandeis University, 1981: University Microfilms International 8126893), chapters 4, 6, 7. The present article, which took shape while I was supported by a generous fellowship from The Society for the Humanities at Cornell University, is based on material from my dissertation.

seems to have been fairly typical in this way; however, it is striking (but not surprising) that most of the changes – indeed, all of the very early ones – are concentrated in Act IV.

Anonymous editors began to tinker with the Act IV *divertissement* (scene ii, part 1) even before the end of the seventeenth century. Apart from the brief instrumental air that introduces the scene (during which the transformation of the desert into a pastoral setting presumably took place), Lully had included two dances, a *gavotte* and a *canarie*; it will be recalled (table 1 above) that the dancers represented 'rustic folk' in an enchanted countryside. Around 1697, a third dance, a brief piece in rondeau form, was added immediately after them. The added piece (example 3) was borrowed from Lully's ballet music of 1660 for Cavalli's opera *Xerxes*;[14] the 1660 score had apparently not specified any particular dance type, but in *Armide* the piece bears the title 'contredanse'. The added

Example 3 Beginning of *contredanse* added to scene ii around 1697

Abbreviations

bc	basse-continue
bsn	basson
b vln	basse de violon
d hb	dessus de hautbois
d vln	dessus de violon
h-c vln	haute-contre de violon
q vln	quinte de violon
t vln	taille de violon

[14] Herbert Schneider, *Chronologisch-Thematisches Verzeichnis sämtlicher Werke von Jean-Baptiste Lully* (LWV) (Tutzing, Hans Schneider, 1981), p. 60: LWV 12/3. I wish to thank Rebecca Harris-Warrick for informing me of the origin of this music. Only the melody was borrowed without change from *Xerxes*. I cannot explain the pieces's four-voice texture in *Armide*; five voices were the norm in French orchestral music until the 1720s.

dance is of little musical interest, but the choreographic implications of its new title are worth noting: the *contredanse*, a French version of the English 'country dance', had developed only recently and differed substantially in style from traditional French ballroom and theater dancing;[15] *contredanses* did not normally appear on the stage of the Opéra at this time, and one wonders if some special effect was intended. Whatever the case, the addition of the *contredanse* began a series of seemingly fussy changes in this scene: in 1703, the new dance was moved to the end of the *divertissement*, which had previously closed with a chorus; in 1713, another dance, a *menuet*, was added after it; later, perhaps not until 1724, the *menuet* was removed, leaving only the *contredanse* in its revised location. Matters of staging, whose significance is unknown today, presumably motivated this continual tinkering with the number of dances and order of events.

There was another change in Act IV during the seventeenth century, one whose purpose is more readily apparent: the removal of one of the two diversionary love affairs. By 1697 – perhaps earlier[16] – all of scene iv, which includes the encounter between Ubalde and Melisse as well as the knights' ensuing dialogue, had been entirely eliminated. Lecerf's remark of 1705 that 'one must cut' the double intrigue evidently was not purely theoretical.

Act IV was performed in this fashion, with minor revisions in its *divertissement* and lacking its final scene but otherwise intact, through 1725. Outside of Act IV, *Armide* underwent practically no change at all during those years; virtually the only textual alterations elsewhere in the opera were cuts of very small scope, generally the elimination of direct repetition of brief passages. It should be mentioned, however, that the disappearance of the traditional five-voice texture of French orchestral music apparently dates from the early 1720s: though the Opéra orchestra still included two *quintes de violon* in 1719,[17] the *quinte de violon* part seems to have been simply dropped when *Armide* was revived in 1724; there was only one small adjustment of the other parts (involving an imitative entry) to accommodate the omission.

Twenty years passed before *Armide*'s next revival. The new editors – François Rebel and François Francoeur, *inspecteurs généraux* of the Académie[18] – crossed out passages somewhat more freely than their early-eighteenth-century counterparts had done; numerous little cuts were made throughout the opera in 1746, and these included not only direct repeats but other bits of text and music as well. Several eighteenth-century commentators attested to the slowing down of

[15] See Anne L. Witherell, *Louis Pécour's 1700 Recueil de danses* (Ann Arbor, UMI Research Press, 1983), pp. 95–6. Pécour's 1700 *Recueil*, containing choreographies for ballroom use, includes this *contredanse* (rebarred in 6/4 and doubled in length by repetition); Pécour was choreographer at the Opéra during the 1690s.

[16] Datable source material from the seventeenth century is scarce: two violin parts from 1686 include scene iv, but a violin part from 1697 omits it; the change could have occurred at any time in between. The same might be said regarding the date of the *contredanse* discussed above.

[17] (Nicholas Boindin), *Lettres historiques sur tous les spectacles de Paris* (Paris, Prault, 1719), p. 118.

[18] Lois Rosow, 'From Destouches to Berton: Editorial Responsibility at the Paris Opéra', *Journal of the American Musicological Society*, XL (1987), pp. 285–309.

operatic performance since Lully's day and the resulting need to shorten older works,[19] but most of the new cuts in *Armide* seem to have had more to do with streamlining than with saving time. These two instances from Act IV should illustrate the point: in scene ii Ubalde's third remark of protest was removed (example 4), and in scene i a linking passage in the basso continuo (connecting the

Example 4 Excerpt from scene ii (bc omitted); bracketed portion was cut in 1746

reprise of the orchestral prelude to the following recitative) was reduced from four bars to one bar. It is particularly interesting that within scenes of dramatic dialogue Lully's typical 'AABb' binary form airs (*b* having the same words as *B* but a firm cadence in tonic, whereas *B* ends in a secondary key) were nearly all short-ened to ABb; the end of such an air retained its feeling of closure, but without repetition of the *A* phrase, the beginning of the air was less clearly set off from the preceding recitative.[20] The editors evidently wanted to minimize Lully's articulation of long scenes into short-breathed units.

But what about the special problems of the troublesome Act IV that year? In keeping with their treatment of *Armide* as a whole, Rebel and Francoeur tried to tighten up the last part of the act by cutting it further. Scene iii, the con-versation between the knights following Lucinde's disappearance, had originally consisted of four airs, preceded by a short orchestral prelude and tagged by a bit of recitative:

> LE CHEVALIER DANOIS (first air: *haute-contre*, basso continuo):
> Je tourne en vain les yeux de toutes parts
> Je ne voy plus cette Beauté si chere.
> Elle eschape à mes regards
> Comme une vapeur legere.

---

[19] For example, Abbé (Jean-Baptiste) Du Bos, *Réflexions critiques sur la poësie et sur la peinture* (1719), 7th ed., 3 vols. (Paris, Pissot, 1770), vol. III, pp. 342–3; and Jean-Jacques Rous-seau, *Lettre sur la musique françoise* (1753), in his *Ecrits sur la musique* (n.p., Pourrat, 1838; repr. ed., n.p., Stock, 1979), p. 301, n. 1.

[20] Act I, scene i, for example, contains four AABb airs that were reduced to ABb: Sido-nie's 'Vous allumez une fatale flame' and 'Vous troublez-vous d'une image legere', and Phénice's 'Si la guerre aujourd'huy' and 'Pour-quoi voulez-vous songer'.

UBALDE (second air: bass voice, two violins, b.c.):
 Ce que l'Amour a de charmant
 N'est qu'une illusion qui ne laisse apres elle
 Qu'une honte eternelle.
 Ce que l'Amour a de charmant
 N'est qu'un funeste enchantement.

LE CHEVALIER DANOIS (third air: *haute-contre*, b.c.):
 Je voy le danger où s'expose
 Un coeur qui ne fuit pas un charme si puissant.
 Que vous estes heureux si vous estes exempt
 Des foiblesses que l'amour cause!

UBALDE (fourth air: bass voice, two violins, b.c.):
 Non, je n'ay point gardé mon coeur jusqu'à ce jour,
 Prés de l'objet que j'aime il m'estoit doux de vivre.
 Mais quand la Gloire ordonne de la suivre
 Il faut laisser gemir l'Amour.

UBALDE (recitative: bass voice, b.c.):
 Des charmes les plus forts la raison me desgage,
 Rien ne nous doit icy retenir davantage,
 Profitons des conseils que l'on nous a donnez.

In 1746, the third and fourth airs were cut, perhaps because they seemed only to reiterate the point made in the second. (A veiled reference to Melisse in the fourth air had been irrelevant for a half-century.) The repetitious sermonizing that characterized the original scenes iii and iv was now reduced to one brief air for Ubalde ('Ce que l'Amour'). Reduction notwithstanding, the audience surely noticed the moral; the trio texture of Ubalde's air ensured that it stood out against its new surroundings.

 There would be one more alteration of this passage that winter; it was not originally copied into the new parts but occurred as an afterthought sometime during rehearsals (though in time for inclusion in the 7 January 1746 libretto): the editors substituted four lines of recitative from Lully's long-defunct scene iv for the three lines (shown above) that had ended scene iii, and the act now ended as follows:

UBALDE:
 D'une nouvelle erreur songeons à nous deffendre,
 Evitons de trompeurs attraits,
 Ne nous destournons pas du chemin qu'il faut prendre
 Pour arriver à ce Palais.

This alteration made sense both dramatically – the conclusion of the act now directed audience attention toward the palace of Armide and Renaud, the site of Act v – and tonally: the new passage is in C major, the key of the rest of scene iii and of the entr'acte preceding Act v, whereas the eliminated recitative had served as a transition to A minor, the opening key of the discarded fourth scene.

 The most striking emendation of *Armide* in 1746 was a major addition to the

Act IV *divertissement* (scene ii, first part); while the dramatic portion of the act continued to shrink, the diversionary portion grew longer and quite different in character. As explained above, the *divertissement* introduces the first episode of seduction: the frightful desert of scene i is suddenly replaced by an enchanted countryside, in which Lucinde and her companions – all actually demons in disguise – dance and sing, luring the Danish knight away from his mission. Lully and Quinault had provided their usual sort of diversionary material for this scene: one large-scale chorus and one brief chorus, each preceded by a short solo (a *récit*) for Lucinde, who simply introduces the choral tune in each case;[21] and the two brief dances mentioned above, a *gavotte* and a *canarie*. They arranged this material in a more-or-less symmetrical construction: the large-scale chorus, preceded by its *récit*, occurs at both the beginning and end of the *divertissement*, acting as a frame around the shorter pieces; and a very short passage of recitative for the two knights – in which Ubalde urges departure but the Danish knight holds back – occurs at approximately the midpoint:

> *récit* and chorus, 'Voicy la charmante retraite'
> *gavotte*; *canarie*
> brief recitative for the two knights
> *récit* and brief chorus, 'Jamais dans ces beaux lieux'
> reprise of *récit* and chorus, 'Voicy'[22]

Between the *canarie* and the recitative, Rebel and Francoeur added not one new piece but four: a pair of airs for Lucinde, separated and followed by a newly-composed dance piece (examples 5–7). To compensate for the length of the insertion, they cut the final *récit* and chorus as well as the *contredanse* that had been added earlier; however, they changed their minds during rehearsals: as performed, the *divertissement* ended with the *récit* (but not the chorus) 'Jamais dans ces beaux lieux', followed by just one phrase of the chorus 'Voicy la charmante retraite'. The portion of the *divertissement* preceding the knights' recitative was now substantially longer than previously, while the remainder was greatly reduced.

We may assume the new music to be by Francoeur or Rebel, or by both; we do not know the author of the poetry. The texts of the airs – 'Everyone must love . . . Even Cupid loved as we do', and 'The birds in these woods breathe only love . . .' – complement the words of Quinault's *récits* and choruses: '. . . Here is the happy place for games and love', and 'In this beautiful place . . . the good things that we want are offered . . .' In 'Les oiseaux' (example 7) the parallel thirds and echo-like imitation between soprano and oboe, the drone bass, and the florid melismas on the word 'warbling' (*ramages*) all aid in evoking the

---

[21] Late seventeenth- and early eighteenth-century musicians and critics often relied on the general term *récit* (meaning any passage for one or more solo voices) to describe those portions of Lully's scores that defy easy classification as either air or recitative. These two pieces for Lucinde are air-like but extremely short,

just a few measures each; some early sources label them 'airs' and others 'récits'.

[22] The 1686 printed score calls for a reprise of only the *récit*; the 1686 libretto calls for a reprise of only the chorus; the violin parts from 1686 specify that both are to be heard again.

Example 5 Beginning of first vocal air added in 1746; bc is lost

Il faut que tout ai - me Rien n'est si doux, Le dieu d'a - mour

mê - me ai-ma _____ com - me nous.

Example 6 Beginning of dance air added in 1746; h-c vln, bsn, and bc are lost

Example 7a Beginning of second vocal air added in 1746

Seul

LUCINDE

Les oi - seaux de ces boc - ca - ges _

Example 7b Another excerpt from 'Les oiseaux de ces boccages', voice part only

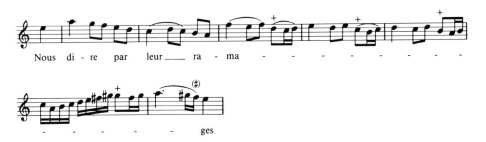

Nous di - re par leur___ ra - ma - - - - - - - - - - -

\- - - - - ges

pastoral setting and bird songs of the text; however, this text is only marginally related to the central plot of *Armide*. The additional attention focused on Lucinde (or, more accurately, on Mademoiselle Fel, the singer of this virtuosic part) pushed this scene much further from the central drama than the original authors had intended; the Danish knight was temporarily forgotten, and Armide and Renaud were far away indeed.

To understand this treatment of the Act IV *divertissement* – in fact, to assess the editors' motives throughout this version of *Armide* – we must place the 1746 production in historical context. The spectators of 1746 arrived at the theater with a very different attitude toward *Armide* from that of 1686, for the style of newly-composed *tragédies-lyriques* had changed considerably since Lully's day.[23] By the turn of the century, the incipient rococo style in the visual arts had already begun to affect opera, and its effects – particularly obvious in the new genre called the *opéra-ballet* but also evident in the *tragédie-lyrique* – gradually increased as the century wore on. In librettos the playful and erotic elements grew in importance at the expense of the dramatic and tragic: *divertissements* grew longer while dialogue scenes shrank, and the romanticized characters who populate the former took ever more attention away from the tragic heroes and heroines; banal hymns to romantic love, like the two added to *Armide* in 1746, seem to have been the rococo librettist's answer to Antoine Watteau's *fête galante* paintings. As for the music, its sensuous and decorative aspects received new emphasis at the expense of subtle text expression: not only in the *divertissements* but even in the scenes of dramatic dialogue, starkly declamatory vocal lines gave way to melodies encrusted with *agréments*; instrumental melodies were affected as well. At the same time, the influence of the Italian opera and cantata complemented that of rococo art: the harmonic vocabulary of French opera grew richer, contrapuntal writing became more prevalent, lengthy Italianate melismas took their place alongside the native *agréments* (but they were still restricted to word-painting purposes, just like Lully's occasional brief melismas), orchestration – which had previously consisted largely of standardized handling of a few

[23] The developments summarized in the next two paragraphs are discussed at greater length by James R. Anthony, *French Baroque Music* *from Beaujoyeulx to Rameau*, rev. ed. (New York and London, Norton, 1978), chapters 9 and 10.

basic textures – grew more flexible, and the use of individual instruments became more idiomatic and technically demanding.

Around the turn of the century programmatic 'noise' pieces and *ariettes* first appeared in the *tragédie-lyrique*, and both soon became clichés. 'Noise' pieces ('tempête',[24] 'bruit de guerre', 'bruit infernal', 'bruit de tonnerre', and the like) were characterized by fast runs, arpeggiated figuration, and tremolos in the strings, and they often had several independent bass parts; Marin Marais composed the most famous early example, the exciting tempest from *Alcyone* of 1706. *Ariettes* werc large-scale da capo *arie di bravura*, but unlike Italian arias they were quite narrow in function: *ariettes* occurred only in *divertissements* and were almost always about romantic love; nearly all of them drew on the same small vocabulary of words to which elaborate melismas were set ('voler', 'régner', 'briller', 'chaîne', 'triomphe', and so on). Although the air 'Les oiseaux de ces boccages' is relatively short (forty-nine measures) and not in da capo form, the elaborate vocal writing, the reliance on pastoral images, and the textural relationship between soprano and oboe are all traits borrowed from the *ariette* style.

The developments outlined here did not occur in great quantity all at once. Some of the new traits were common very early in the century – for instance, obbligato woodwind parts in airs on pastoral or amorous texts (though they became more florid as the century progressed) and a filigree of *agréments* adorning vocal melodies – but others, notably idiomatic writing for strings and daring chromatic harmonies, were introduced only tentatively at first and were, for the most part, reserved for special effect even in the 1720s.

Thus, the first production of Jean-Philippe Rameau's *Hippolyte et Aricie* in 1733 startled Parisian audiences: Italianisms had been creeping gradually into their operas for several decades, but the sheer quantity and intensity of the contrapuntal textures, chromatic harmonies and modulations, virtuosic vocal and instrumental writing, and unusual orchestration[25] in this one opera were unlike anything ever heard before. Rameau's music made unheard-of demands on the performers and, equally significant, on the listeners as well: most highly-trained musicians appreciated his operatic genius from the start (though some were too jealous to express admiration), but much of the general opera-going public needed time to grow accustomed to his style. His works dominated the Académie's calendar during the rest of the 1730s and the 1740s, but they elicited spirited controversy throughout that time.[26]

It is interesting that the conservatives who still complained in the 1740s about Rameau's innovations – Rémond de Saint-Mard, the abbé Mably, Bollioud de Mermet – compared the latest style not with that of the previous generation but with Lully's; Lully's operas had never ceased to be a standard against which all

[24] Caroline Wood, 'Orchestra and Spectacle in the *tragédie en musique* 1673–1715: oracle, *sommeil* and *tempête*', *Proceedings of the Royal Musical Association*, CVIII (1981–2), pp. 40–6.

[25] Graham Sadler, 'Rameau and the Orchestra', *Proceedings of the Royal Musical Association*, CVIII (1981–2), pp. 47–68. Regarding

Rameau's style in general, see Paul-Marie Masson, *L'Opéra de Rameau* (Paris, 1930; repr. ed., New York, Da Capo, 1972).

[26] Paul-Marie Masson, 'Lullistes et Ramistes: 1733–1752', *L'Année musicale*, I (1911), pp. 187–213.

new French operas were measured. By the time *Armide* was revived in 1746, however, Rameau's operas had been generally well accepted, and the so-called 'Lullistes' seemed reactionary – not because they liked Lully's music but because they were too narrow-minded to see the value in a variety of styles. In 1748, Diderot summed up the situation as follows: 'the ignoramuses and the gray-beards were all in favor of Utmiutsol [Lully]; the youth and the virtuosi were all for Uremifasolasiututut [Rameau]; and the people of good taste, young as well as old, had a high opinion of them both'.[27]

We must view the 1746 production of *Armide* in light of these developments. If Rameau's style is the standard of comparison, then the revisions of 1746 seem tame indeed. The many little cuts made throughout the opera bespeak the rococo impatience with Lully's long, static dialogue scenes (and probably compensated for that era's slower, more decorative singing style as well), yet there was only a modest infusion of the elaborate diversionary material that had replaced dramatic dialogue in popularity. The Act II *divertissement* was actually shortened considerably for this production. As for the new pieces added to the Act IV *divertissement* (see examples 5–7), the texture and vocal ornamentation of 'Les oiseaux' clearly post-date Lully, but any of these pieces could have been written decades earlier than 1746. In sum, *Armide* remained untouched by Rameau's innovations in harmony, counterpoint, and orchestration, and was only slightly affected by the innovations of his predecessors.

However, none of this indicates that François Francoeur and François Rebel were unregenerate Lullistes. Their own *tragédie-lyrique* from the Rameau period (*Scanderberg* of 1735) contains enough Italianate airs, contrapuntal vocal ensembles, arpeggiated violin figuration, and rich harmonies to prove otherwise. Their conservative handling of *Armide* indicates little about their attitude toward new compositions and much about their respect for the works of a venerable master. They were apparently not alone:

The Académie Royale de Musique continues the performances of *Armide* with a success that one would not hope for given the wavering uncertainty of taste in this century. It seems from the ovations and from the continually large crowds that the Innovators in Music have not yet conquered the Lullistes and that the Author of harmony loved by the heart had ears on his side as well. If schism reigns in our Concerts, it has not entirely subjugated the Lyric Theatre . . .[28]

In short, in the 1740s an opera by Lully was still expected to sound like an opera by Lully.

Eventually, however, the administrators of the Académie were forced to rethink their handling of the oldest operas in the repertory. The catalyst seems to have been the Guerre des Bouffons of 1752–4. Though the Guerre began with a production of Pergolesi's *La Serva padrona* and led mainly to the development of

---

[27] Denis Diderot, *Les Bijoux indiscrets*, in J. Assézat (ed.), *Oeuvres complètes*, 20 vols. (Paris, Garnier, 1875–7), vol. IV, p. 174. The context is a *roman à clef* about a mythical coun-try that represents France; the composer attributions are Assézat's.

[28] *Mercure*, March 1746 (repr. ed., Geneva, Slatkine, 1970), pp. 152–3.

a new type of comic opera in France, it also raised broad issues having little to do with the merits of *opera buffa*;[29] once again French aestheticians found themselves re-examining their own operatic literature from a new perspective.

While the complexities of Rameau's music had been hard to take in 1733, twenty years later the public was used to them, and Lully's music seemed unbearably simple by contrast. Two of the pamphlets associated with the Guerre des Bouffons include thoughtful prescriptions for a thorough reworking of Lully's operas that would bring them into conformity with contemporary taste. The anonymous editor of *La paix de l'Opéra* (an annotated extract from François Raguenet's *Parallèle des italiens et des français, en ce qui regarde la musique et les opéras* of 1702) praised Quinault's librettos without reservation, but he expressed similar approval of only one portion of Lully's scores: the 'sweet, melodious recitative, well-matched with Quinault's delicate words, with the spirit of our language, and with the sensitive temperament of the French'. He went on to offer the following recommendation:

> A few years ago a plan was proposed to the Directors of the Opéra, which they could make very profitable if they took effective means to carry it out. This plan consisted of going back to work on most of our bygone Operas; it is Monsieur Rameau who was to have been charged with this task, and it is certain that they could not have gone to a better person. This reform would be necessary in many respects; there is nobody who disagrees about that. Lulli, born to excel in all aspects of Composition if he had wanted to embrace them, restricted himself, as it were, to the matter of Song [*Chant*] alone; he neglected almost all the others. . . [Nowadays] his Overtures are found dry and monotonous, his violin airs thin and little wrought, his *ariettes* [*sic*] paltry and trivial. The structure of his Trios and Choruses is rich enough, but the accompaniments are weak, and everything falls short with respect to filling out [*remplissage*]. So long as our old Operas stay in this state of imperfection, it must not be hoped that they could be successfully revived . . . Most of our old Pieces are falling into oblivion. What has become of *Isis, Amadis, Cadmus, Alceste, Atys*? The structure of these Operas is very good, the Recitative is admirable, there are even excellent orchestral pieces. Why deprive ourselves of such a rich heritage? Why renounce a legacy that could be gathered and even expanded at little cost? Why, above all, why let fall into oblivion so many admirable Poems, which would necessarily have the same fate as the Music? . . .[30]

The following year Charles Henri de Blainville published a brief comparison of Lully's and Rameau's operatic writing.[31] Lully, he wrote, is 'filled with soul and action' in his declamation and in many of his 'morceaux de caractère' (pieces depicting particular emotions or character types[32]), but his choruses are 'bare', and his instrumental pieces and *divertissements* cold and uninteresting. Rameau, he continued, is 'warmer and more animated' in his airs and *divertissements*; full of spirit, he seems to have too much of that of which Lully has not enough. Like

[29] See Alfred Richard Oliver, *The Encyclopedists as Critics of Music* (New York, Columbia Univ. Press, 1947), pp. 89–100.

[30] *La Paix de l'Opéra, ou Parallele impartial de la musique françoise et de la musique italienne* (Amsterdam, 1753), pp. 35–40, reprinted in *La Querelle des Bouffons: Texte des pamphlets,* Denise Launay (ed.), 3 vols. (Geneva, Minkoff, 1973), vol. I, pp. 547–52.

[31] C. H. Blainville, *L'Esprit de l'art musical, ou reflexions sur la musique et de ses différentes parties* (Geneva, 1754; repr. ed., Geneva, Minkoff, 1975), pp. 109–13.

[32] Ibid., p. 33.

the editor of *La paix de l'Opéra*, Blainville thought highly of Philippe Quinault, and he even suggested that Quinault's librettos might be reset altogether 'in twenty or thirty years', when Lully's versions would be less recent. In the meantime, he advocated rewriting Lully's operas by preserving the dialogue scenes 'and some other precious excerpts', while replacing 'in a consistent style' (*d'une même main*) the songs and *divertissements* – everything apart from the main dramatic action; 'in a word, refashion all of the ornaments of this building, which displays only a beautiful architectural foundation [but] whose externals all seem neglected'.

In fact, from the mid-1750s to the mid-1770s, numerous operas by Lully and his successors were edited for presentation at the Opéra, and it is clear both from surviving musical sources and from contemporaneous descriptions that these were major reworkings, involving copious adjustments of the original music as well as the addition of many new instrumental pieces and songs. (Rameau is not known to have participated in this activity.) The 1761 version of *Armide* – attributed at the time to Francoeur and Rebel (who were now the co-directors of the Académie) but probably the work of Francoeur alone[33] – seems to have been typical of the genre.

The 1761 revision was remarkably thoroughgoing, involving virtually every piece in the opera: the editor suppressed the prologue, shortened the dialogue scenes even further than before, replaced the overture and some other introductory instrumental pieces with new ones, added a 'bruit' at the end (to accompany the destruction of Armide's palace), supplied a large number of new dances and songs for the *divertissements*, added obbligato instrumental parts to some of Lully's vocal music, rewrote the viola parts in many orchestral settings, altered meters in airs and recitatives[34] and surface rhythms throughout the score, made minor adjustments in Lully's instrumentation, and added a generous layer of *agréments* to most of the melodies. (It might be added that the genesis of this version was tortuous: even after the parts were copied, large and small revisions of all sorts were made in great quantity all through the brief rehearsal period.)

Despite their quantity, however, the additions and alterations evince a certain restraint. The incipient classical style had a firm foothold in Paris in 1761, but there is no sign of it in the new pieces added to *Armide* that year;[35] in fact, many of them – such as the *menuet* in example 8, with its alternating phrases for winds and strings and its unchanging continuo homophony texture – could be placed inconspicuously in an opera written forty years earlier. (The *Mercure* noted approvingly that some of the new dances seemed to conform to the 'fundamental character of the old Music'.)[36] Similarly, the independent violin part added to the duet at the beginning of Act IV (example 9) could have been written around

[33] 'MM. Rebel & Francoeur ont ajouté de nouveaux morceaux à ceux qu'ils avoient placés dans *Armide* en 1746'. *Mercure*, December 1761 (repr. ed., Geneva, Slatkine, 1970), p. 165. Regarding the attribution to Francoeur alone, see the appendix to this article.

[34] I have commented on the metrical alterations in 'French Baroque Recitative as an Expression of Tragic Declamation', *Early Music*, XI (1983), pp. 477–8.

[35] In 1766, Pierre Montan Berton replaced Lully's lengthy *passacaille* (Act V) with three shorter pieces, and these are in the early classical style.

[36] *Mercure*, December 1761, p. 165.

Example 8 Beginning of *menuet* 2 added to Act IV, scene ii in 1761

Example 9 Excerpt from duet, Act IV, scene i; originally scored for voices and bc alone

the turn of the century, and the reworking of the counterpoint in the violas (example 10) seems to have been intended merely to ameliorate the perceived poverty of Lully's inner parts (and to compensate for the missing *quinte de violon*, suppressed nearly four decades earlier), not to introduce noticeably 'modern' harmonies or textures.

On the other hand, as the *gavotte* in example 11[37] shows, Francoeur occasion-

---

[37] The *gavottes* for Act II, as well as an *air en rondeau* for Act I, have been recorded by Jean-François Paillard: François Francoeur, *Symphonies du Festin Royal* [i.e., wedding feast] *de Monseigneur le Comte d'Artois* (1773), Erato, re-leased as Musical Heritage Society 846. (Complete transcriptions of nearly all the pieces added to *Armide* are available in my dissertation, cited in note 13.)

Example 10 Excerpt from orchestral interlude in duet, Act IV, scene ii

a. 1686 version

b. 1761 version

Example 11 Second reprise of *gavotte* 2 added to Act II, scene iv in 1761; melody only

ally ventured into somewhat more modern territory: the division of the phrases into brief repetitive units evokes the busy sound of *opera buffa* and of many dance melodies by Rameau as well. The way the return to tonic is initiated in the ninth measure seems equally remote from the 'fundamental character of the old Music': the leading tone of D is flatted so that an earlier passage can be abruptly quoted out of context (cf. example 12, which is preceded by tonic harmony in G major).

Example 12 End of first reprise of same *gavotte*

Furthermore, the new pieces clearly show that orchestration in French opera had changed considerably as a result of Rameau's influence. Despite the availability of trumpets, timpani, hunting horns, and even clarinets, Francoeur chose not to go beyond the basic collection of strings and woodwinds selected by Lully for this opera; however, his use of the instruments was entirely modern (examples 12, 13, and 14). Multiple stops and rapid string arpeggiation, rare exoticisms in French opera of the 1720s, appeared routinely as a normal part of the language in the 1761 version of *Armide*. The bassoon still played the bass line, its traditional role, in many passages but appeared in others as a tenor instrument. Finally, Lully's almost rigid reliance on two basic orchestral textures – a strong soprano–bass duet for strings and woodwinds with relatively unimportant viola parts as filler, and a trio sonata texture for winds or strings – gave way to a wide range of textural possibilities: the treble group might at any time be divided into two or three parts (something Lully did in trios but only extremely rarely when the full string ensemble was present), the two viola parts (*haute-contre* and *taille de violon*) might occasionally play in unison, and independent woodwind parts might occur in the same texture with the strings, yielding a total of six or seven voices; furthermore, different textures were combined with considerable flexibility within individual pieces.

Example 13 Beginning of *musette* added to Act IV, scene ii in 1761

Example 14 Excerpt from *forlane* added to Act IV, scene ii in 1761

The impulses that led to the transformation of *Armide* – especially the increased emphasis on diversion at the expense of drama and the taste for music of more obvious complexity – led also to a revised understanding of its penultimate act. In 1754, Louis de Cahusac (one of Rameau's librettists) wrote the following about Act IV:

Armide, whom I cannot think calm [about the power of Ubalde and the Danish knight to free Renaud from her enchantment], thus displays at this point all her efforts, all her powers, all the resources of her art, to stop the only enemies that she has to fear. Such is the design of Quinault, and what a design for a Spectacle of Song, Music, and Dance! All that Magic has that is formidable or fascinating – groups of dances of the greatest vigor or the most enjoyable sensual delight; conflagrations, thunder storms, earthquakes; light

Ballets, brilliant Festivals, delicious enchantments – here is what Quinault asked for in this Act. It is the plan that he traced, which Lully should have carried out and completed, as a man of genius, with an Entr'acte in which Magic made one last terrible effort. With this artifice one would have gotten rid of any uncertainty concerning the success of Ubalde's attentions and formed an admirable contrast with the tone of sensual pleasure that dominates the first part of the following Act. Let us imagine such a plan, carried out in Song, Dance, *Symphonies*, Decor, Machines; and let us judge.[38]

The critic who reviewed the 1761 production for the *Mercure* agreed with Cahusac that the emphasis in Act IV should be on terror rather than seduction; however, he felt that the resources of the Académie were inadequate for such an approach:

Monsieur Quinault left a void in the fourth Act, very necessary for the repose of the Actress who represents Armide – even necessary so that the objects of principal interest will not be offered without interruption. This void should apparently have been filled, according to the Poet's intentions, by the magic of the stage machinery, representing the marvels of sorcery and frightening the Danish knights [*sic*]. Open chasms, Volcanos, Monsters of all sorts are indicated in the text. Undoubtedly this idea will one day be carried out, which would engage the interest of [*occuper*] the Audience a great deal – but the presentation of Monsters needs to be improved at our Opéra. Some attempts that have been made so far have produced only a small effect, which exposes them to derision. Very wisely, therefore – and, fortunately, to the satisfaction of the Public – the agreeable has been substituted for the terrible in this Act. It is the act in which most of the additional Music has been placed.[39]

Cahusac and the *Mercure* critic attributed ideas to Quinault that are not evident in the 1686 libretto. It is true that the text in scene i, where the knights trudge across the desert, describes monsters, open chasms, and the like; however, Quinault's instructions for dancing occur later in the act, during the pastoral seduction scene, and the dancers explicitly represent 'rustic folk' (*habitans champestres*); rightly or wrongly, Quinault chose the 'agreeable' rather than the 'terrible' as the major vehicle for song and dance in Act IV. Still, it is significant that mid-century critics were sympathetic to Quinault and preferred to blame others, even the composer, for the failure of Act IV, and that they approved of Act IV's departure from the main plot. Their attitude differed greatly from that of their predecessors.

The 'additional music' mentioned by the *Mercure* critic is concentrated mainly in the *divertissement*: whereas the other *divertissements* were adjusted in relatively minor ways and given one or two new dances each, the one for Act IV was almost completely rewritten and given more new pieces than any other part of the opera. The length of this *divertissement* is remarkable, but the length originally planned for it is truly astonishing: not only was the *divertissement* itself longer in the initial draft than in the final version, but the diversionary material spilled over into the ensuing dramatic dialogue (scene ii, part 2) as well:

---

[38] (Louis) de Cahusac, *La Danse ancienne et moderne ou traité historique de la danse*, 3 vols. (The Hague, Neaulme, 1754; repr. ed.,   Geneva, Slatkine, 1971), vol. III, pp. 90–1.
[39] *Mercure*, December 1761, pp. 168–9.

1. *Divertissement*
   dance: *musette*
   récit (Lucinde) and chorus: 'Voicy la charmante retraite' (retained from previ-
      ous version but much revised)
   *dances: *menuets* 1 and 2
   dance: 'air de pastres'
   air (Lucinde): 'Les oiseaux de ces boccages' (retained from previous version
      but much revised)
   dances: *gavottes* 1 and 2
   air (Lucinde): 'Bergers, qu'assemble un si beau jour'
   dance: *forlane*
   brief recitative (the knights): 'Allons, qui vous retient encore? . . .' (with
      minor revisions)
   *air (Lucinde): 'Dans ces lieux qu'amour vous attire'
2. Seduction Episode
   recitative (Lucinde, Danish knight, Ubalde), punctuated by:
      *air (Lucinde), 'Que ces momens'; and
      *new duet (Lucinde, Danish knight), 'Jouisson' (musically elaborate re-
         placement for simple duet by Lully)

In the course of rehearsals and early performances, however, all the pieces
marked here by asterisks were cut. The dramatic portion of scene ii was thus
greatly streamlined; moreover, the brief recitative that Lully had placed near the
middle of the *divertissement* now signalled its end:

1686:

> *canarie*
> recitative (middle of *divertissement*)
>> UBALDE: 'Allons, qui vous retient encore?/Allons, c'est trop vous
>> arrester'. LE CHEVALIER DANOIS: 'Je voy la Beauté que j'adore:/C'est elle,
>> je n'en puis douter'.
>
> *récit* and brief chorus, 'Jamais dans ces beaux lieux'
> reprise of *récit* and chorus, 'Voicy la charmante retraite'
> recitative (beginning of seduction episode)
>> LUCINDE: 'Enfin je voy l'Amant pour qui mon coeur soûpire,/Je
>> retrouve le bien que j'ay tant souhaité'. CHEV: 'Puis-je voir icy la Beauté
>> qui m'a soûmis à son Empire?' UB: 'Non, ce n'est qu'un charme trom-
>> peur/Dont il faut garder vostre coeur'. (etc.)

1761   (final version):
> *forlane*
> recitative
>> UB: 'Allons, qui vous retient encore:/Allons, c'est trop vous arrester'.
>> CHEV: 'Je vois la Beauté que j'adore:/C'est elle, je n'en puis douter./
>> Je cède à tant d'attraits qui viennent me séduire'. LUC: 'C'est mon amant
>> que je revois'. CHEV: 'O Ciel! Est-ce vous que je vois?' LUC: 'Au rapport
>> de mes yeux je n'ose ajouter foy'. CHEV: 'A mon transport mon coeur ne

peut suffire'. UB: 'Non, ce n'est qu'un charme trompeur/Dont il faut
garder vostre coeur'. (etc.)

As the outline shows, the editor substituted a passionate, if brief, encounter
between the lovers for the original beginning of the seduction episode (example
15); this substitution was apparently part of the 1761 version from its earliest
conception.

Example 15 Excerpt from Act IV, scene ii, 1761 version

The new dances for the 1761 version are longer than Lully's, and the airs for
Lucinde are elaborate pieces, filled with the expected clichés: melismas on words
like 'chantez' and 'regnez', florid woodwind and violin obbligato parts, 'warbling'
broken chord figures in the strings, and echo effects. Pastoral images abound.
What was Francoeur trying to accomplish here? Was this extended retreat into
the world of shepherds and nightingales somehow supposed to strengthen
Act IV, or was the weakest act in the opera simply a convenient place for the sort
of pastoral 'fête' that Opéra audiences had come to expect? Perhaps we should
take the review in the *Mercure* at face value: Act IV represented a 'void' in the
opera; Francoeur had to deal with it somehow, and he chose a method that was
sure to please the crowds and that made use of readily available resources (for
instance, Mademoiselle Lemiere, a soprano who specialized in the *ariette* style).

In view of Cahusac's exhortations, the final emendation of Act IV seems
ironic: the *divertissement* had become so long that it completely dominated the
act, so eventually – around 1764 – scene i was transposed up a whole tone, to
conform to the tonality of the greatly elongated *divertissement* (table 2). The
'terrible' bowed in submission to the 'agreeable'.

Table 2 *Key scheme of Act IV, 1686–1766[a]*

	scene i	scene ii	scene iii	scene iv
1686	Bb–F	C	C–a	a–C
1697	Bb–F	C	C–a	–
1745	Bb–F	C	C	–
1761	Bb–F	C	C	–
c. 1764	C–G	C	C	–

[a] Act III ends in D minor; the entr'acte is in F major.

The history of *Armide's* fourth act must be understood from two points of view: on the one hand, every portion of any opera by Lully that was to be revived, no matter how successful, was likely to be emended in certain ways to make it conform to eighteenth-century taste, and the penultimate act of *Armide* provides an excellent example of these routine procedures; on the other hand, this particular act was considered flawed, and addressing its flaws was a unique editorial problem, not a routine one. It should be clear by now that these two issues are interdependent: editors concentrated on Act IV because it was problematic, but in the 1740s and 1760s they allowed general changes in taste to determine their methods for dealing with its problems. We can do justice to their activities only by considering both issues simultaneously.

APPENDIX: A NOTE ON THE MUSICAL SOURCES

The most important extant source for the Paris versions of *Armide* is the collection of 206 manuscript parts used by the singers and instrumentalists of the Académie during productions of *Armide* from 1686 to 1766: Paris, Bibliothèque de l'Opéra, Mat.18.[27(1–206). This is not a unified part-set but a bewildering array of survivors from an undetermined number of part-sets, prepared over the course of eighty years. Since the preparation of each new production involved the revision of old parts as well as the copying of new ones, the integrity of the part-set for each production was violated at the time of the next. It is perhaps for this reason that a distressingly small amount of this material dates from the seventeenth century, while each successive eighteenth-century production seems better represented among the parts than the last. (Only two parts, both for violin, can be dated to Lully's production; thus, the best source for the 1686 version is the Ballard print cited in note 9.) I have dated the copying and alteration of individual parts by identifying handwriting and watermarks with those in materials that can be dated by other means, by comparing readings among the parts, and by comparing readings between the parts and the dated librettos.

An important source for the 1761 version is the copy of the 1710 engraved score (see note 9) owned by the Marquis de La Salle, along with his personal set of manuscript parts: Bibliothèque de l'Opéra, A.21.b² (the score) and Fonds La Salle 22 and 22bis (the parts). La Salle hired scribes from the Opéra to revise his personal materials in accordance with the 1761 version; though they omitted details in some sections of the opera, they did copy the new version of Act IV, scenes ii–iii, in its entirety. Unlike the Mat.18.[27 parts, which were revised many times in the course of the autumn 1761 rehearsals, the La Salle sources contain fair copies of the new version as it was actually performed. Internal evidence – discarded bits of a different opera found on some of the added paper – suggests that the La Salle sources were revised at the time of the 1761–2 performance run rather than later; thus, the La Salle materials help clarify the state of *Armide* in 1761–2 (as opposed to 1764–5).

One other source requires mention: a manuscript score entitled 'Armide Tragedie en Cinq Actes Mis en Musique par M. de Lully . . . Le Poème est de

M. Quinaut. L'Ouverture, et la plus grande partie des Airs des Divertissements Sont de M. Francoeur Surintendant de la Musique du Roy et Chevalier de St. Michel. Edition derniere. 1781': Paris, Bibliothèque nationale, Cons. Rés. F.564. The music was copied by François Francoeur himself; the cramped style of his handwriting, familiar from other autograph scores dating from his old age, confirms the 1781 date on the title-page. The text was copied by a professional scribe. The contents of the score agree in essence with the 1761–2 version, but many details are different; for instance, the part-writing of the inner voices in many orchestral pieces differs from that of 1761. This score is thus an interesting record of the editor's second thoughts during old age, but it is not an accurate source of the 1761 version of *Armide*. Of special interest, however, is Francoeur's citation of himself alone, with no mention of Rebel (who had died in 1775). During their many years of collaboration, they steadfastly refused to answer questions about their division of labor; in 1780, Benjamin de Laborde complained, 'Each of them used to answer, "That number is by us both"'.[40] Francoeur scrupulously attributed some works to both himself and Rebel after his friend's death – including works that he had revised further on his own – so I am inclined to take seriously his attribution of the *Armide* revision to himself alone.

Further information on these sources, as well as documentation for the dates of individual editorial emendations discussed in this article, may be found in my dissertation (cited in note 13).

[40] (Jean Benjamin de Laborde), *Essai sur la musique ancienne et moderne*, 4 vols. (Paris, Pierres, 1780), vol. III, p. 471.

La Mariée: the history of a French court dance*

REBECCA HARRIS-WARRICK

In 1700 Raoul Auger Feuillet published *Chorégraphie ou l'art de décrire la dance*, a ground-breaking work that set forth the first comprehensive system of dance notation. Feuillet notation made it possible for the beautifully intricate dances of the day to be preserved and communicated, and dancing masters from all over Europe quickly adopted the system. Of the approximately 330 known choreographies in Feuillet notation, most of which appeared between the years 1700 and 1725, at least 52 were set to music of Jean-Baptiste Lully.[1] Some of these were choreographed for revivals of Lully's works at the Académie royale de musique,[2] but many others were published as ballroom dances, even though their tunes were theatrical in origin. This article traces the history of one such dance, known as *la Mariée*, one of the earliest dances to be published in Feuillet notation and also one of the longest lived. Although it was a ballroom dance, investigation reveals *la Mariée*'s history to be intertwined with the *ballet de cour*, the Paris Opéra, and the carnival mascarade. *La Mariée*'s thematic origins lie in a common genre of seventeenth- and eighteenth-century entertainment, and its development as a dance illuminates important relationships between professional and amateur dancing at the French court. The story of *la Mariée* offers not just the history of a single well-loved dance; it serves as a model for the way in which many of the ballroom dances from the period of Louis XIV evolved.

For Feuillet, *Chorégraphie* marked the beginning of a series of projected publi-

* An earlier version of this paper was read at the annual meeting of the American Musicological Society, Philadelphia, Pennsylvania, October 1984. Funding for continued work on ballroom dancing at the French court was provided by a fellowship for the year 1985–6 from the National Endowment for the Humanities, for which I would like to express my very grateful thanks.

[1] Complete bibliographic information regarding all of the known dances preserved in Feuillet notation may be found in Meredith Ellis Little and Carol G. Marsh, *The French Court Dance: An Inventory of Notated Dances* (New York, Broude Brothers, forthcoming). For a discussion of some of the notated choreographies set to the music of Lully, see Wendy Hilton, 'Dances to music by Jean-Baptiste Lully', *Early Music*, xiv/1 (1986), pp. 51–63, and Rebecca Harris-Warrick, 'Contexts for Choreographies: Notated Dances Set to the Music of J. B. Lully', *Proceedings of the Colloque Lully, September 1987* (Heidelberg, forthcoming).

[2] See, for example, Feuillet's *Recueil de dances contenant un très grand nombre des meilleures entrées de ballet de Mr. Pécour* (Paris, 1704). Many of the choreographies in this collection have titles indicating that they were 'dancée à l'opéra de [Persée, Thésée, etc.]' and often giving the names of the dancers. The operas from which such choreographies were drawn were all in the repertoire of the Académie royale de musique in the few years preceding the publication of the collection.

cations.[3] To illustrate his system of 'dance writing', he attached to the book two collections of notated dances, one of theatrical pieces for a varying number of dancers that he himself had choreographed, the other of ballroom dances, each choreographed for one couple.[4] The ballroom dances had all been composed by Louis Pécour, an employee of the king and the principal choreographer for the Académie royale de musique. Feuillet chose them for inclusion because they were either the newest or the most popular of Pécour's dances.[5] *La Mariée*, or 'the bride', a technically demanding dance for a man and a woman, appeared as the second of these nine social dances. *Chorégraphie* and its accompanying dance collections, published in January of 1700, were an immediate commercial success. An article in the *Mercure galant* of May 1700 (pp. 197–200) claimed that sales of the book were so high that a new edition would have to be made soon, and Feuillet rushed into print again with a series of four individual choreographies, also by Pécour, published between May and November of the same year.[6] The tremendous success of Feuillet's *Chorégraphie* can be measured in the number of printings it went through and the number of translations and adaptations of it that were published, both in France and in the other countries of Europe.[7]

La Mariée must have been one of the best received dances of the first publication because the second and fourth of the four individually published dances were entitled *la Nouvelle mariée* and *la Seconde nouvelle mariée* respectively. The procession of brides did not stop there. In 1707 Feuillet published yet another *Nouvelle mariée*, this one of his own composition, and an English *Mariée* choreography dates from 1733.[8] Each of these five choreographies, like the other *danses figurées* in Feuillet notation, is through-choreographed to its own

[3] 'Je donneray dans peu un autre Recueil de ces plus belles Entrées de Ballet, pour homme & pour femme, tant pour une personne seule que pour plusieurs, sans compter toutes les nouvelles Dances de Bal qui se composeront à l'avenir, que je feray graver chacune en particulier, pour l'utilité publique, qu'on pourra envoyer dans une Lettre ainsi qu'on envoye un Air de Musique'. [Raoul Auger] Feuillet, *Chorégraphie ou l'art de décrire la dance* (Paris, 1700), Preface. The new collection was published in 1704. In 1702 Feuillet initiated a series of annual collections of ballroom dances that continued until 1725. See Ingrid Brainard, 'New Dances for the Ball: The *Annual Collections* of France and England in the 18th Century', *Early Music*, XIV/2 (1986), pp. 164–73.
[4] *Recueil de dances, composées par M. Feuillet, Maître de Dance* (Paris, 1700); and *Recueil de dances, composées par M. Pécour, Pensionnaire des menus Plaisirs du Roy, & Compositeur des Ballets de l'Académie Royale de Musique de Paris. Et mises sur le Papier par M. Feuillet, Maître de Dance* (Paris, 1700). In the preface Feuillet states that the first collection consists of 'Entrées de Ballet', and that the second is 'un Recueil des plus belles Dances de Bal, qui ont été com-

posées par Monsieur Pécour'.
[5] 'J'ay chosi les plus nouvelles & celles qui ont le plus de cours'. *Chorégraphie*, Preface.
[6] Feuillet did, in fact, publish a second issue of *Chorégraphie* in 1701. The publication dates of the four individual dances can be traced in the pages of the *Mercure*: the *Pavanne des Saisons* was published in May, *La Nouvelle mariée* in August, and *Le Passepied nouveau* and *La Seconde nouvelle mariée* in November. *Mercure galant*, May 1700, pp. 197–200; August 1700, pp. 212–13; and November 1700, pp. 201–3.
[7] See Elisabeth Huttig Rebman, 'Chorégraphie: An Annotated Bibliography of Eighteenth Century Printed Instruction Books' (unpubl. MA thesis, Stanford University, 1981).
[8] Feuillet's *Nouvelle mariée* appears in the *VIme Recueil de danses et de contredanses pour l'année 1708* (Paris, 1707), pp. 11–18. The English *Mariée* choreography was composed by L'Abbé as *The Prince of Orange: A New Dance for the Year 1733*, in honor of the marriage of Princess Anne on 14 March 1733. See Carol Marsh, 'French Court Dance in England, 1706–1740: A Study of the Sources' (unpubl. PhD diss., City University of New York, 1985), p. 179, n. 26.

tune. However, it was not simply the idea of a dance for a bride that was revived over the years. The first Pécour *Mariée* choreography enjoyed a popularity that lasted for decades: it was republished in 1725 by Pierre Rameau in a collection of Pécour's 'most beautiful dances', and again in 1765,[9] an astounding sixty-five years after its first publication, and almost forty years after its choreographer's death.[10] Even given the notorious conservatism of French taste this dance endured for a remarkable length of time, especially considering that every measure of both the steps and the music was fixed.

The numerous questions raised by this brief account – the significance of the title of the dance, the circumstances of the composition of either dance or music, possible performances, the source of the music, or even the identity of its composer – receive almost no elucidation from the notated choreography itself. As do most dances in Feuillet notation, *la Mariée* simply shows the melody of the piece of music at the top of the page, the corresponding section of the choreography, and the title of the dance, without any further indications (see plate 1, showing its first page).

The identification of the composer as Jean-Baptiste Lully was the necessary first step in tracing the history of the dance.[11] The first known use of this particular piece of music is in the *Ballet des plaisirs* of 1655 where it appears in the second part of the ballet as an 'Air pour le vieillard et sa famille'.[12] However, Lully reused the tune in a ballet he composed in 1663, *Les nopces de village*, or *The Village Wedding*, as an *entrée* for the bride and groom. The livret, published by Ballard that same year, called the ballet a *mascarade ridicule*.[13] Its thirteen *entrées* involved sixty-one performers in 76 different roles. Twenty-seven of the performers were courtiers, thirty-four of them professionals, and all were men. The 'plot', such as it is, can be summarized as follows: after a *récit* sung by Hymen (the god of marriage), dressed as a villager, the bride and groom make their entrance to the same music as the *Mariée* choreography (see example 1). A series of guests,

[9] Pierre Rameau, *Abrégé de la nouvelle méthode...
Seconde partie contenant douze des plus belles danses de Monsieur Pécour* (Paris, 1725), pp. 10–17; and Magny, *Principes de chorégraphie* (Paris, 1765), pp. 174–82.

[10] Pécour died in 1729.

[11] For the known attributions of the music in the first collection of Pécour's dances, see Anne L. Witherell, *Louis Pécour's 1700 Recueil de danses* (Ann Arbor, UMI Research Press, 1983), p. 265. A discussion of *la Mariée*, primarily from the point of view of the choreography, may be found in chapter 2, pp. 35–60. See also Hilton, 'Dances by Lully', p. 53. My interest in the history of *la Mariée* grew out of the opportunity I had to work with both Anne Witherell and Wendy Hilton in their reconstructions of this beautiful dance, and I would like to express my gratitude to both.

[12] *Ballet des plaisirs*, dansé par sa Majesté le 4. jour de Febvrier 1655 [livret] (Paris, Robert Ballard, 1655); the music to those portions of the

ballet presumed to have been composed by Lully may be found in the *Oeuvres complètes de J.-B. Lully*, H. Prunières (ed.), Ballets, vol. I (Paris, 1931). The tune also appears in some early copies of the *Ballet du temps* (1654), but neither Prunières nor Herbert Schneider consider it as having been composed for that work.

[13] *Les nopces de village*, mascarade ridicule dansé par sa Majesté à son chasteau de Vincennes [livret] (Paris, Robert Ballard, 1663); for a list of the musical sources of the ballet, see Herbert Schneider, *Chronologisch-Thematisches Verzeichnis Sämtlicher Werke von Jean-Baptiste Lully* (*LWV*) (Tutzing, Hans Schneider, 1981), LWV 19, pp. 89–92. See also Charles I. Silin, *Benserade and his Ballets de Cour* (Baltimore, The Johns Hopkins Press, 1940), pp. 323–6. A critical edition of the ballet by Rebecca Harris-Warrick is forthcoming as part of *Jean-Baptiste Lully: The Collected Works* (New York, Broude Brothers).

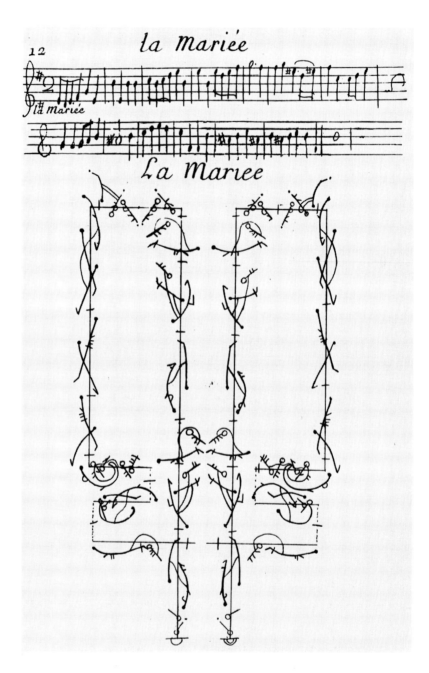

Plate 1. The first figure of Pécour's choreography *la Mariée* as notated by Feuillet
(Paris, 1700). The starting position of the male dancer is on the bottom left,
of the female dancer, immediately to his right. The solid line indicates the path the
dancers trace on the floor, and the short lines at right angles to it show the measures
of the music in relation to the dance steps

Example 1

From J.-B. Lully, *Les nopces de village* (F-Pn: Vm⁶ 6). *Entrée* for the bride and groom

Example 1 (*cont.*)

each dancing their own *entrées*, follows: six old men bearing gifts of kitchen utensils; the caterers; four valets who intend to kidnap the bride; the lord of the
village, who brings along three noble couples, intending to entertain them at the
expense of the bride and groom; the bailiff and other functionaries of the village;
and four men arriving at the wedding directly from their vineyards (and
presumably drunk). The village schoolmaster, played by none other than Lully
himself, then arrives. He sings a comic *récit* in Italian and dances a *bourée* with
four of his pupils. More guests appear: three village girls, one of whom was
danced by the king; six rich bourgeois; four officers who want to flirt with the
pretty girls; the village midwife, whose services, it is hoped, will soon be needed
by the bride and who therefore was one of the first people invited; and a quack
doctor, also played by Lully, who hopes to make some money from the crowd.
The last to arrive, a troupe of gypsies, dance and circulate among the guests tell-
ing fortunes. When a policeman catches some of them snatching purses, a fight
ensues between the gypsies and the upholders of the law. During the confusion
the four valets kidnap the bride. The ballet ends in a general mêlée.

Obviously, the ballet merited its attribution 'burlesque'. However, this particular bride could not have been the *Mariée* of the 1700 choreography by Pécour, despite the connection made by the music, because the ballet dates from 1663 when Pécour was still a child. The choreographer of the ballet was probably Pierre Beauchamp, who played three roles in the ballet, and who had begun his career as a choreographer two years earlier.[14] Nevertheless, the association established in this ballet between Lully's tune and a village wedding is central to the subsequent history of the dance.

The theme of the village wedding appears in many ballets, mascarades, plays, operas, instrumental compositions, paintings, and engravings from the period.[15] Lully's works alone contain no fewer than seven village weddings, ranging in length from a single scene to the entire work: *Ballet des plaisirs* (1655); *Ballet de l'amour malade* (1657); *Les nopces de village* (1663); *Ballet de Flore* (1669); *Le carnaval mascarade* (1675); a mascarade composed for the Carnival season of 1683; and a *divertissement* in the fourth act of the opera *Roland* (1685).[16] Lully's

[14] See Régine Kunzle, 'Pierre Beauchamp, The Illustrious Unknown Choreographer (Part II)', *Dance Scope*, IX/1 (1975), p. 36. Beauchamp was named the *compositeur des ballets du roi* at an unknown date and was responsible for the choreography of many of the *ballets de cour*. He later became the choreographer at the Académie royale de musique. He resigned this post following the death of Lully in 1687 and was succeeded by Louis Pécour.

[15] Some examples of village weddings, other than those by Lully, depicted in France from the mid-seventeenth to the early eighteenth century are: the Carnival mascarades *La noce de village*, mascarade mise en musique par Philidor l'aîné . . . représ. . . . à Marly [livret] (Paris, Ballard, 1700), and *Le lendemain de la noce de village*, mascarade mise en musique par le fils de Mr Philidor l'aîné . . . représ. à Marly [livret] (Paris, Ballard, 1700); two ballets by Michel Richard Delalande, *La noce de village* (1700) and *Ballet de l'inconnu*, 5ᵉ entre, 'Nopce de village' (1719) (see Barbara Coeyman, 'The Secular Works of Michel-Richard Delalande in the Musical-Cultural Context of the French Court, 1680–1726' (unpubl. PhD diss., City University of New York, 1986)), pp. 119–20; the play *La nopce de village*, comédie en un acte, en vers, de M. Brécourt, représenté sur le théâtre de l'Hôtel de Bourgogne (1666), as described in François and Claude Parfaict, *Histoire du théâtre françois depuis son origine jusqu'à présent* (Paris, 1745–9; repr. 1968), pp. 119–20; the opera-ballet *Les Fêtes de Thalie* (1714) by Mouret (in Act II, 'la Femme'); a suite for the musette entitled *La noce champêtre* by Jean Hotteterre (Paris, 1722) with programatic titles for each movement; a piece entitled *la Mariée* in the first suite of the fifth book of Marin Marais's *Pièces de viole* (Paris, 1725); a series of three engrav-

ings by Abraham Bosse, *le Mariage à la campagne*, dating from *c.* 1633 (in Nicole Villa (ed.), *Le XVIIᵉ siècle vu par Abraham Bosse, graveur du Roy* (Paris, 1967), plates 95–7). The theme of a village wedding for entertainments was by no means confined to France; undoubtedly the best known of eighteenth-century staged village weddings is that in Mozart's *Don Giovanni* (1787).

[16] (1) *Ballet des plaisirs* (see note 12 above). The first of the two parts of this ballet, 'Délices de la Campagne', consists of a village wedding; (2) *Ballet de l'amour malade*, in Lully, *Oeuvres complètes*, Ballets, vol. I, pp. 98–110, the tenth and final *entrée*; (3) *Les nopces de village* (see note 13 above); (4) *Ballet de Flore*, dansé par sa Majesté le mois de février 1669 [livret] (Paris, Robert Ballard, 1669), *entrées* VIII and IX; (5) *Le carnaval mascarade* (1675), [score] (Paris, Ballard, 1720), *entrée* VII, 'les nouveaux mariés'. This *entrée* is largely lifted from the village wedding scene in the *Ballet de Flore*. Pécour's choreographies *la Nouvelle mariée* and *la Seconde nouvelle mariée* are both set to music from *Le carnaval mascarade*; (6) the accounts of the *Noce de village* mascarade put on at court during the 1683 Carnival season do not name the composer of the music. However, it seems quite likely that four of the seven dances in the *Plusieurs pièces de symphonie* by Lully, published by Ballard in 1685 together with *L'idylle sur la paix* and *La grotte de Versailles*, were composed for this mascarade. The dances – pavane, gigue, and two menuets – all bear the notation 'Pour Mme la Dauphine (Nopces de Village)'. The 1683 mascarade was arranged by the Dauphin, who along with the Dauphine, was among the performers. See the *Mercure galant*, March 1683, pp. 335–9; (7) *Roland* (1685), Act IV, scene iii.

village weddings, as well as others from the period, do not all share the burlesque characteristics of the 1663 ballet, but exhibit a range of expressive possibilities. At one extreme is the village wedding of low comedy with the bride possibly pregnant, the groom henpecked or drunk, and the guests drawn from ranks of the stock comic characters: the lascivious village lord, the drunk peasant, the self-important bailiff, the rejected suitor, etc. The rustic instruments played for the celebration provide a vehicle for coarse jokes regarding different types of 'fluting'. The other extreme of the village wedding scene, however, conjures up a countryside where contented peasants spend their simple, happy days in singing and dancing, and where true love, free from the intrigues and jealousies of the more sophisticated members of society, reigns triumphant. Many village wedding entertainments drew elements from both the comic and the sentimental traditions and combined them in proportions appropriate to the occasion. For example, *the vers pour le personnage* written for the Marquis de Villeroy who played the groom in the village wedding in Lully's *Ballet de l'amour malade* give some idea of the conception of the role:

So here I am married. But given my size and my age, nothing will be more disparaged than my poor household. And how can I behave in order to avoid being beaten and scolded? Marriage is a burden, and if it weighs everyone down, won't it crush me?[17]

On the other hand, a *Noce de village* mascarade composed for the 1700 carnival season at court by Philidor *l'aîné* presented the bride and groom as young, happy, and in love, but set up some of the other characters as subjects for laughter, such as the lord and lady of the village and a drunk German peasant.[18] The durability of such images of rural life clearly says more about the aristocratic and wealthy bourgeois audiences who patronized such entertainments than about French peasant life in the seventeenth century.

The theatrical convention of the village wedding thus provides the general context for the *Mariée* choreography of Pécour but does not explain the specific circumstances surrounding its creation. Did Pécour simply borrow the tune with its title from Lully's ballet and use it as the basis for an abstract couple dance intended for the ballroom, or does the title mean that the dance was choreographed for a bride and groom, either real or theatrical? If the latter is the case, did the dance retain the burlesque associations imparted to the music by the Lully ballet? The answers to these questions are not only of historical interest but have practical implications for any dancers wishing to perform this choreography. Feuillet notation (see plate 1) reveals only the steps of the dance, the measure-by-measure correspondance between dance and music, and the spatial relationships of the dancers. Questions of interpretation are up to the performers. In only a few choreographies – notably some chaconnes for a Harlequin, which employ false positions of the feet – do the steps themselves reveal a

---

[17] 'Pour le Marquis de Villeroy, representant *le Marié*: Me voilà donc Marié;/Mais vu ma taille et mon age,/Rien ne sera décrié/ Comme mon pauvre ménage;/Et comment me comporter,/Pour ne pas tant meriter/ Qu'on me fouette ou qu'on me gronde?/C'est un fardeau qu'épouser,/Et s'il pese à tout le monde,/Ne doit-il pas m'écraser?' *Les oeuvres de Monsieur de Benserade* (Paris, 1697), vol. II.

[18] Philidor, *Noce.* (See note 16.)

comic intent on the part of the choreographer. The choreography of *la Mariée* as notated by Feuillet lends itself to a variety of interpretations; knowledge of the dance's historical context can thus contribute to an understanding of the affective content of the dance and of Pécour's artistic intentions.

Although the choreography for *la Mariée* was not published until early in 1700,[19] evidence suggests that this dance falls into the category of those selected by Feuillet for their popularity, not for their newness,[20] and that the dance was already ten years old. A number of sources, both choreographic and musical, identify *la Mariée* as being from *Roland*.[21] As mentioned above, Lully's *Roland*, first performed in 1685, does include a village wedding scene as the *divertissement* in the fourth act, but the *Mariée* tune does not appear in the score published by Ballard that same year, nor in any of the later published scores (Baussen, 1709; Mortier (Amsterdam), 1711; Le Cène (Amsterdam), n.d.; Ballard, 1716, 1733, and 1735). However, manuscript additions to several scores of *Roland*, as well as to an undated set of instrumental parts found in the Bibliothèque de l'Opéra, reveal that both this dance and one other borrowed from *Les plaisirs de l'île enchantée* (LWV 22/4) were indeed interpolated into the village wedding scene of the fourth act at some time after the first production of the opera.[22] *Roland* was revived a number of times at the Opéra,[23] but the addition of the two dances can be dated specifically to the revival of 1690, three years after Lully's death, based on their inclusion among excerpts from *Roland* in manuscript Vm⁶ 5 in the Bibliothèque Nationale. This collection, consisting primarily of treble parts of excerpts from French ballets and operas from the second half of the seventeenth century, was compiled in the early 1690s. A heading for the two pieces that reads 'Roland/Nopce de village 1690' explicitly dates their inclusion into the fourth act *divertissement*.[24] Further confirmation comes from the first edition of Ballard's *Parodies bachiques* of 1695, which includes the two pieces with the annotation that they are from *Roland*.[25] Since the next revival of the opera was not until 1705, the enlargement of the *divertissement* has to have taken place in 1690.

[19] The title-page of *Chorégraphie* gives the publication date as 1700, but the book was registered with the *Communauté des imprimeurs & libraires* on 13 December 1699 and the end of the privilege bears the note that it was 'Achevé d'imprimer pour la premiere fois le 31. Decembre 1699'.

[20] See note 5 above.

[21] See, for example, 'La mariée de Roland' in Rameau, *Abrégé*, pp. 10–17; and 'le Mariée et la Mariée de Roland' in *Suite des dances pour les violons et hautbois. Qui se jouent ordinairement à tous les bals chez le Roy. Recueillies . . . par M. Philidor l'ainé, l'An 1712* (F-Pn Vm⁷ 3555), p. 20.

[22] The two added pieces are written out in full in F-Po Fonds La Salle 4 (a set of parts) and A17a¹ and A17a² (both Ballard printed scores from 1685). Other printed scores have manuscript annotations indicating that *la Mariée* and the rondeau were to be included

in the *divertissement* (e.g. F-Pn Rés Vm² 34), and a manuscript copy of the *dessus* parts in *Roland* also incorporates both pieces into this scene (F-Pn Vm² 84). I would like to thank Dr Herbert Schneider for his assistance in my investigations into the enlargement of the *divertissement*.

[23] Revivals of *Roland* occurred in 1686, 1690, 1705, 1708, 1709, 1716–17, 1718, 1727, 1728, 1729, 1743, 1744, and 1755. See Ariane Ducrot, 'Les représentations de l'Académie Royale de Musique à Paris au temps de Louis XIV (1671–1715)' *Recherches*, x (1970), pp. 19–55; and Herbert Schneider, *Die Rezeption der Opern Lullys im Frankreich des Ancien Régime* (Tutzing, Hans Schneider, 1982), pp. 351–4.

[24] F-Pn ms Vm⁶ 5, fol. 232.

[25] *Parodies bachiques, sur les airs et symphonies des opera* (Paris, Ballard, 1695), p. 161.

In testimonial both to the reemergence of *la Mariée* at this time and to its popularity, *la Mariée* can be found in a large number of sources dating from the last decade of the seventeenth century. For example, it appears with various texts in no fewer than five collections of parodies between 1691 and 1700, in several arrangements for harpsichord dating from the same period, and in anthologies of music performed at the French court and elsewhere in Europe.[26]

The context of the fourth-act *divertissement* within *Roland* makes it clear that this village wedding belongs to the happy and bucolic tradition rather than to the ribald and burlesque. At the beginning of the act, Roland has just discovered that Angélique, the woman he loves with what he had mistakenly thought was a shared passion, actually loves another man. He hears the sound of rustic instruments approaching, and waits for them, thinking that Angélique might be watching the shepherds' dance. He hopes desperately that she will tell him that he is the true object of her affection. A troupe of shepherds and shepherdesses enter, singing and dancing in joyful preparation for the wedding of two of their company on the morrow. Their expressions of the joy imparted by love serve to highlight the misery that the same emotion has brought to Roland, a misery that at the end of the act turns to madness.

The *divertissement* as originally composed by Lully contained only three dances: a minuet (LWV 65/65); another dance in triple meter (called '2e menuet' in some sources) that had already been heard earlier in the act (LWV 65/63); and an *entrée de pastres, de pastourelles, de bergers, et de bergères* (LWV 65/67). The interpolation of *la Mariée* (LWV 2/4) following the *entrée de pastres* provided an opportunity for the bride and groom to dance. It is significant that the piece chosen for their dance was one that had already served the same purpose in an earlier work, although one with a very different character. In the 1663 ballet of the *Noces de village*, the dance for the bride and groom was undoubtedly intended to be humorous, but both the context of the *divertissement* and Lully's avoidance of all comic elements in his operas after *Thésée* (1675) make it very unlikely that any such character was attached to the dance tune when it was reused by his successors in *Roland*.

Unfortunately, none of the contemporary sources reveals who was responsible for the enlargement of the *divertissement* in 1690. However, the choreographer of the two new dances, and probably for all of the dances in the revival, was almost certainly Louis Pécour, who had become the *compositeur des ballets* at the Opéra when Pierre Beauchamp resigned following the death of Lully in 1687. The exact date when Pécour assumed his new responsibilities is not yet known, but it was by 1689 at the latest, as the *Recueil général des Opéra* reported in 1703 that all

---

[26] For the parodies, see Schneider, *Verzeichnis* (LWV), p. 24. For arrangements of *la Mariée* for harpsichord see Bruce Gustafson, *French Harpsichord Music of the 17th Century: A Thematic Catalog of the Sources with Commentary* (Ann Arbor, UMI Research Press, 1979), p. 478. Other music collections in which the *Mariée* tune appears, beginning in the 1690s and continuing well into the eighteenth century, are extremely numerous and varied. A far from exhaustive search has uncovered the piece in a very large number of French sources and in collections originating in England, Germany, the Netherlands, and Sweden.

of the works, both new productions and revivals, performed at the Opéra since Collasse's *Thétis et Pelée* (1689) had been choreographed by Pécour alone.[27] It seems quite possible that Pécour, as the person responsible for the dances at the Opéra, would have participated in the decision to enlarge the danced portion of this particular *divertissement*.[28]

Two years after its interpolation into *Roland*, the *Mariée* tune was parodied in a work by Collasse, the *Ballet de Villeneuve Saint-Georges*, performed at the Opéra in 1692.[29] The second piece in the second *entrée* of this ballet, also entitled *la Mariée*, is identical in phrase structure and note values to the Lully dance of the same name (see example 2). Apparently Collasse simply borrowed the very idiosyncratic profile of the Lully original and wrote another melody to fit it. The resulting piece appears in Vm⁶ 5 on f. 230 among excerpts from Lully's *Roland* with the title of the 'Contre mariée' and a note indicating its source as the *Ballet de Villeneuve Saint-Georges*. The title of the dance in Vm⁶ 5 suggests that it may have been intended as a spoof on the dance from *Roland*, but another possibility is that Collasse wrote the piece deliberately to allow Pécour to reuse a favorite choreography in a new context. It is a characteristic of the French dances of this period that each one was choreographed to a specific piece of music and therefore could be danced only to that tune. As the notation indicates (see plate 1), each measure of the music corresponds to a specific measure of the dance, and repetition of a strain of music almost never involves exact repetition of the corresponding choreographic phrase. It would have been possible to reuse a choreography if another tune with the identical phrase structure were to be substituted for the original. However, substitution would not necessarily have been easy, as much of the dance music of the seventeenth century, that of Lully in particular, has irregular phrase lengths. *La Mariée*, with measure groupings of 5+4+5 and 5+2+5 in its two sections is a case in point; it would be difficult to find another tune with the same construction. The parody of Lully's *Mariée* tune may well represent a collaborative effort by Collasse and Pécour to make further use of what appears to have been a highly successful choreography.

In 1700 Feuillet published a choreography by Pécour entitled *la Mariée* set to the music that had been added to *Roland*, but included it in a collection of dances for the ballroom, not for the stage. Could the published social dance of 1700 represent the same choreography as the one performed on the stage of the

[27] *Recueil général des opéra representez par l'Académie Royale de Musique, depuis son éstablissement*, (Paris, Christophe Ballard, 1703), vol. I, Preface, no page number. See also Pierre Rameau, *Le maître à danser* (Paris, 1725), Preface, pp. xiii–xiv.

[28] *La Mariée* is not the only example of a piece taken from a Lully ballet and added to one of his operas after the composer's death and for which a choreography by Pécour exists. A piece labled 'Contredanse' was added to the fourth act *divertissement* of *Armide*, as seen in a part copied for the revival of 1697 (see Lois Rosow, 'Lully's "Armide" at the Paris

Opera: A Performance History: 1686–1766' (unpubl. PhD diss., Brandeis University, 1981), pp. 250–1 and 256–60). The piece, which first appeared as a rondeau (LWV 12/3) in *Xerxés* (1660), was published by Feuillet as a *danse à deux* entitled *la Contredanse* in the same collection of Pécour choreographies as *la Mariée*. It is quite possible that the *Contredanse* choreography owes its existence to the 1697 revival of *Armide*, even though it, too, was published as a ball dance.

[29] Livret in *Recueil général des opéra*, vol. IV. Scores: F-Pn Vm² 117 and Vm² 116.

Example 2

a. *La Mariée* by Lully as the tune appears among excerpts from *Roland* in
F-Pn Vm⁶ 5, fol. 230

b. *La Contre Mariée* by Collasse as the tune appears among excerpts from
Roland in F-Pn Vm⁶ 5, fol. 230

Opéra, in 1690? Or did Pécour compose two choreographies to the same music, one for his professional dancers, the other for use in the ballroom? Unless a dance notation dating from the 1690 revival is found these questions cannot be answered with certainty, but it seems likely that the two dances were indeed one and the same, despite the difference in their settings. There are several pieces of evidence that point to this conclusion. First, not only musical but choreographic sources call this dance 'la Mariée de Roland'.[30] Second, there is the

---

[30] See note 21 above.

choreography itself in comparison with the other dances from the same collection by Pécour. Whereas none of the nine dances could be considered easy, *la Mariée* and one other dance, *la Conti*, stand out from the rest in the technical demands they put on the dancers. Despite their publication in a collection of ballroom dances, they have much more of a theatrical character than do the others.[31] Third, and most important, is the close interrelationship between ballroom and theatrical dancing during this period. The two styles had in common technique, dance types, choreographers, and even to some extent repertory and dancers.[32] Although by 1700, and even well before, there were clear distinctions between the realms of the professional and the court dancers, the two groups often danced together and many social dances began life on the stage. In order to understand how *la Mariée* could have made the transition from stage to ballroom, it is necessary to examine the relationship between these two types of dancing at the French court.

In the *ballets de cour* done at Louis XIV's court in the 1650s and 1660s, courtiers and professionals danced together. Often an *entrée* performed entirely by nobles preceded another danced entirely by professionals, but professionals and courtiers also danced side by side in the same *entrées*.[33] Historians of dance frequently cite the year 1669, the date of the establishment of the Opéra as the time when court and professional dancing separated from each other, after which the professionals were free to develop their art without the confines imposed on them by the amateurs. While the establishment of a professional dance troupe for public performances marked a turning point in the history of dance, it by no means put an end to the close associations between professional and court dancers. First, the charter of the Académie, both Perrin's and the one renegotiated by Lully in 1672, stipulated that nobles would be allowed to perform at the Opéra without jeopardizing their nobility.[34] Occasionally nobles did take advantage of that provision, and appeared on stage with the professional dancers not only in performances by the Académie given at the court, but also in Paris.[35] Second, the *ballet de cour* did not die an instant death when the Opéra was founded, but lived on in two different forms. Genuine court ballets con-

[31] See Anne Witherell's analyses of these dances in *Pécour's Recueil*, chapters 2 and 9; also Hilton, 'Dances by Lully', p. 53.

[32] For information regarding the interrelationships between ballroom and theatrical dancing in seventeenth-century France, see Wendy Hilton, *Dance of Court and Theater: The French Noble Style, 1690–1725* (Princeton, Princeton Book Company, 1981); and Rebecca Harris-Warrick, 'Ballroom Dancing at the Court of Louis XIV', *Early Music*, XIV/1 (1986), pp. 40–9.

[33] See the information regarding casting for all the ballets for which Benserade wrote the livrets in Silin, *Benserade*.

[34] See the *priviléges* of 1669 and 1672, cited in Marcelle Benoit, *Musiques de cour: chapelle,* *chambre, écurie, 1661–1733* (Paris, A. & J. Picard, 1971), pp. 22–5 and 37–8.

[35] In the issue of July 1682, pp. 306–8, the *Mercure galant* reported, 'Le Dimanche dix-neuf de ce mois, on vit sur le Théâtre Royal de l'Opéra, une chose qui surprit agréablement toute l'Assemblée. Le jeune Prince de Dietrichstein, Fils ainé du Prince de ce nom, Grand Maistre de Sa Majesté l'Impératrice regnante, y dansa seul une Entrée de Balet, avec une grace merveilleuse. Il parut sur ce Théâtre magnifiquement masqué selon la coutume, et remplit la place d'un des principaux Maistres qu'employe Mr de Lully. . . . Si l'on a veu quelques Etrangers faire en d'autres temps la même entreprise, il est du moins le premier de la Cour de l'Empereur . . .'

tinued to be produced on an occasional basis well into the eighteenth century,[36] but more important were the smaller forms of balletic entertainment performed at court by professionals and nobles together.

One of these smaller forms was the mascarade, a miniature ballet built around a simple subject, combining acting, singing, and dancing, and generally performed at masked balls held during Carnival season. On such occasions, the usual series of social dances performed one couple at a time would be interrupted by the arrival of a group of costumed performers who would put on a mascarade. Following it the ball would resume the series of social dances, perhaps to be interrupted again later.[37] These mascarades, which ranged from the fairly simple to the very elaborate, were often specially composed, choreographed, and staged for specific balls by the same artists who were working at the Opéra. The composer Lully, dancers Beauchamp and Pécour, and the designer Bérain were all involved at various times in the creation of such mascarades. Either a group of courtiers, or professionals brought in from the Opéra, or courtiers and professionals together, performed the mascarades. An example of the latter type occurred at Versailles during a masked ball in 1683. Lully and his musicians were dressed in Egyptian costumes as was the Princesse de Conti, the king's illegitimate daughter and one of the best dancers at the court. In her role as Queen of Egypt, she danced a chaconne with the professionals Pécour and Létang.[38] Another such mascarade was performed by members of the royal family and by some of the highest ranking nobles from the court during a mardi gras ball held that same year. Its subject was a village wedding. The *Mercure* reported that

This mascarade was executed with all the exactitude and beauty possible. Everyone was dressed in accordance with the character of the person he was representing. Madame la Dauphine [who played the sister of the bride] wore a peasant bodice made of brocade the color of flame, gold, and silver, with the waist marked with black velvet embroidered with diamonds. The lacing of the bodice was of diamonds, and the rest of the dress was made of satin and velvet with gold and silver ornaments. Madame la Princesse de Conti [who played the role of the bride] wore a dress made of cloth with stripes of silver thread and pink flowers and her bodice was laced with diamonds.[39]

The remaining characters wore costumes equally appropriate to their roles. One wonders if these elegant 'peasants' were aware of the ironies of performing a mascarade in celebration of the simple life within one year after the court had officially moved into the chateau of Versailles.

[36] See Barbara Coeyman, 'Lully's Influence on the Court Ballet After 1672', *Proceedings of the Colloque Lully, September 1987* (Heidelberg, forthcoming).

[37] Regarding the role of prepared mascarades in masked balls, see Harris-Warrick, 'Ballroom Dancing'.

[38] *Mercure galant*, March 1683, pp. 322–5. The music for this chaconne could well be the 'Chaconne pour Madame la Princesse de Conty' (LWV 70/5) published among the *Plusieurs pièces de symphonie* attached to the *Idylle sur la paix, avec l'egloque de Versailles*

(Paris, Ballard, 1685).

[39] *Mercure galant*, March 1683, pp. 335–9. The costumes for this mascarade, designed by Jean Bérain, were so impressive that the *Mercure* published an engraving of the costumed cast in its April issue. For a reproduction of this engraving and a discussion of the costume designs, see Jérôme de La Gorce, *Bérain: Dessinateur du Roi Soleil* (Paris, Editions Herscher, 1986), pp. 108–11. Regarding the music for this mascarade, which was probably composed by Lully, see note 16 above.

Besides these carnival mascarades, the production of plays at the court provided other opportunities for courtiers to engage in balletic dancing. In 1684, for example, during the annual fall sojourn of the court at Fontainebleau, the king's actors performed several plays that included dances by courtiers, either as a prologue or between the acts. On one occasion, the Princesse de Conti with two other ladies and one gentleman danced the chaconne from *Amadis*, the latest opera by Lully, as a prologue to Racine's tragedy, *Mithridate*. A few days later, the Italian comedians put together a little comedy that allowed for the insertion of several *entrées* by varying numbers of dancers, performed primarily by nobles, but with the assistance of Pécour and Favier from the Opéra. Other occasions offered dances in the *entr'actes* of plays.[40] The *comédies-ballets* of Molière were also revived at court, with the dances performed by courtiers and professionals.[41]

These different kinds of balletic performances – the occasional *ballet de cour*, other small ballets, the Carnival mascarades, and the balletic *entrées* added to plays – continued at court throughout most of Louis XIV's reign.[42] In many of them, dancers who earned their living on the stage of the Opéra could be seen dancing side by side with nobles. Even those ballets that were danced only by courtiers were choreographed by a professional such as Pécour, and the mascarades danced entirely by professionals were produced in the context of a social event, that is, of a ball. The dancers from the Opéra were not mere figures whom the courtiers watched from the other side of the footlights; they were the people who taught them, choreographed dances for them, and danced beside them. Because the ballroom provided the setting for many of the prepared mascarades, the distinction between the theatrical and social dances is difficult to define. An *entrée* performed at one ball as part of a mascarade may have been done at another as an independent dance. There are recorded instances of courtiers dancing theatrical pieces, such as chaconnes or other *entrées de ballet*, in the course of a ball.[43] This transferal of a dance from stage to ballroom may also be seen in the

[40] *Mercure galant*, November 1684, pp. 228–41, and the *Journal du Marquis de Dangeau* (Paris, 1854), vol. I, pp. 62–3, 67, and 69–70.

[41] See, for example, the following entries from the diary of the Marquis de Dangeau: 'Le roi et Monseigneur, avec beaucoup de dames, allérent dîner à Marly; . . . et l'on eut la comédie du *Sicilien*, de Molière, avec des entrées de ballet, où madame de Bourbon, madame la princesse de Conty, et la duchesse de Roquelaure dansèrent avec les bons danseurs et les bonnes danseuses de l'Opéra . . .' (21 August 1685, vol. I, p. 210); 'Monseigneur y étoit arrivé avant [le roi] avec les Princesses; et, en arrivant, il fit répéter des entrées de ballet qu'on dansera au premier voyage, et qui seront les intermédes du *Bourgeois gentilhomme*, que le roi y fera jouer. Mesdames les Princesses et madame de Seignelay apprirent leur entrée avec le comte de Brionne, Pécourt et Favier.' (19 November 1687, vol. II, p. 67).

[42] The last brilliant Carnival season at Louis's court was in 1708; after then heavy war expenses, a year of extreme cold and famine in France, and the deaths of all those in the direct legitimate line of succession save the infant Louis XV put an end to most court festivities.

[43] See, for example, the following entries from the diary of the Marquis de Dangeau: 'Au sortir du souper, Mlle de Nantes vint avec une troupe de masques chez Mme la Dauphine; elle dansa quelques entrées de ballet et alla ensuite dans le cabinet de Monseigneur.' (26 January 1685, vol. I, p. 112); 'Après les contredanses, Mme la Dauphine fit danser des entrées de chaconne au comte de Brionne et au chevalier de Sully.' (19 January 1685, vol. I, p. 110); 'Mme la duchesse de Bourgogne [at a masked ball] commença par danser une entrée d'Espagnols qui fut fort jolie.' (4 February 1700, vol. VII, p. 243).

published choreographies. In his preface to *la Seconde nouvelle mariée*, published in November of 1700, Feuillet explained that although Pécour had choreographed the dance for the theater, so many people had already started dancing it, and so many dancing masters wanted to have a copy of it, that he had decided to notate and publish it.[44] These accounts clearly show that the reuse of a theatrical dance in the ballroom provided one of the principal mechanisms in the creation of social dances.

Pécour could have choreographed two different dances for a couple to the same Lully tune, one for use in *Roland* by his professional dancers, the other for amateurs in balls, but probably *la Mariée*, with its theatrical character, followed the well-worn route from the stage to the ballroom. The common ground between professional and social dancing occupied by the Carnival mascarade at court offers a logical way for the transferal to have occurred. Perhaps after choreographing it for the 1690 revival of *Roland* Pécour taught the dance to some of his noble pupils for use in a mascarade based on a village wedding. But whatever the path it took, *la Mariée* had become a ballroom dance by 1698 at the latest. In that year John Walsh published a collection of violin airs drawn from the repertory of French dances then current on the London stage and at the English court, and included *la Mariée* among the ballroom dance tunes. The title of the collection suggests that *la Mariée* was among the dances that had been performed at a ball in honor of the birthday of the king, William III (William of Orange).[45]

La Mariée may have been danced at the French court just after its publication, during the Carnival season of 1700. That particular year witnessed one of the most brilliant sets of balls of Louis XIV's reign. Most of the masked balls given at the court included at least one prepared mascarade built around subjects such as an entertainment for the king of China, Amazons, a Venetian Carnival, a great lord in his menagerie, and a game of cards, to name only a few.[46] A village wedding supplied the theme for no fewer than four such entertainments during that one season. The composers of three of them are known.[47] The fourth, a

---

[44] 'Mon dessein n'étoit point de faire graver cette dance pour deux raisons: la première par ce que j'ay donné cy devant une nouvelle Mariée et que celle cy porte le même nom, et la seconde raison est qu'elle n'avoit été faite précisément que pour le Théâtre, mais tant de personnes de qualité se sont adonnée à la dancer et tant de Maître de dances me l'ont demandée que j'ay cru ne pouvoir me dispenser de la donner au Public.' Feuillet, preface to *la Seconde nouvelle mariée* (Paris, 1700).

[45] *Theater Musick, Being a Collection of the newest Ayers for the Violin, with the French Dances performed at both Theaters, as also the new Dances at ye late Ball at Kensington on ye King's Birthday* (London, 1698). The title of the dance, which appears on page 19, is: 'La: maro. a new Dance'. See Marsh, 'Dance in England', p. 236.

[46] Accounts of the balls of this Carnival season can be found in the *Mercure galant*, February 1700, pp. 151–233 and 276–84; *Dangeau*, vol. VII, pp. 235–63; the *Mémoires du Duc de Saint-Simon* (Paris, 1879–1928), vol. pp. 52–62; and the *Mémoires du Marquis de Sourches* (Paris, 1882–93), vol. VI, pp. 218–35. Between 7 January and 23 February (mardi gras) 1700 there were twenty-five balls at Versailles and Marly alone.

[47] The *Noce de village* by Philidor *l'aîné* and the *Lendemain de la noce* by his son (see note 15 above) were performed on two successive days, February 4 and 5, 1700, by professional dancers from the Opéra. A *Noce de village* composed by Delalande, with a text by Rousseau was performed by members of the court on 13 and 21 February.

relatively simple little mascarade performed by high-ranking nobles and members of the royal family, consisted of only two dances – an *entrée* for several peasants and a dance for the bride and groom.[48] Whether the Pécour choreography was danced in this mascarade or not, the fashion at court for village weddings, well publicized in the pages of the *Mercure galant*, undoubtedly contributed to the popularity and commercial success of a dance depicting a rustic bride and groom.

Already well known from its use in *Roland*, *la Mariée* achieved still more popularity as a published ballroom dance. Its success can be seen not only in the offspring it spawned almost immediately after its publication, *la Nouvelle mariée* and *la Seconde nouvelle mariée*, but also in a considerable number of books by dancing masters and musicians, both in France and in other countries, that mention this dance.[49] Pierre Rameau used *la Mariée* as an example of the use of certain steps in his book *Le maître danser* of 1725, and said of it, '*la Mariée*, beside the fact that it is known by everyone, may be justly termed one of the most beautiful dances that have ever been danced'.[50] Rameau renotated the dance and published it in his other book, *Abrégé de la nouvelle méthode*, also from 1725, with the remark that the dances selected for inclusion were Pécour's most popular.[51] Fourteen years later, *la Mariée* still remained a part of the standard repertoire of dances done at court balls. The *Mémoires* of the duc de Luynes report the following sequence of events at a formal ball given by Louis XV in January of 1739. After a long series of couple dances, presumably minuets, a *contredanse* was done:

Then the king asked Mr de la Trémoille, who was sitting behind him, to go and dance *la Mariée* with Mme de Luxembourg. This was followed by another *contredanse*, after which Mr de Clermont d'Amboise and Mme la princesse de Rohan danced a new dance com-

---

[48] This mascarade was performed at Marly by members of the court on 22 January. Contemporary accounts are silent as to the name of either the composer of the music or the choreographer of the dances.

[49] See, for example, Gottfried Taubert, *Rechtschaffener Tanzmeister* (Leipzig, 1717), p. 370; Louis Bonin, *Die neueste Art zur galanten und theatralischen Tantz-Kunst* (Frankfurt and Leipzig, 1711), pp. 135–6; Johann Mattheson, *Der vollkommene Capellmeister* (Hamburg, 1739), part 2, chapter 8, sec. 92, p. 226; Giovanni-Andrea Gallini, *A Treatise on the Art of Dancing* (London, 1762), pp. 176–7.

[50] 'Je vais donc commencer par ceux [i.e. the arm movements] qui se pratiquent dans la Mariée, parce qu'outre qu'elle est connüe de tout le monde; c'est qu'elle est à juste titre une des [plus] belles danses que l'on ait jamais dansé.' Rameau, *Maître*, p. 264. The beauty of the choreography, confirmed by performers of today who have learned the dance, is itself enough to explain the enduring popu-

larity of *la Mariée* during the eighteenth century. But the numerous revivals of *Roland* at the Opéra up until 1755 (see note 23) undoubtedly helped keep the dance (or at least the tune – the choreography may well have been altered) before the eyes of the public. The bride and groom in *Roland* were performed by some of the leading dancers of the Opéra, for example, Mr Balon and Mlle Subligny in 1705; Mr D. Dumoulin and Mlle Prévost in 1709.

[51] 'J'ai même choisi celles qui ont eu le plus de cours'. Pierre Rameau, *Abrégé* (Paris, 1725), part 1, p. 110, as cited in Witherell, *Pécour's Recueil*, pp. 207–9. Before notating these dances in his somewhat modified version of Feuillet notation, Rameau showed the dances to Pécour, who gave them his written approbation. See Witherell, p. 210, for a discussion of the few minor modifications of the choreography between Rameau's notation of *la Mariée* and Feuillet's of twenty-five years earlier.

posed of a menuet and a tambourin. After that, the Dauphin and Madame [his sister] danced *la Mariée*. Then there was another *contredanse*.[52]

It is startling to find that a dance composed in the reign of Louis XIV was still danced at court balls by his great-great-grandchildren.

During the years following the publication of *la Mariée*, the dance gradually lost its village wedding associations to become simply a couple dance for the ballroom. As it became an old chestnut of the repertory, it even found its way into dictionaries of the French language. The 1727 edition of the *Dictionnaire universel* of Furetière defined *la Mariée* as follows: 'A kind of old figured dance done by a man and a woman that is called *la Mariée* because it is generally danced at petty bourgeois weddings. *La Mariée* is gay and agreeable, and it is a pleasure to see it performed by people who dance it well.'[53]

In 1765 *la Mariée* was published in Feuillet notation for the third and last time. At that late date, when the menuet and the *contredanse* reigned supreme, and when the new allemande, an early relative of the waltz, was beginning to sweep Europe, it is difficult to believe that anyone would still be dancing *la Mariée* in the ballroom. Indeed, it is unlikely that anyone actually was. Already in 1754, in an entry that testifies both to the lasting celebrity of *la Mariée* and to its disuse by the middle of the eighteenth century, the *Encyclopédie* had listed *la Mariée* among those dances that had once been fashionable but that were no longer performed at balls.[54] The 1765 book that includes *la Mariée* is yet another version of Feuillet's *Chorégraphie*, published by one of Feuillet's students named Magny, at the end of his career. Magny says in his introduction that he included *la Mariée* and two other old figured dances among the minuets and *contredanses* because they alone are capable of instilling 'the true principles' of dance in students of the art.[55] In other words, *la Mariée* had become what another dancing master, Charles Pauli, referred to in 1756 as a '*danse d'exercise*', a ballroom dance from the good old days, which because it incorporated many more different kinds of steps than the new dances, was practiced as an exercise to give a dancer agility, strength, and the grace necessary for looking well on the dance floor.[56] Thus *la Mariée* ended its days, ignominiously taught to the scrapings of the dancing

[52] 'On dansa donc une contredanse; ensuite le Roi dit à M. de la Trémoille, qui étoit derrière lui, d'aller danser la mariée avec Mme de Luxembourg. Cette danse fut suivie d'une contredanse, après laquelle M. de Clermont d'Amboise et Mme la princesse de Rohan dansérent une danse nouvelle, composée d'un menuet et d'un tambourin. Après cela, M. le Dauphin et Madame dansérent la mariée; il y eut après une contredanse.' *Mémoires du Duc de Luynes sur la cour de Louis XV* (Paris, 1860–5), vol. II, p. 340.
[53] 'Mariée (la). Sorte de vieille Danse figurée, que dansent un homme et une femme, et qui s'appelle la *Mariée*, parce qu'on la danse ordinairement aux noces des petits Bourgeois. La *Mariée* est gaie et agréable, et c'est

un plaisir que de la voir danser à des gens qui la dansent bien.' Antoine Furetière, *Dictionnaire universel*, nouvelle édition (La Haye, 1727). The term is not found in the first edition of 1690.
[54] Cahusac, 'Contredanse', *Encyclopédie ou Dictionnaire raisonné des sciences, des arts et des métiers* (1754), vol. IV. Despite its decline as a ballroom dance, the *Mariée* tune can be found in theatrical works dating from the 1770s and 1780s. See the article by M. Elizabeth C. Bartlet in this volume, p. 291.
[55] Magny, *Principes de Chorégraphie* (Paris, 1765), preface.
[56] See Charles Pauli, *Elémens de la danse* (Leipzig, 1756), part 2, chapter 2, pp. 56–7.

master's *pochette*, nothing more than a textbook example of what ballroom dancing once had been.

Despite this sorry ending, *la Mariée*'s long history – 110 years between the composition of the music and the last publication of the choreography – has much to tell us about how social dances evolved. Like *la Mariée*, many of the ballroom dances in Feuillet notation are set to music drawn from the operas and ballets of the period, and for some of them the theatrical origin of the music may be irrelevent to the choreography itself. Such dances may simply have been composed to tunes that struck the fancy of the choreographer. But, in this as in other cases, the origin of what was ultimately published as a ballroom dance was almost certainly the operatic stage. Pécour did not simply borrow a tune he liked from the corpus of Lully's music and set a dance to it, he choreographed a dance for a specific theatrical event, setting it to a tune that already had associations with the theme of the *divertissement* for which it was intended. Because of the intimate connections between theatrical and social dancing at the time, the dance moved from the stage of the Opéra to the ballrooms of Paris, possibly via the intermediate step of a performance during a ball at court.

The close interrelationship of theatrical and social dancing at court did not, however, survive Louis XIV's reign. In December of 1715, only three months after the king's death, the Académie royale de musique obtained the right to hold public balls at the Opéra,[57] and nobles who formerly had vied for the privilege of attending balls at Versailles now flocked to the opera ball, led by the king's nephew, the duc d'Orléans. The advent of public balls clearly marked the shift from the court to Paris as the center for entertainments, including social dances, and brought to a close the era during which court and professional dancers had frequently found themselves together on the dance floor. Despite occasional reunions of the two groups, as in the court ballets around 1720, social dancing after 1715 confined itself more and more to the minuet and *contredanse*, while the professional dancers developed their art to ever increasing technical heights. During the reign of Louis XIV, however, the centralization of the performing arts at the court had allowed for a mingling of professional and court dancers that resulted in the creation of social dances that were technically demanding, intrinsically beautiful, and intimately allied to the music to which they were composed. The history of *la Mariée* serves to illustrate the close union of social and professional dancing during the *grand siècle*.

[57] See the *Réglement concernant la permission accordée à l'Académie Royale de Musique, de donner des bals publics* (Paris, 30 December 1715) as cited in Durey de Noinville, *Histoire du théâtre de l'opéra en France* (Paris, 1753) vol. I, pp. 148–50, 159–64.

A re-examination of Rameau's self-borrowings*

GRAHAM SADLER

In January 1958 a short article by Cuthbert Girdlestone appeared in *Music & Letters* on the subject of Rameau's self-borrowings.[1] It was to have inaugurated an extensive series devoted to further manifestations of what Hugh Macdonald has described as 'this pelican-like habit',[2] including those of Bach, Handel, Gluck, Rossini, Berlioz, and Mussorgsky. In the event, the only other self-borrowings to be studied in that journal were those of Bizet and, more recently, Vivaldi.[3]

Brief though it was, Girdlestone's article performed a useful service in listing the borrowings he had so far identified and in discussing them in general terms.[4] There are, however, two main reasons for returning to the subject. First, the article gives the impression of having been put together in some haste: by the standards of Girdlestone's other writings on Rameau, many of them still indispensible, it contains a large number of errors, including several spurious entries. One 'borrowing' turns out to be an independent piece by Jean-Jacques Rousseau;[5] another results from a typographical error,[6] while several others can be accepted only as possibilities, since the difficulty in dating items added at revivals of the operas makes it impossible to be sure whether the borrowings were made during or after Rameau's lifetime.

More important, Girdlestone had managed to identify less than half of the borrowings. The majority of those overlooked may be found either in the numerous operas not then available in nineteenth- or twentieth-century editions or in authoritative sources ignored by modern editors. Taking these into ac-

---

* An earlier version of this chapter was read at the American Musicological Society meeting at Boston in November 1981, under the chairmanship of Professor James Anthony.

[1] *Music & Letters*, XXXIX (1958), pp. 52–6.

[2] Hugh Macdonald, 'Berlioz's Self-borrowings', *Proceedings of the Royal Musical Association*, XCII (1965–6), p. 27.

[3] Winton Dean, 'Bizet's Self-borrowings', *Music & Letters*, XLI (1960), pp. 238–44; Eric Cross, 'Vivaldi's Operatic Borrowings', *Music & Letters*, LXIX (1978), pp. 429–39.

[4] Girdlestone also included some of the composer's arrangements, 'since arranging one's own works is but a form of self-borrowings' ('Rameau's Self-borrowing's

p. 55). The present article does not include such arrangements.

[5] The second item in Girdlestone's List (c): 'O mort, n'exerce pas ta rigueur', *Les fêtes d'Hébé*, II, 4. The supposed borrowing, 'O mort, viens terminer les douleurs de ma vie', *Les fêtes de Ramire* (1745), is specifically mentioned by Rousseau (*Les Confessions*, VII, 1745–7; *Jean-Jacques Rousseau: Œuvres complètes* (Paris, 1959), vol. I, p. 333) as one of the pieces which he added to this work. In any case, the resemblance to Rameau's air is very slight.

[6] On page 54, lines 18 and 19 reappear as lines 32 and 33, suggesting a non-existent borrowing from *Acante et Céphise*.

count, the number of incontestible borrowings rises from a mere 36 to 74, while a further 17 may be regarded as probable. Among the additions are at least nine vocal pieces (including almost certainly a section from the 'lost' *tragédie*, *Samson*) and five from the harpsichord collections. The remainder are *symphonies* of various kinds from the operas, and include a second borrowing discovered in the violin part of *Linus*, the sole surviving musical source of this *tragédie*. By no means have all the additional items gone unnoticed by other writers, or even by Girdlestone himself in his subsequent book on Rameau;[7] but the majority have not been identified before, and there has certainly been no previous attempt to survey the borrowings as a whole. Such a survey reveals a number of interesting patterns in Rameau's borrowing habits; it also throws light on matters of chronology and on eighteenth-century French attitudes towards the whole question of self-borrowing.

A composite list of all borrowings so far identified appears as an appendix at the end of this chapter. The contents are limited to those which I feel reasonably certain were deliberate, though the dividing line is admittedly not always easy to draw. In a style that makes much use of certain characteristic turns of phrase, some listeners might hear as self-quotation what I would regard merely as chance resemblance.[8] 'Borrowings' consisting of a single phrase or motive in mid-piece have not been included; nor have items moved bodily from one self-contained *entrée* of an opera to another when a work was revived.

Certain sources, particularly those production scores that preserve the cuts, revisions, and substitutions made for performances at the Opéra or the court until late in the century, contain a bewildering number of borrowings. While some can be shown to date from Rameau's lifetime, most can be eliminated as posthumous by various means. The list of 'Borrowings of uncertain authenticity' (Appendix, no. 80 onwards) includes those which cannot yet be placed with certainty on one side or the other of this dividing line.

In the case of a few operas – *Platée*, for example, or most of *Le temple de la Gloire* – it is still not possible to establish the musical text of the earliest version. In such cases, the dates given in the appendix are of the earliest musical text to include the borrowed item, even though the borrowing may well have appeared in, or been derived from, an earlier version.

While Rameau's borrowings can now be seen to be far more extensive than was formerly thought, they are still of a comparatively minor order by the standards of Bach, Handel and some of his other contemporaries. He seems to have borrowed remarkably little from other composers: the chorus 'Triomphe, victoire' in *La princesse de Navarre* (Appendix, no. 35), first performed in 1745, includes a prominent and hitherto unnoticed 'quotation' from Handel's *Samson*, first

[7] C. M. Girdlestone, *Jean-Philippe Rameau: his Life and Work* (London, 1957; rev. 2nd ed., 1969).

[8] Typical of those resemblances that I have not felt were close enough or extensive enough to justify inclusion are: 'Triste recours des malheureux' (*Les fêtes de Polymnie*, II, 4), 'Je guide un peuple généreux' (*Les fêtes de l'Hymen*, I, 2) and 'Cruelle mère des amours' (*Hippolyte et Aricie*, III, 1); 'Quelle faible victoire' (*Castor et Pollux*, I, 2) and 'Au berger que j'adore' (*Naïs*, II, 6); *La timide* (*Pièces de clavecin en concerts*) and 'Coulez, coulez, ondes' (*Naïs*, III, 5). This last appears in Girdlestone's List (c).

performed two years before.[9] But I suspect that this – like occasional similarities to the work of other composers[10] – may still be a matter of unconscious reminiscence. Moreover, while there is reason to suspect that Rameau re-used some of his earlier music now lost (that for the Parisian Fair Theatres, for example),[11] the first indisputable example of self-borrowing is not found until 1736, his fifty-third year. And a substantial number of works – the cantatas and motets, *Hippolyte et Aricie* (until its final revivals), *Platée*, *Zaïs*, *Pigmalion* and many of the one-act ballets of the 1750s – appear to contain none at all.

Further, Rameau is selective in the sources of his borrowings. There is nothing from the *Pièces de clavecin* (1706), from the motets and most of the cantatas or, for that matter, from at least nine of the operas. Indeed, while the borrowings as a whole originate from between eighteen and twenty-two works or collections, well over half (indeed, two-thirds of the indisputable ones) come from just six (see table 1). As we shall see, there is some significance in the fact that these six

Table 1 *Works from which borrowings are derived*

Title	No. of borrowings ( ) = probable or unconfirmed borrowings
La princesse de Navarre (1745)	16
Pièces de clavecin en concerts (1741)	9
Acante et Céphise (1751)	8 (+1)
Le temple de la Gloire (1745–6)	7
La naissance d'Osiris (1754)	6
Pièces de clavessin (1724)	6
Nouvelles suites de pièces de clavecin (c. 1729–30)	4
Hippolyte et Aricie (1742 revival)	4
Dardanus (1739 and 1744)	3
Zoroastre (1749)	2
Les Paladins (1760)	2
Le berger fidèle (1728)	1
Castor et Pollux (1737)	1
Les fêtes d'Hébé (1739)	1
Les fêtes de Polymnie (1745)	1 (+ 1)
Naïs (1749)	1 (+4)
Platée (1745/9)	1
La guirlande (1751)	1
L'Endriague (1723)	(4)
Samson (mid-1730s)	(1)
Les surprises de l'Amour (1757 revival)	(4)
Zaïs (1748)	(2)

[9] Cf. the aria 'Honour and arms'; the resemblance extends beyond the opening melodic idea. For discussion of another musical link between Handel and Rameau, see Kenneth Gilbert (ed.), *J.-Ph. Rameau: Pièces de clavecin* (Paris, 1979), Preface, p. x., and Graham Sadler, 'Jean-Philippe Rameau', in James R. Anthony *et al.*, *The New Grove French Baroque Masters* (London, 1986), p. 248.

[10] Cf. André Campra, *Tancrède*, Menuet 1 (III, 4) and Rameau, *Les fêtes d'Hébé*, Menuet 1 (III, 7). The resemblance extends to the use of *petites flûtes*. Interestingly, *Tancrède* was revived in 1738, the year before *Les fêtes d'Hébé* appeared.

[11] Girdlestone, 'Rameau's Self-borrowings', p. 55; Graham Sadler, 'Rameau, Piron and the Parisian Fair Theatres', *Soundings*, IV (1974), pp. 13–29.

works fall into two distinct categories: on the one hand, two well-known and widely circulated harpsichord collections; on the other, four of the least performed of the operas.

Let us now consider in turn the three main categories of borrowing: those from the harpsichord collections, instrumental movements from the operas, and vocal items of various sorts.

1. The harpsichord collections. In all, 19 borrowings from these collections may now be identified. Rameau's famous letter of 1727 to the librettist Houdar de La Motte, when the composer was preparing to launch his operatic career, cites eight of the harpsichord pieces as evidence of his ability to characterize.[12] Perhaps even then he was thinking of re-using some of them: at all events, five of the eight (*Les sauvages, L'entretien des muses, Les tendres plaintes*, the Musette and Tambourin) were to re-appear in the operas.

Borrowings from the harpsichord collections are the only ones that Rameau's public seems to have identified. An anonymous writer in *Le postillon français* (1739) claimed that 'everyone agrees that the best parts of the ballet *Les fêtes d'Hébé* are those which Rameau brought in from his old keyboard pieces'; and he adds sardonically: 'this demonstrates the composer's fertility'.[13] Something of the same tone is apparent ten years later in the journalist Clément's remarks on *Zoroastre*: describing the opera as 'more doleful than Maupertuis's treatise on happiness',[14] he concedes that 'from time to time the afflicted ear is consoled by a few fine *symphonies* the majority of which are harpsichord pieces that the composer has stolen from himself'.[15] And mention must be made of two satirical and decidedly vulgar engravings, issued in 1739 by Rameau's detractors at the height of what has come to be known as the Lulliste–Ramiste dispute. The engravings satirize the composer's most recent works, *Les fêtes d'Hébé* and *Dardanus*, and contain disparaging references to the fact that both include prominent borrowings from the keyboard collections.[16] Strategically placed, in plate 1, where Rameau can be seen receiving payment from a demon (under duress, it seems), is a book entitled: 'Old harpsichord pieces for making new operas'. And in a companion engraving, directed at *Les fêtes d'Hébé*, the composer sits astride

---

[12] Published in the *Mercure de France*, March 1765, pp. 36–40.

[13] *Le postillon français*, 30 June 1739: 'Tout le monde convient que ce qu'il y a de meilleur dans le ballet des *Fêtes d'Hébé*, est ce que le Sieur Rameau y a inséré de ses anciennes Pièces de Clavecin. Ce qui marque la fécondité de cet Auteur.'

[14] *Les cinq années littéraires, ou les lettres de M. Clément* (Paris, 1755), lettre xlv, 25 December 1749: 'plus triste que le traité du bonheur de Mr. de Maupertuis'; quoted in Laurence Boulay, '"Lettres de Monsieur Clément": références musicales (1748–50)', *Recherches sur la musique française classique*, VI (1966), pp. 227–32.

[15] Ibid., 'Quelques belles symphonies dont la plupart sont des pièces de clavecin que le musicien s'est volée à lui-même, consolent de tems en tems l'oreille affligée.' Clément continues his attack on Rameau's powers of creativity by repeating an (unjustified) accusation that one of the best airs in Act v was by Hasse.

[16] On the issuing of these and other satirical engravings during the dispute, see Emile Dacier, 'L'Opéra au XVIIIᵉ siècle: les premières représentations du "Dardanus" de Rameau, Novembre-Décembre 1739', *La revue musicale*, III (1903), pp. 163–73. See also Paul-Marie Masson, 'Lullistes et Ramistes, 1733–1752', *L'année musicale*, I (1911), pp. 187–211.

L'allegorie est assez claire.
Pour se passer de Commentaire

Plate 1. F-Pn Estampes, Hennin 8343. Anonymous engraving (1739). Rameau sits
at his desk beneath a Damoclean sword, writing algebraic equations (an allusion
to his music theory). Hanging from the desk is a quotation from *Dardanus*
(Ouverture, bb. 46–7). On the floor are the 'Vieilles Pieces de Clavecin pour faire
des opera nouveaux' and a further, unidentifiable musical quotation.
The demon has a complicated passage in semiquavers tucked into his belt.
The figures falling down the chimney are the composer's supporters – *ramistes* or,
more appropriately here, *ramoneurs* (chimney sweeps)

his indecently attired librettist Montdorge, who is being given literary assistance of an extremely unconventional nature by another writer, the Abbé Pellegrin; in this unflattering context, the presence on the floor of a volume of 'Pièces de clavecin' clearly speaks for itself.[17]

Despite such criticism on the part of the Lullistes, there can be little doubt that Rameau saw these harpsichord borrowings as a way of increasing the popular appeal of his first group of operas. His difficulties in winning over the public in those early years are well known: it took time for audiences to warm to his complex and sophisticated idiom. And while none of his first five operas was a failure (each had between 21 and 71 performances on its first run), the fate of all of them was initially very much in the balance. Yet it was not until 1736, after the appearance of his first two operas, that Rameau realized the potential of borrowing from his already popular harpsichord collections. Faced with the task of composing an additional *entrée* for *Les Indes galantes* – the *entrée* 'Les sauvages', set in the North American forests – he was doubtless prompted by association of ideas to incorporate the keyboard piece *Les sauvages*, which he had written after seeing the dancing of two Louisiana Indians at the Théâtre italien in 1725. The huge success of the new *entrée*, due in no small measure to the inclusion of this famous piece, undoubtedly encouraged him to use others in a similar way. Certainly he makes no attempt to disguise them: most are placed in prominent positions in the prologue, first act or final *divertissement*. And many are given extra prominence by the addition of a vocal *parodie*, in which the instrumental movement is adapted to a poetic text (see nos. 1, 2, 5, 7, 10, 16, and 29). The incidence of such *parodies* is, in fact, very much higher among the harpsichord borrowings than among the others.[18] Moreover, all but one consist not just of a simple vocal re-statement of the music of the dance, but of an often elaborate alternation of a solo voice or voices with the chorus. Table 2 illustrates the complex formed by two interlocked borrowings in *Les fêtes d'Hébé*: here, Rameau alternates the Musette and Tambourin from the *Pièces de clavessin*, the second appearance of the Musette being a sumptuous and extended *parodie*. The whole sequence of movements forms a colossal repetition structure lasting some seven or eight minutes.

By the time of *Zoroastre* ten years later, Rameau's handling of the *parodie* has become far freer and more subtle. Although the borrowed movement in Act II (*L'agaçante* from the *Pièces de clavecin en concerts*) does not appear until scene 4, it is heralded by many brief but unmistakable allusions to its distinctive opening

---

[17] For a reproduction of this second engraving and for further comment on its satirical content, see Graham Sadler, 'Patrons and pasquinades: Rameau in the 1730s', *Journal of the Royal Musical Association* (at press). For more criticism of the borrowings from keyboard collections, see 'Réponse de l'auteur de la "Lettre sur les opéras de Phaéton et d'Hippolyte". . .1743', in J. T. de Booy (ed.), *Studies on Voltaire and the Eighteenth Century*, CXIX, (1974), pp. 341–96, in which the writer criticises as inappropriate Rameau's addition of words to *Les sauvages* when he

incorporated the harpsichord piece into the *entrée* of that name in *Les Indes galantes*: 'Je prends la liberté de critiquer l'acte des *Sauvages*, où une pièce de clavecin charmante, malgré toute l'adresse avec laquelle elle est enchâssée, devient un air déplacé qui n'a aucun rapport avec les paroles que le musicien avait à exprimer' (p. 391).

[18] Of the other borrowings, only nos. 20, 23, and 63 include *parodies*. In a number of cases – nos. 32, 33, 56, 59, (81) – the original has a *parodie* ignored in the borrowing.

Table 2 'La danse', Les fêtes d'Hébé (III, 7)

R=rondeau refrain
C=couplet
ch=chorus

Musette en rondeau:	$R+R+C^1+R+C^2+R$
Tambourin en rondeau:	$R+R+C^1+R+C^2+R+C^3+R+coda$
Chorus, 'Suivez les lois':	R (ch)+R (solo and ch)+C^1 (solo)+R (duo)+R (ch)+C^2 (solo
(=Parodie of Musette)	and duo)+R (duo)+R (ch)
Tambourin en rondeau:	$R+R+C^1+R+C^2+R+C^3+R+coda$

phrase during the huge sequence of solos, duets, and choruses that occupy the previous three scenes. It is a fascinating example of the kind of long-term motivic repetition to be found in a number of Rameau's later works.

Zoroastre is, in fact, anachronistic in containing four movements from the harpsichord collections: by the later 1740s Rameau had all but abandoned borrowings of this sort.[19] Of the other fourteen that can be dated, all but one had been borrowed by 1745. With the Lulliste–Ramiste dispute now largely resolved in his favour, he no longer needed the sort of instant popular appeal that such movements had provided. In any case, he now had a seemingly limitless supply of up-to-date and little-used material readily available in such occasional works as La princesse de Navarre and Le temple de la Gloire. After Zoroastre he returned no more than twice to the harpsichord collections.

It is hardly surprising that the borrowings from the keyboard suites are generally subjected to more (if not necessarily more profound) modification than any other group – the inevitable result of translating into orchestral terms music conceived for harpsichord. We see in reverse the sort of adaptations that Rameau made to the symphonies from Les Indes galantes when he arranged them for keyboard[20] – countless small alterations of melody, harmony, rhythm, ornamentation, texture, and so on. A detailed examination of such alterations is beyond the scope of this paper.[21] There are, however, several other features worth noting.

First, let us consider transposition. If we exclude the keyboard pieces, well under half the borrowings are transposed, and those mostly by no more than a tone or a third. Yet two thirds of the harpsichord borrowings are transposed, and almost all by at least a fourth. Doubtless many of these wide transpositions were prompted by the differences in sonority between orchestra and keyboard or chamber ensemble. For example, when Rameau borrowed the Tambourin from Castor for the Pièces de clavecin en concerts in 1741, he transposed it down from

[19] Zoroastre is one of the operas said to contain music from Samson, abandoned in the later 1730s when the harpsichord borrowings were at their height (see note 27). If at least some of these borrowings came to Zoroastre by way of Samson, that might explain the anachronism noted above.

[20] See Graham Sadler, 'Rameau's Harpsichord Transcriptions from Les Indes galantes', Early Music, VII (1979), pp. 18–24.

[21] Comparison of borrowing and original is made easy in K. Gilbert (ed.), J.-Ph. Rameau: Pièces de clavecin, which includes facsimiles of the borrowed movements alongside the originals. It should be borne in mind that the facsimiles are taken from contemporary editions of the operas rather than from MS sources, and thus normally omit inner parts and indicate scoring in summary fashion.

D to A. But in transferring the movement in its revised form to the 1744 version of *Dardanus* he transposed it back to D. In several more extreme transpositions, the composer accentuates the pitch difference in his choice of texture and scoring. The transformation of *La Livri* from a sombre *tombeau* (it marked the recent death of the Comte de Livry) into a gracious and airy Gavotte in *Zoroastre* was achieved not only by the upward transposition of a major sixth but by the omission of all reference to the dark, low-lying keyboard part. More extreme is the transposition of the second Menuet from the *Nouvelles suites de pièces de clavecin* down a tenth in *La princesse de Navarre*, the pitch change emphasized by the scoring for two bassoons and bass (example 1).

Example 1

a. 2ᵉ Menuet, *Nouvelles suites de pièces de clavecin* (c. 1729–30)

b. 2ᵉ Menuet, *La princesse de Navarre* (1745), I, 7

A second significant feature of the harpsichord borrowings is the fact that few are kept structurally intact. Three of them (nos. 12, 16, and 74) are, indeed, little more than self-quotations consisting of the opening phrase or two; two others use either only the *rondeau* refrain (no. 9) or the first section of a binary movement (no. 3). Two more (nos. 5 and 27) omit the final couplet of the original *rondeau*. Modification of the others ranges from the substitution of a new ending in the *Zoroastre* Sarabande (no. 31) to the numerous small expansions and contractions made to *L'agaçante* (no. 29), the *Castor* Tambourin (nos. 8 and 10), and *La Cupis* (no. 21). The most extreme of these formal changes occur in the borrowing of *La pantomime* (no. 50) as part of the overture for the 1757 revival of *Les surprises de l'Amour*. The original is in an embryo sonata form – short, but with clear-cut first and second subject groups, a brief development and a particularly well-defined recapitulation. Curiously, Rameau blurs or obliterates all the more forward-looking formal features in the process of re-working it; the result is a distinctly old-fashioned if elegant binary form.

Before leaving the harpsichord pieces, I would like briefly to re-examine the suggestion that a number of these pieces may themselves be borrowings – in particular from the music for the Fair theatres, all of it now lost (see note 11). It had been suggested, for example, that the Musette, Tambourin and the pair of Rigaudons in the *Pièces de clavessin* (1724) were derived from Rameau's incidental music to Piron's farce *L'Endriague*, performed the previous year. After all, the play is known to have included a Tambourin (II, 9), a dance not at that date found in keyboard collections, while the others have a distinctly orchestral ring. There is, however, one small piece of evidence that adds weight to such speculation. In his preface to the *Pièces de clavessin*, Rameau states that 'there are several pieces in this book that may be transposed; for example, the Musette may be put into C, above all for playing with the Violle; and the Rigaudons [may be put] into D.'[22] It is, of course, possible that Rameau suggested such transpositions to make the pieces easier for beginners. But it seems more likely that they were originally conceived in these keys – the Rigaudons in D minor and major, the Musette (as a *pièce de viole?*) in C – and that they were eventually transposed to E major or minor to fit the tonality of the first suite in the collection. It seems too much of a coincidence that the composer should have singled out three of the four pieces already suspected of being borrowings. At all events, I have felt justified in including these pieces, with the Tambourin, under the heading 'Probable borrowings' in the appendix (nos. 75–8).

2. Instrumental borrowings from the operas. With 46 firmly identified and 11 further possibilities, this is by far the largest and most varied group. Interestingly, none of these predates 1745, twelve years after Rameau's debut as an opera composer. His approach here differs considerably from that to the harpsichord pieces, and indeed seems to undergo a significant change during the last few years before his death in 1764. From 1745 to 1760 (by far the greater part of the period), Rameau derives borrowings from only eight operas. In striking contrast to those from the keyboard suites, these borrowings tend to be taken from lesser-known sources: Rameau chooses movements not included in contemporary editions, or movements no longer in the current form of a work; above all, movements from occasional works that either had a restricted number of performances before court audiences (*La princesse de Navarre*, *La naissance d'Osiris*) or, if played in Paris, were never considered among his best works and never revived (*Le temple de la Gloire*, *Acante et Céphise*).

During Rameau's last four years, this pattern alters abruptly. Not only do the new borrowings effectively double the total number of 'parent' works, but they now involve some of his best-known operas, such as *Castor et Pollux*, *Zoroastre*, *Platée*, and *Zaïs*. Parallel with this, the number of borrowings involving virtually no re-working rises from almost negligible proportions in the earlier period to form the majority in the later one.

---

[22] Ibid., p. 19. 'Il y a quelques piéces dans ce livre, qu'on peut transposer; par exemple; la *Musette* peut être mise en C. sol ut, sur tout pour être jouée avec la Violle; & les *Rigaudons* en D. la ré.'

An important clue as to why this might have happened is provided by the *Mercure de France*, in a review of the revival of *Les surprises de l'Amour* in 1757. Noting that the *divertissement* of the *entrée* 'Les sibarites' had already been reviewed on an earlier occasion, the jounalist continues: 'we will merely add that MM. Rebel and Francoeur [the directors of the Paris Opéra] have enriched it with several *airs* [*de ballet*] which they have borrowed from M. Rameau himself. (These airs are taken from *Le temple de la Gloire* and *Acante et Céphise*.) It may be said that [the directors] have served this great man as he deserves, and that they have adorned him with his own beauty.'[23] This *entrée* does indeed contain borrowings from the two operas named, as well as from *La princesse de Navarre* (nos. 45–9). The tone of the *Mercure's* review suggests that it was something of a new departure for the Opéra directors to have done Rameau's borrowing for him. Significantly, none of the pieces from *Acante et Céphise* and *Le temple de la Gloire* involve any real re-working. It is thus difficult to avoid the conclusion that a certain proportion of the late borrowings – particularly those from well-known works and with little or no revision – were not made by Rameau himself. This is, after all, the pattern that continues after the composer's death. It would be a mistake, however, to assume that all the late borrowings were made by others: autograph additions to sources of his last two operas (*Les Paladins* and *Les Boréades*) show him taking an active part in the final preparations despite extreme old age and ill health; and he is known to have attended rehearsals right up to the final year of his life.

As Girdlestone observed,[24] Rameau seems to have regarded the *symphonies* in the operas rather like stage properties that could be moved from one opera to another: just as a Temple of Venus in one work might, with a coat of new paint, become a Temple of the Muses in another, so an *Air de triomphe* might become an *Entrée des guerriers*, and so on. Not surprisingly, the majority of borrowings in this category involve comparatively modest changes: the 'new paint' takes the form of small modifications of melody, harmony or rhythm, changes of scoring, ornamentation and the like. In view of the ease with which dances and other *symphonies* could be taken over from earlier works, it says much for Rameau's powers of invention that he did not indulge in the practice more often.

3. Vocal borrowings. Whereas Girdlestone lists only 2 borrowings from vocal sources, the total now stands at 11 or possibly 12 – still a small enough number. This is a little strange, in view of contemporary reports that Rameau had confessed to finding vocal music more difficult than instrumental[25] – an idea that receives some support from the distribution of revisions and corrections in the

---

[23] *Mercure de France*, August 1757, p. 159: 'Nous avons rendu comte de ce divertissement; nous ajouterons seulement que MM. Rebel et Francoeur l'ont enrichi de plusieurs airs qu'ils ont emprunté de M. Rameau même (ces airs sont tirés du *Temple de la Gloire* et d'*Acante et Céphise*); on peut dire qu'ils ont servi ce grand homme comme il le mérite et qu'ils l'ont embelli de ses propres beautés.'

[24] 'Rameau's Self-borrowings', p. 53.

[25] Hugues Maret, *Eloge historique de M. Rameau* (Dijon, 1766), p. 72; Michel-Paul-Gui de Chabanon, 'Essai d'Eloge historique de feu M. Rameau', *Mercure de France*, October 1764, vol. I, p. 169.

autograph manuscripts; strange, too, when one thinks of the countless times that he was called upon to set almost identical words. In at least one case Rameau even ignores the opportunity for self-borrowing provided by his librettist: the text of the ariette 'Heureux oiseaux' from Cahusac's libretto for *Les fêtes de l'Hymen et de l'Amour* (I, 8) is found verbatim in the same author's *La naissance d'Osiris* (see F-Po, Rés. 208, between pp. 28 and 29); yet Rameau, either deliberately ignoring or, more likely, failing to recognize it, composes a totally different setting.

There can be little doubt that this general unwillingness to re-use vocal numbers is connected with the marked reluctance in France to re-set existing libretti (at least before the late 1750s) and with the lack of a *pasticcio* tradition quite comparable with that in Italian opera. It is true that the Paris Opéra management would frequently arrange for the refurbishing of works long established in the repertory, but not normally before the composer and librettist were already dead. In any case, the refurbishments usually consisted either of additional accompaniments, ornamentation and so on, or of the replacement of airs or choruses by settings of wholly new texts.

It is equally rare for a French librettist to appropriate the work of another living librettist. Authors were all too aware of the likelihood of charges of plagiarism and accusations of lack of invention in a country where librettos were closely scrutinized by the literary world and subjected to at least as much critical comment as the music.[26] It is particularly significant, for example, that when Cahusac borrowed an eleven-line passage from Voltaire's *La princesse de Navarre* (II, 11) for the 1753 revival of *Les fêtes de Polymnie* (III, 6), he had the whole passage printed within double commas (plate 2). This might at first sight be taken merely as an example of *versi virgolati* (lines retained in the libretto but omitted in the performance), which in Italian *opera seria* were commonly indicated thus. But the French convention for showing discarded passages of that sort was a thick brace; the double commas were reserved for the pronouncements of gods or oracles, and for direct quotations – though not normally from other librettos. In this context, then, Cahusac's use of the device must be seen as an acknowledgement of his borrowing from Voltaire – for which, one assumes, he had the author's permission.

This attitude to the re-setting of words helps explain why only three or four of Rameau's vocal borrowings retain essentially the same words as their originals. Of the others, two have texts with a certain amount in common, while the remaining seven either have completely different texts or are linked by comparatively flimsy connections.

Naturally, the practice of altering texts in such instances makes it harder to trace borrowings from works like *Samson*, *Linus*, and *Lysis et Délie* for which the librettos survive but not the music. In the case of *Samson*, various attempts have been made to match passages of Voltaire's text with approximate equivalents in

---

[26] See, for example, 'Lettre de M. de Cahusac à M. Remond de Saint Albine, sur les bruits qui courent que M. de Cahusac n'est point Auteur de nouvel Opera de Zoroastre', *Mercure de France*, December 1749, vol. I, pp. 202–3; Ibid., September 1748, p. 222.

other works by Rameau, but without wholly convincing results.[27] There is, however, one remarkable correspondance, so far overlooked, between a short passage in *Samson* (III, 5) and another in *La princesse de Navarre* (II, 11). The latter is, in fact, identical with the above-mentioned passage borrowed by Cahusac for the revival of *Les fêtes de Polymnie*, and can thus be seen in plate 2. Voltaire's original is set out below:

> Écho, voix errante,
> Légère habitante
> De ce beau séjour,
> Écho, monument de l'amour,
> Parle de ma faiblesse au héros qui m'enchante.
> Favoris du printemps, de l'amour et des airs,
> Oiseaux dont j'entends les concerts,
> Chers confidents de ma tendresse extrême,
> Doux ramage des oiseaux,
> Voix fidèle des échos,
> Répétez à jamais: Je l'aime, je l'aime.[28]

After the first four lines, which are virtually identical, the two texts continue independently; even so, the last line of the *Samson* extract has some similarity to the last but one of the other.

Without the score of *Samson* we cannot be entirely sure that the passage in *La princesse de Navarre* is Rameau's as well as Voltaire's self-borrowing. The author does, after all, use some similar imagery in *Le temple de la Gloire* (III, 5), though Rameau's setting bears only a passing resemblance to that of the passage from *La princesse de Navarre* referred to above:

> Répondez à leur chant, voix errante et fidèle,
> Écho, frappez les airs de sons harmonieux,
> Répétez avec moi: ma gloire est immortelle.

Yet Voltaire himself acknowledges in the 'Avertissement' to his *Oeuvres* (1752) that Rameau 'has since used almost all the airs from *Samson* in other lyric compositions'.[29] And the fact that the composer clearly thought enough of the piece to re-use it with only minor modifications in the 1753 revival of *Les fêtes de Polymnie*[30] strengthens the possibility that the first part of this 'Écho' air is a musical borrowing from the sadly stillborn *Samson*. I have therefore included it among the probable borrowings (no. 79). As Girdlestone remarked when

[27] See, for example, C. Saint-Saëns, C. Malherbe et al. (eds.), *Jean-Philippe Rameau: Oeuvres complètes* (Paris, 1895–1924, repr. New York, 1968), vol. VII, pp. liv–lv; vol. IX, pp. lxxiii–lxxiv; Mary Cyr, *Rameau's 'Les fêtes d'Hébé'* (unpubl. PhD diss., University of California, Berkeley, 1975), p. 27f. For further on *Samson*, see C. M. Girdlestone, 'Voltaire, Rameau, et "Samson"', *Recherches sur la musique française classique*, VI (1966), pp. 133–43; R. S. Ridgway, 'Voltaire's Operas', *Studies on Voltaire and the Eighteenth Century*, CLXXXIX (1980), pp. 119–51.

[28] L. Morland (ed.), *Voltaire: Oeuvres complètes*, vol. III (Paris, 1877–85), pp. 26–7. For an earlier variant of this passage, see Theodore Besterman (ed.), *Voltaire: Correspondence and Related Documents* (Geneva, 1968–77), Letter D.971.

[29] 'Le musicien employa depuis presque tous les airs de *Samson*, dans d'autres compositions lyriques que l'envie n'a pas pu supprimer.'

[30] This later version, in which Rameau has added parts for *petit choeur*, clearly follows the text and music of the version in *La princesse de Navarre*.

Z. I M É S.

Quels charmes inconnus!..Eſt-ce un ſonge flatteur!..

On danſe.

ARGELIE alternativement avec le C H œ u r.

» Echo , voix errante ,
» Legere habitante
» De ce ſéjour :
» Echo , fille de l'Amour.
» Roſſignols amoureux , onde brillante & pure
» Repetez avec moi ce que dit la Nature.
» Il faut aimer à ſon tour.

On danſe.

Z. I M É S.

Que d'attraits !

Plate 2. Passage quoted by Cahusac (*Les fêtes de Polymnie*, 1753 revival) from Voltaire's
La princesse de Navarre, 1745

speculating that parts of the work might eventually be located: 'This may not console us for the loss of the music as a whole, any more than the salvaging of fine sculptures, displayed in a building for which they were not conceived, can make up for the loss of the cathedral to which they once belonged.'[31] Even so, the present fragment has a stronger claim to be such a 'sculpture' than any of those so far tentatively identified. The opening bars are given in example 2.

[31] 'Voltaire, Rameau, et "Samson"', p. 143. 'Ceci ne saurait nous consoler de la perte de la musique dans son ensemble, pas plus que le sauvetage de chefs-d'oeuvre de sculpture, recueillis dans un édifice pour lequel ils n'ont pas été conçus, ne compense celle de la cathédrale à laquelle ils appartenaient.'

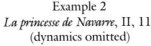

Example 2
La princesse de Navarre, II, 11
(dynamics omitted)

Perhaps because there are so few of them, it is not easy to discern any clear pattern in Rameau's approach to vocal self-borrowings. In only a very few instances does the motive seem to have been the desire to provide singer and audience with a sure-fire 'hit' number – though that is certainly true of the ariette 'Non, non, une flamme volage' (no. 44): when it first appeared in *La naissance d'Osiris* (performed once before the French court in 1754), the *Mercure de France* singled it out as 'that ariette whose simple melody expresses the ingenuousness of the words in such a fresh way'.[32] Later, after it had been given a wider audience in the 1756 version of *Zoroastre*, the *Sentiment d'un harmoniphile* declared it to be 'an air that the whole of Paris has applauded', and reproduced the melodic line.[33] The ariette 'L'objet qui règne dans mon âme' (no. 4) enjoyed

[32] '. . .cette ariette dont le chant simple exprime d'une manière si neuve la naïveté des paroles', *Mercure de France*, II (December 1754), p. 193.

[33] 'C'est un air que tout Paris a applaudi', A. J. Labbet de Morambert and A. Léris, eds., *Sentiment d'un harmoniphile sur différens ouvrages de musique* (Paris, 1756/R1972), p. 148.

a similar popularity: not only was it often performed as a separate piece, but it appears as an example in Rousseau's *Dissertation sur la musique moderne* (1743) in the author's numeral notation, in Bérard's *L'art du chant* (1755), as well as in such publications as Clément's *Journal de clavecin* (1764).

For the remainder of the vocal borrowings, however, such outright popularity seems not to have been a primary factor. Here the musical material has been re-worked to a much greater degree, suggesting either that the composer saw marked new possibilities in the material or that he used the stimulus of existing ideas to set his imagination working. In the case of the chorus 'Triomphe, victoire' (no. 35), Rameau borrows no more than the words and music of the opening phrase. Similarly, the ariette 'Eclatez, fières trompettes' (no. 42) uses little more than the first and second ritornellos of a quite different ariette, 'Rég-nez, régnez en paix'. In the other vocal borrowings, material from the model is more evenly spread, though rarely taken over without modification.

An intriguing example of Rameau's re-working of vocal material is provided by the borrowings listed as nos. 17 and 72. Here, we have a duet found in three distinct versions: in *La princesse de Navarre* and *Les fêtes de Polymnie* (both of 1745) and in the undated and incomplete *acte de ballet*, *Io*. Comparison of the three raises interesting questions concerning the librettist and the dating of this latter work.

All three versions of the duet have different texts (set out below), though those in *Io* and *Les fêtes de Polymnie* begin the same and have much in common:

Voltaire, *La princesse de Navarre* (III, 5)

Dans vos mains gronde le tonnerre,
Effayez [rassurez] la terre,
Frappez vos ennemis,
Répandez vos bienfaits!

Cahusac, *Les fêtes de Polymnie* (Prologue, sc. 1)   Anon., *Io* (sc. 4)

Jupiter, lance la foudre   Jupiter, lance la foudre,
Sur les ennemis de la paix!   Vange l'amour méprisé.
Éclate, reduis en poudre   Éclate, reduis en poudre
Les peuples orgueilleux,   Cet orgueilleux tyran
Jaloux de tes bienfaits.   De mon coeur abusé.

At first sight the strong connection between these latter two texts might suggest that Cahusac was the author of the otherwise anonymous libretto of *Io*. He was, after all, Rameau's most faithful collaborator; further, most of the other borrow-ings with unchanged or little-changed texts are found in works which have the same librettist as the 'parent' work. Unfortunately, however, that is not always so: as we have seen, the 'Echo' air was moved almost verbatim from Voltaire's to Cahusac's libretto. Thus the present evidence can be little more than a first, tentative contribution towards establishing the identity of *Io*'s librettist.

It is when we compare the music of the three duos that we find evidence that might have a bearing on the dating of this work. Although little work has been done on the subject, the general assumption has been that *Io* is a comparatively late work; Paul-Marie Masson even wondered if it might be Rameau's last, since all known sources break off at the same point – before what would have been the final *divertissement*.[34] Because the surviving sources are posthumous,[35] dating can be established only by internal evidence.

The three duets are of approximately the same length (68–9 bars) and share the same largely contrapuntal texture; all are scored for two high voices, unison violins and continuo. Nevertheless, there are many important differences between them. The least closely related are the versions in *La princesse de Navarre* and *Les fêtes de Polymnie*: only in the opening fifteen or sixteen bars could it be said that one is modelled on the other, and even then many details (notably the violin part and, of course, the verbal rhythms) differ considerably. For the remaining fifty bars or so, the duos develop independently, though both continue to develop the thematic ideas of the opening.

The *Io* version, however, is more closely related to both the others, though in different ways. On the one hand, its first twenty-seven bars compare remarkably closely with the equivalent bars in *La princesse de Navarre* (and its first seventeen bars thus relate, though less closely, to those in *Les fêtes de Polymnie*). On the other, the final thirteen bars (with the exception of the violin part) correspond not to the duo in *La princesse de Navarre* but to that in *Les fêtes de Polymnie*.

Now, for the *Io* version to have been composed last, as might until now have been assumed, we must suppose one of two possibilities: either that Rameau had both earlier versions before him as composed, and selected different passages from each (rather an unlikely idea), or that he was conflating elements of both from memory (possible, but also unlikely, given the often complex four-part polyphonic texture). If the dates of all three were unknown, we should probably conclude (i) that the *Io* duet was the earliest, (ii) that from it Rameau borrowed, fairly literally, the first twenty-seven bars for *La princesse de Navarre*, and (iii) that later, and more freely, he borrowed the first seventeen and the last thirteen bars for *Les fêtes de Polymnie*. This last is much the most highly finished, and thus likely to be the latest in date. At the same time, it seems less probable that the opening melodic ideas were conceived for the words 'Dans vos mains gronde le tonnerre' (*La princesse de Navarre*) than for 'Jupiter, lance la foudre' (*Io* and *Les fêtes de Polymnie*), which fit altogether more happily in rhythmic terms. Some further, if limited, support is provided by the only other 'shared' movement in *Io* (no. 73). Compared with the version in *La guirlande* (1751), it seems more discursive, less well integrated, and could easily be taken for the earlier.

[34] *L'opéra de Rameau* (Paris, 1930; repr. 1972), p. 86. The fact that the composer's son, in what is presumably a reference to the autograph score now lost, describes *Io* as 'sans divertissement' (see G. Sadler, 'A Letter from Claude-François Rameau to J. J. M. Decroix', *Music & Letters*, LXIX (1978), p. 142) seems to confirm that the ending is not simply lost but was never composed. The abandoning of *Io* could, however, have happened at any time during Rameau's operatic career.

[35] A score (F-Pn Vm² 316) and parts (Vm² 324) were prepared after Rameau's death for the private collection of J. J. M. Decroix. (See R. Peter Wolf, 'An Eighteenth-century *Oeuvres complètes* of Rameau', in Jérôme de La Gorce (ed.), *Jean-Philippe Rameau: Dijon 1983* (Paris and Geneva, 1987), pp. 159–69.)) A nineteenth-century copy (F-Pc D.8173 (4)) is derived from these.

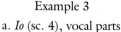

Example 3

a. *Io* (sc. 4), vocal parts

b. *La princesse de Navarre* (III, 5), vocal parts

Thus, inconclusive though it may be, this evidence must suggest the possibility that Rameau composed the enigmatic *Io* considerably earlier than was previously supposed. Indeed, if it predates *Les fêtes de Polymnie*, it must presumably belong to that long fallow period between the completion of *Dardanus* in 1739 and Rameau's return to operatic production in 1745.

Paul Henry Làng[36] once pointed out that in Ancient Rome the practice of moving portions of one play to another was known as contamination – a term which many a nineteenth-century critic would have thought eminently suited to the widespread borrowings of the previous century. Yet few eighteenth-century composers would have agreed with Racine that 'All invention consists of making something out of nothing.'[37] Thankfully the days are long gone when making something out of something else was regarded with censure. Today, we would consider the practice merely one of many facets of the creative process, to be studied and valued for the light it might throw on various aspects of a composer's output. In this, the self-borrowings of Rameau are no exception.

[36] Paul Henry Lang, *Handel* (New York, 1966), p. 558.   [37] Quoted in ibid., p. 569.

Appendix: Rameau's self-borrowings

Symbols and abbreviations:
+ borrowing not listed in Girdlestone (1958)
* information incorrect in Girdlestone
r revival
v/vv voice/voices
Prol Prologue
sc scene

Borrowing			Origin	
1		Danse du Grand Calumet de la Paix [g]	Les sauvages [g]	
Les Indes galantes [Parodie, 'Forêts paisibles', 2vv / chœur]	1736*	'Les sauvages' sc.6	*Nouvelles suites de pièces de clavecin*	*c.* 1729–30
2		P.er menuet [D]	[Premier] menuet [G]	
Castor et Pollux [Parodie, 'Naissez, dons de Flore', 1 v / chœur]	1737	Prol. sc.2	*Nouvelles suites de pièces de clavecin*	*c.* 1729–30
3		Air tendre [d]	L'entretien des Muses [d]	
Les fêtes d'Hébé [In original version of 2e *entrée*]	1739	II 5	*Pièces de clavecin*	1724
4		Air, 'L'objet qui règne dans mon âme' [E]	Air, 'L'amour qui règne dans votre âme'* [E flat]	
Les fêtes d'Hébé	1739	III 7	*Le berger fidèle*	1728
5		Musette en rondeau [E]	Musette en rondeau [E]	
Les fêtes d'Hébé [Parodie, 'Suivez les lois', 2vv / chœur]	1739	III 7	*Pièces de clavecin*	1724
6		Tambourin en rondeau [e]	Temborin (*sic*) [e]	
Les fêtes d'Hébé	1739	III 7	*Pièces de clavecin*	1724
7		Air en rondeau [D]	Les niais de Sologne [D]	
Dardanus [Parodie, 'Paix favorable', 2vv / chœur. See also no. 74.]	1739	III 3	*Pièces de clavecin*	1724

Appendix: Rameau's self-borrowings (*cont.*)

Borrowing		Origin		
8 *[music notation]*	P[er] tambourin [A]	Tambourin [D]		
Pièces de clavecin en concerts [See also no. 10]	1741 IIIe Concert	*Castor et Pollux* [Girdlestone lists the *Castor* version as a borrowing from the *Pièces de clavecin en concerts*, rather than vice versa.]	1737	Prol. sc.2
9+ *[music notation]*	Air pour les plaisirs [a]	La timide, 1er rondeau [a]		
Dardanus	1744[r] Prol. sc.1	*Pièces de clavecin en concerts*	1741	IIIe Concert
[music notation]	1er tambourin [D]	P[er] tambourin [A]		
Dardanus [Parodie, 'Chantons tous', 1 v / chœur]	1744[r] III 6*	*Pièces de clavecin en concerts*	1741	III[e] Concert
		[*Dardanus* version clearly derived from *Pièces de clavecin en concerts* rather than from *Castor* (1737). See no. 8.]		
[music notation]	2[e] tambourin [d]	2[e] tambourin en rondeau [a]		
Dardanus	1744[r] III 6*	*Pièces de clavecin en concerts*	1741	III[e] Concert
+ *[music notation]*	2[e] menuet [e]	2[e] menuet [g]		
La princesse de Navarre	1745 I 7	*Nouvelles suites de pièces de clavecin*	*c.* 1729–30	
+ *[music notation]*	Loure [D]	Loure [D]		
La princesse de Navarre	1745 III 5	*Les fêtes d'Hébé* [In F-Pn Vm² 342; part of 'Suplement de M[r] Rameau. Airs dansez par Melle Barbarine', p. 195ff.]	1739	

Appendix: Rameau's self-borrowings (*cont.*)

Borrowing				Origin		
14		P^{re} gavotte [D]		P^{er} gavotte [D]		
	La princesse de Navarre [See also no. 69.]	1745	III 5	*Hippolyte et Aricie*	1742^r	Prol. sc
15		Deuxième gavotte [d]		2e gavotte [d]		
	La princesse de Navarre [See also no. 68.]	1745	III 5	*Hippolyte et Aricie*	1742^r	Prol. sc
16+		Musette [D]		L'agaçante [G]		
	La princesse de Navarre [Parodie, 'Ces beaux noeuds', 2 vv. See also no. 29.]	1745	III 5	*Pièces de clavecin en concerts*	1741	IIe Concer
17+		Duo, 'Jupiter, lance la foudre' [D]		Duo, 'Dans vos mains gronde le tonnerre' [D]		
	Les fêtes de Polymnie [See also no. 72.]	1745	Prol. sc.1	*La princesse de Navarre*	1745	III 5
18		Chaconne [C]		Chaconne [D]		
	Les fêtes de Polymnie [Text of vocal section changed from 'Amour, Dieu charmant. . .' to 'Dans ce beau séjour. . .'.]	1745	I 2	*La princesse de Navarre*	1745	III 5
19		2e menuet [g]		2eme menuet [g]		
	Les fêtes de Polymnie	1745	I 4	*Pièces de clavecin en concerts*	1741	IIe Conce
20		Air vif [G]		Entrée des Bohémiens [A]		
	Les fêtes de Polymnie [Parodie, 'Dieu de la tendresse', 1 v / chœur]	1745	II 7	*La princesse de Navarre*	1745	I 6

Appendix: Rameau's self-borrowings (*cont.*)

	Borrowing			Origin		
1		Air tendre pour les Muses [c*]		La Cupis [d]		
	Le temple de la Gloire	1745–6	Prol. sc.2	*Pièces de clavecin en concerts*	1741	v^e Concert
2+		Passepied en rondeau [E flat]		Air tres vif [G]		
	Le temple de la Gloire [See also no. 52.]	1745–6	Prol. sc.3	*Dardanus* [In 2nd version of 1st run. See F-Pn V^m 349, MS with printed title (Paris, J. B. C. Ballard, 1739).]	1739	IV 1
3		Gavotte vive [D]		Tambourin en rondeau [E]		
	Le temple de la Gloire [Parodie, 'Bacchus, fier et doux vainqueur', 1 v / chœur]	1745–6	II 2	*La princesse de Navarre*	1745	I 7
+4+		Air de triomphe [D]		Entrée des guerriers [D]		
	Le temple de la Gloire [Survives minus last 19 bars in F-Po A.157a (i–iv). Probably used in 1745 version, but later omitted.]	1745	III 4	*La princesse de Navarre*	1745	I 7
+		Entrée [D]		Entrée [D]		
	Les fêtes de l'Hymen et de l'Amour	1747	III 3	*La princesse de Navarre*	1745	III 5
		2e gavotte [a]		2e gavotte en rondeau [a]		
	Naïs	1749	II 6	*Les fêtes de Polymnie*	1745	Prol. sc.2
		Air tendre en rondeau [g]	Les tendres plaintes [d]			
	Zoroastre	1749	I 3	*Pièces de clavessin*	1724	

Appendix: Rameau's self-borrowings (*cont.*)

Borrowing			Origin		
28 [musical notation]		Gavotte vive en rondeau [g]	Gavotte [g]		
Zoroastre	1749	I 3	*La princesse de Navarre*	1745	II 11
29 [musical notation]		Entrée d'Indiens et d'Indiennes [D*]	L'agaçante [G]		
Zoroastre [Parodie, 'Pour la fête', 2 vv / chœur. See also no. 16.]	1749	II 4	*Pièces de clavecin en concerts*	1741	II[e] Concert
30 [musical notation]		Gavotte en rondeau gracieux [a]	La Livri [c]		
Zoroastre	1749	III 7	*Pièces de clavecin en concerts*	1741	Ier Concert
31 [musical notation]		Sarabande [E*]	Sarabande [A]		
Zoroastre	1749	III 7	*Nouvelles suites de pièces de clavecin*	*c.* 1729–30	
32+ [musical notation]		Air gracieux [A]	Musette en rondeau [G]		
La guirlande [In F-Pn Vm² 310, Recueil de ballets . . . copiés sur les partitions originals de l'auteur.]	1751	sc.1	*Le temple de la Gloire*	1745–6	I 2
33+ [musical notation]		1er menuet [A]	P[er] menuet en musette [G]		
La guirlande [Same source as no. 32.]	1751	sc.1	*Le temple de la Gloire*	1745–6	I 2
34+ [musical notation]		2e menuet [a]	2e menuet [g]		
La guirlande [Same source as no. 32.]	1751	sc.1	*Le temple de la Gloire*	1745–6	I 2

Appendix: Rameau's self-borrowings (*cont.*)

	Borrowing			Origin		
5+		Chœur, 'Triomphe, victoire' [D]		Chœur, 'Triomphe, victoire' [D]		
	Acante et Céphise	1751	III 3	*La princesse de Navarre*	1745	III 4
6+		Ariette, 'Un Bourbon ouvre sa carrière' [D]		Ariette, 'Un héros ouvre sa carrière' [D]		
	Ariette pour la naissance de M. le duc de Bourgogne [F-Pn Vm⁷ 3620]	1751		*Acante et Céphise*	1751	III 3
				[Probably removed from *Acante* before its first performance. See G. Sadler, 'A Letter from Claude-François Rameau to J. J. M. Decroix', *Music & Letters* LIX (1978), pp. 139–47.]		
7+		Sarabande [c]		Sarabande [c]		
	Linus [See also no. 45.]	before 1752	III	*La princesse de Navarre*	1745	II 11
8		Gavotte. Rondeau un peu gay [c]		Rondeau gavotte [c]		
	Linus	before 1752	III	*La princesse de Navarre*	1745	II 11
9+		Air, 'A la beauté tout cède sur la terre' [C]		Air, 'Lorsque Vénus vient embellir la terre' [D]		
	Les fêtes de Polymnie	1753ʳ	I 4	*La princesse de Navarre*	1745	I 6
0+		'Echo, voix errante' [C]		'Echo, voix errante' [C]		
	Les fêtes de Polymnie [Clearly borrowed directly from *La princesse de Navarre* rather than from *Samson*. See no. 79.]	1753ʳ	III 6	*La princesse de Navarre*	1745	II 11

Appendix: Rameau's self-borrowings (*cont.*)

	Borrowing			Origin		
41+			Bruit de guerre [C]	Bruit de guerre [C]		
	Castor et Pollux	1754[r]	Entr'acte between I and II	*Dardanus*	1744[r]	Entr'acte between IV and V
42+			Ariette, 'Eclatez, fières trompettes [C]	Ariette, 'Régnez, régnez en paix' [D]		
	Castor et Pollux	1754[r]	II 5	*La princesse de Navarre*	1745	III 5
43+			Ariette: 'Des Zéphirs que Flore rapelle' [D]	Ariette: 'Du printems sur l'herbe fleurie'		
	Anacréon (ii)	1754	sc.3	*La naissance d'Osiris*	1754	sc.1
44			Air gracieux, 'Non, non, une flamme volage' [D]	Ariette andante et lourée, 'Non, non, une flamme volage' [D]		
	Zoroastre	1756[r]	I 3	*La naissance d'Osiris*	1754	sc.1
45			Sarabande [d]	Sarabande [c]		
	Les surprises de l'Amour [See also no. 37.]	1757[r]	'Les sibarites' sc.1*	*La princesse de Navarre*	1745	II 11
46			Air gracieux pour les Sibarites [g]	2[e] gavotte en rondeau [g]		
	Les surprises de l'Amour	1757[r]*	'Les sibarites' sc.4	*Acante et Céphise*	1751	I 1*
47			P[er] air, mouvement de chaconne* [g]	P[er] air, mouvement de chaconne [g]		
	Les surprises de l'Amour	1757[r]*	'Les sibarites' sc.4	*Acante et Céphise*	1751	I 6
48+			2e air [G]	2e air [G]		
	Les surprises de l'Amour	1757[r]	'Les sibarites' sc.4	*Acante et Céphise*	1751	I 6

Appendix: Rameau's self-borrowings (*cont.*)

	Borrowing			Origin		
49+		Forlane [G]		Forlane gay [D]		
	Les surprises de l'Amour	1757[r]	'Les sibarites' sc.4	*Le temple de la Gloire*	1746[r]	II 2
50+		Ouverture (3rd movt.) [F]		La pantomime, loure vive [B flat]		
	Les surprises de l'Amour	1757[r]		*Pièces de clavecin en concerts*	1741	IV[e] Concert
51		Sarabande [d]		Sarabande [d]		
	Les surprises de l'Amour	1757[r]	'Anacréon' sc.4	*La princesse de Navarre*	1745	III 5
52+		2[e] passepied [G]		Air très vif [G]		
	Les surprises de l'Amour [In *La lyre enchantée . . . avec les changemens qui ont été fait* [sic] *en 1758* (Paris, 1758). For an earlier borrowing see no. 22.]	1758[r]	'La lyre enchantée' sc.3	*Dardanus*	1739	IV 1
53+		Loure [g]		Loure [g]		
	Les surprises de l'Amour [Same source as no. 52.]	1758[r]	'La lyre enchantée' sc.6	*Acante et Céphise*	1751	I 6
54+		[1er] tambourin [G]		1er tambourin [G]		
	Les surprises de l'Amour [Same source as no. 52.]	1758[r]	'La lyre enchantée' sc.6	*Acante et Céphise*	1751	I 6
55+		Mineur [2e tambourin] [g]		2e tambourin [g]		
	Les surprises de l'Amour [Same source as no. 52.]	1758[r]	'La lyre enchantée' sc.6	*Acante et Céphise*	1751	I 6

Appendix: Rameau's self-borrowings (*cont.*)

Borrowing			Origin		
56+		(a) Ouverture (3rd movt.) [F] (b) Air gai [G]	(a) Ouverture (1st movt.) [F] (b) Contredanse [D]		
Les Paladins	1760	(b) III 4	*La naissance d'Osiris*	1754	(b) sc. dernière
57		Première gavotte gaye [C*]	P^re gavotte [D]		
Les Paladins	1760	I 5	*La naissance d'Osiris*	1754	sc.3
58		2^cme gavotte [c*]	2eme gavotte [d]		
Les Paladins	1760	I 5	*La naissance d'Osiris*	1754	sc.3
59+		[Air] très gay [D]	Air vif pour les Héros [E flat]		
Les Paladins	1760	II 9	*Le temple de la Gloire*	1746^r	Prol. sc.2
60+		Air gay [D]	Air gay [D]		
Les Paladins [In F-Po Rés. A. 201]	1760	II 10	*Le temple de la Gloire*	1746^r	II 2
61+		Air très gay [G]	Air très gay [G]		
Les Paladins	1760	III 4	*Le temple de la Gloire*	1746^r	III 6
62+		Loure [e]	Loure [d]		
Les Boréades	c. 1763	II 6	*Les Paladins* [In F-Po Rés. A.201, incomplete.]	1760	I 6

Appendix: Rameau's self-borrowings (*cont.*)

	Borrowing			Origin		
63+		Air un peu gay [A]		Rondo gracieux [D]		
	Les Boréades [Parodie, 'Eh pourquoi se deffendre', 1 v.]	*c.* 1763	III 3	*La naissance d'Osiris*	1754	sc.1
64+		Air de triomphe [C]		Air de triomphe [D]		
	Castor et Pollux	1763[r] or 1764[r]	II 5	*Naïs*	1749	I 7
65		1er rigaudon [A]		1er rigaudon [A]		
	Castor et Pollux	1764[r] [?1754[r]]	V 7	*Zoroastre*	1749	V 4
66		2[e] rigaudon [a]		2[e] rigaudon [a]		
	Castor et Pollux	1764[r] [?1754[r]]	V 7	*Zoroastre*	1749	V 4
67+		Air gracieux [D]		Air gracieux pour les Génies et [les] Fées [D]		
	Naïs	1764[r]	III 5	*Acante et Céphise*	1751	III 3
68		Gavotte légère [d]		2[e] gavotte [d]		
	Naïs [Order of gavottes reversed. See no. 69 and nos. 14 and 15.]	1764[r]	III 5	*Hippolyte et Aricie* [Quite possibly derived direct from *La princesse de Navarre*; see nos. 14 and 15.]	1742[r]	Prol. sc.5
69		Majeur [2[e] gavotte] [D]		P[re] gavotte [D]		
	Naïs	1764[r]	III 5	*Hippolyte et Aricie* [See comments on no. 68.]	1742[r]	Prol. sc.5

Appendix: Rameau's self-borrowings (*cont.*)

	Borrowing			Origin		
70		1ᵉʳ loure [d]		Loure [c in most sources]		
	Naïs	1764ʳ	III 5	*Les Paladins*	1760	III 5
71+		Loure [d]		Loure [d]		
	Naïs	1764ʳ	III 5	*Platée*	1749ʳ	III 5
72+		Duo, 'Jupiter, lance la foudre' [D]		Duo, 'Dans vos mains gronde le tonnerre' [D]		
	Io	Date unknown	sc.4	*La princesse de Navarre*	1745	III 5
	[Not yet possible to determine which is borrowing and which is original. (Dating discussed in text, pp. 273–5.) See also no. 17.]					
73+		Entrée [G]		Pantomime noble [G]		
	Io	Date unknown	sc.6	*La guirlande*	1751	sc.7
	[See 1st comment on no. 72.]					
74+		Pʳᵉ gavotte [G]		Les niais de Sologne [D]		
	Zéphyre	Date unknown	sc.8	*Pièces de clavessin*	1724	
	[See also no. 7.]					

Probable borrowings (See text pp. 267 and 270f.)			Origin		
75+	Musette en rondeau [E]	[Musette ?C]			
Pièces de clavessin	1724	*L'Endriague* or *pièce de viole*	1723		
[See also no. 5.]					
76+	Tembourin [*sic*] [e]	Tambourin			
Pièces de clavessin	1724	*L'Endriague*	1723	[II 9]	
[See also no. 6.]					

Appendix: Rameau's self-borrowings (*cont.*)

Probable borrowings (See text pp. 267 and 270f.)			Origin	
77+	1er Rigaudon [e]		[?d]	
Pièces de clavessin 1724			*L'Endriague* 1723	
78+	2e Rigaudon [E]		[?D]	
Pièces de clavessin 1724			*L'Endriague* 1723	
79+	Air, 'Echo, voix errante' [C]		[Air] 'Echo, voix errante'	
La princesse de Navarre 1745	II 11		*Samson* mid-1730s III 5 [1st four lines in *Samson* libretto (Paris, 1745). See also no. 40.]	

Borrowings of uncertain authenticity

80+	3e Air de Furie [F]		Air vif [C]		
Hippolyte et Aricie 1757^r or 1767^r [In F-Po A.128a, much modified for final revivals.]	II 3		*Acante et Céphise* 1751 III 2		
81+	Air gay [G]		Air, fièrement [G]		
Hippolyte et Aricie 1757^r or 1767^r [Same source as no. 80.]	III 8		*Naïs* 1749 I 7		
82	Premier menuet [G]		1er menuet [G]		
Hippolyte et Aricie 1757^r or 1767^r* [Same source as no. 80.]	III 8		*Naïs* 1749 I 8		
83+	Air, 'Au dieu des mers' [g]		Air, 'Au dieu des mers' [g]		
Hippolyte et Aricie 1757^r or 1767^r [Same source as no. 80.]	III 8		*Naïs* 1749 I 8		

Appendix: Rameau's self-borrowings (cont.)

				Borrowings of uncertain authenticity				

84

Premier tambourin [G] — P[er] tambourin [G]

Hippolyte et Aricie   1757[r] or 1767[r*]   III 8   *Naïs*   1749   I 8
[Same source as no. 80.]

85+

Gavotte légère [a] — 2e gavotte [a]

Dardanus   1760[r] or 1768[r]   V 4   *Les surprises de l'Amour*   1748   'Adonis' sc.9
[In F-Po Rés. A.145b, much modified for final revivals.]

86+

1er air vif [E] — P[er] air vif en rondeau [E]

Dardanus   1760[r] or 1768[r]   V 4   *Les surprises de l'Amour*   1748   'Adonis' sc.6
[Same source as no. 85.]

87+

2e air [e] — 2e air [e]

Dardanus   1760[r] or 1768[r]   V 4   *Les surprises de l'Amour*   1748   'Adonis' sc.6

88+

Contredanse [G] — Contredanse [G]

Les Indes galantes   1761[r] or 1770–2[r]   Prol. sc.1   *Les surprises de l'Amour*   1757[r]   'La lyre enchantée' [new version] sc.7

[In F-Po A.132a; contains additions, substitutions made at various dates. The version in *Les Indes* may even pre-date that in *Les surprises*.]

89+

Air vif [G] — P[er] air des chasseurs [G]

Les Indes galantes   1761[r] or 1770–2[r]   Prol. sc.1   *Les fêtes de Polymnie*   1745   III 2
[Same source as no. 88.]

Appendix: Rameau's self-borrowings (*cont.*)

				Borrowings of uncertain authenticity			

90

| | | Gavotte gracieuse [e] | 1er gavotte [e] | | | |

Les fêtes d'Hébé   reprise   III 7   *Zaïs*   1748   Prol. sc.3
[In F-Po A.143b, used for revivals   unknown
until 1770.]

91+

| | | 2e gavotte [E] | 2e gavotte [E] | | | |

Les fêtés d'Hebé   reprise   III 7   *Zaïs*   1748   Prol. sc.3
[Same source as no. 90.]   unknown

A musician's view of the French baroque after the advent of Gluck: Grétry's *Les trois âges de l'opéra* and its context*

M. ELIZABETH C. BARTLET

In the eighteenth century, operas went out of fashion and out of the repertory quickly in most European cities. Few audiences tolerated works more than several seasons old. An exception to this general rule was found at the Académie royale de musique (the Opéra) in Paris. Here some operas by Jean-Baptiste Lully, the favourite composer of Louis XIV, remained in the repertory a century after their premières. Several of the most popular operas by Jean-Philippe Rameau (1683–1764) held the stage for more than four decades – outlasting their author by over twenty years.

Foreign visitors found this situation puzzling. In 1789 that Gallophobe Englishman, Dr Charles Burney, for example, wrote:

[The people of] this nation [France] so frequently accused of more volatility and caprice than their neighbours, have manifested a steady persevering constancy to their Music, which the strongest ridicule and contempt of other nations could never vanquish. . . . The long and pertinacious attachment to the style of Lulli and his imitators [including Rameau] in vocal compositions, to the exclusion of those improvements which were making in the art in other parts of Europe, during the first fifty years of this century, have doubtless more impeded its progress, than want of genius in this active and lively people, or defects in their language.[1]

By 1789 Burney's remarks were, in reality, several years out of date. The French had new operatic idols – Christoph Willibald von Gluck and Niccolò Piccinni especially – and as the *surintendant du spectacle*, the government official in charge of the Opéra, pointed out the same year, the current limited repertory at the theatre resulted from the public's intolerance of old works (that is, those composed before 1770).[2] Indeed, after Gluck's first Parisian success, *Iphigénie en Aulide* (première Académie royale de musique, 19 April 1774), his supporters credited him with starting a musical revolution,[3] and many modern scholars concur, labelling his French works 'reform operas'.

* This chapter is an expanded version of a paper read at the annual meeting of the Society for Eighteenth-Century Studies, 28 April 1984. The author acknowledges with thanks Graham Sadler's helpful suggestions.

[1] *A General History of Music from the Earliest Ages to the Present Period, to which is prefixed, a Dissertation on the Music of the Ancients*, vol. IV (London, 1789), pp. 610, 607.
[2] [Denis Pierre Jean Papillon de La Ferté], *Précis sur l'Opéra et son administration et réponses à différentes objections* ([Paris, 1789]), p. 77.
[3] See especially [Gaspard Michel, *dit* Le Blond, (ed.)], *Mémoires pour servir à l'histoire de la révolution opérée dans la musique par M. le chevalier Gluck* (Naples and Paris, 1781, reprint ed., Amsterdam, 1967 and Geneva, 1984), which includes many of the Gluckistes' letters to newspapers, replies to reviews, pamphlets, etc.

During the period from 1774 (the première of *Iphigénie en Aulide*) to 1785 (the last performance of *Castor et Pollux*), attitudes towards Lully, and towards Rameau in particular, changed. This article investigates the shift in the context of rising historical consciousness by outlining the opposing views of the Ramistes and the Gluckistes (the supporters of Rameau and Gluck respectively) about the older composers in the mid-1770s, by examining a work – *Les trois âges de l'opéra* ('The Three Eras of Opera') – commissioned from André Grétry in 1778 by the Académie royale's director in an attempt to placate the factions, and finally, by summarizing the critical reception to that work and a few later contributions to the Ramiste–Gluckiste debate.

I

In the early 1770s Rameau's operas still set the genre's standards for the French, who often judged new works by comparison with those of Rameau and nearly always found the former wanting.[4] After one revival of his masterpiece, *Castor et Pollux*, the critic of the influential *Mercure de France* wrote:

> Cet Opéra qui réunit tous les moyens en quelque sorte de tous les autres Opéra, la pompe du spectacle, l'intérêt de la scène, la variété des événemens, le contraste des effets, une poësie facile & lyrique, une Musique savante & toujours gracieuse . . . enfin la Tragédie de *Castor & Pollux* fera toujours l'admiration & les délices des amateurs éclairés.[5]

> This opera that, as it were, unites all the means of all other operas: pomp of the spectacle, interest of the staging, variety in events, contrast of effects, fluent and lyric verse, music skilfully written and always graceful . . . in short, the tragedy of *Castor et Pollux* will always inspire admiration and delight in well-informed lovers of music.

Yet, his prophecy of immortality must have seemed false a dozen years later when this and all other Rameau operas disappeared from the stage of the Académie royale de musique.

Before Gluck's arrival in Paris, the librettist of *Iphigénie en Aulide* in an open letter published in the *Mercure* sought to align the composer with the Italians by citing Gluck's success in Italy (and thus to take advantage of a recent attempted revival of the 1750s *querelle des bouffons* debate,[6] the last serious challenge there

---

[4] See, for example, the review of Etienne Joseph Floquet's *L'union de l'amour et des arts* (première Académie royale de musique, 7 September 1773) in the *Journal des beaux-arts et des sciences*, Paris, February 1774, pp. 377–83. 'There is no one today who would not agree that it is to Rameau's genius that our music owes its progress: it is from him that it gained a new character suitable for creating images, for expressing feelings, and for reproducing thoughts.' Floquet suffers in the comparison: he has written a charming work, which, however, does not rise 'to the summit of art' (pp. 378–9, 383). This opera was the most successful new work at the time, although it did not remain in the repertory

long.

[5] *Mercure de France*, Paris, February 1772, p. 178.

[6] Michel Paul Gui de Chabanon's critique of *Castor et Pollux*, ibid., April 1772, pp. 159–79; partially reprinted in Charles Malherbe, 'Commentaire bibliographique', in Jean-Philippe Rameau, *Castor et Pollux*, Auguste Chapuis (ed.), Oeuvres complètes, vol. VIII (Paris, 1903), pp. cii–cvi, omitting many of the specific references to Italian music and misdated August 1778. It sparked a spirited reply from an anonymous Ramiste: *Réponse à la critique de l'opéra de Castor & observations sur la musique* ([Paris], 1773).

had been to Rameau's operatic supremacy). Du Roullet emphasized both Gluck's intention to reform Italian abuses and the composer's admiration of the French dramatic tradition.[7] This and other advance publicity prepared the audience to find a different type of opera from the Rameau norm in *Iphigénie en Aulide*. 'This new form of dramatic music' drew mixed critical reactions. As the *Mercure* noted, some found that 'the composer deviated from [the norms of] art and verisimilitude'; that is, he no longer conformed to the accepted model. Others, including the reviewer, thought *Iphigénie* 'a work of genius', in which there was a mixture of styles:

Le récitatif a paru étrange et imité des Italiens, tandis que le chant presque entièrement modulé, était dans l'ancienne simplicité françoise.[8]

The recitative seemed odd and imitative of the Italians, whereas the melody, almost always inflected [according to the text], was in the old French [intentionally] simple style.

Already, critics lauded Gluck for capturing the spirit of the French aesthetic tradition in his airs by avoiding Italianate ornamentation, extended repetition without dramatic purpose, and useless instrumental *ritornelli*. Another reviewer, generally favourable to *Iphigénie*, pointed out that some of the ideas the Gluck supporters claimed as new inventions were also found in Rameau operas.[9] Of course, Gluck's most ardent advocates emphasized the differences in this work.[10]

Gluck's next opera for Paris, *Orphée* (libretto adapted and translated by Pierre Louis Moline after *Orfeo* by Renieri Calsabigi, première Académie royale de musique, 2 August 1774), prompted specific comparisons between the two composers. The similarities in the plot between it and *Castor et Pollux* – the people's mourning, and especially, the hero's defiance of Hades to rescue someone from the Elysian Fields – invited it.

According to the *Mercure*, Rameau, the master of the dance, handled these scenes better:

Nous croyons même que la musique du Compositeur François est mieux sentie, plus appropriée, &, pour ainsi dire, plus locale que celle de M. le Chevalier Gluck. Elle est ici empruntée du genre pastoral; & il lui falloit peut-être une autre nuance.[11]

We even believe that the French composer's music is better expressed, more appropriate, and has, so to speak, more 'local' colour than that of M. le Chevalier Gluck's. [The style of the latter] is borrowed from the pastoral genre; perhaps it should have had another nuance.

---

[7] [François Louis Gand Le Bland, bailli du Roullet], Letter to M. D[auvergne], director of the Opéra, *Mercure de France*, October 1772, vol. II, pp. 169–74; reprinted in [Le Blond (ed.)], *Mémoires*, pp. 1–7; translated by Oliver Strunk, *Source Readings in Music History from Classical Antiquity through the Romantic Era* (New York, 1950), pp. 676–80.

[8] *Mercure de France*, May 1774, pp. 157–79. The recitative caused a sensation because,

unlike current French practice, it was accompanied by the orchestra throughout and ranged from *récitatif simple* to *récitatif animé* to *récitatif obligé*.

[9] *Journal des beaux-arts*, June 1774, pp. 496–500.

[10] See, for example, the report in *Correspondance littéraire, philosophique et critique par Grimm, Diderot, Raynal, Meister, etc.*, Maurice Tourneaux (ed.), vol. X (Paris, 1879), p. 416.

[11] *Mercure de France*, September 1774, p. 196.

But Gluck had his supporters; Grimm, who had taken the Italian side in the *querelle des bouffons*, made a special point of praising his noble and sustained style.[12]

Though a moderate Gluckiste, the critic of the *Journal des beaux-arts*, Jean Castilhon, found the demons' chorus and dance in *Castor* superior.[13] Yet he avoided prolonged comparison and concluded with a dismissal of the current insulting 'demi-Castor' epithet for *Orphée*, stating that:

> Les moyens dont Rameau & M. Gluck, se sont servis pour réussir également, sont si différents, qu'il seroit presqu'impossible d'en faire une comparaison tant soit peu exacte.[14]

> The means that Rameau and Gluck used in order to be equally successful are so different that it would be almost impossible to make a fairly exact comparison.

For Castilhon, then, both composers wrote good operas; that is, they composed works that met certain absolute aesthetic standards. He recognized differences, but these he attributed to qualities in the libretto and to the composers' personal styles.

The newspaper reviewers tried to maintain an even tone, whatever their personal convictions. Yet, several contemporaries remarked that heated debates between Ramistes and Gluckistes dominated conversations in Paris.[15] Both factions issued pamphlets that reflected the spirit of these discussions.

Though praising a few pieces in *Iphigénie en Aulide*, the Ramiste Saint-Alphonse insisted that, compared to the standards set by Rameau's *Castor et Pollux* and *Dardanus* (and Lully's *Armide*), Gluck's opera did not measure up throughout. The French composers' recitatives were 'much more moving and truer', whereas Gluck often rendered the declamation false by exaggeration. Rameau proved the importance of variety in opera. Gluck mistakenly neglected the effect of fine *divertissements* and the possibilities allowed by the *merveilleux*; his consistency in tone led to monotony. An opera should not aspire to be a pure tragedy. In conclusion, Saint-Alphonse outlined his ideal opera:

> Réunissons, s'il est possible, les talens de Quinault pour la composition du Poëme; de Lully, pour le récit débité; de Rameau, pour la danse & les choeurs; & joignons-y le génie ardent & sublime, & vraiment tragique, de l'Auteur d'*Iphigénie*, & nous pourrons hardiment avancer que nous possédons l'Ouvrage le plus parfait qui ait existé.[16]

> Let us unite, if it is possible, Quinault's talents for libretto writing; Lully's, for declaimed recitative; Rameau's, for the dances and choruses; let us join to these the fervent, sublime,

---

12 *Correspondance littéraire*, vol. x, p. 473.
13 September 1774, pp. 529–30, 533.
14 Ibid., pp. 545–6. That Gluck's opponents called *Orphée* nothing but a 'demi-Castor' was widely reported in the press and literary correspondence; see, for example, *Correspondance littéraire*, vol. x, p. 473.
15 According to the *Correspondance littéraire*, 'For the past two weeks in Paris everyone thinks and dreams only of music. It is the topic of all our debates, all our conversations, the soul of all our dinner parties; and to be interested in anything else would even seem ridiculous'. Vol. x, p. 416.
16 [Alphonse Marie Denis Devismes de Saint-Alphonse], *Lettre à Madame de ***, sur l'opéra d'Iphigénie en Aulide* (Lausanne, 1774), p. 22. See also pp. 8, 10, 11, 19–20. The pamphlet is reprinted in François Lesure (ed.), *Querelle des Gluckistes et des Piccinnistes*, vol. II (Geneva, 1984), pp. 7–27.

truly tragic genius of the author of *Iphigénie*, and we shall be able to claim boldly that we have the most perfect work that has ever existed.

Less than four months later, Saint-Alphonse wrote another pamphlet, this one on *Orphée*. He, too, compared *Orphée* and *Castor et Pollux* – to the former's disadvantage. Above all, he defended Rameau against the Gluckiste charge of inexpressivity, particularly in dramatically intense scenes, and he stressed the wider range of emotions in Rameau's scores:

Ce *Rameau* est, à la fois, le *Rubens*, & le *Corrège* de la musique, & s'il n'a jamais su arranger une partition, au moins a-t-il su arranger ses compositions sur toutes les impressions de la sensibilité. Savant, harmonieux, terrible, énergique, déchirant dans le quatrième Acte de *Zoroastre*, dans le second de *Castor*, voyez comme il est doux, tendre, sensible, voluptueux dans le quatrième Acte de *Dardanus*, dans celui de *Castor*, dans les *Indes Galantes*, dans les *Talens lyriques*. Je crois l'*Autuer d'Orphée* un très-grand Peintre, mais je crois aussi, qu'il n'a qu'une couleur, & plus je l'entends, plus je me le persuade. Il fait agiter le poignard de la Tragédie, avec une énergie vraiment sublime; mais la palette, où les grâces exercent leurs pinceaux, je doute qu'il la parcoure jamais.[17]

This Rameau is at one and the same time the Rubens and the Correggio of music, and if he never knew how to orchestrate fully [one of the Gluckiste charges], at least he knew how to adapt his compositions to all sensations of feeling. Skilful, harmonious, terrifying energetic, heart-rending in the fourth act of *Zoroastre*, in the second act of *Castor*, see how sweet, tender, sensitive, voluptuous he is in the fourth act of *Dardanus*, in the fourth act of *Castor*, in *Les Indes galantes*, in *Les talens lyriques* [*Les fêtes d'Hébé*]. I believe the author of *Orphée* to be a very great painter, but I also believe that he has only one colour, and the more I listen to him, the more I am persuaded of this. He brandishes tragedy's dagger with a truly sublime energy; but I doubt that he will ever use the palette from which the Graces fill their brushes.

In summary, the Ramistes saw in the operas of their favourite composer the embodiment of an absolute musical beauty, since they conformed to universal, and therefore, unchanging standards. They judged ahistorically; for them, the music's effect in the 1770s, as they perceived it, was all that mattered.

Gluck, too, had eloquent and active champions. Moline, his collaborator for *Orphée*, was one of the most strident critics of Lully and Rameau. His contribution to the debate takes the form of an imagined dialogue in the Elysian Fields between the two French composers.[18] In it, each lauds his own achievements and often speaks slightingly of the efforts of the other.[19] In both, Gluckiste points are raised. Thus, Rameau congratulates himself on a profound knowledge of harmony, while belittling Lully's too simple melodic declamation. Lully

---

[17] [Saint-Alphonse], *Lettre à M. le chevalier de M ***, sur l'opéra d'Orphée* (Lausanne and Paris, 1774), pp. 21–2. See also pp. 5–9, 17–19. The pamphlet is reprinted in *Querelle*, vol. II, pp. 79–106.

[18] [Pierre Louis Moline], *Dialogue entre Lulli, Rameau et Orphée dans les Champs Elisées* (Amsterdam and Paris, 1774).

[19] In real life, Rameau expressed high regard for Lully; for example, he described Armide's monologue, 'Enfin il est en ma puissance', as

music of genius and fine expression in his *Code* and analysed it at length in the *Nouveau systême* and *Observations*. *Code de musique pratique* (Paris, 1760), p. 168; *Nouveau systême de musique théorique* (Paris, 1726), pp. 80–90; and *Observations sur notre instinct pour la musique* (Paris, 1754), pp. 69–114. Facsimile editions of the three treatises are available in Jean-Philippe Rameau, *Complete Theoretical Writings*, Erwin R. Jacobi (ed.), vols. II–IV (n.p., 1967–9).

retorts with the charge of unnecessary erudition in Rameau's *Traité d'harmonie* and lack of expression in his operas. Lully does allow that his successor's *airs de danse* merit their popularity – this was a frequent Gluckiste concession.[20] The arrival of Orphée, who has entered this forbidden land by the artistic talent of one of Europe's most famous musicians, namely Gluck, cuts short their discussion.[21] Orphée vaunts the achievements of *Iphigénie en Aulide* and lectures Lully and Rameau on the need to abandon old rules in order to achieve greater dramatic verisimilitude. He gives them the score so that they can see 'how he [Gluck] knew how to make himself the master of the stage by the superiority of his genius, united with the force of expression'.[22] Lully frets and asks Orphée to tell him frankly what their reputations are since the success of *Iphigénie*. Orphée replies with a strongly partisan assessment:

Toutes les personnes de goût disent que M. Rameau a mis trop d'art dans son harmonie, & que vous [Lully] n'en avez pas mis assez dans votre mélodie; au lieu que l'Auteur d'Iphigénie a sçu réunir à vos sublimes talens la fraîcheur du coloris, la variété des nuances & la vérité de l'expression: en un mot, c'est par la perfection de l'art soumis à la nature qu'il a eu l'avantage de l'emporter sur vous.[23]

All people of [good] taste say that Rameau put too much art [artifice] into his harmony, and that you [Lully] did not put enough into your melody; whereas the author of *Iphigénie* knew how to combine with your sublime talents a fresh colouring, variety in nuances, and truth in expression; in a word, it is by the perfection of art obedient to nature that he had the advantage to surpass you.

Unlike the case of Lully, who is partially excused because of the defective state of music at the time he lived,[24] all Moline's judgements of Rameau are ahistorical. Instead of associating styles with different eras, this collaborator places Gluck above Rameau in an absolute aesthetic sense.

In *La soirée perdue à l'Opéra*, another ardent Gluckiste, probably abbé François Arnaud, also raised the issue of Rameau's science and its effect on his musical composition:

Quant à Rameau; ce fut sans doute, un grand homme; on ne peut lui contester la gloire d'avoir révélé le premier les secrets de l'harmonie, & enlevé la musique aux tâtonemens de la routine. Mais ce fut la profondeur même de ces connoissances dans la théorie, qui l'égara dans la pratique: trop souvent il substitua la science à l'art, & l'art au génie.[25]

As for Rameau, he was doubtless a great man; one cannot dispute his glory as the first to have revealed the secrets of harmony and raised music from the gropings of routine. But it was the very depth of his knowledge in theory which led him astray in practice: too often he substituted technique for art, and artifice for genius.

---

[20] [Moline], *Dialogue*, pp. 12–14.
[21] Ibid., pp. 23–4. The choice of character is, of course, a blatant reference to Moline's own collaboration with Gluck (no doubt the reason Moline chose to publish this pamphlet anonymously).
[22] Ibid., pp. 25–9. The frontispiece depicts this scene. Lully and Rameau seem startled by Orphée's spirited defence; while *Castor et Pollux* lies ignored on the ground, people in the background are enchanted by Gluck's

music. The engraving is reproduced (without explanation) in Paul-Marie Masson, *L'opéra de Rameau* (Paris, 1930), plate 16, opposite p. 560.
[23] [Moline], *Dialogue*, p. 30.
[24] Ibid., pp. 11–12.
[25] [François Arnaud], *La soirée perdue à l'Opéra* (Avignon and Paris, 1776), p. 8. This pamphlet is also attributed by some to another Gluckiste, Pascal Boyer. It is reprinted in [Le Blond (ed.)], *Mémoires*, pp. 46–61.

This author, too, found in Rameau's music an expressive neutrality. He sharply criticized the French opera performance tradition, which, he argued, attempted to hide the defect.[26]

The Gluckistes spoke of revolution in music, stressing their composer's genius and superiority, especially in his view of the drama in opera and its musical realization in solo recitatives and airs. They could still accept as valid models some of Rameau's pieces for their formal clarity and solid harmonic framework, but only in places, such as *divertissements*, not requiring any rapid development in dramatic action. Although they arrived at different conclusions, they held assumptions similar to those of their opponents during the early years of the debate (1774–6): music could and should be judged by absolute criteria with reference only to contemporary norms (on which, of course, they did not agree). No consideration need be given to the fact that Rameau wrote at a different time for different conditions. In short, Gluckistes and Ramistes both judged ahistorically.

II

The battle lines were clearly drawn.[27] Some accused the Ramistes of mounting a cabal against *Orphée*; others saw underhanded Gluckiste pressure in the lack of performances of *Castor et Pollux* at the Académie royale de musique in the period 1774 to 1777 and in the problems before its revival in 1778.[28] For these and other reasons, the Académie royale was in a state of crisis by the late 1770s. To try to improve matters at the theatre, the Council of State appointed a new director, Anne Pierre Jacques Devismes du Valgay.[29] At the outset Devismes concerned himself with the reforms necessary to turn the Opéra into a viable operation. He wanted to increase attendance and thereby the audience's share in contributions to revenue. Three improvements seemed to him essential: to give performances six or even seven days a week, instead of the traditional three or four; to mount new and lavish productions employing the best set and costume designers available as well as excellent materials; and to promote a varied repertory that had appeal for all the factions.[30] For the latter, he imported an Italian

[26] Ibid., p. 9: 'The performers had to do everything for the music [i.e., to make it expressive]; thus, those movements of the head, arms, eyebrows, those languorous portamentos, those feminine cadences, those *inhuman* shrieks, those sounds torn from the depths of the soul and accompanied by long rattling trills, and all that huge accumulation of affectations and simpering gestures that one had the kindness to take for *expression*.'

[27] The partisan nature of the Ramiste–Gluckiste debate sparked some satirical comment on the blindness of both sides to any merit in the other composer's music. Among the wittiest is 'L'in-promptu du Palais Royal, dialogue entre deux amateurs, Gluck et Orphée', probably by Le Fuel de Méricourt, published in *Le nouveau spectateur, ou examen des nouvelles pièces de théâtre servant de répertoire universel des specta-*

cles vol. I (1776), pp. 401–24.

[28] See, for example, *Correspondance littéraire*, vol. X, p. 472 (entry for August 1774); and [Louis Petit de Bachaumont, attrib.], *Mémoires secrets pour servir à l'histoire de la république des lettres en France, depuis MDCCLXII jusqu'à nos jours; ou journal d'un observateur*, 36 vols. (London, 1777–89), vol. XII, p. 135 (entry for 30 September 1778), and p. 154 (entry for 22 October 1778).

[29] The best study of his activities at the Opéra is Arthur Pougin, *Un directeur d'opéra au dix-huitième siècle: L'Opéra sous l'ancien régime, l'Opéra sous la Révolution* (Paris, 1914).

[30] [Jean Benjamin de Laborde], *Essai sur la musique ancienne et moderne*, 4 vols. (Paris, 1780), vol. I, pp. 401–3. (Laborde was Devismes' brother-in-law.)

troupe to perform *opera buffa* and commissioned new works from Gluck and Piccinni. Still, he did not forget the supporters of Lully and Rameau.[31] Even before the theatre opened for his first season as director (1778/9), Devismes announced his plans to stage a new French opera one day, an old one the next, an *opera buffa* the day after, and finally a ballet or concert or an evening of short works, because 'this is the way to conciliate all tastes and to allow all talents to shine'.[32]

To promote his programme, Devismes decided to commission for the reopening of the Académie royale after the Lenten closure a new work of frankly sermonizing intent. He chose as the librettist his own brother, Saint-Alphonse.[33] This selection of one who but four years earlier was an ardent Ramiste may seem somewhat surprising; however, even in 1774 Saint-Alphonse had found qualities worthy of admiration in Gluck, and by now he seemed reconciled with the 'reform' opera style. To help ensure the success of the prologue, the brothers turned to the one popular Parisian composer not directly involved in the current operatic battles: André Ernest Modeste Grétry. This decision led to *Les trois âges de l'opéra*.[34] In it, the authors supported the director's aim to placate the warring factions by a re-evaluation of views on French baroque music and Gluck's place in the continuation of the French lyric tradition. In other words, Gluck, in some sense, appeared as the heir of Lully and Rameau.[35]

[31] On views of Lully and the performance of his music in the eighteenth century, see Herbert Schneider, *Die Rezeption der Opern Lullys im Frankreich des Ancien Régime* (Tutzing, 1982), especially chapter D; Lois Rosow, 'Lully's *Armide* at the Paris Opéra: a Performance History: 1686–1766' (unpubl. PhD diss., Brandeis University, 1981); and William Weber, '*La musique ancienne* in the Waning of the Ancien Régime', *Journal of Modern History*, LVI (1984), pp. 58–88.

[32] *Mercure de France*, January 1778, p. 168. Although the repertory was varied during his tenure as director, it did not exactly follow the pattern stated here. *Opéra buffa* proved unpopular, as did revivals of older works with the exception of *Castor et Pollux* (see below).

[33] Saint-Alphonse was a tax farmer, an officer in the artillery, a reader for the prince de Condé, and an amateur *littérateur*. Neither of his revisions of libretti (Lemonnier's *Hellé*, set by Floquet, and Quinault's *Amadis de Gaule*, set by Johann Christian Bach) was successful. See Pougin, *Un directeur*, pp. 40–1. In spite of his efforts, Saint-Alphonse could not persuade the Opéra to perform his three other works (a revision of La Motte's *Omphale*, and *Daphnis et Thémire* and *Osroès*, set by Louis Joseph Saint-Amans). See the documents, Paris, Archives Nationales [F-Pan], O¹ 614, vol. III, pp. 77–8; O¹ 620, nos. 38 and 112.

[34] The main sources for this opera are two MS scores: F-Po, A. 249, 77 fos. (mostly autograph) (originally entitled 'Le génie de

l'opéra'); and F-Pn Vm. (5) 202, 62 fos. (missing part of scene iii) (entitled 'Les trois âges de la musique'); and the printed libretto: *Les trois âges de l'opéra, prologue; représenté pour la première fois, par l'Académie-Royale de Musique, le lundi 27 avril 1778, suivie de l'acte de Flore* (Paris, 1778). In the F-Po MS, all the newly composed music and most of the borrowed pieces that required arrangement of more than the text are in Grétry's hand. Copyists, following instructions, filled in the rest, including the Lully duo, all the choruses and dances except the instrumental marches, and part of the Rameau air, and recopied two pages of recitative for clarity. The MS has numerous changes, mostly from the time of rehearsals. The F-Pn MS is a fair copy of the final version of the F-Po score (with some variants, principally rhythmic). It also has full realization of some passages in the prologue presented in an abbreviated form in the F-Po score (except for the dances where only incipits are given). It was prepared by a court copyist, probably the year of the première. The modern edition in the *Collection complète des oeuvres de Grétry*, vol. XLVI, Sylvain Dupuis (ed.), is a confused and inaccurate conflation of the two MS sources, in which the revisions in the autograph especially are misunderstood. Unless otherwise indicated, all examples below are taken from the final version as presented in the F-Po score.

[35] Originally Saint-Alphonse had planned to include the *bouffons* in the final scene, but as

In the first scene, the presiding Génie de l'Opéra summons the Artistic Talents, who contribute to the splendour of the genre, and the three muses who protect its creators. Saint-Alphonse counted on his audience to recognize the clear symbolism. For the eighteenth-century French, the word 'muse' derived from the Greek word meaning one who explained mysteries 'because they [the muses] taught men very interesting and important matters, which are beyond the understanding of common people'.[36] Furthermore, muses could perceive the past, present, and future. Their presence as central figures is, thus, appropriate for a work celebrating the history of opera, a genre that in France usually offered subjects deliberately chosen from outside the mundane and embellished by the *merveilleux*. The Génie evoked the muses most closely associated with the genre: Polymnie, the inventor of harmony; Melpomène, the patron of tragedy; and Terpsichore, the muse of dance. Each sings a solo illustrating her special gifts. Polymnie offers an Italianate air with the typical flourishes for words like 'triomphe': her victory results from 'pleasure's charm'. Melpomène's *récitatif obligé* in the Gluckian mould emphasizes her power to astonish. Terpsichore's air presents a pair of stylized dances (the first returns with variation and new text after the second, resulting in the standard ternary form). The choice is a suitable one for Terpsichore, the muse who 'knows how to charm and to please without the attraction of speech'. Grétry included a part for obbligato flute, an instrument frequently depicted in representations of Terpsichore. In a trio, all three promise to join forces for the sake of art.

In the second scene, Polymnie, who promotes the study of history, introduces Lully as one of her favourites. As the muse of oratory and eloquence, she becomes the natural advocate for this composer, still admired for his mastery of lyric declamation. She points out that:

. . .dans ces lieux C'est lui qui fonda ma puissance,	. . .in this place He was the one who laid the foun- dations of my power,
Et je lui dois trop de reconnoissance, Pour ne pas la prouver en ces momens heureux.	And I owe him too much, Not to show it at this happy time.

'Reconnoissance' for past achievements becomes the key word in the Lully scene. The composer regrets the imperfections of the musical resources of his time (echoing the remarks of Moline and others), but insists that since he introduced music (that is, opera) to the French, he merits some consideration. Although the Génie de l'Opéra reassures Lully that he will always be 'one of the models for the stage', Lully is depicted as resigned to the fact that his best days, the period of his fame, are gone: 'In turn all passes; such is fate's law', he sings.

he himself stated in the preface to the libretto, such a reference would have been foreign to the opera (and thus damaging to the unity of the work required by French dramaturgy). The F-Po score has remnants of this scene on fos. 73v–75r.

[36] For the current definitions of the muses cited here, see *Encyclopédie, ou dictionnaire raisonné des sciences, des arts et des métiers*, 17 vols. (Paris and Neufchâtel, 1751–80), vol. x, pp. 894–5 (s.v. 'Muses'), p. 323 (s.v. 'Melpomène'); vol. xii, p. 944 (s.v. 'Polyhymnie ou Polymnie'); vol. xvi, p. 162 (s.v. 'Terpsichore'); all are by Louis de Jaucourt.

Table 1 *Borrowed music in* Les trois âges de l'Opéra

Piece in *Les trois âges*	Composer	Work, Act: Scene	Original piece
Scene 2			
Marche for Lully and his suite (characters from his most famous operas: Renaud, Phaëton, Atys, Armide, Médée, Sangaride)	Lully	*Thésée* (1675), 2:6	Premier air for the triumphal entry of Thésée sung by the chorus of Athenians, 'Que l'on doit estre', LWV 51/39
Air for Lully: 'Faites grâce à mon âge en faveur de ma gloire'	Lully	*Thésée* (1675), 1:8	Air for King Egeus: 'Faites grâce à mon âge en faveur de ma gloire', LWV 51/26
Duo for Lully and one of his followers: 'Pour le peu de bon tems qui nous reste'	Lully	*Thésée* (1675), 2:6	Duo for two old men: 'Pour le peu de bon temps qui nous resté', LWV 51/42
Marche for everyone: 'Que l'on doit être'	Lully	*Thésée* (1675), 2:6	As première air cited above
Scene 3			
Annonce and two gavottes for the entry of Rameau and his suite (characters from his most famous operas: Castor, Zoroastre, Dardanus, Thélaire, Mélite [Amélite], Iphise)	Rameau	*Castor et Pollux* (rev. of 1754), 3:4	Two gavottes for Hébé's followers, the Celestial Pleasures
Air for Rameau: 'Des effets de l'harmonie'	Rameau	*Hippolyte et Aricie* (1733), prologue:5	Two gavottes for Amour and the chorus of forest inhabitants: 'A l'Amour rendez les armes'
Choeur en rondeau for everyone: 'Suivés les loix'	Rameau	*Les fêtes d'Hébé* (1739), 3ᵉ entrée, 'La danse':7	Choeur en rondeau for Terpsichore and her followers: 'Suivés les loix'
Annonce	Rameau	*Les fêtes d'Hébé* (1739), 3ᵉ entrée, 'La danse':7	Entrée for Terpsichore and her followers (first four bars only)
Choeur for Rameau's suite and Artistic Talents: 'Du beau génie'	Rameau	*Les Indes galantes*, nouvelle entrée (1736), 'Les sauvages':6	Rondeau for Zima, Adario, and chorus of savages: 'Forests paisibles'
Scene 4			
Instrumental introduction to récitatif	Gluck	*Iphigénie en Aulide* (1774)	Opening of the overture's second section
Récitatif obligé for Melpomène (and Artistic Talents): 'La haine, la pitié, la tendresse, l'horreur . . . Un mortel a surpris mes secrets'	Gluck	*Armide* (1777), 1:4	Quotation from the récitatif obligé for Aronte, Armide, and her supporters: 'Un guerrier indomptable les a délivrés tous'
Choeur for everyone: 'Chantés, célébrés votre reine'	Gluck	*Iphigénie en Aulide* (1774), 2:3	Choeur for Achille and the Thessalians: 'Chantés, célébrés votre reine'

Divertissement

1. Menuet	Lully	*Thésée* (1675), 4:7	Menuet for a shepherd and his companions: 'L'amour plaist malgré ses peines', LWV 51/67
2. La mariée [et le marié]	Lully	*Les noces de village* (1663), 1re entrée	Entrée for the bride and groom, LWV 19/3
3. Gigue	Rebel and Francoeur	*Pirame & Thisbé* (1726), 2:4	Air and rondeau for the Egyptians
4. Ariette and choeur for the Génie de l'Opéra (and Artistic Talents): 'Muses, j'implore vos bienfaits'	Grétry	–	Newly composed
5. Two gavottes	Rameau	*Les fêtes d'Hébé* (1739), 3e entrée, 'La danse':6	Two gavottes en rondeau for Eglé and shepherds
6. Polonnoise	Rameau	*Les Indes galantes* (1735), prologue:2	Air polonois for two Poles
7. Menuet	Gluck	*Orphée* (1774), 3:3	Menuet in the final divertment
8. Gigue	Grétry	*Céphale et Procris* (1773), 2:5	Gigue for Aurora's followers
9. Two tambourins	Grétry	*Céphale et Procris* (1773), 1:5	Two tambourins for Diane's nymphs
10. Marche	Rameau	*Castor et Pollux* (rev. of 1754), 2:4	Marche for the triumphal entry of Pollux and his men

As table 1 shows, throughout this scene Grétry and Saint-Alphonse incorporated contrafacta of several pieces from Lully's *Thésée*.[37] The choice of opera was not fortuitous; Devismes staged this work later in the season. In the solos' original context, old men sang of respect for age, of the virtues experience offers, and of the pleasure in life still possible for the old.[38] In general outline Saint-Alphonse preserved in *Les trois âges* the spirit of the original, as a comparison of the air's verses demonstrates:

Thésée	*Les trois âges de l'opéra*
Faites grâce à mon âge en faveur de ma gloire,	Faites grâce à mon âge en faveur de ma gloire;
Voyez le prix du rang qui vous est destiné;	Voyez tous les plaisirs que j'ai sçû préparer;
La vieillesse sied bien sur un front couronné,	La vieillesse offre encore des traits à révérer,
Quand on y voit briller l'éclat de la victoire.	Quand les plus beaux lauriers attestent sa victoire.
Excuse my age because of my glory,	Excuse my age because of my glory,
See it as the price of the rank intended for you,	See all the pleasures which I knew how to prepare;
Old age becomes a crowned brow,	Old age still offers features to be revered,
When one sees shining there the brilliancy of victory.	When the most beautiful laurels bear witness to its victory.

Lully's triumphal march to welcome back a victorious hero in *Thésée* becomes one to honour 'a master whose laws are cherished' in *Les trois âges*. The Artistic Talents close the scene with the wish that:

Qu'à jamais dure sa gloire,	May his glory last forever,
Et qu'au Temple de Mémoire,	And may in the Temple of Memory,
Des lauriers toujours nouveaux	Forever fresh laurels
Soient le prix de ses travaux.	Be the reward for his labours.

In the third scene, Terpsichore's favourite, Rameau, arrives. Whereas Lully received the deference due a respected old man, whose contribution to art, though considerable, is now decidedly dated, the welcome for Rameau has a more contemporary ring. Indeed, the lines assigned the Génie de l'Opéra reflect the Ramistes' position of timeless beauty found in their composer's music

[37] In his autograph, Grétry abbreviated the march by writing out only the first violin and bass line, though clearly this was meant to stand for the full string scoring (as in the modern edition). The composer was careful to notate as dotted-quaver – semiquaver the *notes inégales* of the original and to include here and in other numbers the old-fashioned ornamentation appropriate to the performance of French baroque music (unfortunately, these indications are often omitted in the edition). For the air, Grétry added a four-bar introduction (later deleted) and altered the rhythm slightly for the sake of the declamation. Except for the addition of a filler part (in the violin, not viola as transcribed in the edition) and instrumental doubling of the voices, the duo is very close to the original as printed.

[38] When Gossec later reset the *Thésée* libretto (première Académie royale de musique, 1 March 1782), he also reworked Lully's music for 'Faites grâce à mon âge'.

(despite reference to 'progress' – a word of significance for later views of Rameau, as we shall see below):

Est-ce vous, immortel Rameau?	Is that you, immortal Rameau?
De la Scène lyrique, appui	The lasting support of the
toujours durable,	lyric stage,
Venez jouir d'un triomphe nouveau	Come enjoy a new triumph.
Vos Choeurs savans, pompeux, &	Your skilful, stately choruses,
votre Danse aimable,	and your pleasant dance,
Quels que soient les progrès	Whatever the progress of which
dont l'art sera capable,	art is capable,
Vous placeront toujours dans	Will always place you in the
le rang le plus beau.	highest rank.

Significantly the Génie de l'Opéra chooses to single out the dances and choruses – pieces in Rameau operas that Saint-Alphonse (and others) particularly admired (see table 1). Rameau rather petulantly complains that, because of his research in harmony, he stands accused of lacking melody and inspiration. As we have seen, this was a Gluckiste charge, but now it is flatly denied. Again, the authors of *Les trois âges* assigned the Génie de l'Opéra the role of spokesman:

Vous, Rameau, sans Mélodie!	You, Rameau, without melody!
Eh! qui l'osa dire jamais!	Who ever dared to say that!
. . .	. . .
Grand Rameau, vous serez	Great Rameau, you will be
long-tems	for a long time
De vos successeurs le modèle.	Your successors' model.
Allez, soyez sûr que le tems,	Be reassured that the
	passage of time,
Loin de nuire jamais à vos rares	Far from harming your
talens,	exceptional gifts,
Ne fera qu'ajoûter encore	Will only add further
A l'éclat des lauriers	To the brilliancy of the
brillans	splendid laurels
Qu'a pour vous cueillis	Which Terpsichore has gathered
Terpsichore.	for you.

Everyone expresses their admiration for the composer by singing two of his choruses. For the first, Saint-Alphonse kept the original text: its moral, 'Follow the laws, which Love himself has dictated to us', seemed entirely appropriate for the affection that many Frenchmen still felt for Rameau's music. The second has a new text in praise of the composer (note that Lully's muse has also blessed Rameau with her gifts):

Du beau génie	Of the fine genius
Que Polymnie	That Polymnie
Se plût à couronner de ses	Was pleased to endow with
rares bienfaits,	her unusual blessings,
Chantons la gloire.	Let us celebrate the fame.
Que sa mémoire	May the memory of him
Pour nous soit à jamais le	Be ever for us the sign of
gage des succès.	success.

I shall return to the significance of these specific pieces in Grétry's opera, and his changes to them after a brief survey of the rest of the prologue.

Finally, in the fourth scene, Melpomène, the most important muse and the mistress of dramatic art, takes up the cause of Gluck, who does not appear on stage (that would have been a violation of French convention because he was still living). Without naming the composer directly, but identifying him by quotations from his music, Melpomène extols Gluck's ability to depict a wide range of passions from hate to pity, tenderness to horror, jealous love and plaintive innocence, and so on. The text is reminiscent of Armide's famous monologue, 'Enfin, il est en ma puissance' (*Armide*, Act II, scene v). Grétry, who had written only basso continuo accompaniment for the recitatives of Lully and Rameau[39] and chordal string support (*récitatif simple*) for the Génie de l'Opéra, took the opportunity to include here a vigorous *récitatif obligé* clearly modelled on Gluck's which had so stunned French audiences. The passage reaches its climax when Melpomène confesses that 'a mortal has discovered unexpectedly my secrets'. At this point, Grétry presents a quotation from Gluck's most recent opera, *Armide* (to Quinault's libretto originally set by Lully). Just as Renaud emerged victorious against impressive odds, so too has Gluck triumphed in his field.[40] Melpomène then calls for a performance of Gluck's 'Chantés, célébrés votre reine'. According to the muse, this chorus, always pleasing to the French, not only offers a tribute to the composer, but also serves as a touching homage to the Opéra's most influential patron, the queen, Marie-Antoinette.[41]

At the suggestion of the Génie de l'Opéra, the work concludes with a *divertissement* portraying the different eras of ballet. Except for a newly composed solo air requesting the muses' continued blessings on the arts for the delight of men, Grétry selected dances from a variety of works and, but for the last, arranged them in chronological order by composer. Lully is represented not only by a piece from *Thésée*, but also by 'La mariée', perhaps his best-known dance in the late eighteenth century (it appears in several *divertissements* of the 1770s and 1780s in Gossec's arrangement: F-Po Recueil XI (MS copy with autograph corrections)). A gigue from a François Rebel and François Francoeur opera is a compliment to the reputation of these two mid-century Opéra directors. Even though Gluck often drew criticism for his ballet music,[42] the nature of the subject required his representation: Grétry chose the charming menuet from *Orphée*. Grétry also included two of his own dances from his most recent work for the Académie royale de musique. Rameau, the master of the dance, has three

---

[39] By 1778 such recitatives were decidedly old-fashioned. Grétry himself adopted the modern recitative procedures for *Andromaque*, the opera he was then composing (première Académie royale de musique, 6 June 1780).

[40] Contemporaries recognized the reference and praised Grétry for the aptness of the quotation. See, for example, the *Journal de Paris* 28 April 1778, p. 471. Grétry rewrote the solo line to adapt the passage to the new text and simplified the parts of the lower strings; still, the quotation is unmistakable. The citation from the overture, too, is exact, although it is more fully scored in *Les trois âges*.

[41] There are no musical differences. The original text was slightly altered to make the compliment even more obvious.

[42] See, for example, the *Journal des beaux-arts* (May 1774), pp. 374–5.

numbers – more than anyone else – the last having pride of place as the final piece of *Les trois âges*.[43]

Returning to the third scene, we can glean further information about the authors' view of Rameau in the late 1770s. Although throughout this scene Rameau's achievements appear in a favourable light, and just a few years earlier the librettist was an avowed Ramiste, the authors have, in fact, accepted the Gluckiste analysis as their starting-point. To be sure, Grétry and Saint-Alphonse differ on the interpretation and evaluation of it from the Gluckistes. For the Ramistes, the dances offered but one praiseworthy aspect of the composer's *oeuvre*. The Ramistes also stressed the beauty of solo airs and dramatic recitatives while the Gluckistes dismissed these as inexpressive. Grétry borrowed only *airs de danse* from Rameau scores, even adapting a pair of gavottes as a solo air.[44] The choruses, too, are *choeurs dansés* in the original. The selection of some specific pieces helps to underline the dominance of the theme of Rameau's association with the dance. The first pair of gavottes comes from *Castor et Pollux*, an opera praised for the superiority of its *divertissements*. In that work, they appear in the scene where the Celestial Pleasures through dance try to entice the hero away from his resolution to challenge Hades. Even more significant is the presence of three items from the third entrée of *Les fêtes d'Hébé* – a celebration of the dance – for these are all associated with Terpsichore, the muse sponsoring the composer in *Les trois âges*.

Some Gluckistes grudgingly admired Rameau's theoretical contribution in harmony, but not his practical application, which they judged to be too academic. In spite of his own aversion to treatises,[45] Grétry set out to emphasize the positive side of Rameau's theoretical understanding for his composing. For Grétry, the art/artifice dichotomy was a false one. In his *Mémoires*, he wrote:

En effet, *Rameau* fut un des plus grands harmonistes de notre siècle. Il fit des choeurs magnifiques, où l'harmonie non-seulement est savante, mais très-expressive. . . . Son harmonie servira de modèle, parce que le cachet du maître y est empreint.[46]

Indeed, Rameau was one of the greatest harmonists of our century. He wrote magnificent choruses, in which the harmony is not only erudite, but very expressive. . . . His harmony will serve as a model, because the stamp of the master is impressed on it.

To accompany Rameau's entry in *Les trois âges*, Grétry chose a pair of gavottes whose thematic material is little more than a strong harmonic progression with

---

[43] Because nos. 1–3 and 5–9 contained no musical changes, the F-Po score abbreviated them as either the first violin part or a short score. No. 4 was newly composed and therefore is present in autograph in this source. No. 10 is a special case to be discussed below.

[44] In Rameau, these gavottes are played first by the orchestra and then sung by the soloist accompanied by the basso continuo with the chorus and orchestra on the repeats. Grétry later wrote that he much admired Rameau's ballet music. See *Mémoires, ou essais sur la musique*, 3 vols. (Paris, an V [1797]; reprinted New York, 1971), vol. I, p. 427.

[45] According to the composer, 'After having read the harmony treatises by Tartini, Zarlino, Rameau and d'Alembert, I said to myself: "That's surely enough theory." Before practice exhausts all these rules and these boundless calculations, there is enough to keep artists busy for several centuries. May only this accumulation of erudition give us a melodic phrase that arouses a tender sensation consoling for sensitive souls!' Ibid., p. 419.

[46] Ibid., pp. 427–8.

emphasis on and prolongation of the tonic chord: much of the fastest moving part (in the violins of the first gavotte) presents arpeggiations of the tonic. These gavottes are atypical for Rameau: most of his dances of this type have clearly defined melodic interest as well as well-crafted harmonic structure. Compare the opening of the first gavotte in *Castor et Pollux* quoted in *Les trois âges* (example 1a) to that of another gavotte, also at a sprightly tempo, written for the same Rameau opera and more representative of his usual style (example 1b). By his choice, Grétry sought to prove not only Rameau's mastery of harmony, but also the fine musical results that he obtained because of it, even when he chose to elevate it to the thematic foreground.[47]

Example 1a The opening of the first gavotte from *Castor et Pollux* used in *Les trois âges de l'opéra*

Example 1b The opening of the gavotte from Act IV, scene vi of *Castor et Pollux* (based on the MS parts, F-Po, Fonds La Salle 23)

[47] In *Les trois âges*, the versions are identical to Rameau's originals.

The director doubtless influenced the choice of the Lully opera quoted in *Les trois âges*, but more Rameau works remained in the current repertory. Grétry selected pieces from some of his most popular operas performed during the 1770s – *Les fêtes d'Hébé*, *Les Indes galantes*, and *Castor et Pollux*. The less popular *Hippolyte et Aricie*, last given in 1767 before Grétry came to Paris, may have been chosen for a symbolic reason: to show the older composer's steadfast championing of his art – the subject of 'Des effets de l'harmonie' – the authors wanted music from this, Rameau's first opera, one that had generated criticism of him as too learned even at the première.[48] (On the other hand, these gavottes had entered the repertory of opéra-comique *timbres* and were, therefore, well known.) Whereas the originals of Lully's passages were for characters closely paralleling the portrayal of the composer in *Les trois âges*, and thus the librettist could keep several lines the same or almost the same, the originals of Rameau's passages lack this dramatic correspondence: the text of 'Des effets de l'harmonie' shows the metrical equivalence necessary for parody, but complete disregard for the mood set in Rameau.[49]

Hippolyte et Aricie	*Les trois âges*
A l'Amour rendez les armes;	Des effets de l'harmonie
Donnez-lui tous vos momens.	J'ai cherché les tons divers.
Chérissez jusqu'à mes larmes;	On reproche à mon génie
Mes allarmes ont des charmes;	D'être sec, sans mélodie,
Tout est doux pour les Amans.	Et sauvage dans ses airs.
La tranquille indifférence	Des accords que l'âme inspire,
N'a que d'ennuyeux plaisirs.	Si j'ai mal connu l'emploi,
Mais, quels biens l'Amour dispense	Est-ce à moi de vous le dire?
Pour prix des premiers soûpirs!	Soumis tous deux à ma loi,
Il fait naître l'espérance,	Dardanus et Télaïre
Aussi-tôt que les désirs.	Vous répondront mieux que moi.
Lay down your arms before Love,	In the matter of harmony's effects
Give him all your time!	I searched for the varied [combinations of] sounds.
	My genius is criticized
Cherish even the tears [he causes]	For being dry, unmelodic,
His alarms have charms,	And barbarous in the airs.
Everything is sweet for lovers.	
	If, of chords inspired by the soul,
Calm coolness	I misjudged the use,
Has only boring pleasures.	Is it up to me to tell you so?
But what benefits Love gives	

[48] The controversy is mentioned in the generally favourable review in the *Mercure de France*, October 1733, pp. 2248–9. See also the later *Lettre de M. de *** à Madame de *** sur les opéra de Phaëton et Hyppolite et d'Aricie* ([Paris], 1743), pp. 13–14. The question is examined in Paul-Marie Masson, 'Lullistes et Ramistes, 1733–1752', *L'année musicale* I (1911), pp. 187–211.

[49] This contravenes Grétry's normal practice in parodying; usually he scrupulously maintained the same spirit in the new piece as in the model. For an example of his self-parody, see M. Elizabeth C. Bartlet, 'Politics and the Fate of *Roger et Olivier*, a Newly Recovered Opera by Grétry', *Journal of the American Musicological Society*, XXXVII (1984), pp. 108–14.

At the cost of first sighs!	Since both are under my control,
He causes hope to arise	Dardanus and Télaïre
At the same time as desire.	Will answer you better than I.[50]

Grétry viewed some of Rameau's melodies as vague, that is, expressively neutral.[51] Through his changes to the *Hippolyte et Aricie* gavottes, he sought to make them emotionally specific by his standards and thus suitable for *Les trois âges*. Instead of the original spritely dance, 'Des effets de l'harmonie' has a plaintive quality, partly because of the tempo marking, 'lentement'. The bass voice, replacing the soprano solo, and a transposition downward make the tessitura lower and darker, and therefore, by eighteenth-century aesthetic standards more dismal.[52] For the orchestral accompaniment, Grétry used the two parts, first violin and bass (published by Rameau for the dance version and the choral repetition after the solo), and added to them a new second violin part, which acts as a filler, in the first section. Minor alterations in rhythm and ornamentation help the text setting (see examples 2a and 2b).

Example 2a The opening of the soprano solo of 'A l'Amour rendez les armes' from *Hippolyte et Aricie* (based on the 1733 printed score)

Example 2b The opening of 'Des effets de l'harmonie' from *Les trois âges de l'opéra*

[50] Dardanus is the hero in Rameau's opera of the same name (1739, revised 1744), and Télaïre is the heroine of *Castor et Pollux* (1737, revised 1754).

[51] As he later wrote, 'The turns of phrase in his vocal line have become antiquated, but such will always be the fate of all indefinite melody.' *Mémoires*, vol. i, p. 427.

[52] For the *annonce* from *Les fêtes d'Hébé*, transposition has the opposite effect. To make the piece even brighter, Grétry put the upper strings up a perfect fourth and reorchestrated it to put greater weight on the melody (now played by the flute and first and second violins); divided violas take over the second violin and viola parts of Rameau's dance.

The most important change was Grétry's decision to almost double the size of the middle section (in minor) for the second verse (that of *Les trois âges* is now sung twice). To accomplish this, he inserted ten bars between Rameau-based sections (example 3). Here Grétry was careful to use some motives related to Rameau's rhythms, and harmonic progressions similar to those of the older composer's and intentionally archaic ornamentation. Although Rameau's original is

Example 3 The opening of the minor section of 'Des effets de l'harmonie' from *Les trois âges de l'opéra* (the clarinet doubling the voice and the viola doubling the cello to bar 17 are omitted)

to be preferred, Grétry made a conscious effort to adapt his style to the older
composer's. Example 4 gives a portion of the continuation of the second section
based on original Rameau material. Grétry generally intended his modifications
to match the music to the mood of the text.

Example 4 The continuation of the minor section of 'Des effets de l'harmonie'
(based on Rameau material) from *Les trois âges* (the inner string part missing
from the short score in the F-Po MS is supplied from Rameau's original
as in the MS parts, F-Po, Fonds La Salle 46)

The emphasis on the chorus contributes to the larger plan. To remind the
audience of Rameau's superiority in such pieces, the Génie de l'Opéra calls on
the Artistic Talents to perform 'Suivés les lois'.[53] Grétry chose to end the third
scene with his own favourite, the famous rondeau from *Les sauvages*.[54] The next
scene presents, after a bow to Gluck's novel recitative style, an extensive quotation from his *oeuvre* – a dramatically static chorus – the type of piece that, according to some critics and the composer himself, owed much to the French
model.[55] *Les trois âges* emphasizes the connection; by it, Saint-Alphonse and
Grétry intentionally reinforced the view that in some ways, Gluck continued the
Lully–Rameau lyric tradition. By 1778, Gluck became naturalized in the sight
of many French opera-goers in a way that Piccinni, in spite of his popularity,
never was.[56]

[53] Except for continuing the oboe line (doubling the first violin) in the solo passages,
Grétry maintained Rameau's version (with
its ornamentation, unfortunately sometimes
omitted in the modern edition).

[54] Grétry, *Mémoires*, vol. III, pp. 448–9. For *Les
trois âges*, Grétry kept Rameau's orchestral
part (the short score for strings only in the
F-Po MS is correctly realized for strings with
woodwinds doubling in the F-Pn MS, unfortunately not indicated in the modern edition); because of the new text, he was obliged
to change the rhythm, the ornamentation,

and in one place the phrasing, more than in
the other borrowed numbers.

[55] See, for example, the *Mercure de France*, 6 July
1782, p. 42.

[56] In the late 1770s, even some Piccinnistes
viewed Gluck within the French tradition,
although, according to them, this was a fault.
See, for example, [Jean François Marmontel],
Essai sur les révolutions de la musique en France
([Paris], 1777), pp. 10–11, 19–21, 25. This
pamphlet is reprinted with editorial commentary in footnotes in [Le Blond (ed.)],
Mémoires, pp. 153–90.

Grétry's final homage to his French predecessors, the *divertissement*, highlights baroque composers. Indeed, this part of the Rameau repertoire remained in current use during the 1770s and 1780s. *Divertissements* by other musicians often included at least one of his dances. The final number is a special case. Grétry's autograph shows that he originally intended the march to represent the French tradition as a whole, to be a summing up of the moral of *Les trois âges de l'opéra*. To accomplish this aim, he used as the basis the triumphal march from *Castor et Pollux*, which he scored more fully. To it, he added a two-bar introduction using the main theme from the *Thésée* march; the piccolo, oboes, and clarinets have its continuation with modifications after the rest of the orchestra enters (see example 5). The second section is treated in a similar fashion: the woodwinds have

Example 5 The original version of the Marche, no. 10 of the *divertissement* of *Les trois âges de l'opéra* (the timpani part is omitted)

Thésée or imitation-*Thésée* material while the strings play the *Castor et Pollux* march. Although in the abstract, the plan has a symbolic logic, in practice the idea is not successful. The marches are in different keys: a minor for Lully's and C major for Rameau's. The combination results in a tonally odd and unsatisfactory binary form because of the first section that starts in a minor and ends on G as the dominant of C major (the second section, as usual, moves from G to C major). Grétry rejected his experiment and corrected the autograph to remove the Lullian references.[57] Thus, in the end, the last word or, in this case, music is Rameau's.

To sum up Grétry's attitude to his task in *Les trois âges de l'opéra*, the composer himself makes a good spokesman. In a public letter to the *Journal de Paris* (an influential newspaper that frequently supported Gluck), he wrote:

[57] The F-Pn MS correctly identifies the final version as the march from *Castor et Pollux* and gives only the incipit. The modern edition presents Grétry's original and labels it as (only) the march from *Thésée*.

Quelques personnes me reprochent, dit-on, de m'être occupé de cet Ouvrage du moment. Mais lorsqu'il s'agissoit de la gloire de l'Art que je cultive, pouvois-je refuser mes efforts pour y contribuer, & n'étoit-ce pas une heureuse occasion de payer mon tribut d'admiration au génie et aux talens de ces illustres Artistes, sur le Théâtre même de leur renommée?[58]

Some people, it is said, criticize me for bothering with this ephemeral work. But since it concerned the glory of the art that I practise, how could I refuse my efforts to contribute to it, and was it not a fortunate opportunity to pay my tribute of admiration to the genius and talents of those illustrious composers in the very theatre of their fame?

III

By most accounts, *Les trois âges de l'opéra* was a success. Whereas occasional prologues usually received one or two performances, this prologue was presented a dozen times in all – a surprising total – and the gate receipts were quite good.[59] In spite of some reservations, notably about the depiction of Rameau as a complainer,[60] most critics applauded the work for its choice of subject.[61] They generally accepted the thesis of three revolutions in French opera credited to Lully, Rameau, and Gluck, and several singled out for special praise the new director's programme:

Ce Prologue est ingénieux, & ne pouvoit mieux annoncer le zèle & l'intelligence de la nouvelle Administration, qui s'occupe de multiplier & de varier les Spectacles & les plaisirs de la Scène lyrique.[62]

This prologue is ingenious and could not better demonstrate the zeal and intelligence of the new administration, which is dedicated to increasing and varying the works and the delights of the lyric stage.

The challenge for Grétry was duly noted, and the reviewer of the *Mercure de France* expressed the consensus:

La Musique nouvelle de ce Prologue, est de la composition de M. Grétry qui a su plier, avec autant d'adresse que de franchise, son génie à tous les genres de Musique qu'il célébroit, & en saisir avec tant de vérité les formes, &, pour ainsi dire, le costume, qu'il est impossible de ne pas s'y méprendre.[63]

[58] 9 May 1778, p. 515; reprinted with minor inaccuracies in Georges de Froidcourt (ed.), *La correspondance générale de Grétry* (Brussels, 1962), p. 99.
[59] Although gate receipts must be used with caution (for they do not include revenue from the boxes), they are, nevertheless, a good barometer of the popularity of an opera. When they fell below a certain level (2000 *livres* during this period), the theatre administration often suspended the work. Because admission prices stayed fairly steady from 1778 to 1785, they are a useful measurement of the rise and fall in popularity from season to season. *Les trois âges* earned on average 2752 *livres* (compared to a daily average of 2446 *livres* for the first five months of Devismes' administration). It was last performed on 14 June 1778. F-Po usuel 201 vol. vi ('Journal des entrées journalières').
[60] See, for example, *Affiches, annonces et avis divers*, Paris, 6 May 1778, p. 72.
[61] Only two were lukewarm: the Gluckiste, Friedrich Melchoir Grimm, and the Piccinniste, Jean François de La Harpe. Their remarks are found in MS literary correspondence of limited circulation in the eighteenth century. *Correspondance littéraire, philosophique et critique*, vol. xii, pp. 96–7. La Harpe, *Correspondance littéraire adressée à Son Altesse Impériale*, 6 vols. (Paris, 1801–7), vol. ii, pp. 229–30.
[62] *Mercure de France*, May 1778, p. 155. See also *Affiches*, 6 May 1778, p. 72.
[63] May 1778, p. 155.

The new music of this prologue is by M. Grétry, who knew how to adapt his genius with as much dexterity as candour to all the types of music that he celebrated, and to grasp with so much exactitude the forms, and, so to speak, the dress, that it is impossible to misunderstand it.

Beyond these points of general agreement, the journal articles often show strong biases, reflecting their authors' position in the Ramiste–Gluckiste debate. The account in the *Journal des théâtres*, in the form of a provincial's letter to the editor, shows one extreme.[64] It deplored the lack of a sufficiently noble deportment and heroic style in the Lully scene, and for the treatment of Rameau a few dances hardly conveyed the variety and wealth of expression in this composer's *oeuvre*. Why not extend the scene by introducing some of his dramatic choruses and solo airs from *Castor et Pollux* and *Dardanus*?, the writer asked rhetorically, and he proved his point by citing specific examples. Above all, he took exception to the association of the muse of tragedy and the expression of emotions that she cites with Gluck alone: masterpieces by both Lully and Rameau 'are beautiful trage-dies, which have scenes where all the passions mentioned by her reign supreme'.[65] But this writer stood virtually alone.

More influential papers took up other themes. The chronological structure and the references to a composer's improvements of techniques and forms that he inherited from his predecessors, implicit in *Les trois âges*, become explicit and emphasized in several reviews. The *Journal de Paris* thought the work could be improved by having the character Rameau assign Gluck an appropriate place in the Temple of Immortality (by implication one higher than Rameau's).[66] The *Journal encyclopédique*, too, noted that for Rameau only dances were used, but this did not strike the critic as an inappropriate choice. Whereas in the opera, a quotation from Gluck's overture to *Iphigénie en Aulide* prompts the reaction 'What new sounds!', the reviewer reported that the Génie de l'Opéra 'asks from whence comes a harmony superior to all heard up till now'.[67] Later he raised the question of progress in art:

Cette variété d'opinions bien reconnue relativement à l'art de la musique, ne pourroit-elle pas faire penser que les principes de cette science des sons n'ont rien d'absolument décidé; que c'est un art d'illusion, de mode & de pur caprice, puisqu'il est susceptible de tant de variété, & que dans son état naturel, après avoir cherché a détruire les sensations agréables que nous faisoit épreuver notre ancienne musique, il peut à son tour faire place dans la suite à d'autres chants qu'on aura toujours de bonnes raisons de croire meilleurs, parce qu'ils seront plus nouveaux?[68]

Could not this well-known variety of opinions with regard to the art of music make us think that the principles of this science of sounds have nothing absolutely fixed; that it is an art of illusion, fashion, and pure caprice, since it lends itself to so much variety, and that at its most basic, after having sought to destroy the pleasant feeling that our old music caused us, it could in its turn cede the place to other airs which one will always have good reason to believe better, because they are newer?

[64] *Journal des théâtres, ou le nouveau spectateur*, Paris, 1 May 1778, pp. 120–8.
[65] Ibid., p. 127.
[66] 28 April 1778, p. 471.
[67] *Journal encyclopédique ou universel*, Bouillon, July 1778, pp. 127–8.
[68] Ibid., p. 128.

His own opinion emerges clearly in the conclusion: unlike other arts and literature, '[musical] masterpieces of one century will unfailingly cease to be those of the following centuries'.[69]

The emphasis on chronology, on seeing Rameau's music as representative of an earlier generation's now removed from current norms, has important implications. In this view we find a sense of judging historically: an opera is a product of its age as well as a work of art by an individual composer. However, for the late eighteenth century, placing an opera in a continuing tradition, in which the most recent exponent, in this case Gluck, had the benefit of changes for the better, was but a short step away from condemning it as obsolete. The writing of *Les trois âges de l'opéra* and its reception reflect some common concerns of the late 1770s.

Just before the revival of Lully's *Thésée*, Devismes argued that he proposed 'to draw together the most chronologically disparate works . . . and by that means to give the public at large the opportunity to compare and to judge more precisely the progress that this art [music] had made among us'.[70] According to one critic, people came to the première of the revival out of curiosity:

Les connoisseurs l'ont écouté avec cette curiosité qui cherche à distinguer le point où un Art a commencé, de celui auquel il est arrivé.[71]

Connoisseurs listened to it with that inquisitiveness which seeks to distinguish the point where art began from that at which it has arrived.

By the 1770s, few disagreed with the assessment of Lully's music as old-fashioned (though, some maintained, still worthy).[72] But now Rameau, too, was drawn into this category. The equation of progress with improvement in the late 1770s and the early 1780s became an increasingly stronger theme in Rameau criticism, especially of *Castor et Pollux*. In 1777, the year before the première of *Les trois âges*, the ardent Ramiste of the *Lettre à M. le baron de la Vieille-Croche* allowed that music had progressed, particularly in the style of accompaniment, although he went on to attack Gluck's orchestral writing as too complex. Why not, he argued, remedy the defects in Rameau by cutting scenes no longer conforming to modern dramatic tastes, rewriting and speeding up the recitative, and replacing the basso continuo with simple orchestral support? After all, Rameau had a much better understanding of French language declamation, and above all, good taste, than any foreigner could possibly acquire.[73] Patriotism, too, required support of national artists; the modern love of things foreign was a disgrace:

[69] Ibid., p. 129.
[70] *Journal de Paris*, 15 February 1779, p. 183. Although Devismes promised a production as Lully wrote it, others composed the overture, dances, and accompaniment for Médée's monologue at the end of Act II. Critics, too, complained of inappropriate ornamentation and too slow tempi for the recitatives. Ibid., 24 February 1779, p. 219.

[71] *Mercure de France*, 5 March 1779, p. 50.
[72] See, for example, remarks in the reviews of Gluck's *Armide* in the *Journal de Paris*, 24 September 1777, pp. 3–4 (reprinted in [Le Blond (ed.)], *Mémoires*, pp. 257–8), and the *Journal encyclopédique*, December 1777, pp. 297–308.
[73] *Lettre à M. le baron de la Vieille-Croche, au sujet de Castor & Pollux, donné à Versailles le 10 mai 1777* ([Paris], 1777), pp. 2–4.

Le ciel me préserve, M. le Baron, de vouloir heurter de front les intrépides Spectateurs de M. le Chevalier G[luck] ni même de faire de la peine aux fanatiques de bonne-foi, qui veulent tout sacrifier aux *musettes* étrangers, en foulant aux pieds les muses patriotiques; mais j'ose élever ma foible voix au milieu de ces réformateurs indécens, pour dire, qu'à mérite inférieur, je donnerois encore la préférence aux artistes nationaux.[74]

Heaven help me, my lord baron, if I want to launch a frontal attack against the fearless audience of Sir G[luck] nor even to vex the sincere fanatics who wish to sacrifice everything to the little foreign muses at the same time as they tread underfoot the national ones; but I dare to raise my feeble voice amid these indecent reformers to say that even if less worthy, I would still give preference to French artists.

When Devismes staged a revival of *Castor et Pollux* at the Opéra 11 October 1778, the *Mercure de France* took issue with some of these arguments. The appeal to national sentiment was false, according to the critic; rather, it masked the supporters' preference for the music of one's youth and showed the force of habit.[75] The reviewer attributed the opera's popularity to the curiosity aroused by the Ramiste–Gluckiste debate, although he admitted it was generally considered the masterpiece of French opera, and he still praised a few choruses and dances.[76] La Harpe agreed and continued:

Nul opéra n'avait eu plus de succès sur notre théâtre lyrique [que *Castor et Pollux*], et cela devait être dans un temps où nous ne connaissions pas encore le chant. Mais depuis que nous avons entendu la musique expressive et dramatique des bons compositeurs italiens et de leur imitateurs, depuis que les beaux airs de *Lucile* [de Grétry], de *Sylvain* [de Grétry] et d'*Orphée* [de Gluck] nous ont fait verser des larmes; enfin depuis qu'on a entendu le *Roland* de Piccini, et qu'on a vu dans *l'Iphigénie* [*en Aulide*] de Gluck un ensemble plus intéressant que *Castor*, soutenu d'une musique plus variée, quoiqu'encore un peu allemande, il était difficile de nous charmer avec le chant monotone et criard qui a régné si longtemps à l'opéra. Ces cadences éternelles, ces ports de voix, ces hurlemens, tout ce qui faisait extasier les Français, il y a vingt ans, est aujourd'hui passés de mode.[77]

No opera had more success on our lyric stage [than *Castor et Pollux*], and that is as it should be in a period when we did not yet know true melody. But since we have heard the expressive, dramatic music of good Italian composers and their imitators; since the fine airs of [Grétry's] *Lucile* and *Sylvain*, and [Gluck's] *Orphée* have made us weep; finally since we have heard Piccinni's *Roland* and seen in Gluck's *Iphigénie* [*en Aulide*] a more interesting general effect than in *Castor*, sustained by a music more varied, even if still somewhat Germanic, it is difficult to charm us with the monotonous and shrill song that held sway for so long at the Opéra. Those interminable trills, portamentos, howls, everything that twenty years ago enraptured the French, is today out of fashion.

Thus, both reviewers emphasized the temporal – and aesthetic – distance between the time of Rameau and their own day. Clearly, for them the changes in style were generally improvements.

Others were more favourable to Rameau, but even they no longer considered *Castor et Pollux* as a currently valid example of its genre. The strongly Gluckiste *Journal de Paris* wrote with respect about this work, which 'has always been

[74] Ibid., p. 2.
[75] *Mercure de France*, 25 October 1778, p. 296.
[76] Ibid., pp. 294–6.

[77] *Correspondance littéraire adressée à Son Altesse Impériale*, vol. II, pp. 303–4.

considered as the masterpiece among French operas for the pomp and variety of the staging, for the different styles that the subject seems to require, finally for the grand effects of tragedy', and side-stepped the debate on progress by saying that generally it was unjust and even ridiculous to compare works that were so different.[78] It was no longer necessary to support Gluck by challenging Rameau.

Like the author of the *Lettre à M. le baron de la Vieille-Croche*, the critic of the *Journal encyclopédique* recommended changes so that today's audience would enjoy *Castor et Pollux* as much as Rameau's did before recent developments:

Les courtes observations que nous avons faites des vraies beautés que s'y trouvent, ont suffi pour conserver à cet opéra l'estime dont il avoit joui avant que nos oreilles eussent connu de nouveaux prodiges en musique, & la lui conserveront encore longtems, surtout si quelque jour une main habile, pour plaire à la nation, daigne échauffer un peu le dialogue chantant & en varier les mouvemens.[79]

The brief remarks that we have made about the true beauties found in this opera suffice to maintain for it the esteem which it enjoyed before our ears heard new wonders in music, and will maintain it still for a long time, above all if some day a skilful hand, in order to please the nation, deigns to revise a little the recitative and to vary the tempi.

Contrary to the *Mercure de France*'s assertion of 'little success', *Castor et Pollux* was very popular indeed in the 1778/9 season. It received thirty-six performances, and the gate receipts averaged almost 4000 *livres*. (For comparison, Gluck's most recent opera, *Armide*, was given thirteen times during the same period, and its takings averaged under 3000 *livres*. Piccinni's *La buona figliuola*, a novelty for Paris this season, earned just over 2000 *livres* on average for its ten performances, while his successful *Roland* during its first season was staged twenty-seven times and took in just over 3500 *livres* on average.)[80] A handful of die-hard conservatives and a few curiosity seekers could not have sustained *Castor et Pollux* to this extent. Some critics may have thought Rameau's masterpiece obsolete; the Parisian opera-going public did not agree.[81]

Less than two years later, however, there was a marked shift. Revived on 7 May 1780, *Castor et Pollux* was withdrawn later that month when at the sixth performance the gate receipts fell below the 2000 *livres* barrier (a level achieved only after thirty-five performances in 1778/9).[82] The tone of the review in the *Mercure de France* had changed as well. Whereas in 1778 the critic tried to prove Rameau's music was too old-fashioned, now he assumed that battle was won. Rameau was nonetheless worthy of respect for his contribution to the national heritage. The critic's conclusion – that the baroque master could no longer serve as a model – stands in sharp contrast to the generally held position on the eve of

[78] 12 October 1778, p. 1143. The critics had praise for some of the choruses and dances.
[79] December 1778, p. 507. He also maintained that the opera needed a few more airs and improved orchestral accompaniments, although he, too, lauded some choruses and dances.
[80] 'Journal des entrées journalières'. The figures for Rameau's opera are also given in Malherbe, 'Commentaire', pp. lxxxvii–lxxxviii.
[81] The critics who supported Rameau's opera were not slow to use its enthusiastic reception as evidence; see, for example, the *Journal encyclopédique*, December 1778, p. 497. In contrast, *Thésée* was performed only five times in 1779; in spite of initially high gate receipts, by the last performance they had fallen below 2000 *livres*.
[82] 'Journal des entrées journalières' and Malherbe, 'Commentaire', p. lxxxviii.

Gluck's arrival in Paris.[83] In 1781 *Castor et Pollux* received only five perform-ances.[84] By the following year, its image as a national monument was well entrenched. When the Tsarevitch of Russia (later Paul I) expressed a desire to see an example of French opera, it was the natural choice. As critics remarked, it was the only work 'that seems to have survived the ruins of what one calls French music'[85] and which, 'considered as the masterpiece of the leader among our national composers, is, so to speak, hallowed'.[86] Now in an almost apologetic fashion, the *Mercure de France* singled out a few pieces of 'timeless beauty'. He also sounded a note of alarm about a style of performance inappropriate to this music. The first performance was a gala event very well attended; by the fourth, the gate receipts had dwindled to the point that the run was suspended. Another revival in the autumn was a little more successful, but of limited duration.[87]

Special events for three performances in the winter and spring of 1784 secured full houses: the first two were charity benefits (for the poor and for the actors), and the third, again a royal gala, entertained the King of Sweden. Although the *Journal de Paris* described the opera as the 'lyric tragedy generally acknowledged as the first among old works', most of the review praised the efforts of the singers, dancers, and orchestral members, who with limited rehearsal, could mount so difficult an opera, and by implication, one not likely to be given often.[88] After a final brief run of six performances from 29 October 1784 to 7 February 1785, Rameau's *Castor et Pollux* disappeared from the stage of the Académie royale de musique.[89] By the following year the administration of the theatre considered having it revised and largely rewritten by the leading opera composers in Paris: Langlé, Gossec, Piccinni, Sacchini, and Grétry. Lack of funds prevented carrying out the project.[90] Finally, Pierre Candeille undertook a new setting using with modifications a few Rameau pieces.[91] This *Castor et Pollux* (première Académie royale de musique, 14 June 1791) was last performed there on 10 March 1816.

The gradual change in attitude towards Rameau operas from current models to historic relics during the period 1774 to 1785 was paralleled by another, less

[83] *Mercure de France*, 20 May 1780, pp. 128–9.
[84] It was given from 2 to 18 January 1781. By the fifth performance, the gate receipts were under 2000 *livres*. 'Journal des entrées journalières' and Malherbe, 'Commentaire', p. lxxxviii.
[85] *Mercure de France*, 6 July 1782, pp. 41–5.
[86] *Journal de Paris*, 15 June 1782, p. 673.
[87] The performances took place between 14 and 25 July and between 6 September and 24 November 1782; there were fourteen in all. See 'Journal des entrées journalières' and Malherbe, 'Commentaire', p. lxxxviii.
[88] 2 March 1784, p. 283. The performances were given 1 and 8 March and 24 June 1784.
[89] There were six performances during this period; the gate receipts were very high on average, but the early withdrawal indicates

that the administration believed that its success could not be sustained. 'Journal des entrées journalières' and Malherbe, 'Commentaire', p. lxxxix.
[90] The project was outlined in a proposal to the minister of the *maison du roi* in charge of the Opéra; transcribed in Malherbe, 'Commentaire', pp. lxvii–lxviii.
[91] He often reorchestrated and sometimes expanded, especially towards the conclusions, the pieces borrowed; these include: the chorus 'Que tout gémisse' (Act I, scene ii), the air 'Tristes apprêts' (Act II, scene ii), the *marche triomphale* (Act I, scene iv), the demons' chorus 'Brisons tous nos fers' (Act III, scene iv), and two dances (one each in the *divertissements* of Act II and Act IV).

clearly marked reassessment of his contribution to music in general. At the time of his death, his contemporaries recognized him as a composer and as a theorist, but for them his operas were the most important part of his *oeuvre*.[92] By the 1780s Laborde, Rameau's former student and admirer, fell back on the continuing significance of Rameau's writings now that his operas no longer dominated the repertory:

Mais l'avantage immense que Rameau a . . . c'est d'avoir écrit sur son art, d'en avoir découvert les vrais principes, & par-là d'avoir mérité à jamais l'estime de la postérité. Sa Musique, celle qui l'a précédée, & celle qui la suivra, n'existeront probablement plus dans quelques siècles; . . . mais son traité de l'harmonie, sa génération harmonique, &c. seront connus dans deux milles ans, & laisseront de lui le souvenir qu'il mérite.[93]

But the immense advantage that Rameau has . . . is to have written about his art, to have discovered its true principles, and because of that to have merited posterity's esteem forever. His music, that which preceded it, and that which will follow, will probably no longer exist in several centuries; . . . but his *Traité de l'harmonie*, his *Génération harmonique*, etc., will still be known two thousand years from now and will leave for him the reputation that he deserves.

This lopsided view of Rameau's achievements persisted well into the nineteenth century.[94]

An increasing historical awareness was not paralleled by an understanding for older works. Perhaps Burney would have been pleased that the French had finally accepted as valid the principle of judging music in terms of progress; though no strong supporter of Gluck, the English historian would have found their application of it eccentric.[95] Ironically, the institutionalization of Rameau's operas as French National Art of a previous age was concomitant with their withdrawal from active repertory, for in the late eighteenth-century public's estimation, such a status was incompatible with the entertainment value that the genre should have.

[92] This balance was typical of obituaries; see, for example, Charles Palissot de Montenoy, 'Eloge de Jean-Philippe Rameau, compositeur de musique du cabinet du Roi', *Le nécrologe des hommes célèbres de France pour 1765* (Paris, 1767), pp. 83–113. On the other hand, several epitaphs in verse stress Rameau's contribution to the study of harmony; see Lionel de La Laurencie, 'Quelques documents sur Jean-Philippe Rameau et sa famille', *Mercure musical et bulletin français de la S. I. M.* vol. III (1907), p. 573.

[93] *Essai sur la musique*, vol. III, pp. 465–6.

[94] As in François-Joseph Fétis, *Biographie universelle des musiciens et bibliographie générale de la musique*, 2nd ed., vol. VII (Paris, 1864), pp. 167–76, s.v. 'Rameau (Jean-Philippe)'.

[95] Indeed, in Burney's view, Gluck's popularity in France was largely due to his 'flattering the ancient national taste'. He continued, 'though there is much real genius and intrinsic worth in the dramatic compositions of this master, the congeniality of this style with that of their old national favourites, Lulli and Rameau, was no small merit with the friends of that Music'. *A General History*, vol. IV, pp. 618–19.

A bibliography of writings by James R. Anthony

DORMAN SMITH

This bibliography lists in chronological order James R. Anthony's writings on French baroque music following the completion of his dissertation in 1964. The scope of Anthony's writings has been obscured in some measure because much of his scholarly contribution has been to monumental works like the *The new Grove dictionary of music and musicians* and the *New Oxford history of music*. Regrettably, the fullest extent of his contributions over the past twenty-two years cannot be documented because to do so would require a listing of the many colloquia, panels, and conventions in which he has participated. Furthermore, Anthony has exercised considerable influence as a reviewer of dissertations, grant proposals, and manuscripts for many monographs and journal articles.

Books, articles, and reviews

'The opera-ballets of André Campra: a study of the first period French opera-ballet' (unpublished PhD dissertation, U. of Southern California, 1964)

'The French opera-ballet in the early 18th century: problems of definition and classification', *Journal of the American Musicological Society*, XVIII (1965), pp. 197–206

'Thematic repetition in the opera-ballets of André Campra', *Musical quarterly*, LII (1966), pp. 209–20

Review of *Documents du Minutier Central concernant l'histoire de la musique (1600–1650)*, vol. I, ed. M. Jurgens (Paris, 1968), *Notes*, XXVI (1969–70), pp. 511–13

'Some uses of the dance in the French opera-ballet', *Recherches sur la musique française classique*, IX (1969), pp. 75–90

'Printed editions of André Campra's *L'Europe galante*', *Musical quarterly*, LVI (1970), pp. 54–73

Review of G. Seefrid, *Die Airs de danse in den Bühnenwerken von Jean-Philippe Rameau* (Wiesbaden, 1969), *Notes*, XXVII (1971–2), pp. 697–9

French Baroque music from Beaujoyeulx to Rameau (London, B. T. Batsford; New York, W. W. Norton, 1973; rev. ed., New York, W. W. Norton, 1978; paperback ed., New York, W. W. Norton, 1981; French ed., *La musique en France à l'époque baroque*, B. Vierne (trans.), Paris, Flammarion, 1981)

Review of A. Campra, *Les festes vénitiennes*, M. Lutolf (ed.), (Paris, 1972), *Journal of the American Musicological Society*, XXVIII (1974), pp. 144–8

Bibliographies for chapters III 'Origins of French opera', IV 'French opera from Lully to Rameau', and VII 'Church music in France' in *New Oxford history of music*, vol. V (London, Oxford University Press, 1975), pp. 788–96, 806–12

'Church music in France: 1661–1750', with N. Dufourcq, in *New Oxford history of music*, vol. v (London, Oxford University Press, 1975), pp. 437–92

Review of D. Tunley, *The eighteenth-century French cantata* (London, 1974), *Musical quarterly*, LXI (1975), pp. 611–15

'French music of the XVIIth and XVIIIth centuries: a checklist of research in progress', *Recherches sur la musique française classique*, XV (1975), pp. 262–9

Review of R. M. Isherwood, *Music in the service of the king: France in the seventeenth century* (Ithaca, N.Y., 1973), *Journal of Modern History*, 47 (1975), pp. 347–9

'French Baroque music: an introduction', in the English Bach Festival 1976 *Souvenir programme* (London, 1976), pp. 10–11

'French binary air within Italian aria da capo in Montéclair's third book of cantatas', *Proceedings of the Royal Musical Association*, CIV (1977–8), pp. 47–55

'Aux-Cousteaux, Artus', in *The new Grove*, S. Sadie (ed.) (London, Macmillan, 1980), vol. I, p. 742

'Ballet de cour', in *The new Grove*, vol. II, pp. 88–90

'Ballet-héroïque', in *The new Grove*, vol. II, pp. 90–1

'Bourdelot' (family), in *The new Grove*, vol. III, pp. 109–10

'Brossard, Sébastien de', in *The new Grove*, vol. III, pp. 336–7

'Cambert, Robert', in *The new Grove*, vol. III, pp. 637–9

'Campra, André', in *The new Grove*, vol. III, pp. 662–6

'Campra, Joseph', in *The new Grove*, vol. III, pp. 666–7

'Collasse, Pascal' in *The new Grove*, vol. IV, pp. 534–6

'Collin de Blamont, François', in *The new Grove*, vol. IV, pp. 562–3

'Comédie-ballet', in *The new Grove*, vol. IV, pp. 588–9

'Desmarets, Henry', in *The new Grove*, vol. V, pp. 390–2

'Destouches, André Cardinal', in *The new Grove*, vol. V, pp. 400–2

'Divertissement', in *The new Grove*, vol. V, pp. 506–7

'Du Mont, Henry', in *The new Grove*, vol. V, pp. 712–14

'Duval, Mlle.', in *The new Grove*, vol. V, p. 762

'Entrée', in *The new Grove*, vol. VI, pp. 209–10

'Foliot, Edme', in *The new Grove*, vol. VI, pp. 692–3

'Fuzelier, Louis', in *The new Grove*, vol. VII, pp. 46–7

'Gantez, Annibal', in *The new Grove*, vol. VII, p. 148

'Gobert, Thomas', in *The new Grove*, vol. VII, p. 481

'Intermède', in *The new Grove*, vol. IX, pp. 257–8

'Lalande, Michel-Richard de', in *The new Grove*, vol. X, pp. 381–5. Revision in *The new Grove French baroque masters* (New York, W. W. Norton, 1986), pp. 119–48

'Lambert, Michel', in *The new Grove*, vol. X, pp. 397–9

'Le Rochois, Marthe', in *The new Grove*, vol. X, p. 685

'Lully, Jean-Baptiste', in *The new Grove*, vol. XI, pp. 314–29. Revision in *The new Grove French baroque masters* (New York, W. W. Norton, 1986), pp. 1–70

'Mazarin, Jules', in *The new Grove*, vol. XI, p. 863

'Montéclair, Michel Pignolet de', in *The new Grove*, vol, XII, pp. 508–10

'Motet. III. Baroque. 4. France', in *The new Grove*, vol. XII, pp. 641–4

'Mouret, Jean-Joseph', in *The new Grove*, vol. XII, pp. 654–6

'Opera. III. France. 1: The *tragédie lyrique* and kindred forms', in *The new Grove*, vol. XIII, pp. 568–72. Revision to be included in forthcoming *The new Grove opera*

'Opera-ballet', in *The new Grove*, vol. XIII, p. 647

'Parfaict, François', in *The new Grove*, vol. XIV, p. 182

'Paris. III. 1600–1723', in *The new Grove*, vol. XIV, pp. 193–8

'Paris. v. Music at court outside Paris. 1(i). Versailles, 1664–1715', in *The new Grove*, vol. xiv, pp. 201–6

'Paris. v. Music at court outside Paris. 3. Saint-Cyr', in *The new Grove*, vol. xiv, pp. 207–8

'Paris. v. Music at court outside Paris. 4. Sceaux', in *The new Grove*, vol. xiv, p. 208

'Perrin, Pierre', in *The new Grove*, vol. xiv, pp. 545–6

'Quinault, Jean-Baptiste Maurice', in *The new Grove*, vol. xv, p. 507

'Quinault, Marie-Anne-Catherine', in *The new Grove*, vol. xv, p. 507

'Quinault, Philippe', in *The new Grove*, vol. xv, p. 508

'Récit', in *The new Grove*, vol. xv, p. 643

'Robert, Pierre', in *The new Grove*, vol. xvi, p. 66

'Sicard, Jean', in *The new Grove*, vol. xvii, p. 291

'Sommeil', in *The new Grove*, vol. xvii, p. 477

'Tragédie lyrique', in *The new Grove*, vol. xix, pp. 114–15

'French music of the XVII and XVIII centuries: a checklist of research in progress', with J. Hajdu, *Recherches sur la musique française classique*, xx (1981), pp. 261–74

Review of J. A. Sadie, *The bass viol in French Baroque chamber music* (Ann Arbor, 1980), *Journal of the Viola da Gamba Society of America*, xviii (1981), pp. 124–7

'Letter to the Editor', *Fontes artis musicae*, xxix (1982), p. 141. (Response to L. Sawkins on the spelling of M.-R. de Lalande)

'A source for secular vocal music in 18th-century Avignon: MS 1182 of the Bibliothèque du Muséum Calvet', *Acta musicologica*, liv (1982), pp. 261–79

Review of G. E. Vollen, *The French cantata: a survey and thematic catalogue* (Ann Arbor, 1982), *The American Recorder*, xxiv (1983), pp. 73–5

'La structure musicale des récits de Michel-Richard Delalande', in J. Mongrédien and Y. Ferraton (eds.), *Actes du Colloque International sur le Grand Motet Français* (Paris, Centre National de la Recherche Scientifique, 1986), pp. 119–27

'Lully's airs – French or Italian', *The Musical Times*, cxxviii (March, 1987), pp. 126–9

'More faces than Proteus: Lully's *Ballet des Muses*', *Early Music*, xv (August, 1987), p. 336–44

Editions

Montéclair, Michel Pignolet de, *Cantatas for one and two voices*, with D. Akmajian, Recent Researches in the Music of the Baroque Era, vols. xxix-xxx (Madison, Wisconsin, A & R Editions, 1978)

Delalande, Michel-Richard, *De profundis: grand motet for soloists, chorus, woodwinds, strings and continuo*, Early Musical Masterworks (Chapel Hill, University of North Carolina Press, 1980)

Forthcoming

Article on the dance in French baroque stage music, in S. J. Cohen (ed.), *International encyclopedia of the dance* (New York, Charles Scribner & Sons, forthcoming)

'Towards a principal source for Lully's court ballets: Foucault vs. Philidor', *Recherches sur la musique française classique*, xxv (1987)

Campra, André, *Le carnaval de Venise* (facsimile with extensive introduction and performance history), in French Opera in the 17th and 18th Centuries (New York, Pendragon Press, 1988?). Scheduled to contribute: Campra's *Idoménée* and *Les âges*; and Mouret's *Les fêtes de Thalie* and *Les amours de Ragonde*

Lully, Jean-Baptiste, *Ballet des amours déguisez* and *Ballet des muses* to appear in the new
    Broude Brothers edition of the Collected Works
'The Musical Structure of Lully's Operatic Airs' to appear in the *Actes du Colloque Lully*
    (September 1987), University of Heidelberg
Review of Lully, J.-B. and M. Marais, *Trios pour le coucher du roy*, H. Schneider (ed.),
    'Le Pupitre' LXX (Paris, 1987), to appear in *Music and Letters* (July, 1988)

Index

N.B.: This index does not list names or compositions in the tables in this volume (see particularly pp. 9–10, 21, 44–9, 104–5) or names in Julie Anne Sadie's index of musicians mentioned in the Parnassian works of Titon du Tillet (see pp. 149–57).

Académie Royale de Musique
  Lyon 188
  Paris 103, 146, 183, 197n, 239, 257, 291, 298
  Rouen 192
  Strasbourg 198
alexandrine verse form 1, 3
Amaulry, Thomas 191
Amsterdam
  editions of Lully's orchestral suites 113–30
  performances of Lully's operas 199–202
Angelis, Francesco-Paolo d' 207
Anne, of Austria, widow of Louis XIII
  7, 12, 15, 30
Anthony, James R. xii–xiii, 4–5
  bibliography 319–22
  on Dumont 58, 63
  on Lambert 38–9
  on Lully 95, 97, 183, 186
  on Mazarin 8
  on Perrin 42
Antoine, Jean 197
Antoine, Michel 196
Antwerp, performances of Lully's operas 202–7
Arnaud, François 296
Arnault, Jean 163
Audran, Jean 134–6
Auld, Louis 42–3, 50
Avignon, performances of Lully's operas 185

Bach, Johann Sebastian 113, 128–9
Bacilly, Bénigne de 32, 37
Ballard, Christophe, publications 36–7, 43
  ballets 241
  livrets 100
  motets 64, 68, 82–6
  operas 201, 236, 247
  orchestral suites 114
ballets de cour 251–3
Barberini family 7, 21
  Cardinal Antonio 8, 13–14, 20
  Cardinal Francesco 14
Baroni, Leonora 8, 14, 16, 21–2
Bauyn d'Angervilliers, Prosper 162–3

Bavière, Marie-Anne-Christine-Victoire de 103
Beauchamp, Pierre 245, 248, 252
Benedetti, Elpidio 13
Benoit, Marcelle 107, 108n, 109
Benserade, Isaac de 9–10, 21, 26–7, 35, 183
Bérain, Jean 100–2, 252
Bérard, Jean-Antoine 273
Bernier, Nicolas 143–4
Bibiena, Francesco 197
Bichi, Cardinal Alessandro 13, 15
Blainville, Charles Henri de 227–8
Blamont, François Colin de 65, 142
Boësset, Antoine 36–7
Boësset, Jean-Baptiste? 10
Boileau Despréaux, Nicolas 3, 132
Bombarda, Giovanni Paolo 203
Borrel, Eugène 184, 189, 194, 202, 204–6, 208
borrowings
  Grétry 300–12
  Rameau 259–89
Bourdelot, P. 25–6
Bourot de Valroche, Antoine 169
Brebion, Charles 185
Brossard, Sébastien de 88–91, 97
Brunet, musician 33
Brussels
  collection of Lully motets 95
  performances of Lully's operas 202–7
Burney, Dr Charles 291, 318
Buti, Francesco 9–10, 17, 20–3

Cabart de Villeneuve, M. 177
Cahusac, Louis de 232–3, 269–71, 273
Callières, François de 99, 108
Calsabigi, Renieri 293
Cambefort, Jean de 30–1
Cambert, Robert 3, 9–10, 25, 146
Campra, André 111, 114, 134, 141, 146, 197, 198, 207
Candeille, Pierre 317
Caproli, C. 9, 21
Carissimi, Giacomo 12, 43, 45, 47
Casaubon, Jean Maurice de 169

Castellani, Giulio 14
Castilhon, Jean 294
Cavalli, F. 9–10, 21, 218
Certain, Marie-Françoise 146, 171
Chapelle royale 41, 64–5, 69, 81, 83
Chappe, Marie 143
Charles I, King of England 8
Charpentier, Marc-Antoine 4, 114, 143, 147
Cheilan-Cambolin, Jeanne 184, 186–7, 189
Chéron, Elisabeth-Sophie 147
Clément, journalist 262, 273
Clérambault, Louis-Nicolas 141
Colasse, Pascal 146
  ballets 249
  and Lully 64–5, 166, 171, 193
  motets 43–51 passim, 64–5, 71, 76–7
  operas 111
Colbert, Jean-Baptiste 30, 43, 81, 166, 185
Collignon, Gaspard 180
Conti, Princesse de 252–3
Cordey, Jean 168–9
Corneille, Pierre 50
Costa, Anna Francesca (Signora Checca) 15, 22
Cotton, Michel 180
Couperin, François 141–2, 147, 167
Couperin, Louise 143
Couperin, Marguerite-Antoinette 147
Coupillet, N. 43, 49, 64–5
Coysevox, Antoine 180
Crébillon, Prosper de 138
Crépy, Louis 134
Curé, Simon 134

Dandrieu, Jean-François 143
Danglebert, père et fils 107
Dassoucy, C. 9
Delacroix, Pierre 188
Delalande see Lalande
Deschamps, Armand 163
Descoteaux, René-Pignon 33, 103–4, 109
Desmarets, Henry 114, 144, 196–8
Desrochers, Étienne 138
Destouches, André Cardinal 134, 144–5, 191, 196–7, 207
Destouches, Michel 33, 104
Devismes du Valgay, Anne Pierre Jacques 297–8, 302, 314–15
Dijon, performances of Lully's operas 195, 198
doubles 37–8
Duhallay, Mme and Mlle 145
Du Mesny, Louis de Golard 192–3
Dumont, Henri 43–63 passim, 68–71, 91
Dupont, Pierre, scribe 88–90, 94–7
Dupré, Laurent 104, 107, 109
Dupuis, Hilaire 26, 30–1, 35, 160–2, 166, 173–4
Dupuis, Michel 27
Du Roullet, François Louis Gand le Bland 293

Ecorcheville, Jules 32, 114
England 3
  Lully's operas in 208
Expilly, G. 43, 45, 47–8, 50n

Fabri, Alessandro 15
Favier, Jean 253
Fel, Mlle 224
Fétis, François-Joseph 30, 63
Feuillet, Raoul Auger 239–40, 249, 254
Fiocco, Pietro Andrea 203
Fischer, Johann Caspar Ferdinand 114
Fontainebleau 183
Fonteaux de Cercamanan, Anne 38
Fontenay 63
Foucault, Henry 32, 95, 97–8, 114
Fouquet 26
France
  and Italian opera 7–23
  spread of Lully's operas 183–211
Francine, Nicolas de 161, 171, 174, 181, 188
Francoeur, François 219–22, 226–9, 235, 237, 268, 304
Fransen, Jan 199–201
Fréron, Élie 142, 148
Furetière, Antoine 256

Garnier, Louis 133
Garnier, Joseph 197n
Garros, Madeleine 52
Gatti, Jean Theobalde de 103, 105, 146
Gautier, Jacques 185
Gautier, Pierre 114, 146, 185, 188
Germany, Lully's operas in 208
Ghent, performances of Lully's operas 202–7
Gigault, Nicolas 25
Gillot, Pierre 168
Girdlestone, Cuthbert 259–60, 268, 270
Gittard, Daniel 162
Il giuditio della Regione tra la Beltà e l'Affetto 16–23
Gluck, Christoph Willibald von 291–2, 310
  Armide 213, 304, 316
  Iphigénie en Aulide 291–3, 313
  Orphée 293–5
  success in Italy and France 292–4
  in Les trois âges de l'opéra 304, 313, 316
Gobert, Thomas 43, 45, 47–8, 50, 63
grand motet, evolution of 41–79
  Livres du Roi 51–64
  Lully and the sous-maîtres 64–74
  Perrin's lyrics 41–51
  see also under Lully
Grétry, André Ernest Modeste xii, 292
  Les trois âges de l'opéra 292, 298–318
Grignon 177
Gros, Étienne 27–8, 186, 188, 201
Guichard, Henri 166
Guise, Henri II of Lorraine, duc de 29
Guldiman, Antoine Léonard 174

Hague, The, performances of Lully's operas 199–202
Handel, George Frederick 113, 128, 145, 260–1
Hesselin, Louis 29
Heus, Jean Philip 113, 115, 117–19, 199
Heyer, John Hajdu 68n
Hotteterre family 33, 103–4, 109

Huyghens, Constantin 63

Innocent X, Pope 20
Isherwood, Robert 43, 63
Italy
  influence on Lully 2
  Italian opera in France 7–23
  Lully's operas in 208
Itier, Léonard 108–9

Jacquet de la Guerre, Elisabeth-Claude *see*
    La Guerre, Elisabeth-Claude Jacquet de
Joannis, Joseph 203

La Barre, Anne de 26, 35
La Barre, Pierre Chabanceau de 108–9
Laborde, Jean Benjamin de 63, 237, 318
Lacroix, Paul 28
La Fontaine, Jean de 28, 112
La Fosse, Antoine 147
La Gorce, Jérôme de 192–4, 197
La Guerre, Elisabeth-Claude Jacquet de 133–4,
    144, 147
La Guerre, M. de 9
La Harpe 315
Lainez 143
Lajoüe, Jacques de 138–9
Lalande, Michel-Richard de
  ballets 65, 245n
  and Lully 4, 64–5, 146, 171
  motets 43, 49, 51, 58–60, 64–5, 68–74, 143
  and the *Parnasse François* 133–4, 142–3
La Laurencie, Lionel de 25
Lalouette, Jean 146
Lambert, Madeleine (Lully's wife) 28, 30–1,
    160–1, 180–1
Lambert, Michel
  and Lully 25–39, 160–2
  and the *Parnasse François* 145–6
  residences 31, 160, 166, 169, 173, 181
La Motte, Houdar de 262
Lang, Paul Henry 275
La Pierre, Paul de 108
Largillière, Nicolas de 132, 138
La Salle, Marquis de 236
Laurain-Portemer, Madeleine 7
Le Brun, Charles 111
Le Camus, Sébastien 36–7
Lecerf de la Viéville, J. L. 25, 31, 36–8, 71, 145,
    214, 219
Lefebvre, Léon 195, 197–8
Le Gras, H. 20
Lemiere, Mlle 235
Le Moyne, Étienne 104, 107, 109
Léopold, Duke of Lorraine and Bar 196
Le Rochois, Marthe 141, 146
Le Tellier, Cardinal Maurice 83
Le Vasseur, Nicolas 188
Lhotte, Gustav 198
Liebrecht, Henri 202–7
Lille, performances of Lully's operas 195, 197–8
Livres du Roi, motet texts 41, 43, 51–64

Loewenberg, Alfred 183, 186–7, 189–90, 195,
    200, 204–6, 208
Lorenzani, Paolo 11, 166, 171
Loret, Jean 25, 26
Louis XIII 7, 12, 178
Louis XIV 178
  and the arts 183, 251–4, 257
  balls 254–5
  chapel 41–79
  hunting 175
  and Lully 30, 144, 159, 185, 207, 291
  and Mazarin 7
  motets for 64–5, 81, 83, 91, 143
  palaces 178–9
  and the *Parnasse François* 133
Louis XV 89, 134, 140, 183, 255–6
Louis XVI 183
Louvencourt, Marie de 143, 147
Louvois, Marquis de 144
Lully, Caterine Madeleine de 174, 181
Lully, Jean-Baptiste 1–4, 8, 50
  ballets 9–10, 21, 28–30, 38, 245n
  and Buti 21, 23
  compared with Rameau and Gluck 226–7,
    294–6, 315
  death 64, 81, 180–1
  grands motets 43–7, 64–74, 78–9, 81–98
  and Lambert 25–39
  and Louis XIV 30–1, 144, 159, 185
  and *La Mariée* 239–57, 304
  marriage 28, 160
  operas, spread of 183–211
  orchestra 99–112
  orchestral suites, Amsterdam, editions 113–30
  and the *Parnasse François* 133–4, 137, 142, 146
  and Quinault 3–4
  residences 31, 159–82
  and *Les trois âges de l'opéra* 304, 307, 311
  ballets and comédies-ballets
    Ballet d'Alcidiane 29, 32, 106
    Ballet de l'amour malade 245–6
    Ballet des amours déguisés 32–4, 95, 97
    Ballet des arts 31–3
    Ballet des bienvenus 29
    Ballet de Flore 32, 38, 245
    Ballet de la galanterie du temps 29
    Ballet de l'impatience 21, 29–32
    Ballet des muses 32, 38
    Ballet de la naissance de Vénus 32–4, 38
    Ballet de la nuit 28–9
    Ballet des plaisirs 29, 241, 245
    Ballet de Psyché et la puissance de l'amour 21, 29
    Ballet de la raillerie 29, 32
    Ballet du temps 29
    Les amantes magnifiques 178
    Le bourgeois gentilhomme 108, 144, 196–7, 207
    Le carnaval masquerade 245
    Les fêtes de l'Amour et de Bacchus 94, 115,
      196, 201
    George Dandin 38, 207
    La grotte de Versailles 32, 38
    Le mariage forcé 32

Lully, Jean-Baptiste (*cont.*)
  Monsieur de Pourceaugnac (Divertissement de
    Chambord) 38, 197
  Les nopces de village 30, 33, 241, 244–5
  Pastorale comique 106
  Les plaisirs de l'ile enchantée 106
  La Princesse d'Elide 108, 178
  Le Sicilien 38
  Le temple de la paix 115, 118, 121
  Le triomphe de l'amour 100, 107, 109, 115,
    144, 166, 178, 185
  grands motets:
    De profundis 65, 93, 146
    Domine salvum fac Regem 87, 93, 95
    Exaudiat te, Domine 68, 71, 81, 84, 93–4
    Jubilate Deo 68, 84, 93
    Miserere 63, 68, 81–2, 93, 94
    Notus in Judaea 68, 71, 81, 84, 87, 90–1,
      93–5, 97
    O Lachrymae 68, 87
    Plaude laetare 68, 81
    Quare fremuerunt 68, 71, 81, 87–8, 93–6
    Te Deum 81, 84, 171
  operas:
    Acis et Galathée 115, 118, 167, 171, 189,
      193, 196, 203
    Alceste 100, 106, 115, 123–4, 178, 191, 197,
      203
    Amadis 115–20, 125, 128, 171, 185, 193,
      196, 199–201
    Armide: Amsterdam editions of suites 115,
      120–1, 125; fourth act 213–37; perform-
      ances 65, 185, 191, 196–7, 201, 207
    Atys 100, 103, 107–9, 115, 118, 127, 178,
      185, 193, 197–9, 201–3
    Bellérophon 100, 115, 117–18, 178, 185, 188,
      198, 207
    Cadmus et Hermione 35, 37, 100, 106,
      115–18, 120, 166–7, 178, 191, 193,
      199, 203
    Isis 100, 102, 115, 118, 178, 202
    Persée 115, 118, 120, 185, 188, 191, 201,
      203, 207
    Phaëton 115–16, 120, 185, 188, 193,
      198, 202
    Proserpine 100, 115–16, 118–20, 193, 201
    Psyché 94, 100, 115, 118, 202
    Roland 115, 118, 171, 186, 188, 191, 193,
      197, 199, 203, 245, 247–9, 254
    Thésée 100–1, 107, 109, 178, 191, 196–8,
      201, 203, 207, 302, 304, 311
Lunéville, performances of Lully's operas 194,
  196
Luynes, Duc de 255–6
Lyon, performances of Lully's operas 188–92

Macdonald, Hugh 259
Magny, Claude-Marc 196, 256
Mailly, Abbé 9
Maintenon, Mme de 65, 81, 144
Maisonneuve, Alexandre 137–9
Malte, François 198

Marais, Marin 103–4, 107, 133–4, 142–3,
  146–7, 225, 245n
Marais, Mlle 147
Marazzoli, Marco (Marco dell'Arpa) 12–14,
  16–17, 20–3
Marchand, Claude 143, 160
Mariée, la (dance) 239–57, 304
Marie-Thérèse, Queen, wife of Louis XIV 30, 65
Marseille, performances of Lully's operas 185–7
Martinozzi, Laure 29
Mascranny, Paul 162
Masson, Paul-Marie 274
Matho, Jean 144
Maximilien, Elector of Bavaria 203
Mazarin, Cardinal Jules, and opera 7–23, 30
Medici family 15
Melani, Atto 8, 15–16, 22
Melani, Jacopo 15–16
Mersenne, Marin 110
Metru, Nicolas 25
Metz, performances of Lully's operas 194, 197
Minoret, Guillaume 43, 45, 47, 49, 64–5
Molière, Jean-Baptiste Poquelin 2, 166, 179, 253
Molin, André 191
Moline, Pierre Louis 293, 295–6
Montéclair, Michel Pignolet de 147, 192
Montespan, Mme de 144
Montpensier, Mlle de (Anne-Marie-Louise
  d'Orléans) 25–6, 167–8
Moreau, Jean-Baptiste 144
Moreau, Jeanne 143
Morineau, Catherine and Anne 31
Motteville, Mme de 22
Moulinié, Étienne 26, 32
Mouret, Jean-Joseph 197, 245n
Mozart, W. A. 245n
Muffat, George 114
Musique de l'Écurie 33

Nancy, performances of Lully's operas 194, 196
Netherlands, Amsterdam editions of Lully's
  suites 113–30
Normandin, Dominique 31
Nyert, Pierre de 28, 30, 145

opera buffa 226–7, 231, 292–4, 297–8
orchestra, Lully's 99–112
Orléans, Anne-Marie-Louise de, *see* Montpensier,
  Mlle de
Orléans, Gaston, duc d' 26
Orléans, Philippe duc d' ('Monsieur') 166, 175,
  179

Paisible, Guillaume 197
Pajou, Augustin 138
Palais-Royal 21, 159–67
Pamphili, Prince Camillo 14
Pamphili, Gian Battista (Pope Innocent X) 20
Paris
  early opera 7–23
  Lully's residences 31, 159–71
Parnasse François 131–57

Paul, Tsarevitch of Russia 317
Pauli, Charles 256
Pécour, Louis 240–2, 245–6, 248–55, 257
Pergolesi, G. 226
Perrault, Charles 27–8, 99
Perrin, Pierre 9–10, 41–51, 55, 162, 266
Pestel, Joseph de 207
Petit, Gilles Edme 138
Philidor, André-Danican (*l'aîné*)
  composer 246
  copyist 68, 84, 88, 91, 94, 97–8
Philidor (musicians) 103, 105, 109
Piccinni, Niccolò 291, 310, 316
Pièche family, musicians 33, 105, 109
poetry, France 1, 3, 50
Pogue, Samuel 115
Poilly, Nicolas de 134–5
Pointel, Antoine 113, 115–18, 120, 199
politics, and opera 7–23
Popelinière, Marquis de 163
Portet, Mariette 174–5
Predo, Jean-Baptiste 162
Prunières, Henry
  on Lully 25, 32, 164–6
  on Mazarin 8, 11, 15
  on Perrin 43
Puteaux 31, 171–4

Quinault, Philippe 3–4, 27–8, 133, 166, 183, 188, 197
  Armide libretto 213, 227–8, 233
Quittard, Henri 63

Racine, Jean 171, 275
Radet, Edmond 163–4, 168, 179–80
Raguenet, François 227
Rameau, Jean-Philippe
  and fashion 295–7, 305, 315–17
  operas 225–8, 260–75, 291
    Castor et Pollux 265, 292, 294–5, 305–7, 311, 313–17
    Dardanus 262–3, 266, 308n, 313
    Les fêtes d'Hébé 262, 264, 305, 307
    Les fêtes de Polymnie 269–70, 273–4
    Hippolyte et Aricie 225, 307–8
    Les Indes galantes 264–5, 307
    Io 273–5
    Linus 260
    La naissance d'Osiris 269, 272
    Platée 260
    La princesse de Navarre 260, 266, 268, 270, 272–5
    Samson 260, 269–70
    Les surprises de l'Amour 266, 268
    Le temple de la Gloire 260, 268
    Zoroastre 262, 264–6, 272
  opinion of Lully 295
  and the *Parnasse François* 141
  Pièces de Clavessin 261, 264–7
  popularity 292–3
  self-borrowings 259–89
    harpsichord collections 262–7

instrumental passages 267–8
vocal borrowings 268–75
and *Les trois âges de l'opéra* 305–11
Rameau, Pierre 241, 255
Rebel, François 219–22, 226, 228, 237, 268, 304
Rennes, performances of Lully's operas 192–4
Richelieu, Cardinal 7, 12, 20, 26–7, 30, 166
Roberday, François 25
Robert, Jean 185
Robert, Pierre 43, 45, 47–8, 51, 64–71, 74, 147
Rochechouart-Mortemart, duc de 30
Rochefort, Jouvin de 172
Roger, Estienne 113, 115–21, 123–9, 199
Rondel, Auguste 188
Rose, Gilbert 197
Rosow, Lois 82
Rospigliosi, Giulio 17
Rossi, L. 9, 15, 21
Rouen, performances of Lully's operas 193–4
Rousseau, Jean-Baptiste 132, 138, 143
Rousseau, Jean-Jacques 259, 273
Roux, François 191
Royer de Marainville, Charles-Antoine 143, 196

Sablières, Jean Granouillet de la 43, 45, 47
Sacrati, F. 9
Saint-Alphonse, Alphonse Marie Denis Devismes de 294–5, 298–9, 302–18
Saint-Christophe, Mlle de 31, 35, 38
Saint-Germain-en-Laye 100, 103, 111, 144, 178, 183
Saint-Mard, Rémond de 225
'St Vallier' collection 91–4, 97
Salomon, Joseph-François 105, 107, 144–5
Sawkins, Lionel 87–8
Schelte (family) 201
Schneider, Herbert 183–95 *passim*
Schott, Gérard 201
Schütz, Heinrich 71
Sévigné, Mme de 81
Sèvres 174–7
sommeil 4
Sornique, Dominique 138
Spain 3
Strasbourg, performances of Lully's operas 195, 198–9

Tallemant des Réaux, G. 27–8
Tannevot, Alexandre 142, 146
Tardieu, Nicolas Henri 134, 136
Tessier, André 107
Theobalde (de Gatti), Jean 103, 105, 146
Thibault collection 32, 94, 98
Titon du Tillet, Évrard 131–57
  writings 141–8
Toulouse, Comte de 94
tragédie lyrique 4, 81

Urban VIII, Pope 7, 13, 20

Vallas, Léon 184, 188–91
Veillot, J. 48

Verdi, Giuseppe 106
Verdun, Jean François 174
Verger, Félix du 168
Versailles 179, 183, 252
Vigarani, Carlo 166
Ville-l'Évêque 167–71
Villeroy, Marquis de 245
Voltaire (François Marie Arouet) 4, 138, 141,
    269–71, 273

Walleau, Antoine 224
Wallon, Simone 52
Walsh, John 254
Wolfgang, Abraham 201, 202n
Wright, Craig 198